UNLIKELY PURSUITS

SIX ROMANCES OF FAITH, CHANGE,
AND IMPROBABLE ACHIEVEMENTS

Unlikely Pursuits

AWARD-WINNING AUTHOR
CONSTANCE SHILLING STEVENS
WITH
JALANA FRANKLIN
JULANE HIEBERT
EILEEN KEY
KIM VOGEL SAWYER
RALPH VOGEL

Published by Wings of Hope Publishing Group
Established 2013
www.wingsofhopepublishing.com
Find us on Facebook: Search "Wings of Hope"

Printed in the United States of America

Franklin, Jalana; Hiebert, Julane; Key, Eileen;
Stevens, Constance Shilling; Vogel, Ralph; Sawyer, Kim Vogel
Unlikely Pursuits
Wings of Hope Publishing Group
ISBN-13: 978-1-944309-05-3
ISBN-10: 1-944309-05-5

Cover artwork and typesetting by Vogel Design in Hillsboro, Kansas.

Table of Contents

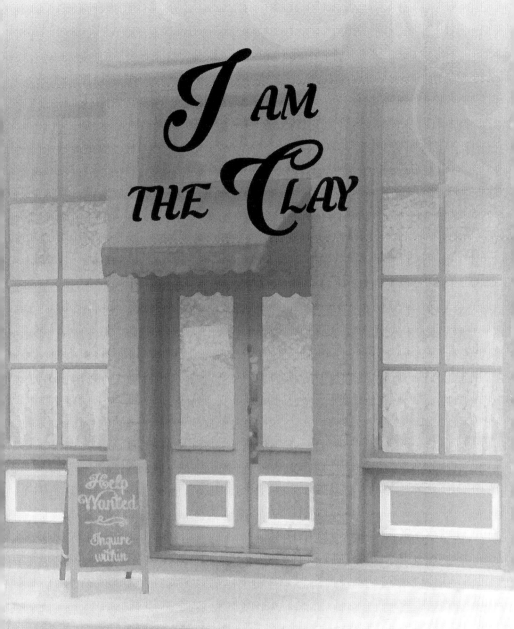

I AM THE CLAY

CONSTANCE SHILLING
STEVENS

Then I went down to the potter's house, and behold, he
wrought a work on the wheels.
And the vessel that he made of clay
was marred in the hand of the potter:
so he made it again another vessel,
as seemed good to the potter to make it.
Then the word of the Lord came to me, saying,
O house of Israel, cannot I do with you as this potter?
saith the Lord. Behold, as the clay is in the potter's hand,
so are ye in mine hand.
JEREMIAH 18:3-6

Chapter 1

Stonecliffe, Maine 1886

B ryn Sinclair curled her fingers into a fist beneath the folds of her skirt and clenched her teeth. She swallowed hard and fixed her steady gaze on her father. Preston Sinclair sat like a king on a throne, flicking his cigar ashes and scowling at his only daughter.

But Bryn refused to cower under her father's glare. "Father, neither Edgar or August has the slightest interest in running the *Clarion*. You've said yourself you wished at least one of your offspring would—"

"There is no need to remind me neither of my sons desire to follow in my footsteps." Father snapped the words off like breaking glass. He rose and strode to the window. "Newspaper ink has flowed in my veins all my life." The timbre of his voice modulated to a mutter. "A father's legacy means nothing."

The very thought of stepping into her father's shoes as publisher and editor of the *Clarion* sent sparks of excitement coursing through her, but she had to convince him. She gulped and went on. "I've loved writing since I was a child, and tagged along with you to the *Clarion* office more times than I can count. Why shouldn't I have a chance to prove I can be a successful newspaper publisher?"

From her chair across the room, Bryn's mother released a huff. She patted her upper lip with a dainty handkerchief. "Why? Because it's unseemly for a woman, that's why. No proper suitor would have anything to do with you if you insist on pursuing a career no genteel woman in New England has ever held before." Faye Sinclair sniffed behind her lacy handkerchief and leaned back against the red velvet cushion. "You would be blackballed from every social event of the season."

"So you've said repeatedly, my dear." The impatience in Father's tone communicated far more than his reply. "But this is about more than your society friends." He shifted his focus to Bryn. "This is about the reputation of the *Clarion*. A woman publisher? It's unheard of."

Bryn couldn't let this discussion come to a close without one last effort to convince her father she could handle the job. "Father, there's no rush to sell the *Clarion*, is there? You don't have any prospective buyers on the horizon. All I'm asking for is a chance. How do you know I'm not capable?"

"Desire and ability are not the same thing." He returned to his chair and set his cigar in a nearby bronze ash tray.

"But, Father." Bryn scooted to sit on the ottoman in front of him. "Doesn't it make more sense to keep the *Clarion* operating when you and Mother leave for Martha's Vineyard?"

Mother sputtered and flapped her hand. "What do you mean, when your father and I leave? You are accompanying us, young lady. Why, I've already responded to a half dozen invitations to cotillions and garden parties, and the most eligible young men will be in attendance. I'll not permit you to throw away this opportunity to make a suitable match."

The prospect of a suitable match held no enticement for Bryn. She appealed again to her father's business sense. "Am I right, Father? Wouldn't the *Clarion* be much more attractive to a buyer if it was operating on schedule with a list of satisfied readers and advertisers?"

Father pressed his lips into a thin line and drummed his fingers on the arm of the chair. He leveled an unblinking stare at her, as if scrutinizing her argument and motives. Oh, how she wished she could read his mind.

Just as Bryn thought she might go mad waiting for his answer, he finally interlocked his fingers and leaned forward. "When did you get to be so shrewd?" He lifted his gaze to the ceiling, eyes narrowed as he formed his verdict. "If I entrust the *Clarion* to you during the time your mother and I are away"—he shot a look at Mother to halt any interruption and then returned his focus to Bryn—"I will expect a smooth continuation of publication in my absence. You will be named editor and publisher pro tem, and as such will have full responsibility, both literary and business decisions—"

"Preston, how can you possibly consider such a ridiculous notion?" The veins in Mother's neck protruded and her face reddened as she turned to Bryn. "Imagine the gossip that will ensue. I'll not allow you to bring disgrace on our family's respected name."

Bryn rose and held her ground. "How can pursuing the same respected vocation as my father bring disgrace?"

"Ah." Mother fanned herself. "Do you see? She is determined to humiliate me and tarnish our family's reputation."

"Mother, I'm not trying to humiliate you. I'm merely asking for a chance to do what I love."

"Bryn." Her father's voice gained an edge, and he cocked his head toward the door—her signal to go and leave her mother to him. But even as she slipped out the library door and up the spiral staircase, she knew Mother could be a formidable contender.

She entered her bedroom and crossed to sit on the window seat overlooking the side yard. A pair of robins had begun building a nest in branches of a majestic spruce just a few feet from her window. Each bird flitted to and fro, bringing bits of dried grass and small twigs to add to their unified goal of a place to raise their young. Neither bird—the male or female—did more work than the other. After a time, Bryn lost track of the number of trips the pair made, or how many contributions to the construction of their home were made by each bird.

Bryn studied the female robin. Muted browns and grays gave her a slightly drab appearance in comparison to the male's more pronounced markings and colors, but there was nothing diminished about the way the female labored over her nest. Bryn smiled. "You aren't sitting by watching your husband do all the work, are you?"

As if in response, Mrs. Robin cocked her head and flew off, no doubt in search of more grass to line the nest for her soon-to-be-born babies. Why couldn't it be that way with people?

She heaved a sigh. Was her father making any headway convincing her mother? Unable to sit still any longer, she paced across the room. Her eyes fell on the Bible sitting on the bedside table. To her shame, she'd not opened it for weeks. But surely there must be something within its pages describing the work of a woman's hands. She settled into a chair with the book and flipped the pages. She had no trouble locating scriptures that spoke of a woman taking care of her home and children, of being subject to her husband. Weren't there any women in the Bible who wanted to step outside the lines of convention and dare to do something most women didn't?

If Bryn believed her mother's predictions, she might never marry or have a place in society. She pondered the prospects and found neither of them as distasteful as her mother apparently did. The thought of managing the *Clarion*, however, accelerated her pulse and pulled a smile onto her face.

Two raps on the door drew her attention. When she opened it, her father's imposing figure filled the doorframe. She held her breath as he entered the room and slid his thumbs up his suspenders.

"Your mother is still fretting about damage to our family's social standing, but I've appeased her by promising we will stay in Martha's Vineyard through the summer. But that means you must carry the responsibility of operation for three months."

Elation flared in Bryn's middle, and she threw her arms around her father's neck. "Oh, Father, thank you. I—"

Father patted her back awkwardly. "*Ahem.* I'm not finished."

Bryn reined in the joy dancing in her middle.

Father narrowed his eyes at her. "I expect to return to a thriving newspaper. Don't let me down, daughter."

She straightened her shoulders and stiffened her spine. "I won't, Father. I have the same ink flowing through my veins that you do." Though her tone was resolute, a betraying tremble in her voice brought heat to her face.

The corner of her father's mustache twitched. "Yes, well, that may be, but your mother will never let either of us forget it if you fail." He turned and exited.

In his wake, the thrill of anticipation swelled through her once more. The first female newspaper publisher in New England. She'd show him she could perform the task so well, he'd change his mind about selling the *Clarion* when he returned home at the end of summer.

The hardest thing Drew Montgomery ever had to do was face his best friend's widow. He watched as she moved around the tiny kitchen, her hands moving woodenly, pouring tea into chipped cups. What could he say to her? She must know as well as he that as captain of the *Stalwart*, he alone was responsible for the death of her husband. His first mate. His best friend. His foolhardy decision to alter their course to save time had put the *Stalwart* in a collision course with the spring storm that took Garth Henshaw's life.

He wished she would say something—rail at him, throw something at him, order him to leave her cottage. But she did none of those things. She set his cup of tea in front of him and paused to peer into the cradle in the corner before sitting across from him.

"Felicity—"

"Drew—"

Let her speak. He braced himself for her tirade.

"Drew, nobody is to blame. The sea takes sailors every year. Garth knew that, and so did I. Seafaring is a dangerous occupation." She sipped her tea, closing her red-rimmed eyes for a moment.

"Felicity, I'm not here seeking pardon. I am the *Stalwart*'s captain. When Garth signed on as my first mate, he put his trust in me." He stared at the steam rising from the amber liquid in his cup. "The safety of the crew is the captain's responsibility. I didn't pay close enough attention to the signs—the way the clouds were forming, the wind currents, the dampness in the air, the way the gulls—"

A whimper from the cradle halted his litany, a reminder that Garth not only left a widow, but also a child. Felicity rose and crossed the room to the cradle. She lifted her daughter and cuddled her against her shoulder, patting her back and bouncing gently.

Drew stared at the child while Felicity tried to soothe her. "I don't remember her being that big. She was such a tiny thing."

Felicity turned, a sad smile on her lips. "Babies grow, and this one is growing like a weed. Would you like to hold her?"

"M-me? N-no, I might break her, or drop her, or something." He stood and paced across the tidy room. On one end of the table, several folded garments sat stacked beside a sewing basket. He reached into his inside coat pocket and withdrew a leather pouch, placing it on the table beside the basket. "Garth's wages."

Felicity gave a single nod and shifted the baby. "I started taking in washing and mending. I'll make do."

Something stirred deep in Drew's gut. If her husband were still here to provide for his family, she wouldn't have to take in laundry or mend other people's clothes. The thought only served to reinforce his decision.

He would no longer be the captain of the *Stalwart*—or any other ship, for that matter. His moral responsibility stood directly in front of him. Garth's family. Felicity and baby Lenora would not be left alone in this world. Not if Drew could help it.

CHAPTER 2

Drew signed the documents the clerk shoved in his direction, carefully avoiding the scorn he knew was written across the man's face. The same scorn he'd seen on a dozen faces in the past several days. When he'd stepped into the courthouse a half hour ago, silent accusations rang out from the knowing looks of every person in the place, including the man across the table who was purchasing the *Stalwart*.

Selling the ship wasn't as hard as Drew anticipated. His heart no longer had room for the sea. That part of his life was best passed on to the man now adding his signature to the bill of sale. Mr. Monroe mentioned he planned to change the *Stalwart*'s name—no doubt to avoid the stigma attached to its legacy. It didn't matter. If every person in town forgot about the *Stalwart*, the weight of blame would remain around Drew's shoulders every time he looked at Garth's wife and daughter.

While the courthouse clerk finished the paperwork, Drew took in the profile of the ship's new captain. Mr. Monroe's black hair hung across his forehead and curled over the stained collar of his shirt. His knuckles tapped impatiently on the edge of the table as his piercing black eyes glanced up at the clock. Drew could tell him impatience wasn't a partner to take to sea, but he doubted Mr. Monroe cared a whit about anything Drew thought, and the man would be right. A negligent ship captain didn't have a right to give advice.

Final papers for the sale were filed and the bank draft was folded and tucked in Drew's pocket. There was nothing left to do except to bid good day to Mr. Monroe and take his leave. He extended his hand. "Thank you, sir. You'll find the *Stalwart* a fine ship."

Monroe tossed a careless glance at Drew's hand and frowned. "As soon as I can hire someone to scrape off the name, she'll be the *Regent.*" The man turned on his heel and walked out, leaving Drew standing there holding out his hand.

A muffled snort came from the direction of the clerk who quickly turned and attended to a stack of papers. Drew stuffed his hand in his pocket and headed for the door.

It was done. Sorrow and relief mingled and twined their way up his throat. Perhaps he was a coward, but he never intended to pursue another occupation in which he was responsible for another man's life. He'd entertained the notion of moving away for a fresh start in a place where nobody knew him. But every time the thought crossed his mind, his conscience pierced his heart. Unless Felicity Henshaw remarried, it was up to him to look after her and little Lenora. He owed it to Garth.

Drew crossed the street and entered the bank. The teller and his customer both turned to look at him and then inclined their heads toward each other and lowered their voices to a whisper. Drew wanted to tell them they needn't bother whispering. He knew what they were saying—*How could a competent sea captain be so negligent as to sail his ship directly into a storm?*

The bank manager, Mr. Colquitt, stepped toward him. His paunch protruded between his vest buttons, and his thick hair lay plastered against his scalp with Macassar oil. Condescension clouded his gaze. "Captain Montgomery. Is there something you need?"

Drew gestured toward the office. "May we speak privately?"

With a curt nod, the banker strode toward his office. Drew followed, taking note of the elegant furnishings. Drew took the chair across from Colquitt's large mahogany desk and withdrew the bank draft from his pocket.

"I've sold the *Stalwart* and I wish to set up accounts for Garth Henshaw's widow at the dry goods store, the mercantile, the grocer, and the butcher. Those bills with be paid through my account here." Drew paused. "I assume you can do that."

16

Colquitt nodded. "Of course."

Drew pushed the bank draft across the desk. "I want to deposit this. I plan to set up the accounts today for Mrs. Henshaw with the merchants I mentioned. So bills could begin coming in as early as next week. Is that acceptable?"

Colquitt glanced at the bank draft. "A tidy sum. Yes, we can do that. I'll put a notation in your account."

If the banker speculated anything beyond what Drew had told him, he didn't let on. Drew rose. "I will expect you to keep this matter entirely private. Mrs. Henshaw has been through quite enough without gossip spreading around town."

Colquitt's face reddened. "It has always been the policy of this bank to keep its clients' personal business private, sir." He cleared his throat. "I'll get a receipt for this." He snatched the bank draft from the desk and stalked out to the teller, muttering under his breath.

Drew leaned against the chair back. The money from the sale of the *Stalwart*, added to the comfortable bank account he already had, would see to Felicity's needs as well as his own, for a good while. But he'd run mad if he didn't have something to occupy his time. Given the attitudes and opinions of the people he'd encountered in the past week, however, his chances of finding employment in Stonecliffe were slim. Some sea captains he knew went into ship building or opened a ship chandler store when it came time for them to retire from the sea. Drew doubted many mariners based in Stonecliffe would be inclined to do business with him. No, whatever work he found to fill his hands would have nothing whatsoever to do with seafaring.

Ten minutes later, with his receipt in hand, Drew walked down the boardwalk to speak with Jim Shilling at the lumber mill about supplying Felicity with firewood. By lunchtime, he'd set up the accounts for her with the area merchants, all of whom nodded their agreement with Drew's plan.

He began retracing his steps toward home, relatively confident he'd done all he could to provide for Garth's family. A young boy stood at the end of the boardwalk, the tip of his tongue sticking out while he tapped a tack into a flyer on a post. When Drew stepped closer, he saw it was a Help Wanted advertisement.

THORNDIKE PAPER MILL

IS SEEKING TO HIRE

TRADESMEN AND LABORERS.

FAIR WAGES.

SEE LANGLEY THORNDIKE.

Drew knew a little something about aluminum sulfate used in the paper-making process since he'd hauled the chemicals to a mill in Old Town on occasion. Thorndike Paper Mill wasn't far—up the hill and outside of town. When the wind blew the right direction, one could smell it. He set out in the direction of the mill, hoping his limited knowledge might give him an advantage.

Langley Thorndike gripped Drew's hand after agreeing to the employment terms. He seemed to Drew a fair man—at least he didn't look upon his newest employee with disdain. For that, Drew was grateful. Thorndike's explanation of the job didn't sound challenging or adventurous, but adventure wasn't what Drew sought. Constructive work to occupy his time would keep him from brooding and getting too soft.

"Be here by seven o'clock Monday morning." Thorndike clapped him on the shoulder. "I like to train new hires myself, so I am assured they learn the process correctly."

Drew nodded. "Yes, sir."

Thorndike nailed Drew with a scrutinizing look. "I don't like to poke my nose into another man's affairs, but I have a question. I know you captained your own clipper ship for a time. And I heard like everyone else in town that you lost a crew member. Does that mean you've given up seafaring? Because I don't want to waste time training you in the paper manufacturing business, only to have you quit me and go back to sailing."

Drew sucked in a deep breath. It was a fair question. "I've sold the *Stalwart*. I have no plans to ever return to the sea."

Thorndike studied him for a long moment, no doubt forming his own speculations. "All right. The reasons aren't any of my business. You work hard for me, and I'll treat you fairly." He offered Drew his hand once more.

"Thank you, sir." Drew released some of the tension in his shoulders. "I'll see you Monday morning."

Thorndike arched his eyebrows. "I hoped I'd see you Sunday—in church."

The statement hit Drew like an indictment. He'd skipped church last Sunday, only three days after the *Stalwart* had docked. News of Garth's death had spread faster than a plague of diphtheria, and the judgmental stares were more than Drew could stand. If the town folk continued to treat him with contempt, could he find the peace for which he yearned in a church filled with those stares?

He bit back a sigh. "Sunday." With a tug on the brim of his cap, he strode down the hill back toward town. He still had one more stop to make.

The sun had begun its descent when Drew knocked on the door of Felicity's cottage. Laundry flapped on the clothesline beside the little house, and he could hear Lenora fussing as Felicity lifted the latch.

"Drew, come in." She managed a smile, but the dark circles under her eyes spoke louder.

He pulled his cap from his head and stepped across the threshold. "Lenora sounds unhappy."

Felicity crossed to the small stove and pulled the kettle forward. "She's cutting a tooth and wants me to hold her all the time. But I have work to do." She nodded toward the pile of mending. "I'll make some tea, but I'm sorry I don't have any sugar."

Drew waved his hand. "None for me, but thank you. I just stopped by to talk to you about something."

She frowned and sent him a puzzled look while she picked up the fussy baby.

He returned her look with one he hoped brooked no argument. "I set up accounts for you today at Stiples Dry Goods, Pittman Mercantile, Appleby's Grocer, and at Walter Sims butcher shop."

"Drew—"

He held up his hand. "There will also be a load of firewood delivered tomorrow."

She opened her mouth again, but Drew stopped her. "Garth would do the same for me. Please. I want to do this."

Felicity shook her head. "I wish you could understand that it was nobody's fault. You are under no obligation to—"

"I know." He knew no such thing, but at least it got her to be quiet. Knowing she was working so many hours, she barely had time to pick up her baby when she cried tore at his insides. "Please use the accounts, Felicity. And if you need anything else, you will let me know."

Her eyes brimmed with unshed tears, and he knew...

She needed her husband.

CHAPTER 3

Spending her leisure hours at the *Clarion* office during her youth wasn't the same as running the operation, nor did it prepare Bryn for the long hours she'd spent her first week as editor and publisher. While her mother continued to rail at her at home, her father took on a sink-or-swim approach. He'd not made an appearance at the office since Bryn took over, saying she needed to get used to him not being there, since he and Mother were leaving the first of next week.

Bryn glanced up and found Homer, the typesetter and press man who had worked for Father for seventeen years, leaning against the work table with his frowning gaze fixed on her. He'd not said much all week, but she could tell he'd been mulling over the situation.

"Is something wrong, Homer?"

Homer's thick mustache twitched along with his jaw muscles. "Well, I been wonderin' why the boss ain't come in all week. He sick or somethin'?" His eyes narrowed, as if he dared her to offer any other explanation.

She chewed on her lip. "Homer, I told you on Monday I was stepping in as editor and publisher."

"Yep." He ran ink-stained fingers through his salt and pepper, scraggly hair. "I 'member you said that. Figured he'd be in to talk to me, though. I ain't broke my back here for seventeen years for nothin'."

Bryn pulled in a deep breath and shifted her eyes toward the clock. She had a deadline to meet. "Homer, can we talk about this tomorrow after the next edition is run?"

A heavy silence hung in the air for several seconds. "When you said you was steppin' in as editor and publisher, you didn't mean for good, did you?" He wiped his hands on his grimy apron.

Tension twined up Bryn's shoulders and neck. "My father has plans to sell the *Clarion*, but I convinced him to let me run it for the time being. I am the new editor and publisher."

Homer pursed his lips and Bryn was about suggest they get busy firing up the press. But the man shook his head. "No." He pulled off his apron. "No, I ain't workin' for no woman." He snatched his cap from a nearby peg and slung it atop his head. "I'll be back for my wages." The door slammed in his wake.

Bryn fought the urge to run after him and beg him to reconsider. Homer was much more skilled than she at setting type and running the press. But she'd not allow anything to stop her from proving herself capable to her father. If she had to do it all herself, then so be it.

Muttering, she pulled the pieces of type for the headline.

TRAGEDY ABOARD THE STALWART

Surely Father would be impressed with her first edition. A grim smile pulled on the corner of her lips as she inserted the type into precise rows to form the story. Yes, Father should certainly be pleased.

Bryn's ears still burned the following morning from her mother's tirade last night. Leaving the house before anyone else was up, she found sanctuary in the *Clarion* office. As she inked the type, Bryn recalled the argument and scowled. Mother hadn't let an evening go by all week without haranguing her daughter about damaging her reputation or scaring off every potential suitor within a hundred miles. What did Bryn care about suitors? Her only interest in social events was covering them for the newspaper.

The pages slid off the press and into the tray. Her first front page. A thrill tickled away her aggravation. She pulled the lever back and inserted another folio sheet of paper. Before long, she found a rhythm—slow compared with Homer's skill, but steady.

By early afternoon, her first edition of the *Clarion* sat proudly on the work table, all folded and bundled. A satisfied sigh blew past her lips as she ran her fingers over the headline. A swell of pride filled her.

As soon as the young boys who delivered the newspaper carried off the last bundle, Bryn checked her reflection in the window and smoothed her hair. The idea she'd rolled over in her head half the night and most of the day chafed to be put into place. A visit to her aunt, Miriam Pierce, might put an end to her mother's diatribes.

She crossed Penobscot Street and headed down Evergreen Lane to the white clapboard house with the picket fence in front. Her mother's sister had lived here for as long as Bryn could remember. The house wasn't as grand as her parents' home, not by half. Aunt Miriam was a crusty, outspoken woman, who scorned the society soirees and teas that Mother attended. As a result, Mother and Aunt Miriam rarely saw eye to eye. Regardless, Bryn sent up a prayer that she'd catch her aunt in a good mood.

The door opened before Bryn could knock, and her silver-haired aunt stood in the doorway. Flour dotted her faded, yellow apron.

"Bryn? Saw you coming from the kitchen window. What are you doing here?"

Not the greeting she was hoping for. "Hello, Aunt Miriam. May I come in?"

"Of course." Her aunt stepped aside and dragged a sleeve across her forehead. With her elbow, Aunt Miriam pointed toward the rear of the house. "Well, come into the kitchen so I can work while you talk. I don't have time for tea parties."

The aroma of cinnamon and apples teased Bryn's senses as she followed her aunt to the kitchen. "Apples pies?"

"Turnovers. For the orphanage." Aunt Miriam poured two cups of strong coffee and set one in front of Bryn. "Now, what is it you need to talk about?"

No sense wasting time on small talk. "I'm working at the *Clarion* now. Mother isn't at all happy about it."

Aunt Miriam harrumphed. "Giving you a hard time, is she?"

Bryn raised her gaze to the ceiling. "That's an understatement."

"So, what do you want from me? If you think I can change her mind..." Aunt Miriam shook her head and rolled out a ball of pastry dough.

"No, it's not that. Actually, I wondered—" Bryn gulped. Perhaps her plan needed a bit more thought.

Aunt Miriam sent her a sharp look. "You wondered what? Spit it out."

Bryn drew in a deep breath. The worst her aunt could do was say no. "I hoped that I could move in here with you. Since you live in town, it's much closer to the *Clarion* office, and I wouldn't—"

"You wouldn't have to listen to my sister yammer at you."

Bryn swallowed back a giggle. Aunt Miriam had a way of getting right to the point.

"Well, yes." Bryn lifted her shoulders. "I hoped Mother would be more accepting if I wasn't living at the house alone when they leave for Martha's Vineyard next week. I wouldn't expect you to put me up without compensation, of course. I'd pay rent."

Aunt Miriam halted the motion of her rolling pin and sniffed. "Yes, it's about that time of year, isn't it? Faye likes going off with her snooty friends." She ran a flour-dusted hand across her chin, leaving a white streak. "You said alone. Don't tell me Faye is dragging your father with her this year."

Bryn suppressed a smirk. "Yes, they're both going. Father wants to retire and sell the *Clarion*, but I convinced him to allow me the opportunity to prove to him I can run the newspaper. If he is satisfied when he and Mother return, perhaps he'll change his mind about selling."

Aunt Miriam rolled out another pastry crust. Finally, the older woman pursed her lips and laid aside her rolling pin. "Does your mother think your staying with me makes the whole arrangement more proper?"

Bryn pulled her lips in between her teeth. "I hope so."

"How much?"

Bryn blinked. "How much...what?"

"Rent." Aunt Miriam wiped her hands on her apron. "You said you'd pay rent."

Bryn hadn't given the amount much consideration. "Uh, wh-what do you think is fair?"

She could have sworn the corners of Aunt Miriam's lips twitched when she picked up the rolling pin and went back to work. "Two dollars a week, and you help out with the household chores."

Her father had said he'd leave her funds for expenses, but she hoped the newspaper would do so well, she'd not have to touch his money. She extended her hand. "It's a deal." She'd ask later what the chores entailed.

Aunt Miriam shook her head. "I'll bet you've never washed a dish, made a bed, or done laundry in your life." She punctuated the statement with an unladylike snort.

Bryn drew her hand back. No, she hadn't done those things. Her mother always had hired help. "But I'm willing to learn."

Aunt Miriam looked up from assembling the turnovers and fixed her unblinking gaze on her, as if examining her from the inside out. "Fair enough."

Relief washed over Bryn like a gentle rain. "Thank you, Aunt Miriam."

Operating machinery wasn't that different from steering a clipper ship. One had to stay alert and keep the beast on course, not allowing it to stray from its appointed mission. Drew's muscles ached from the unaccustomed labor, lifting heavy barrels and feeding the wood fiber into the jaws of the vat where it was beaten and then heated to a liquefied state. The rank odor of the wood pulp combined with sulfite chemicals turned his stomach the first few days, but he gradually became used to the smell.

This morning, however, Langley Thorndike informed Drew that

the man who drove the delivery wagon had an accident and would be laid up for at least six weeks. Thorndike assigned the delivery tasks to Drew. Escaping the noise and heat of the mill for a couple of hours each day held an appeal, and with the wagon loaded and the sea-scented breeze in his face, he could almost imagine himself riding the waves again.

He delivered packages of paper to the courthouse, an attorney's office, the school, and Stiple's Dry Goods. His final stop was the *Clarion* office. Hoisting the reams of folio size paper to his shoulder, he pushed open the office door. A woman worked at the desk.

He glanced around the cramped office. "Is the boss here?"

She turned, and Drew hiccupped. The startlingly dark brown eyes that stared back at him held a hint of offense when she rose and walked toward him.

"Bryn Sinclair. I am the editor and publisher of the *Clarion*. May I help you?"

Drew swallowed. This woman looked too fragile, too pampered, and too spoiled to be a businessman—er, businesswoman. He pulled his gaze elsewhere before his eyes gave away his thoughts.

A fresh-off-the-press newspaper lay at the corner of a work table. The headline caught his eye. TRAGEDY ABOARD THE STALWART. He shifted the weight of the load of paper on his shoulder and picked up the newspaper in his free hand. His eyes raced along the typewritten lines. Before he reached the end of the third sentence, Miss Sinclair pulled the paper from his hand.

She cleared her throat. "Perhaps you would like to purchase a copy?"

Umbrage rose up from his belly. "I have a right to know what is being said about me."

CHAPTER 4

Drew gritted his teeth when Miss Sinclair raised her eyebrows. If she didn't know who he was when he walked in the door, she did now.

"Captain Montgomery?"

Drew couldn't tell if she spoke a greeting or an inquiry as to his identity. No matter, since he had no intention of debating the authenticity of the article he'd not been permitted to read. He dropped the ream of paper on the floor with a scowl and a thud. "At your service, ma'am." He didn't even try to rein in the sarcasm from his tone.

He turned on his boot heel and returned to the low-sided market wagon for the second bundle. When he returned, Miss Sinclair still stood in the same spot she'd occupied a minute before, staring at him when he reentered with the remainder of her order. He deposited the second ream beside the first one with more force than necessary, and pulled the Thorndike Mill invoice from his pocket. He slapped the bill on the table. The breeze from the open door caught the paper and whisked it across the work surface. Miss Sinclair caught it just before it took wing.

"Am I supposed to pay you?" The thread of uncertainty in her voice didn't go undetected, but it wasn't enough to assuage his ire.

"Sign at the bottom." He achieved a smidgen of enjoyment over the gruffness of his voice. The niggling nudge to his conscience, however, hinted he'd been more than a tad rude. He shoved the feeling aside.

She pushed the paper back to him without so much as an apology for yanking the newspaper from his hand, or for printing the front page story about him and his ship. He snatched the invoice and glanced at her perfectly penned signature: Bryn Sinclair. Unusual name. Unusual occupation for a woman. But then, judging by the lift of her chin and the squaring of her shoulders, he got the distinct impression Miss Bryn Sinclair wasn't an ordinary woman.

He stuffed the invoice back into his pocket and strode out the door. As it swung closed behind him, he thought he heard her speak.

"Could you—" The slamming of the door cut off the rest of her words.

He secured the short tailgate and stalked to the front end of the wagon. When he passed the *Clarion*'s window, he caught a glimpse of Miss Sinclair struggling to lift the heavy reams of paper. Clamping his teeth and jutting out his jaw, he ignored her and released the brake.

Guilt poked him knowing he'd left the woman to carry the load for herself when he was going out of his way to help Felicity Henshaw. But the two weren't even similar. Felicity was struggling under a much different burden—one he'd caused.

Resentment still clawed at him over the article that emblazoned the front page of the *Clarion*. Without reading it, he couldn't say with any certainty whether or not Miss Sinclair had her facts straight or if she'd stretched the truth. Remorse drooped his shoulders. Either way, the blame still lay with him, regardless of the slant of the news article.

He turned the team toward the mill and urged them to pick up the pace. The same recurring thought slipped through his mind again. Would it be so wrong to move away? He could go west where nobody knew the role he'd played in his best friend's death. He could set aside money at the bank for Felicity and her baby to make sure her accounts were paid. Wasn't that enough? Or was he only trying to pay her off to dispel his guilt?

The answer manifested itself in his heart before he could entertain the notion for longer than the space of three heartbeats. He was responsible to not only provide for Garth's family, but to watch over them. No, like it or not, he was staying in Stonecliffe.

Bryn leaned back in the desk chair and rubbed three weeks' worth of ache from her shoulders. Father's account ledgers were meticulous, balanced to the penny. Trouble was, the figures recorded on a week by week basis for the past years showed profits growing in significant increments, but the proceeds from her first two editions hadn't come close to matching the weekly amount the newspaper brought in when Father was at the helm.

After she'd paid Homer and the young boys who hawked the paper on street corners, rent to Aunt Miriam, and the invoice from Thorndike's, she had less than twelve dollars left. The boys had all returned unsold copies, and the places in town that normally sold out of the *Clarion* by the weekend still had a significant stack of newspapers sitting on their counters this afternoon.

Had she missed something? An outlet for selling papers she'd omitted? One notable was a reduction in the advertising revenue. A thorough scrutiny of the advertisers list showed three that had not renewed their usual ads last week. An oversight on her part, or a coincidence?

Late afternoon sunlight streamed in the front window and glinted off the gold-plated ornament hanging from a decorative hook above the desk. Bryn reached out and ran her finger over the one-of-a-kind piece. Two Christmases ago, she'd commissioned it done—a special gift for her father to show her love of the newspaper. Larger pieces of type, the size used to print headlines, spelled out THE CLARION. A local jeweler had gold-plated the unique memento. As Bryn's fingers caressed the letters, she determined to draw perseverance from the piece—a daily reminder of her goal.

She straightened the ornament and closed the ledger. If she hurried, she could likely catch the mayor before he left his office for the day. His version of the proposed raising of taxes was certainly front page news to interest the readership. The short articles she'd written on the happenings down by the docks, a break-in at Pittman's

Mercantile, and an update on the planned spring festival lacked the punch her Father would expect from a lead story. She grabbed her notebook and stubby pencil.

She pulled her cape about her shoulders against the spring chill, and hurried down the street toward the courthouse. If the mayor's story panned out, there was still time this afternoon to get started on the front page article. Homer's absence meant she not only had to gather and report the news, she also had to do the layout, set the type, ink the press, and feed paper into the monstrous machine, all of which required a lot more time. She'd intended on putting a Help Wanted sign in the front window, but in view of the unexpected reduction in her budget, perhaps she ought to wait.

The long afternoon shadows had faded and disappeared hours ago when Bryn finally dragged herself up the front porch steps. Lamplight spilled from the parlor windows. Aunt Miriam met her at the door.

"Supper was at six o'clock." Her aunt leveled a look at her that could have intimidated a bull moose. "Just like yesterday, and the day before that." She pointed to the settee. "Sit down."

All Bryn's weary body wanted was to go upstairs and collapse on her bed, but defying her aunt wasn't an option. She sat.

Aunt Miriam plunked down in a chair across from Bryn and cleared her throat.

"When I agreed to let you move in with me, it was with the understanding that you would help with the household chores, like doing the supper dishes and sweeping the kitchen floor." She folded her arms across her chest and tapped her fingers on her arm. "But you haven't come home for supper for the past four evenings, nor have you been around to help with any cleaning or laundry. You even disappeared on Sunday instead of attending church." Aunt Miriam leaned forward. "Since you're living in my house, I have a right to ask. Have you been fiddling around in that newspaper office until nearly nine o'clock at night?"

Bryn closed her eyes for a moment, her face in her hands, too tired to answer Aunt Miriam's question and too frustrated not to. "That is exactly where I have been, but I'm not 'fiddling around.' I'm writing the articles, arranging the newspaper layout, and working on the typesetting. I'm also going over the accounts and tracking the advertisers." She uncovered her face and sighed.

Aunt Miriam's brows dipped. "What in the world... Why are you doing all that? Doesn't your father have a man in his employ?"

"Not anymore." Through her exhaustion, she explained the tentative nature of the deal she'd made with her father while her aunt listened with wide eyes and rapt attention.

"So for now, I am the editor and publisher, but I only have until the end of the summer to prove to him I can run the paper as well as he did." Her shoulders sagged. "The trouble is the *Clarion* didn't sell the usual number of copies for the past two weeks, and I've lost advertisers."

"My, my." Aunt Miriam blinked as she took in Bryn's explanation. "When you said you were working at the *Clarion*, I didn't realize you'd be doing everything yourself." She shook her head. "Why?"

A tiny spark of renewed energy flared in Bryn's chest. "Because I love the newspaper business, and I want to be the first female newspaper publisher in New England."

Aunt Miriam tapped her fingers on the arms of the chair. "That's a...lofty goal." She tipped her head to the side and narrowed her eyes. "Have you written your father about the drop in sales and advertisers?"

"No." Her aunt's question didn't douse the spark completely, but dampened it a bit. "I plan on speaking with the owners of those businesses tomorrow and encourage them to renew their ads. After I finish the front page story and the article on the spring festival." After a moment's pause, she added, "And after I've helped you with the chores."

"Tsk, tsk." Aunt Miriam waved her hand. "Don't worry about that. If you'd told me all that you were doing in the first place, I'd have cheered you on." A tiny smirk found its way to the woman's face. "I imagine my sister must be reveling in your struggles."

Exhaustion slumped Bryn's shoulders. "I think she is hoping I'll fail so she can be proven right."

Aunt Miriam's smirk dissolved. She rose and planted her hands on her hips. "Is that so? Well, I, for one, think you can do whatever you set your mind to do. In fact, I think maybe you should write an editorial about perseverance to achieve your ambitions." She gave a sharp nod to punctuate her statement. "And come Sunday, you're going to be sitting with me in church."

The idea of publishing such an editorial stoked the fire within her. But church? Her mother was embarrassed by her. The weight of responsibility Father placed on her shoulders tightened its grip. Her overwhelming schedule precluded time for reading her Bible. Could she expect God to smile on her church attendance?

CHAPTER 5

Drew navigated his way through the Saturday shoppers and tipped his hat to a lady exiting Appleby's Grocer. The woman responded with lowered eyes and a polite nod. At least she didn't glare at him with scorn.

He stepped into the grocer where the aroma of pickles, spices, and cheese tickled his nose. Frank Appleby looked up from the crate over which he was bending. His bald head gleamed in the sunlight from the wide front window, and his paunch hung slightly over his apron ties. The merchant was civil, if cool. After all, Drew was spending money in his store as well as providing an account for the Henshaw family.

"Montgomery." He dusted off his hand on the seat of his pants. "What can I get for you today?"

Drew handed over his list. "I don't need much, and I have other business in town. Can I pick up these things later?"

Appleby took Drew's list, glanced over it, and grunted his agreement. "It'll be ready in an hour."

Not the friendliest conversation. Drew nodded. "That'll be fine." He hesitated. "Has Mrs. Henshaw been in and used the account I set up for her?"

Something in Appleby's eyes softened, and he laid the list on the counter. "Mrs. Henshaw came in yesterday. She got a few things and pulled out a few coins to pay for 'em, like she was afraid to ask about that account. I told her I'd take care of it for her. Hope that was all right."

Relief bloomed in Drew's chest. "Yes, that was fine. Thanks for doing that." He turned toward the door.

"Captain Montgomery?"

Drew halted. He supposed most folks in town knew by now that he'd sold the *Stalwart* and was no longer a sea captain, but he had no inclination to correct Frank Appleby. He turned and waited to hear what the grocer had to say.

Appleby ran his hand over his beard. "I just wanted to tell you I think it's a real decent thing you're doing for Mrs. Henshaw." He jerked his thumb in the direction of Drew's list. "I'll get these supplies packaged up for you."

Decent? If the man only knew how Drew had made the wrong decision, the wrong choice as a ship's captain. Hadn't he ignored doing the decent thing that fateful day on the ocean? His stomach twisted into a knot as the haunting echo of Garth's scream, swallowed up by the tumultuous sea, resounded through his memory. He couldn't bring himself to acknowledge Appleby's kind comment.

"I'll be back by in an hour."

Spring air hit him in the face the moment he stepped onto the cobblestone street. He pulled a breath deep into his lungs. After stops at the post office and bakery, he dropped off a pair of boots to be repaired at the cobbler. Retracing his steps back uptown, he passed the *Clarion*. Through the window, he spied Miss Sinclair wadding up a sheet of paper and throwing it across the room. His steps slowed. He owed her an apology, but she didn't appear to want company. He paused with his hand on the doorknob, and asked God to give him the right spirit.

His eyes slid closed. The brief prayer stung. Had he prayed before setting the *Stalwart*'s course the day of the storm, Garth might still be alive.

He put gentle pressure on the door and it swung on silent hinges. Miss Sinclair leaned forward in her chair and ran her fingers over a gold ornament of some kind that hung just above the desk.

She didn't appear to realize he was there, so he cleared his throat. Startled, she sniffed and pulled the back of her hand across her face before rising and turning to face him. Had she been crying?

Drew pulled off his hat, hoping he was wrong. Being in the presence of a weeping woman always made him want to run the other way.

"Captain Montgomery. Good afternoon." Her words belied the evidence of distress in her eyes.

"Good afternoon. I just wanted to stop by to apologize for my rudeness the other day." He curled the brim of his hat as he turned it in his hands. "I shouldn't have left those heavy reams of paper for you to lift by yourself."

Her slim shoulders lifted. "I managed. I admit I wasn't very polite to you, either."

Drew took a tentative step forward and pointed his hat toward the gold ornament he could now see was pieces of news type that spelled out THE CLARION. "Don't think I've ever seen anything quite like that before."

A soft sigh met his ears. "It was a gift."

The wistfulness in her voice reminded him she'd been teary-eyed when he came in. Perhaps he should just leave. After all, he'd said what he came to say, and there was no point in hanging around. "Uh, is there...is there anything I can do for you?" He shifted his gaze left and right to see who'd spoken the entreaty, and realized it was him.

Her downcast eyes fluttered up and met his, a combination of unease and hope reaching out from their dark brown depths. A strange stirring traveled through his chest.

"Do? For me?" Pink crept into her cheeks.

He shouldn't stare at her, but he couldn't seem to pull his gaze away. "I have some...time b-before my order is ready to be picked up at Appleby's. I'd like to make up for my bad manners."

Something akin to a tiny smile tipped the corners of her mouth. The earlier stirring in his chest doubled in intensity and spun into a whirlwind. He grasped his hat with both hands.

She walked to the press and pulled a freshly printed sheet from the tray, holding it away from her and frowning at it. "I just finished running three hundred copies of this page and it has four typesetting mistakes." A distinct lament threaded her voice.

Drew hung his hat on a nearby peg, took off his coat, and rolled up his shirtsleeves. "Show me what to do."

Her eyes widened and her lips parted. "You would really help me?"

Somewhere in the inward part of his spirit, he found a smile and tried it on. Perhaps it was time to get reacquainted with a more pleasant countenance, and helping Miss Sinclair brought it out of hiding. He nodded. "Show me."

She demonstrated, he followed. Together, they slid the pieces of type out and reinserted them correctly, working in tandem. Each letter snugged up against the next in a meticulous row.

"It looks fine." Her scrutinizing gaze studied the replaced type. "I just wish I hadn't been in such a hurry. I wasted a half ream of paper before I noticed the mistakes." Despair carved lines across her brow, and she heaved a deep sigh of self-incrimination.

Drew surveyed her for a few moments. Certainly paper wasn't cheap, but what he saw as an easily-remedied error, she apparently saw as a crisis. Either she was over-reacting, or there was something he didn't know. Why was she trying to do all of this by herself, anyway?

"Don't you have a man to do the typesetting and printing?"

Storm clouds gathered in her eyes, and she stiffened. "Why do men always think a woman is incapable of anything more complicated than embroidery?"

A woman's place is in the home.

The red-painted words scrawled across the front door of the *Clarion* office greeted Bryn on the morning she planned to run the next edition of the newspaper with her newest editorial on page two. Broken glass littered the floor from a shattered window. After last week's editorial stated how women should be allowed the freedom to choose between being a housewife or pursuing a career, four more merchants in town discontinued their advertising and newspaper sales dropped again.

Suspecting the majority of newspaper purchasers were men, she'd written a follow-up editorial imploring the men of Stonecliffe to open their eyes to the talents and skills of the women around them. But she hadn't suspected this kind of retaliation. Anger curled a fist in her stomach. Who would do such a thing?

She stepped gingerly over the glass shards to inspect the press and trays of type. A whisper of relief blew over her. At least her equipment wasn't damaged. If they thought she'd be intimidated, they were wrong. Well, maybe they were a little right, but she didn't intend to display fear or weakness. Her next editorial on the prejudicial intolerance demonstrated by the men of the community still awaited the ink and press. But first, she had a mess to clean up.

She had no intention of writing Father about the vandalism, but that didn't mean someone else wouldn't. Before she sought out a bucket and rags, however, she determined to show the constable the damage.

Less than thirty minutes later, she gritted her teeth at the indifference shown by the law enforcement officer. In essence, he'd said she had asked for it by printing those articles and asserting herself in a "man's job."

She welcomed the sting of the strong lye soap on her hands as she scrubbed the terse message from the door. The burn fueled her anger, and she mentally set the type in her head for her next editorial.

As the scrawled words gradually disappeared under the vigorous scouring, the day Drew helped her reset the type wandered into her mind. She slowed the motion of her rag. The memory of his gentle voice soothed her distressed spirit. She still couldn't figure out why he'd helped her, especially after she ran the story about the *Stalwart*. She considered Captain Montgomery's inquiry about her not having a typesetter and press man. Perhaps her response had been overly sensitive, but with every other man in town holding her in disdain, she could only assume Captain Montgomery felt the same way.

"What happened here?"

She jerked her head in the direction of the now-familiar voice. "I found this when I arrived this morning."

Captain Montgomery's gaze slid to the window and back. His eyes locked onto hers. "Are you hurt?"

She shook her head. "Just my pride." She aimed a puzzled look at him. "Pardon me for asking, but what are you doing here?"

The deep scowl on his face gentled. "I was making deliveries and noticed you hadn't placed an order for more paper this week."

Bryn bit her lip and turned back to continue scrubbing. She didn't have the money to order more paper—unless Thorndike Paper Mill would extend her credit. And now she needed to pay for the window repair.

Her hands remained busy. "Do you think Mr. Thorndike would agree to a trade? A free ad in the *Clarion* in exchange for paper?"

Captain Montgomery rubbed his chin. "I don't know, but Thorndike is a fair man. I'll certainly ask him. Pardon me." He slipped past her through the door.

She watched as he navigated the glass on the floor. "What are you doing?"

"Have you a broom?"

"In the back corner."

He returned with the broom in his grip. Without a word, he went to work, sweeping up the broken glass.

She dropped the rag into the bucket. "I don't understand you. Why are you doing this when every other man in town thinks I'm a fool for trying to run the *Clarion*?"

He paused, a soft look aimed her way. "A person is a fool for not pursuing what they want, provided it's what the Lord wants them to do."

CHAPTER 6

D rew nearly choked on his own words. How dare he lecture anyone else on seeking God's will? A rush of heat filled his face, and he turned away from Miss Sinclair as he swept. The nagging memory of piloting his ship into the teeth of the storm that took Garth's life taunted him again.

No, he'd not sought God's guidance then, nor had he prayed before selling the *Stalwart* or taking the paper mill job. Working at Thorndike's Paper Mill merely provided him something to do—an occupation that freed him from further guilt and responsibility for the lives of others.

Seek Me. I long to speak to you.

A nudge so distinct he turned to see who had elbowed him, whispered to his spirit.

From childhood, Drew knew that God spoke to His believers through His word. But he'd neglected his Bible ever since that fateful voyage. Perhaps it was time. There was no use in ignoring the nudge. God's entreaty lingered in his heart, and would, no doubt take up permanent residence until Drew acted on it.

He pulled a rubbish barrel across the floor and scooped glass shards into it. "Miss Sinclair, is someone coming to replace the glass?"

She made a few more swipes on the nearly-clean door with her rag before answering. Between the noise filtering in from the street and her soft voice, he barely heard her, but thought she said something about having to check on the cost first. She wrung her rag out into the scrub bucket and straightened. The soft smile she aimed in his direction did strange things to his insides—it being the first gift she'd ever given him.

She propped one hand on her hip. "You've helped me re-set type and now have swept up broken glass. I suppose, under such circumstances, you might as well call me Bryn."

What a lovely name.

His heart hiccupped, and he couldn't stop the grin from spreading across his face. "I'm Drew."

"Thank you for your help, Drew." She bent and curled her fingers around the rope handle of the bucket. Her head tilted toward the door. "That's the best I can do for now. I'm just going to dump out this water." She edged past him and carried the bucket to the rear door.

Drew spied a measuring rule hanging on the side of the work table. He snatched it and made a quick calculation of the window's dimensions before Bryn returned.

He hung the ruler back in its place as light footsteps announced her reappearance.

"Thank you, again, for your help. You didn't have to do that." She tipped her head and regarded him in a way that made him wish he could linger.

"Pleased I could help. I must be going, but I hope you will allow me to help again if you need it." The instant the words crossed his lips, he experienced a heartbeat of regret, hoping she'd not misinterpret his meaning.

"I would be appreciative." A repeat of her smile accompanied her reply.

He tipped his hat and went on his way. The doors to Acherman's Hardware, adjacent to Appleby's Grocer, were propped open to welcome customers. Drew entered and greeted the proprietor.

"I need a pane of glass, thirty inches by forty inches."

Mr. Acherman's thick mustache twitched beneath his smirk. "Heard you took up a new profession, but I didn't think workin' at a paper mill involved workin' with glass. Leastwise you can't hurt nobody but yourself."

Drew's fingers curled into fists, but he anchored his feet to the floor and refused to take Acherman's bait. "Do you have the glass in stock or should I try Pittman's Mercantile?"

Acherman released a snort. "I got glass in stock. When do you need it?"

"As soon as possible." Drew leveled a hard stare at the merchant. "I'm going to check down at the docks. There's always a sailor or two looking for handyman work between sea voyages. When I hire someone, I'll send him back here to pick up the glass." He wasn't two steps away from the gaping doors when Acherman's chortle stopped him.

"So that sassy female running the *Clarion* has you cleaning up her messes, has she?"

Drew turned on his heel and crossed his arms. "I never said what the glass was for. What makes you think it's for Miss Sinclair?"

Acherman's face turned beet red. "W-well, you j-just— you said you n-needed— I just figured—"

"What did you figure, Mr. Acherman?" Drew dragged out a long pause, waiting for the man to incriminate himself. "Do you know how her front window got broken?" He walked over to a wall of shelves displaying paint and brushes. The dusty shelf revealed a dust-free circle, evidence that a can had recently been removed. He drilled a glare through the hardware proprietor. "You sell a lot of red paint?"

Acherman muttered something under his breath. "I'll get that glass cut."

"Oh, by the way, Mr. Acherman, didn't you used to run a regular, weekly ad in the *Clarion*?"

The man halted and growled, "Like I said, I'll get that glass cut."

Drew watched the man disappear through the stockroom door before he set out for the docks.

The ticking of the mantle clock in the parlor tapped out the minutes. Drew stared through the darkness and despised the memories that kept him awake. He threw back the covers and swung his legs over the edge of the bed, abandoning his futile desire for sleep.

Fumbling for the box of wood matches beside the lamp, he lit the wick and adjusted the flame. Shadows played against the wall as he picked up the lamp and carried it to the parlor. A few coals still glowed in the fireplace. He tossed a handful of kindling over them and added a log.

The big leather-covered chair beside the fireplace invited him to settle in. Was it purely coincidence that his Bible sat on the adjacent table? The Bible he hadn't opened in more than a month. The same Bible his sea captain father read from every day. But it wasn't the disappointment he knew his father would feel that kept him awake. It was the whisper of God's voice he kept hearing in his heart.

Seek Me. I long to speak to you.

"Lord, I'm here, but I can't imagine why You want to speak to me, or why You even still care about me." He ran his fingers over his father's Bible before picking it up. A thin ribbon marked the place where he'd last read—a scripture he couldn't even recall.

Drew opened the sacred pages and set the ribbon aside. The eighteenth chapter of Jeremiah. He pursed his lips and began reading aloud.

"'Then I went down to the potter's house, and, behold, he wrought a work on the wheel. And the vessel that he made of clay was marred in the hand of the potter; so he made it again another vessel, as seemed good to the potter to make it.'"

He scowled at the verses. Perhaps he should flip the pages and read something else. If God really wanted to speak to him, Drew was sure it had nothing to do with a clay pot. But the scripture wouldn't let him go. He continued reading in a whisper.

"'Then the word of the Lord came to me, saying, O house of Israel, cannot I do with you as this potter? saith the Lord. Behold, as the clay is in the potter's hand, so are you in My hand.'"

He laid the Book in his lap. Surely this wasn't what God wanted to speak to him. The scriptures were full of much more encouraging verses. Maybe he was simply too tired to hear from God right now.

"Lord, I know I haven't been as faithful as my father was. I've read

Your word and prayed, but not like I should. It's no great surprise I'm confused and off-balance. I admit I haven't sought Your guidance in a great many areas of my life. I was the captain of my ship long before I ever sailed the *Stalwart*. I thought I was in control—I made the decisions. Why did I think that?"

He ran a hand over his chin. The warmth of the fire didn't chase the chill from his soul. Had he drifted so far from the God he once loved? When had he stopped viewing God as the Lord and Master of his life? He slipped from the chair to his knees.

"Oh, God, forgive me. I can't even remember the last time I prayed for Your guidance. I didn't seek You the day I set the course that took us into the storm, or in any of the decisions I've made since. I've tried to do everything by myself to take care of Garth's family—everything except pray for them."

Tears fell and dampened his nightshirt. "Lord, Felicity told me Garth's death wasn't my fault, wasn't anyone's fault. I want to believe her, but how can I not be to blame? You may have forgiven me, God, but I don't think I can forgive myself."

You must not claim ownership of what I have forgiven.

Drew laid his head down on his crossed arms and sagged against the chair. Guilt bled profusely until he was empty. Every sin he confessed—every offense against him—was blotted out, and God declared him free. Scarred by the wounds, certainly, but free of the infection.

The picture painted by the scripture he read manifested in his mind. The clay—the marred, broken clay...in the Potter's hand. "I am the clay, Lord Jesus. Make me over again."

CHAPTER 7

Bryn tore off the calendar page and crumpled it. Six weeks into her coveted position at the newspaper, and already the account ledger showed she was in financial trouble. She had to admit she never realized all that went into the business of running the publication. She wasn't incapable of learning. There was simply more to learn than she'd expected.

Regaining her advertisers and rebuilding her readership required a plan. Perhaps more human interest stories, or follow up stories on last week's reports. She could ask the local ministers to provide articles with a spiritual bent, or interview seamen for recent updates on the sailing and fishing industries. Anticipation of gathering information to report and writing the articles sent a thrill through her. The obstacles she'd encountered as publisher, however, were quite unforeseen. While she jotted down notes for promotional ideas, the one thing she refused to do was quit.

Hanging above the disarray of papers on the desk, the gold-plated pieces of news type spelling THE CLARION mocked her. She closed her eyes to shut out the prospect of disappointing her father.

Nothing changed when she opened her eyes. The dismal numbers in the account ledger remained the same. The wadded up calendar page reminded her the next edition of the *Clarion* was due out in a few days. She'd stayed up late last night penning her editorial. As she'd read it to Aunt Miriam that morning over breakfast, her aunt had cautioned her, suggesting perhaps she should alter the tone of her articles, and be more informative and less critical.

When Bryn pointed out that Aunt Miriam had been the one to encourage her to publish the editorials in the first place, her aunt had quickly responded, *"I didn't tell you to call every man in Stonecliffe ignorant."* But how else should she describe those who broke windows and painted callow messages?

Bryn read over the thoughts she'd scribbled last evening. The narrative compared the work of a woman to that of a man, pointing out that gender did not make one capable or incapable. Her eyes skimmed the over the draft, searching for anything untrue or far-fetched.

> *A person's talents and skills do not depend on their sex,*
> *and if a woman has the determination and fortitude*
> *to pursue an occupation traditionally held by men,*
> *they should applaud her. If they cannot find it within*
> *themselves to do so, perhaps they are plagued by a*
> *malady called Ignorance.*

Bryn tossed the paper back on the desk. She'd heard the crass and cynical remarks, demeaning her for presuming to think she could step into her father's job and do it as well as he had. While hurtful, they didn't possess the power to make her admit defeat.

Drew hadn't thought her presumptuous. He'd not uttered a single critical word, not even when she ran the story about the death of his first mate. Not even when he'd helped clean up messes—unless she included his inquiry about her needing a man to run the press. She stared at the table where he'd worked beside her to reset the type. Perhaps she'd misinterpreted his meaning.

She crossed to the new front window. A man had arrived only this morning, saying he was there to install a pane of glass. Despite telling him she hadn't ordered it, he assured her it was already paid for.

She bit her lip. Had Father somehow been made aware of recent events? She'd not contacted him. But who else would have hired someone to replace the glass? It had to be Father. After all, he was planning on selling the *Clarion* upon his return. No doubt he'd want the building to be in good repair.

On the other side of the glass, people scurried back and forth, wagons and carriages rattled down the cobblestone street. There were other news stories out there. Did anyone but her care whether or not a woman was free to pursue whatever she chose?

She donned her bonnet and picked up her market basket. Her errands included a stop at the mercantile to pick up a few things for Aunt Miriam and perusing the newest yard goods at Stiples. Maybe she'd have time to walk down to the docks and get some insight from the sailors for an article on this season's shipping business. Surely such a piece would be of interest to the residents of Stonecliffe. She dropped her notebook and pencil into her basket.

A handful of men lounged on the boardwalk in front of Pittman's Mercantile, swapping stories and exaggerating over who had caught the biggest fish. When Bryn neared, they fell silent and stared as she entered the yawning doors. Mr. Pittman looked up from a shelf he was dusting. His thick, black eyebrows merged together with skepticism, and the frown lines around his mouth deepened. He acknowledged her with a grunt.

She pulled Aunt Miriam's list from her basket and slid it across the counter to the merchant. "Mr. Pittman, I've noticed you haven't renewed your ad in the *Clarion* for the past three weeks." She glanced around at the nearly empty store. "Advertising will increase your business, as I'm sure you already know."

The storekeeper muttered something about his reputation before snatching up Aunt Miriam's list. Bryn didn't need a mind reader to understand. Clearly, he wanted her business, but was unwilling to connect the name of his establishment to the *Clarion*.

"I'm running a special on ads this week." The words tumbled from Bryn's lips before she had a chance to think about them. "Half price."

Mr. Pittman halted his hands as they gathered her items together, and glanced at her. His thin mustache curved into a downward arc. "Don't need no advertisement." He set the last item down and totaled up her purchases. "Two dollars and forty cents."

"You always advertised when my father ran the paper." Bryn halted the escape of a more accusing statement by drawing in a deep breath. "The special price goes through this week if you'd like to think about it."

"No need thinkin' on it." The man's jowls flapped at he shook his head. "I have a lot of loyal customers."

Bryn raised one eyebrow. "Loyal customers who might turn disloyal if you were to advertise in a newspaper run by a woman? Doesn't sound very loyal to me." She picked up her purchases and deposited them in her basket. "Please put these on my aunt's account."

Without waiting for Mr. Pittman's reply, she gripped the basket handle and stepped outside, where a brisk breeze coming off the water tousled her hair. She paused to tuck the errant strands into her bonnet.

To her right, a few guffaws drew her attention. The men lounging against the building cast speculative looks her way. She didn't catch every word they said, but the wind carried enough of their conversation to her ears to understand the gist of their comments.

"... woman ... *Clarion* ... ought to wear britches if she's gonna..."

"...doing a man's job..."

"I heard Homer up and quit..."

"...how long she thinks she's gonna last..."

"...by the end of the month."

"End of the month? It ain't gonna take that long!"

"I bet Pittman ten dollars..."

"I'll cover that bet and put another ten..."

Bryn froze in place as the men pulled out their wallets and slapped money down on a crate. Tears stung her eyes and she forced her feet to hasten in the opposite direction. Their laughter followed her until she rounded the corner.

Gambling. They were laying down wagers on how long she would remain as publisher of the *Clarion*. The knot in her stomach generated a surge of anger, and the basket handle cut into her fingers under her tight grip.

The sun had already dropped below the trees, painting the sky to the west with shades of gold, orange, purple, and crimson. Most of the businesses in town were already closed and shuttered, except for a couple of taverns. Drew strode past them on his way home. Up ahead, lamplight spilled from the front window of the *Clarion* office.

His chest stirred like a storm over the ocean. He'd kept his distance from her for several days—not because he didn't want to see her, but rather he needed to hear from God before pursuing anything more than friendship. Spending time in prayer each day overflowed his soul with joy, and asking God to order his steps brought peace to his heart in nearly every area of his life—except one. He'd not yet grasped sure direction regarding Bryn. He'd prayed and asked God to not let him fall in love with her...yet. Whether his heart took note of that prayer, he couldn't say.

He peered into the *Clarion*'s window. Bryn sat at the desk, focused on the work before her. He twisted the doorknob and pushed, tapping his knuckles on the door to gain her attention as he did so.

Bryn jerked around in her chair with an audible sharp intake of breath. She dropped her pen and clutched her hand to her throat, her dark brown eyes widened.

"Oh, Drew." Strain edged her voice even as relief sagged her shoulders.

Drew crossed to the desk. "I'm so sorry. I didn't mean to startle you."

She leaned back in the chair. "No, no. I thought it was those men returning. I'm glad it's you."

"What men?" Drew spun and stared hard out the window before returning his full attention to her. "What happened?" He touched her shoulder. "Did somebody harm you? Threaten you?"

She hunched her shoulders and shook her head. "No, they didn't hurt me, and I didn't recognize them. Their faces were covered." He followed her gaze back to the window where the street was bathed in the glow of a nearby gaslight.

Drew tightened his fingers into fists at his sides. "What did they do?"

"They said some ugly things. Threw some papers on the floor." She turned her head so he couldn't see her face, but he detected a slight tremble in her voice.

"Bryn, look at me."

She straightened and lifted her chin.

"Did you report this to the constable?"

She blew out a quiet, but disgusted laugh. "I didn't bother. I went to him when the window was broken, but he said I'd brought it on myself, and I should have expected as much."

Drew ground his teeth. "Until we find out who is doing these things, it's not safe for you to be here after dark."

"But—"

He pulled out his best sea captain tone. "No buts. Either let me help you do whatever needs done, or I'm taking you home right now. Then I'm going to speak to the constable myself."

Frustration pressed her lips into a tight line and her eyes darkened. "This is my fight, not yours. I don't mean to sound ungrateful, but I have to handle this myself."

Drew leaned forward and placed two fingers under her chin. The gentle contact sent a wave of an indescribable emotion through him. He pushed it aside. There would be time later to identify it, but for now, he intended to ensure her safety. "Bryn, I do not think you're incapable. Quite the contrary. But I won't leave you here alone."

CHAPTER 8

Drew pulled off his hat and ran his fingers through his hair as he steered the market wagon down the slope from Thorndike's Paper Mill. Only two deliveries today—at least two from paying customers. The third bundle in the wagon bed had been purchased with his own money, but Bryn didn't need to know that. He slapped his hat back over his disheveled hair.

Bryn's stubborn pride frustrated him, but he couldn't help admiring her tenacity. On the short walk to her aunt's home the other night, she'd let down her guard and admitted running the *Clarion* was a struggle. Between her mother's haranguing and her father's intention to sell the *Clarion*, he'd formed a better picture of what she was up against. Summer was more than half over. Her parents would return soon, and she despaired over the decline of the *Clarion*.

Drew frowned and clucked to the horses. The first two deliveries were only a few blocks apart. Drew hoisted the reams to his shoulder and toted them to their recipients at the bookbinder and the courthouse. If he hurried, he'd have a few minutes to stop and check on Felicity before delivering Bryn's bundle of paper. The merchants with whom Drew had set up accounts for Felicity had reported she'd only used the accounts once or twice, if at all.

He released the wagon brake and set the horses in motion, his thoughts drifting to Bryn again. He had the funds to help her, but knew her pride would never allow her to accept such an offer. There had to be another way. Her aunt had seemed supportive, but Bryn needed an advocate. Drew hoped that advocate was him.

He pulled the horses to a halt in front of Felicity's cottage. Tempting aromas tickled his nose as he strode to the door. Felicity answered his knock, wiping her hands on her apron.

"Drew, how nice to see you. Please, come in."

Drew removed his hat. "Hello, Felicity." He glanced toward the cradle in the corner. "How is little Lenora?"

A smile graced Felicity's face. "Doing better now that the tooth she was cutting has broken through." She gestured to the stove. "Would you like a cup of tea? I made scones to go with them this morning."

The fact that she had tea and the ingredients to make scones reassured him. "No, thank you. I can't stay."

She stirred the contents of a pot on the stove—a rich stew if his nose was correct. Fresh loaves of bread sat on the back of the stove, and the table held a crock of butter and a bowl of apples. "Are you sure you can't stay for dinner? It's almost ready."

Drew held up his hand. "Thank you, but no. I just stopped by to—"

The back door opened and a man Drew had never seen before stepped inside with an armload of firewood. He and Drew locked eyes.

"Drew, this is Garth's cousin, Kent Henshaw. Kent, Drew Montgomery."

Garth's cousin deposited the firewood in the box beside the stove and reached to shake Drew's hand. "Pleased to meet you."

Drew gave the man a cautious nod. "Likewise."

Felicity's gaze rested on Mr. Henshaw for a long moment before returning to Drew. "Kent has a farm just outside of town, and he brings us fresh vegetables, eggs, milk, and even a cured ham and some chickens."

Drew raised his eyebrows. "That so? Very kind of you, Mr. Henshaw."

The man shrugged. "It's nothing. Felicity has told me how you've helped her and the baby." He dropped his gaze. "I know you and my cousin were best friends."

Pain sliced through Drew. "Yes, we were." He cleared his throat. "Well, I have to be going. Felicity, it's good to see you doing well." He gave Henshaw another nod. "A pleasure meeting you, Mr. Henshaw."

Felicity walked Drew out to the wagon. "It's not what you think, Drew. Kent has been very good to me. Besides bringing food and chopping wood, he helped me plant my garden, repaired a window frame, re-hung the back door so it's more secure, and last week he brought over sacks of flour, cornmeal, coffee, and tea. This morning he hung another clothesline for me."

Drew paused by the wagon. "I'm grateful he's been so helpful. But I hope he's not—"

She stopped him. "He's not pressuring me at all. He told me when I'm ready to love again, he'll be here."

Her eyes still held fragments of grief for her husband, but at least Drew took assurance Garth's widow and daughter were being cared for. "Goodbye, Felicity."

She rose up on tiptoe and placed a light kiss on his cheek. "Thank you for caring, Drew."

He squeezed her hand and climbed up over the wheel, his heart a little lighter.

Bryn paused on the boardwalk to adjust the weight of the stack of newspapers in her arms—most of which she'd hoped to drop off at several places around town by now. The fact she was still toting them testified of the number of merchants who had turned her away.

Perhaps the depot agent at the end of the street would allow her to leave some papers to sell. She continued down to the end of the boardwalk. Up ahead, a wagon sat parked by a white picket gate in front of a small cottage. Drew and a woman Bryn did not recognize stood beside the wagon.

Her feet slowed. Drew and the woman appeared engaged in an intimate conversation. She stumbled to a stop and couldn't tear her eyes away. The one person she needed right now to reassure and encourage her, but his attentions were occupied elsewhere.

The woman stood on tiptoe and brushed a kiss across Drew's

cheek. A fist grabbed Bryn's heart and squeezed until she could barely breathe. Drew smiled down at the woman and climbed aboard the wagon. With a tug on the brim of his hat, he nudged the horses forward.

Bryn stepped into the alley beside the depot, leaned against the brick wall, and hugged her stack of newspapers.

Why shouldn't Drew be attracted to that other woman? Lovely blonde hair, pretty blue dress that probably matched her eyes, even her apron was neat and tidy. Compared to her, Bryn's appearance was downright shabby.

Her self-conscious gaze fell to her fingers gripping the bundle of newspapers. Ink-stained and broken, stubby nails defined her occupation. Even her dress bore evidence of brushing against the printing press. It couldn't be helped. Without a press man or typesetter, she was the *Clarion*. If she had a choice between wearing spotless gowns and having soft, beautiful hands or doing what she loved, she'd still choose the newspaper regardless of the obstacles and opposition. Today, however, she simply wished for a few less obstacles.

She dragged in a deep breath. Seeing Drew with another woman wasn't exactly an obstacle, but the image blurred the threads of hope to which she'd clung—hope that often carried her through difficult days. She searched for a shred of resolve and continued down the street.

Up ahead, the door of the dressmaker's shop opened and two familiar figures stepped out. Bryn halted her steps, tension stiffening every muscle.

Not now. Not today. Not with everything else she'd endured. What were they doing here? It was barely a week into August. She braced herself as they approached.

"Mother. Father. You're home early. I didn't expect you until..."

Mother's eyes swept over her, from her hastily pinned hair and ink-smudged hands to her ruined gown. A gasp hissed from her mother's lips, and the woman teetered on the boardwalk, fanning herself with her handkerchief.

"Bryn Rebekah Sinclair, how dare you disgrace this family by carrying on in such a degrading manner?" Her face paled as her glance darted back and forth, presumably to see if their confrontation was being witnessed by anyone her mother deemed important. "I cannot imagine why you've persisted in this ridiculous charade. The humiliation you've brought down on our family's name will ostracize us from the pinnacle of society for generations to come." A flush of red replaced the paleness in her face. Her lips opened and closed like a fish out of water as she turned to Father. "Preston, do something at once."

"Faye, that's enough." Displeasure etched lines in Father's expression. He eyed the stack of newspapers Bryn held. "Shouldn't these papers have already been distributed yesterday? Where is Peter and the other lads who peddled the *Clarion* each week?"

"H-he... I-I couldn't..." No, she wouldn't voice reality—that Homer had quit, and her finances were so anemic she'd had to let the boys go.

He arched his thick eyebrows. "I had to see for myself if what Homer had written to me was true."

She should have known the former press man would find a way to contact Father to air his complaints. It wasn't as if she'd fired him, but even if he'd stayed, she wouldn't have been able to pay him.

"Homer sent me copies of the editorials you've been printing." Father shook his head. "Bryn, what were you thinking, printing something so outrageous?"

Mother shook her finger in Father's direction. "I told you this would happen. You wouldn't listen."

Father silenced her with a look. Bryn waited for the anger she knew was coming. Instead, she saw intense disappointment in her father's eyes.

"We need to discuss this privately." His tone crackled with ice. "I'm taking your mother home. I will send the carriage for you in one hour."

"But, Father, you agreed to let me have the entire summ—" She bit off her words before all the frustration inside her came pouring out, creating a public spectacle. She blew out a disheartened sigh. "An hour."

Bryn wanted to scream from the depth of her lungs as she watched her parents walk to their carriage. She could have predicted her mother's reaction, but her father's disapproval burned. Learning they had cut their summer plans short to return home made her throat ache. She wanted to throttle Homer. Her gaze slid from side to side. Several stares were aimed her way, reigniting the heat in her face.

If she thought her day couldn't get any worse, she was mistaken.

CHAPTER 9

Drew pulled up in front of the *Clarion* office at the same moment Bryn walked up the boardwalk from the opposite direction, her expression unreadable. He'd come to look forward to her welcoming smiles, and disappointment pricked him this time. Her eyes only lit on his for a fraction of a moment before turning to unlock the front door. He hopped down from the wagon seat and strode to the tailgate.

"Hello. I have a delivery for you." The very sight of her accelerated his pulse. He wished God would tell him clearly one way or the other if His will for Drew's life included Bryn Sinclair. He earnestly hoped it was so.

She pushed the door open and dropped the key into her reticule. "I didn't place an order." She held the door open while he carried the paper inside. "I suppose this means Mr. Thorndike accepted my proposal—paper in exchange for free advertising. Please thank him for me."

Drew deposited his load on the work table with a brief nod. Should he tell her his boss had not agreed and insisted on cash on the barrel? He shrugged. What she didn't know wouldn't hurt her, and the resolve to protect her swelled within him. She'd withstood adversity with courage, but she shouldn't have to face it alone. Besides, it was his money. He could spend it any way he pleased.

She dusted her hands and sat at the desk, her back to him. "I know you're busy, so I won't keep you."

The abruptness of her statement gave him pause. He'd hurried through his deliveries so he'd have a few minutes to spend with her. The aloof tone of her voice indicated she wanted him to leave. He hoped he was wrong.

"Are you angry because I insisted on walking you home the other night?"

Her hands halted mid-motion and she hesitated before replying. "No, I'm not angry." Did her voice just tremble? She quickly turned back to the desk, but not before Drew caught sight of her rapid blinking.

He took a step closer. "Is everything all right?"

Sniff. She cleared her throat. "Yes, of course. Thank you for bringing the paper."

What had he done to offend her? Had he misread her feelings for him? He'd hoped the growing attraction in his heart was mutual. What if she only desired friendship and nothing more? The idea punched him in the stomach.

"Bryn, you will call on me if you need anything, won't you? Help with setting the type, or..." Did he sound like he was begging?

When she turned to speak, her tight, brittle smile didn't reach her eyes. "You've done more than enough already. I'm obliged."

He didn't want her obligation. He wanted her heart.

He reached out to touch her shoulder, but his fingertips stopped inches from their destination. Her expression was shuttered.

He withdrew his hand and shoved it in his pocket. "Well, I'll let you get back to work." The request for permission to call on her fought for release, but he forced it back. "Good day, Bryn."

Lead weights in his feet hindered his exit, and once seated in the wagon, he allowed the horses to plod their way back to the mill. Their gait reflected his mood. He couldn't shake the feeling something had happened to dampen Bryn's goodwill toward him. Was that all it was after all? A platonic association?

Misery accompanied him back to the mill. He doubted whether hard work would relieve the ache in his chest, but at the very least, keeping his hands busy might provide a distraction.

After spending two hours in intense discussion with her father, Bryn returned to the office emotionally bruised. Homer had embellished the truth, but for the most part, his description of the current situation was accurate.

Father's ultimatum was clear. He'd not let her do any more "damage" to the newspaper before he had a chance to find a buyer. At least he wasn't shutting her down entirely. He'd stated he would come by the office tomorrow afternoon to read over what she planned to print.

Typesetting tomorrow's lead story was finished and ready for the press. She rolled her head from side to side to work the kinks from her neck.

She gathered her papers and reticule, paused to straighten THE CLARION gold type that hung askew, and extinguished the lamp on the desk. The gaslight on the street shed enough of a glow through the window to show her the way to the front door. Her key turned easily in the lock, and she jiggled the doorknob to make sure the office was secure.

Drew's admonishment about working late alone tugged at her. The only people out this time of night were Stonecliffe's lamplighter and a few men coming and going at the tavern down at the far end of town. At least those were the only ones she could see. An involuntary shiver ran through her. She gripped the strings of her reticule and hugged her sheaf of papers to her. Despite her weariness, she pushed her feet into a trot, watching and listening as she hurried.

Nearly breathless by the time she reached Aunt Miriam's house, she entered as quietly as possible, certain her aunt must be sound asleep by now. The bottom step creaked under her weight.

"Bryn, is that you?"

Bryn cringed. "Yes, Aunt Miriam. I'm sorry I awakened you."

"You didn't. I was waiting for you."

Oh, dear. Bryn climbed the stairs and stopped in the open doorway of Aunt Miriam's bedroom. The older woman sat in her rocking chair beside the bed, her dressing gown wrapped around her ample figure.

"Come in, child. The tea is still hot." She reached for the china teapot on her bedside table and poured tea into a second cup. "Sit down."

Since the rocker was the only chair in the room, Bryn perched on the side of the bed and took the fragrant cup of rose hips tea her aunt held out to her. No scowl marred Aunt Miriam's face—no ire laced her tone.

"I'm sorry to be so late. I had to finish up—"

Aunt Miriam waved her hand. "It's all right, dear." She peered over her spectacles. "Although I would worry a lot less if you could see fit to come home at a decent hour."

Debating with Aunt Miriam was futile. "Yes, ma'am, I'll try."

The corners of Aunt Miriam's mouth twitched and she took a sip of tea. As she replaced the cup in her saucer, she leveled a look at Bryn. "You had a visitor this evening."

"I did?" Had Father stopped by and told her about their meeting?

"That handsome sea captain came to see you. He wanted to know if everything was all right." Aunt Miriam set cup and saucer on the table. "Is there perchance anything you'd like to tell me?"

Bryn let her shoulders slump. If she couldn't confide in Aunt Miriam, there was no one else on earth she could trust. Besides, she suspected her aunt wasn't going to let her go to bed until Bryn revealed what was on her heart.

She sighed and deposited her teacup beside her aunt's. "I suppose I should have done a better job guarding my heart."

Aunt Miriam's brows rose. "Why, child? What has happened?"

Fatigue wrapped itself around the anguish that had plagued her all day, and twined up her throat to choke off her words. All she could manage was a shake of her head.

"Ah, I see." Aunt Miriam leaned back and set the chair into its rocking motion. "You're in love with him."

Was she? How could she know? She twisted her fingers. "Drew—that is, Captain Montgomery—hasn't made any advances or done anything improper. I suppose I...I hoped he felt the same way about me as I do about him."

Aunt Miriam pressed her fingertips together and continued to rock. "And you think he doesn't."

"It's just as well." Bryn hated the way her voice broke as she told her aunt about her meeting with her father. "The newspaper has taken all my attention. I don't have time for a man in my life."

"It sounds as though you're trying to convince yourself, not me." Aunt Miriam's insightful tone nailed Bryn in place.

Tears burned behind her eyelids. "I saw him. Drew and a woman. They kissed. That is, she kissed him." She rubbed her eyes with the back of her hand and faced her aunt again. "It was a very chaste kiss. On the cheek. But..."

"But?" The rhythm of the rocking chair never diminished.

"But, he seemed...pleased. He smiled."

"I see." Aunt Miriam folded her gnarled fingers together in her lap. "And then what happened?"

Bryn lifted her shoulders. "He got into the wagon and left."

Her aunt gave a slow, thoughtful nod. "So, do you know who the woman is?"

"No." Bryn rose and collected the tea cups and tea pot, placing them on the tray. "I don't remember ever meeting her." She leaned down and kissed her aunt, and then picked up the tray. "I'm awfully tired. I'm going to bed."

How was it possible to be so tired but unable to fall asleep?

The glow of sunrise coming in Bryn's bedroom window barely shed enough light for her to see which gown she was donning, but she didn't feel like lighting the lamp. As she fastened the buttons, she leaned closer to the small mirror and examined the dark smudges under her eyes. She stifled a groan.

"I look hideous." Not that it mattered. There was no one she needed to impress.

Her fingers fumbled through the task of braiding her hair, twisting it around the back of her head, and pinning it in place. The aroma of coffee teased her from the kitchen below her room.

She hurried down the stairs and gave her aunt a peck on the cheek. "Good morning."

Her aunt eyed her in much the same way one might scrutinize the fruit at Mr. Appleby's grocery. "Didn't sleep well?"

Unwilling to engage in an extension of last night's discussion, Bryn shrugged and poured herself a cup of coffee. "I have a busy morning planned. The front page type is already set, and Father is coming to proofread the inner pages before I can run this week's edition."

Aunt Miriam fussed about her not eating a proper breakfast, but Bryn gulped down the coffee, snatched her reticule and bonnet, and scurried out the door with a promise to be home for supper.

Stonecliffe was stretching and yawning as she approached the office. She turned her key in the lock and pushed the door, but it banged against something before it opened more than a foot. What in the world? Bryn pushed her shoulder against the door and squeezed through the opening.

The carnage strewn across the office stole her breath.

Chapter 10

D rew drove the wagon toward the wharf to pick up barrels of aluminum sulfite for Thorndike. The sun barely peeked over the treetops but already the street teemed with people.

"Mr. Montgomery."

Drew pulled the horses to a halt to see Bryn's aunt waving and hurrying toward him. "Good morning, Mrs. Pierce."

"Good morning to you, sir." She dabbed her forehead with her handkerchief. "My niece will shoot me if she finds out I'm telling you this." She proceeded to tell Drew that Bryn had seen him with another woman.

Puzzlement snagged him for a moment, but then he remembered and explained his association with Felicity Henshaw. "I had merely stopped by to see how they were doing."

Enlightenment colored her expression, and Mrs. Pierce nodded. "I know Felicity Henshaw. Taking it upon yourself to look after her and the little one is commendable." She sent him a pointed look. "You might want to tell Bryn about Felicity—just to erase any confusion."

Chagrin popped Drew upside the head. "I believe you're right."

Mrs. Pierce smiled. "Of course I am. I happen to know she is getting ready to run the next edition this morning. She might even need some help."

Drew tipped his hat. "Thank you, Mrs. Pierce." He slapped the reins down on the horses' backs, and the wagon lurched forward. In minutes, he pulled up in front of the *Clarion* office.

The door stood ajar and he barged in, but halted in his tracks. Trays of type lay strewn across the floor, ink splattered several reams of paper. Even the desk was turned over.

Bryn sat on the floor in the middle of the wreckage, weeping.

Emotions crashed into each other head on--even more than the anger that immediately seethed through him, an overwhelming desire to comfort and protect this woman who had endured so much injustice. He was beside her in three strides, on his knees, pulling her into his arms. He held her and let her cry.

"Why?" The anguish in her broken word tore at his heart. Her tears soaked the front of his shirt. After a time, when her sobs waned, he tenderly blotted her face with his shirttail.

She hiccuped. "I n-needed you, and y-you c-came."

He tightened his embrace. Controlled rage raced through him at the thought of anyone doing such a thing to the woman he loved. Yes, he loved her. He knew it. He couldn't deny it.

He thumbed away another stray tear that escaped. "Do you know who did this?"

She nodded. "I did."

Surely he didn't hear her correctly.

"It's my fault. If I hadn't insisted on getting my own way and trying to run the *Clarion*, this never would have happened." The words tumbled out along with more tears.

Drew righted the desk chair and settled Bryn into it. He cupped her face with both hands. "Don't you blame yourself for this. No one has worked harder, been so diligent, or strived for approval more than you have. No one can accuse you of not doing your best."

She shrugged. "Perhaps not. But there are some who think I've committed some kind of atrocity by daring to cross the line in a profession reserved for men."

He grasped her shoulders. "You listen to me. You don't have to prove yourself to anyone, because God accepts you for who you are. You are His child. He loves you. And so do I."

Her eyes widened and her lips parted.

Drew stroked his finger down the side of her cheek. "Besides, whoever made such a ridiculous statement?"

"My mother, my brothers, former advertisers, even people on the street." Her list made his heart ache. But she wasn't finished. "Some are even taking bets on how long I will last at the *Clarion*."

Drew jerked backwards. "What?"

"It's true. I heard them. They were putting down money on the length of time until I'm intimidated enough to quit."

"Who? Can you name these men? Do you know who they are?"

Her brows dipped. "I know who a couple of them are. The others I would recognize if I saw them again."

Drew grasped her hands and pulled her to her feet. "We're going to the constable's office right now." He tugged her toward the door.

She resisted. "What for? The constable didn't lift a finger when the window was broken."

He took her chin between his thumb and forefinger. "He will this time. There is enough damage here to prosecute, and we have possible suspects who had a motive."

She stared at him with wide, dazed eyes. "Do you mean those men who were placing wagers did this? So they could win the bet?"

"Come on. Let's go see the constable."

Constable Lovell was just coming out his office door when Drew and Bryn arrived. The law officer tipped his hat. "Miss Sinclair." He nodded in Drew's direction. "Montgomery."

Drew returned the nod. "Glad we caught you, Constable. There's been an incident at the *Clarion* office."

Lovell smirked. "Again?" He sent a disparaging look toward Bryn. "What's happened this time? Someone leave a frying pan and an apron hanging on the front door?"

His scoff grated on Drew's nerves. He took a step forward. "This is a bit more serious. The entire office has been ransacked, furniture turned upside down, the type destroyed, the press damaged, ink strewn all over the place, the—"

"All right, I get the idea." The constable glanced left and right. A small crowd was beginning to gather. "Why don't we step inside and—"

"No."

Bryn jerked her focus to Drew. No?

Drew gestured to the town folk stepping up to listen. "No, I think we need to have this discussion right here so everyone can hear about it."

A few more people scurried over to join the growing audience.

Drew placed his hand on Bryn's shoulder. "Tell the constable what you found this morning when you arrived at the office. Don't leave anything out. And speak up so all these fine folks can hear you."

"Now, see here, Montgomery—"

A woman in the crowd called out. "Yes, we want to hear." Murmurs of agreement floated through the gathered group.

In a halting voice, Bryn described everything she'd encountered, right down to the jimmied back door and trays of type tossed across the room. As Drew prompted her, she related what she'd heard from the men who were placing bets. Gasps rippled through the onlookers as they expressed disgust over what had happened.

Clearly uncomfortable, Constable Lovell rubbed his hand over his whiskers. "Well, I've seen men do worse for monetary gain. I suppose I'll have to write up a report."

"A report, Lovell?" Drew used his sea captain voice so people at the back of the crowd could hear. "I would like to point out this woman has done nothing wrong. She did not bring this on herself. There is nothing written in the constitution forbidding a woman to run a newspaper. The freedom of occupational choice has been in place for well over a decade, and in fact, there are women in this very town who own their own businesses. I see a few of them in this crowd."

Drew caught Bryn's hand and squeezed as cries of agreement and jeers regarding the constable's performance of his duty rose to a din.

Lovell raised his hands and bellowed. "All right, all right. Everyone go about your business while I launch an investigation into this matter. Miss Sinclair, if you and Captain Montgomery will accompany me to the *Clarion* office, I'd like to take some notes."

As Drew ushered Bryn past the constable, Lovell harrumphed. "Montgomery, maybe you should write the next editorial."

Bryn smiled up at Drew as he tucked her hand securely in the crook of his arm. Constable Lovell had taken his time looking over the damage, inspecting the broken door latch, and documenting every detail before he returned to his office. Finally, they were alone surrounded by the jumbled mess.

"Won't Mr. Thorndike be wondering where you are?"

Drew nodded. "Yes, I need to get back, but I promise I'll return just as soon as I can to help you clean up."

She shrugged. "Why bother? The *Clarion* doesn't have the revenue to repair or replace anything that has been destroyed. Furthermore, when Father learns what has happened, he will no doubt close everything down and put the newspaper on the auction block." Her voice broke. "I'm finished."

Drew cupped her chin and caressed her cheek with his thumb. "Didn't your father give you until the end of summer?"

She resisted the desire to lean her head into his hand. "Yes, but—"

Drew laid his finger over her lips and bent to brush a soft kiss across her forehead. "Then we have three more weeks."

Bryn watched him step over the rubble and slip out. She shook her head at his retreating figure. "Drew Montgomery, you are an incredible man."

CHAPTER 11

The emotions storming through Bryn's chest created a hopeless tangle. Sorting the despair and anger over the destruction to the apprehension over her father's ultimatum drained her of the will and energy to keep going. In the middle of it all, however, hope glimmered in the form of Drew's smile and gentle kiss. Did she dare cling to the encouragement he offered that she could still make the *Clarion* work?

The memory of seeing him standing by the gate, that other woman standing on tiptoe to kiss his cheek, crashed over her. Who was that woman? Had Drew already committed his heart to her? If so, why then, would he give the gifts of his smiles, his time, his energy, and his support to Bryn?

And his kiss.

She touched her fingertips to the spot on her forehead where his lips had tenderly brushed, and her heart fluttered like a hummingbird's wings. Drew could have joined forces with the other men in Stonecliffe, especially when she ran the story about the *Stalwart*. But he didn't. Oh, how she wanted to believe he cared for her, but by all appearances, the woman at the gate already had his heart. The ache in her chest swelled. Contemplating the idea of Drew being nothing more than a friend sent a shard of pain through her, but she would not be guilty of stealing him away from another woman.

Bryn sidestepped the debris-cluttered floor and locked the *Clarion* door. She dug through the scattered papers and found a sheet that didn't bear too many stains. In large, block letters she wrote:

DUE TO VANDALISM
THE NEXT EDITION
OF THE CLARION
WILL BE DELAYED

Delayed or cancelled? She studied the message for a long minute and weighed her situation. Father would, no doubt, have something to say as soon as he learned what had transpired. For now, delayed carried a thread of hope. She put the sign in the window and turned to survey the mess.

What made her think she could put out the next edition at all? Until she sorted through everything, there was no way to tell how much damage was repairable or estimate the cost. She set to work gathering up pieces of type into their respective compartmental drawers.

She hauled the trash bin from the back alley into the office and tossed in ruined paper, destroyed ink pads, and broken type set trays. After two hours of non-stop work, she glanced around. She'd barely made a dent in the wreckage.

A sigh, born in the depth of her soul, sought freedom. Her eyes closed as she lifted her heart to heaven.

"God, I've been chasing after my own dreams and desires without even considering You. I've been striving to do what I want, but I didn't ask You what You want. I thought I had to prove myself— to my father, to the citizens of Stonecliffe...but I never stopped to realize I don't have to prove myself to You. Forgive me.

"You aren't a God who holds threats or imposes stipulations over my head. You don't withhold Your love and acceptance based on whether or not others validate my efforts." Another sigh whooshed from her lips. "You love me even when I make mistakes, and even when I forget to love You back."

Bryn sank to her knees, surrounded by the evidence of her failure. Her heavenly Father's unconditional love rained down and saturated her being. "I had hoped to prove myself capable, but I can't do anything without You. Oh, Father, I need Your strength. Give me the grace I need this hour."

Drew strode down the cobblestone street on his way to the *Clarion* office. His errand had taken longer than he expected, but the last piece finally fell into place.

Up ahead, Constable Lovell hailed him, and Drew hastened to meet the man.

"Just wanted to let you know I've already made two arrests in relation to the vandalism at the newspaper office."

Pleasant surprise arched Drew's brows. "Indeed? Found them rather quickly, did you?" He didn't point out that the constable might have prevented the damage from occurring in the first place had he been more diligent about his duty when the window had been broken. The underlying implication seemed to escape the constable's notice.

Lovell puffed out his chest. "Yes, based on the testimony of several men, all of whom witnessed the wagering, I located the two culprits. Neither of them had viable alibis and both had ink stains on their hands." He reached inside his vest. "Oh, and this." He withdrew a gold-plated ornament and held it out to Drew. THE CLARION piece glittered in the sunlight. "This was in the pocket of one of the thugs. No doubt he expected to scrape off the gold and sell it. Can you make sure Miss Sinclair gets it?"

Drew's heart soared as he took the piece. "It will be my pleasure."

"Tell Miss Sinclair she will likely be called upon to testify." Lovell tucked his thumbs behind his suspenders and strutted down the street.

Bryn dragged her sleeve across her forehead and plunged back into the clean-up. Her father had yet to make an appearance, and she hoped to have the place back in order—at least as much as possible—before he arrived. Given the extent of the damage she continued to uncover, the likelihood of putting out the next edition in a halfway-timely manner looked more remote by the minute. Regardless of the turmoil around her, her recent conversation with God left her with a quiet peace.

The door rattled and she glanced up. Drew peered through the glass, and her heart skipped. She twisted the key in the lock to let him in.

He grasped both her hands in his and fixed his gaze on her. Not on the mess, but on her.

"How are you doing?" His deep voice rumbled with an emotion she didn't dare try to name.

"All right."

He cocked his head and studied her. "I can see that you are. There is something different about you." He brushed his fingers against her cheek.

Heat filled her face as she glanced down to her dress and ran her hand over her hair. "I must be a mess."

Drew squeezed the hand still in his possession and smiled. "You're beautiful." After a long moment, he released her hand and tucked his fingers into his belt. "I have news." He relayed what Lovell had told him and she nodded.

Relief trickled through her. "I'll testify. The sooner, the better."

"There's more." Was that unease she heard in his voice? "Let's sit." He cupped her elbow and guided her to the chair. He upended a crate and perched on it.

"What is so consequential that I must sit down to hear it?" She braced herself.

He placed his elbows on his knees and interlaced his fingers. She'd not seen him struggle for words before, but just now he hesitated, as if trying to protect her from something she didn't want to hear.

"Your father has sold the *Clarion*."

Despite his gentle tone, the statement still hit her like a bucket of cold water. Disappointment skewered her, but she couldn't truly claim surprise. She slumped against the back of the chair. "I see." She blew out the pent-up breath she'd been holding. "I can't help wishing he had at least notified me."

Drew dropped his gaze. "He didn't have time to notify you. The buyer made an offer and your father accepted it."

That didn't sound like Father—to make a hasty decision without taking time for negotiations.

"But Father doesn't know about...this." She cast a sweeping gaze about the room that still lay in much disarray despite her work all morning.

"Yes, he does."

Ah, so that's why he was in such a hurry to accept the offer. "I assume the constable reported the incident to him." She lifted her shoulders in resignation. "He will probably arrive any minute to take me back home."

"Bryn—"

"It seems we didn't get those last three weeks, after all, did we?" She tried her best to force a smile, but the lump in her throat pulled at her effort. "Well, if I must leave here for good, there is one thing I'm taking with me." She turned in the chair and reached for the gold THE CLARION ornament, but her hand halted in mid-air. The piece didn't hang in its usual place.

She bent and pushed aside papers and other debris, searching for the keepsake.

"Looking for this?"

She glanced toward Drew's outstretched hand. "Yes. Where did you find it?"

A small smile tweaked Drew's mouth. "Constable Lovell found it in one of the miscreant's pockets."

"Oh..." She cradled the piece in her hands like a precious thing. "I'll clean up the office the best I can, but the new owner isn't getting this." She ran her finger over the golden edge.

Drew rose. "I'll help you clean."

She sent him a questioning look. "But don't you have to work? Mr. Thorndike—"

"Accepted my resignation this morning." He lifted his shoulders. "He said under the circumstances, it was the right thing."

Under the circumstances? He must refer to the woman whom Bryn had seen.

"Drew, there is something I must know." She took in a deep breath. "I saw you with a woman a couple of days ago."

He looked her straight in the eye. "Her name is Felicity Henshaw. She is the widow of my best friend. Until now, I've been looking after her and her baby daughter, making sure they want for nothing. It was the right thing to do."

Understanding dawned, and Bryn nodded. "Until now?"

"Her late husband's cousin has shown a great deal of interest, and Felicity seems to welcome his attention. I have been assured he can be relied upon to see to their needs."

She blinked away the tears that welled behind her eyelids as a sudden lightness seeped into her being. A bubble of laughter rose to her throat and she allowed it freedom. Her presumption regarding the woman was inaccurate. She was never so happy to be wrong.

Drew sent her a quizzical look. "What is it?"

Heat filled her cheeks and she lowered her gaze. "I was just wondering if I'll get to meet the *Clarion*'s new owner."

"You already have. I'm the new owner."

Bryn yanked her focus back to Drew and blinked her widened eyes. "You? But..." She shook her head in an effort to joggle the conflicting emotions into some sort of order. "But I thought..."

He shuffled his feet, pushing papers and trash away.

Confusion assaulted her. "Wh-what are you doing?"

He continued kicking clutter out of the way. "Clearing a spot."

A spot? "What for?"

Drew lowered himself to one knee on the newly cleared space and took her hand—the one still holding THE CLARION ornament—within both of his. "Bryn Sinclair, I love you with all my heart, and I wonder if you'd be willing to work at two jobs. One as the editor-in-chief of the *Clarion*, and the other as my wife."

She covered her mouth with the fingers of her free hand. "Oh, Drew." Her words were a breathless whisper. "Yes. Oh, yes."

He rose and enfolded her in her arms. "I hope you won't mind teaching me about the newspaper business."

She pressed the gold news type piece into his hand and snuggled against his chest. "I don't mind at all."

RODEO GIRL

EILEEN KEY

Greater love hath no man than this,
that a man lay down his life for his friends.
JOHN 15:13

Chapter 1

Gravel pinged under the truck as Erin Storm swung onto the rodeo grounds. She maneuvered around a pothole, glancing in the rearview mirror at the trailer carrying her dad's prized stock. "Keep calm, buddies." She bit her lower lip and let her eyes rove over the lot to locate the alleyway leading to the holding pens.

When she stopped, Carl Owens approached, a clipboard in hand. "Unloading?"

Erin nodded.

"Then I'll guide you in."

Drawing in a deep breath, Erin tugged her cap low and tight and readied to line up the trailer with the alleyway opening. She backed up slowly, watching Carl's hand signals. Once the trailer was in the right spot, she exhaled and set the brake. Storm Stock Contractors had arrived. She'd call her daddy as soon as the eight bulls were unloaded.

She swung down from the dually's cab and strode to the end of the trailer, a hot June wind kicking up dust. The cowboy opened the gate and she lifted the latch. The lead bull turned and spotted the opening. He shook his huge head, his horns almost catching the trailer railing. With a snort, he started down the ramp.

"Okay, Killer, you take 'em in." Erin slapped the bull's hide as he passed. "Hiyah, let's move." She reached inside and slapped another bull. He turned and followed. Within seconds the captives moved down the alleyway toward their holding pen.

"Have your paperwork right here, Erin." Carl held out the clipboard.

Erin smiled. "Appreciate your—" Out of the corner of her eye, she spotted movement. Someone standing inside her holding pen. "Mister!" She almost strangled on the word. Killer might head his way. Panic threaded through her middle—not another accident. "Mister!" The word strangled from her throat, and she ran toward the pen. "Get out of there!"

The man turned then noticed the approaching animals. His eyes widened and his jaw dropped open. With three strides, he hit the side of the chute and climbed up. His fancy shoes slipped on each slat, but he made it to the top. Erin leaned over and clapped her hands on her thighs, relief flooding her.

"Hey, driver. Are you crazy?"

Erin lifted her head.

The man clambered over the chute, dropped to the ground and stomped toward her. "What in blue blazes do you think you're doing?" He flapped his arms above his head. "Didn't you see me?" His perfectly groomed appearance had taken on a ramshackle look. Dirt coated the front of his suit coat and his probably-expensive shoes were caked in mud and manure.

Erin twisted her lips to keep from laughing.

Carl chuckled. "Well, sir, I didn't see you just like Erin. And you ain't got no business inside the grounds, as I see it."

The gentleman brushed his coat and proceeded toward them. "This idiot driver Aaron should've seen me." He drew within a few feet of her. "What outfit are you with, mister?"

Erin straightened and drew her shoulders back. She glared at the man. Into wonderfully dark eyes. A flush crept up her neck. "Storm Stock Contractors."

"I'm lodging a complaint at your recklessness." He leaned forward. "A man ought to survey the area before he lets out dangerous animals."

A man? Erin suppressed another laugh, then lifted her cap and let her hair trail down. She shook the unruly mane and waited.

The man's face reddened. "Oh." He slipped a finger inside the collar of his shirt. "Sorry. I thought—" He stared at her then whispered, "I'm sorry. Shouldn't have called you an idiot."

"Why? Because I'm a girl?" Anger tinged her words. "You had no business inside that pen." She pointed at the cowboy. "Neither he nor I are at fault here." She shook her finger at the man. "You are. And if I was in the name calling business, like you, I could think of a few." She raised her head, shot him another look and reached for the clipboard. "I'll sign out now." With a few strokes of the pen, she was done. Time to move out and park.

"Wait." The man held out his hand. "Let's start over. Conrad Butler."

Erin stared at him. She debated the handshake. Her daddy told her she was entering a man's world, but with three months of deliveries under her belt she'd proven herself capable of hauling stock. What was this handsome city slicker with the dark eyes and perfectly coifed hair doing at the arena?

She blinked. Where had her mind gone?

She reached for his hand. "Erin Storm of Storm Stock Contractors." Her fingers tingled at his touch, and she jerked her hand away. She slapped her cap against her leg and turned. "Gotta move to the parking area."

"Would you like to grab a cup of coffee?"

"Thanks" —she threw the word over her shoulder—"but I've got work to do." She reached for the truck door handle, tugged it open and clambered inside.

Conrad grabbed the door and leaned in. "Maybe I can see you later?"

Erin rubbed her hand across the steering wheel. "Sticking around for the rodeo?"

Conrad nodded.

She stared out the windshield then down at him. "Then you'll see me." Conrad stepped back, closed the door, and nodded. Erin started the motor and drove to the back parking lot, the handsome man in her rearview mirror.

Jack "Dusty" Bolton watched the scene from his truck. Erin looked mad enough to chew nails. She'd even shaken her finger at the fancy dressed dude. Dusty had seen him at the last two rodeos. He watched the girl shake her head and climb into her truck. Good. She was done with the guy. Dusty shifted in the seat. Why should he care?

But he did. He'd met Erin six weeks ago and liked her easygoing manner. Not like a lot of buckle bunnies who hung around cowboys looking for a good time. Erin's quiet demeanor set her apart from the rest.

He sighed. Not that he'd ever get to know Erin Storm. She was light years above his reach. Her daddy owned the biggest spread in the area, a truck business, plus the arena in front of him. He'd never have the kind of money she was accustomed to. He shoved his hat tighter on his head and jerked the gear shift into drive. He'd best check into the motel before all the cheap rooms disappeared.

Dusty rounded the end of the parking lot and spotted the fancy man climbing into a sports car. Figured. Probably a doctor or a lawyer. Wonder what he was doing here?

He shook his head. The guy left Erin alone—that was enough for him. Dusty pulled onto the highway leaving thoughts of city slickers behind. Only a beautiful truck driver danced through his mind.

Chapter 2

E rin stood in the saddle and slid the flag into the flag boot on her stirrup. The strap held the pole straight. She glanced up at the red, white, and blue, and a shiver ran down her spine. Riding in the rodeo entry always engulfed her emotions.

Memories of her mom on this same palomino signaled the lump in her throat to tighten. Every time Erin donned the familiar gold satin shirt with white fringe, topped her head with the white cowboy hat, climbed into the silver coated saddle and settled the flag, her heart nearly burst with pride. The Storm Arena, the stock trucks, the bawling of the cattle, horses snorting, the overpowering smell of popcorn from the concession stand tinged with dirt from the rodeo—spelled home. There was no where on earth she would rather be than Higly, Texas.

The screech of the microphone caused Buttermilk to dance, and Erin reined her in tighter. She awaited Calvin Woodlee, the announcer, to signal her entrance.

"Ladies and gentlemen, if you'd please stand—"

The rest of the words were lost on the wind as Erin spurred Buttermilk through the gate, around the sides of the arena, flag held high and rippling in the breeze. One circle then they pulled up in the center of the arena as the "Star Spangled Banner" stirred the air. Cowboys removed their hats and held them against their hearts, wizened faces, young girls and boys—patriotism was alive and well on this night.

Dismissed from her ride, Erin left the arena, passed off the flag, and turned Buttermilk toward the trailer.

"Looked mighty fine out there, Miss Erin."

Erin accepted the compliments and ignored the catcalls. Being backstage on the rodeo grounds meant being in a man's world again. She dismounted, tied up her horse, and dragged the saddle to the backseat of her cousin's pickup truck. Her Storm Contractor uniform lay in a heap on the floorboard. She grabbed the shirt and headed for the restroom to change. Satin was fine when you rode in the wind, but not for watching a rodeo.

"You looked wonderful out there, Erin." Conrad materialized in front of her on the walkway, a crooked smile on his face. "Will you ride in other events? Maybe barrel race?"

Erin shook her head. "No, sir. Nowadays, I'm strictly here for show." Snarky, Erin. Quit. But it seemed true. No time for practicing, no money for entry fees. She was just a driver and a flag girl.

"Time for coffee or a drink now?"

Erin paused, one boot on the cracked concrete sidewalk leading to the ladies' room. She tapped the denim shirt on her arm. "Grab me a soda while I change." She opened the door and stepped inside the musty room. Fluffing her hair, rubbing a smudge of dirt from her cheek, she donned the trucking shirt. Staring in the mirror she groaned. "Face it. You are now a truck driver, no longer the high school rodeo queen. Get over yourself."

A woman entered the restroom breaking Erin's mood. She straightened her shoulders and marched out the door. It had been a long while since a nice looking gentleman had taken any interest in her. Maybe life was taking an unexpected turn.

Dusty's heart had swelled with pride when he watched Erin ride into the arena, the flag held high. Tears welled and he struggled to sing the anthem. Man, she was beautiful. Her brown hair cascaded down her rigid back as her palomino struck a pose. A sight to behold. Then she rode away.

He meandered to his truck to get ready for the evening. He'd carb up and dress. He grabbed a bag of Fritos and settled back into the seat, a flat soda in the drink carrier.

He chomped on a chip. He wished he had the courage to visit with Erin Storm. He'd only met her as Dusty the bullfighter, covered in grease paint. Would she even recognize him without his makeup? Dusty glanced in the mirror at his pock-marked skin. Acne had caused him such agony in high school. Would he ever outgrow his unease? He sipped the warm soda and then screwed the bottle cap on. Time to get a move on. He had a lot to do before his rodeo appearance. And his focus could not be on a pretty woman with curly brown hair.

Dusty wrapped the trash in a plastic bag and tossed it in the backseat. He opened the console and reached for his Bible where he found his verse, John 15:13, and closed his eyes. "Lord, I hope I don't have to lay down my whole life tonight, but whatever happens it's in Your hands. I trust in You."

He smiled. How many times had he uttered those words before he stepped into an arena? Many called him crazy for waltzing in front of monsters, but it was his passion, his livelihood and he loved it. Sure, the adrenaline rush was there, but more than that, he protected guys who were giving it their all as they seated themselves on the back of a ton of animal. Protect the cowboy, protect his partner and protect himself, the bullfighter mantra. He closed his Bible and placed it back in the console.

With swift movements, he cleared the front seat and jerked his prep bag from the floorboard. A few swipes of greasepaint and he soon wore his rodeo face. He slid from the truck and donned his padded shorts and protective vest. His droopy, baggy clothes—which would tear away from a bull's horns—would wait until just before show time.

He slammed the door of the truck and rounded the bed, colliding with a man carrying two drinks. The cups crumpled and a dark stain ran down the man's shirt, coat and pants. The guy strangled out a curse word and shoved Dusty.

"Hey, man." Dusty reached over the tailgate and grabbed a greasy rag. "I'm truly sorry. Didn't see you." He held out the towel. "Let me buy you another round."

"Don't touch me, idiot. You...you..."—his lips turned up in a snarl—"clown!" He dropped the cups and stomped away.

"The stranger." Dusty shook his head and rubbed his jaw. "Seems like he's in everybody's way today."

CHAPTER 3

"Erin, I apologize. I was accosted by the rodeo clown." Conrad swiped at his wet shirt then glanced at her. "Was looking forward to a visit." He leaned closer. "I'd like to get to know you better." He smiled but it didn't seem to reach his eyes.

A skitter of worry ran down her spine. Unease settled in her stomach. His dark eyes peered out from his hooded brow. "Accosted? By our clown?" Her voice sounded shrill. "Daddy doesn't put up with any craziness on the rodeo grounds. Do I need to call security?" She tucked the gold shirt under her arm.

Conrad held up a hand. "No, no. I guess that was too strong a word." He jerked his shirt front from his chest, fanning it a bit. "More like he wasn't watching where he was going." He pointed to a set of empty bleachers. "Maybe I'd dry out better if we sat in the breeze. Do you mind? Want another drink?"

Erin licked her lips and tried for a smile. Her gaze roved the area and settled on Dusty. He was watching. True blue Dusty. He gave a slight nod, his floppy hat half covering his face.

If she needed anything—

"Let's sit." She climbed up to the second row and sat, plunking her boots on the row in front of her. Truth be told, this spot was exactly where she wanted to be. Her favorite to keep an eye on the chutes and the arena. "So what brings you to the rodeo tonight?" She pointed at his shoes. "See you got those clean."

Conrad tilted toward her until their shoulders bumped. "Just wanted to hear the national anthem."

Erin jerked forward. "I'm sure it's played on the radio." She fanned fringe from her mom's gold shirt across her knees. "Why are you at the rodeo?" She lifted a brow. "Dressed like a banker."

Conrad cleared his throat. "Because I am a banker."

"I see." Nausea trailed through her middle, but she turned and faced him. "Business or pleasure visit?"

"I think you know, Miss Storm." Conrad reached inside his jacket pocket. "I came looking for Mr. Storm, but I heard he's been in an accident." He fixed her with a level stare. "Please tell him to get well." He stretched out his hand and tapped an envelope on her knee. "However, this is a matter that must be addressed by the end of the quarter." He let go of the envelope and it dropped in her lap. He twisted his arm toward his face to look at a shiny gold watch. "Today's date is the twelfth." Conrad scooted from the end of the bleacher and stood. "I really would like to get to know you better, Erin. But maybe tonight's not the best time." He saluted with two fingers, turned and disappeared behind the chutes.

Erin held the envelope against her chest, tears welling and the lump in her throat trying to choke her to death. Her brother in the military, deployed, her daddy injured and her mom gone. A tear spilled over her lashes down her cheek. "Guess you're the lucky Storm."

Dusty spotted the couple when he approached the chutes. He nodded when Erin glanced his way. He placed his foot on a rung and watched as the stranger pressed an envelope into Erin's hand, then left. Dusty cocked his head and stared. "She's crying." He angled away from the chute and headed in her direction.

The microphone squealed. "And he's about to enter the arena. Give a warm Higly welcome to our bullfighter, Dusty."

Dusty jerked to a stop. Show time? He watched Erin swipe a tear then give him a thumbs up. He returned the gesture and stomped into the arena. His moment to comfort her had evaporated. And it was time to get his head on straight. Total attention was needed to protect these boys, the other bullfighter Trevor, and himself.

"Okay, Lord. We're in Your hands." Dusty waved to the crowd, stationed himself to Trevor's right and planted his feet. With a nod from the cowboy on the bull, the chute gate opened.

Two thousand pounds of beef shook the ground when he landed after a buck. Dusty counted five seconds before the rider shot from the beast's back. He ran straight at the bull, straining for his attention so the boy could scoot to safety. One up and down safely. "Thanks, Lord."

Within minutes the second chute opened and another rider bit the dust. Then the gate flew open for the third bull. Dusty felt his mouth go dry. He knew this bull. Killer. Every rider and bullfighter recognized the mean animal. The rider on his back lasted one or two seconds before he disentangled his hand, slung a leg over and gave up the ride. The bull pounded the ground and the terrified cowboy scrambled away. Trevor started toward Killer then jerked and climbed the chute, leaving Dusty in the arena.

"So we want a show?" Dusty grit his teeth. Killer pawed the ground and slung drool in the air. He bellowed and charged.

"Go around him," Trevor yelled, waving one hand. "Head around."

Dusty made his way past the bull garnering a rough nudge in the side. A pain shot down his hip. He slipped and Killer whirled about. For a moment he was face to face with the beast. His chips and cola threatened to spill out. The pain rippled through him, but he regained his footing. As the beast shot forward, Dusty cut right, spinning the animal in a tight circle. Dusty froze in front of the bull again, waiting. At the charge, Dusty cut left, and ran to the fence. With a hop and a skip he was over. Cowboys on horseback rounded up Killer, and the audience cheered. Another successful performance.

Dusty lay against a bleacher and ran his hand down his hip. He'd been run over and stomped on before, so pain was no stranger.

Trevor pounded across the metal bleacher. "You okay?" He bent over to poke at Dusty's chest. "You handled that good, buddy."

"Thanks." He ran a hand over his face. "How many riders left?"

Trevor looked toward the chutes. "Three loaded. But Killer was the only show. The rest are just rides."

Just rides. Lord, let them be safe ones. Maybe I'm getting too old for this.

"Dusty! Dusty! Are you okay?" Erin appeared before him, the arena lights casting a glow about her head—angel-like. She dropped to the bleacher seat and peered into his eyes.

Heat crept up his face under his makeup. "Doing fine, thanks." He wiped the front of his vest and shuffled to his feet. "That old bull of yours didn't take me out." He forced a chuckle. "Not yet, anyway."

Trevor reached for the top fence slat. "Let's go, partner. Cowboy's up." He slid into the arena.

"If you need to rest—"

"Thank you, Erin, for checking on me." Dusty swung his leg over the fence and dropped into the dirt. "See you later."

Get your head back in the game. Rodeo queens don't end up with ugly clowns.

CHAPTER 4

The screen door crashed against the wall as Erin stomped down the steps and yanked open the truck door, scouring the front seat of the truck. "Where is that envelope?" She had searched her purse, the gold shirt, her jeans, and nothing. She propped her elbow on the door and sighed. The thought of a stranger reading the contents made her sick to her stomach. Perspiration dotted her lip. She pulled the truck keys from her pocket and slid in the seat. "Nothing to do but go look." Tears stung her eyes as she drove toward the rodeo grounds.

Once parked, she darted to the bleachers where Conrad had handed her the bad news. Nothing. She searched under the seats and found popcorn bags and other garbage, but no envelope. "Oh, Lord." The words escaped her lips before she could catch them. So far He hadn't heard any of the other prayers she'd cast upward. Especially the ones for her daddy. She slumped against a chute. "Where else?" Erin ran fingers through her hair. A bull bellowed in the night air. Bull riders. "Dusty."

Erin shot around the chutes and holding pens to the other side of the arena. She clumped down the bleacher row until she reached the place where she'd talked with the injured bullfighter. Drawing in a breath and holding it, she searched the area. Nothing.

She sat down and pinched the bridge of her nose, a sinking feeling in her stomach. Once again, tears threatened. She dreaded the idea of asking Conrad for another copy of the letter.

"Miss Erin?"

She opened her eyes. Trevor stood in the arena. He dusted dirt from his jeans. "You okay, Miss Erin?" Concern tinged his look.

"Yeah, yeah." Erin straightened. "By any chance did you spot—"

"An envelope?" Trevor grinned. "Sure did."

Erin's breath caught in her throat.

He climbed the fence, dug into his back pocket and produced a wrinkled envelope. "Was saving this until tomorrow." He handed it to her.

Relief flooded her. "Thank you so much." She held the letter against her chest. "Really appreciate the help." She stood and held out a hand for him to shake.

He gripped her fingers in a tight squeeze then released them. "You staying for services?"

Erin resisted the urge to rub her hand against her thigh to restore circulation. "Services?"

Trevor jabbed a thumb at the end of the arena. "Cowboy church." He slid back into the dirt. "You missed the singing, but Pastor Jack just began preaching. I spotted you and slunk out for a minute." He chuckled. "In that crowd, I won't be missed." He waved a hand. "Come on and join us."

Erin shook her head. "I appreciate the invitation, Trevor, but I'm exhausted and have to haul bulls to Ridgely in the morning. Guess I'd better turn in." She waved the envelope. "I'll sleep better now that this is in hand."

"Well, good night. Maybe next time." Trevor loped toward the end of the arena and through a gate where a large group of people sat in a semi-circle.

She flapped the envelope in the air. "Guess I owe you a thanks for this one, God." A breeze lifted her hair and she smiled.

Dusty closed his Bible. "We've been blessed this night. No injuries of any kind." He pointed to a cowboy. "Except for a small rope burn where a glove should've been." He lifted his hands. "Let's rise and close with a song." He tipped his head toward a keyboard player.

"What do you think, Roger?"

A chord sounded and the notes of "Amazing Grace" filled the air. The motley group of cowboys and cowgirls poured out the words. Dusty shut his eyes. *It is Your grace, Lord, that calls us here. Thank you.*

After the music, people streamed from their seats toward the parking lot. Dusty gathered up his notes and Bible careful to keep them from pressing against his clean white shirt. If luck held, he'd avoid the cleaners and wear it tomorrow night. Changing persona quickly after the rodeo had become an art. Why he felt comfortable with no makeup before a church crowd still baffled him. It had to be a calling.

He followed the crowd and circled a holding pen then jerked to a stop. Erin's truck sat there. She was behind the wheel with her head on the steering wheel. Dusty's heart began a fast rat-a-tat. He stepped nearer. The driver's window was down.

"Erin?" Dusty sidled closer, not wanting to scare her, but desperate to know she was all right. "Erin?"

She lifted her head and stared at him. No. Stared through him. She was not all right.

Dusty placed his Bible on the hood of the truck and leaned toward her. "You look like you could use a friend." He smiled.

Eyes blurry with tears, Erin nodded. "I think I could," she whispered. She glanced at the Bible and tilted her head. "Are you Pastor Jack?"

Dusty nodded. His throat tightened. Without his bulky protective gear and makeup, she hadn't recognized him. "What might I do to help?" He placed a hand on the door.

"No one can help." Erin shook her head. "Not one blasted person can help keep this place alive."

"Not sure what you mean." Dusty tipped his head. "Would you like to grab a cup of coffee and visit?" He pointed toward the diner across the road.

She eyed him then shook her head. "I think I'm too tired. And this pile of junk won't start. And I have to haul cattle in the morning." Her voice grew thick. "And I need to go see my daddy."

Dusty straightened. "One thing at a time." He smiled. "Let's start with the truck. Can you turn the key and we can listen?" She flipped the ignition key. The grinding led him to believe it was an alternator. "Don't think this is something that we can fix at night in the arena." Her lips drew tight. "But I know what to do. The auto parts store on Highway 9 has what we need."

She pressed her forehead to the steering wheel. "Did I mention I have to haul cattle?"

He suppressed a grin. "You did. What time?"

"About ten, ten-thirty." Erin raised her head.

Dusty reached for the door handle and opened it. "We'll have her running by then. Come on, let me take you home." Dusty picked up his Bible.

Erin grabbed her purse and slid from the truck. She paused and her eyes roved over his face. Dusty fought the urge to cover his cheek or forehead and hide a few scars. A smile drew her lips up. "I'm so grateful for your help, Pastor Jack."

Dusty nodded and touched her elbow. "My truck's this way." He strode a few feet in front of her so he could swipe stuff from the passenger seat. "Climb aboard."

Erin did just that. Dusty closed the door and bit his lip. Erin Storm was in his truck. How many times had he watched her in the last few weeks and wished to spend time with her? And here she was. His mouth grew dry. What would he talk about? Would she spot his scars and shy away?

Only one way to find out, dummy. He pulled keys from his pocket and climbed behind the wheel. "Which way?"

Erin toyed with her purse strap. "I guess home." She sighed. "I can visit Daddy tomorrow."

"I'd be glad to take you now." Dusty started the motor.

"No, not today. I need to assimilate some bad news." She glanced at him, a sad smile playing on her lips.

Dusty pulled onto the road. "I'm sorry."

She leaned her head against the seat and closed her eyes. "Very bad news." She pinched the bridge of her nose. "Looks like the bank wins. They'll take the arena."

CHAPTER 5

Erin choked on a sob and stared out the window as they drove the familiar ranch road. How she wished for her mother's calming influence, her brother's wise words, or her dad's strong embrace. She'd never felt so lonely in all of her life. She glanced at Pastor Jack's hand gripping the steering wheel.

"I'm always hungry after services." His words jerked her from reverie. "We could grab a bite."

As though on cue, Erin's stomach growled. She slapped a hand over it to quell the noise a second too late.

Pastor Jack gave a snort. "Sounds like someone else is too." His pleasant voice had a calming effect on her jangled nerves.

Suddenly she was ravenous. "A bite sounds really good." She settled against the truck's seat and felt tension drain from her shoulders. One thing at a time, he'd said. Maybe he was right.

The diner's old fashioned red vinyl booths were almost empty, but a few latecomers hailed a hello to Erin or the pastor as they walked by. The familiar aroma of a greasy grill and burned coffee filled the air. As a regular, Erin had memorized the menu and quickly placed her order for a burger and fries. The pastor ordered the same.

Running his finger around the condensation on his water glass, the pastor smiled. His kind eyes seemed to caress her face. Another pound of stress melted away. He held her gaze a moment longer and then stared at the table. A flicker of a memory tickled her brain. She closed her eyes then nudged the thought to the side. Surely she'd come across him at the arena and not known his profession.

Pastor Jack cleared his throat garnering her attention. "So we have the truck problem figured out." He leaned forward and placed his folded arms on the table. "What's next? Do you need to stop in to see your dad?"

Erin shook her head. "I am too tired for that at the moment. But thank you." She tipped her head. "Guess everyone at the arena knows about the accident." She pictured her dad on the ground, crumpled and bleeding, the raging bull stomping his middle. A chill ran down her spine.

Pastor Jack said, "We've been praying for him. How is he doing?"

"He's on the mend." Erin shrugged. "Getting really grouchy, so that signals getting well, I think." She sat back as the waitress set her plate on the table. "Separated shoulder. Rotator cuff tear. Two broken ribs. Some cuts and lots of bruises. Won't slow him down for long." She shuddered at what could have been.

Pastor Jack pulled his food closer to him and paused. "I'd like to say a blessing, if you would care to join me." He held out a hand.

Erin stared into his large brown eyes, crinkles at the corner tipped up, accompanying the smile on his face. What was it about this man that made her so at ease? So—calm? She reached for his hand and intertwined their fingers. "I'd like that."

He quietly said grace, thanking God for the time they had together as well as their dinner. When he squeezed her fingers and let go, Erin felt adrift. She longed to grab his hand once again, but picked up her napkin instead. Dropping it into her lap, she swallowed hard. Her insides were dancing and it was not from hunger.

Dusty could barely focus on the food in front of him. Seconds before he'd clasped the hand of the only woman who had ever made him feel so— He shifted in the seat and reached for a French fry. So what? Like he could rescue her from a dragon? Or face down Killer once again? He chewed slowly lest his closed throat cause him to choke.

Erin bit into her burger and stared at him. Dusty stilled. Would her eyes rove over his face and cause her unease? A flush crept up his cheek. Great. Now the scars will glow.

She sipped from her water glass then said, "Thank you."

Dusty tipped his head. "For what?" He ate another French fry, striving for nonchalance.

Erin leaned back. "My rescue." She smiled. "I needed a helping hand hero tonight."

Dusty slapped his napkin over his lips to hold in a laugh. She said he had rescued her. A tingling ran between his shoulder blades. Hero. First time for everything. "You're welcome. Glad to be of service." He bit into his burger, then placed it on the plate. He chewed, swallowed and lifted a hand. "One. We will get you home tonight." He held up a finger. "Two." He ticked the count. "Work on the truck in the morning. Three. Your dad visit can wait." He smiled at her. "What was left? Oh, yeah. Hauling cattle." He drank a sip of water. "Want a ride along? I'm not busy."

"Oh, no." She dabbed her lips with the napkin. "I couldn't ask—"

"But you didn't. I offered." Please say yes.

"Sure. I'd love a ride along. As long as you don't mind a bunch of bawling cows and the smell of manure." Her lips tipped up in a smile. "Then again, you are the pastor of Cowboy Church, guess it goes with the territory."

Dusty nodded. "Love it all."

They ate the remainder of their meal in silence. Dusty could see weariness tug at Erin's shoulders. When he drew in a deep breath, his ribs reminded him he'd been knocked down. The waitress placed the check on the table and both reached for it. Dusty's hand clamped on top of hers. "My treat." He held her stare for a beat or two, and she finally drew her hand back.

She nodded. "Then breakfast is on me."

They strolled to Dusty's truck, the humid air thick and sticky. He opened the door, and she climbed in and pulled it shut. He rounded the front of the truck and paused. Across the road, at the dark arena, a glow from headlights bumped along. Low to the ground headlights.

Not truck height. A chill ran down his back. He watched as the car swerved around the end chute and shot out the side gate onto the highway. Strange.

He turned toward Erin to mention the sight. He smiled. She had tipped her head against the seat and closed her eyes. He got into the truck and turned the key in the ignition. No way would he cause her any more worry.

CHAPTER 6

Breakfast proved to be tacos on the road. The truck repair took a bit longer than Jack anticipated but wasn't costly, to Erin's relief. They'd made it to the ranch, loaded six bulls, and gotten on the road by ten thirty. Plenty of time to make it to the Ridgely arena. Once this load was delivered, she'd have to do some figuring, and hope to meet costs.

Two cowboys on horseback loped around the arena practicing team roping. One rider threw a lasso around a steer's head while the other rider aimed for the back heels. Neither made it. Jack snorted a laugh. "Bet those two are green to this event."

Erin smiled. "Harder than it looks."

"Most things are in this business." Jack stared out the window.

She swung into the parking lot and began to back toward the alleyway. Once situated, the arena boss appeared, clipboard in hand. He counted the six bulls, jerked the gate open and let Erin unload. Jack shoved the trailer gate shut, dust coating his jeans and shirt. He slapped it away and climbed back into the cab.

Erin signed the invoice, breathed a sigh of relief at the amount to be paid, and joined Jack in the cab. "Thanks again for your help." She folded the slip of paper and tucked it into the console.

He nodded.

Pulling on to the highway, Erin settled in for the fourteen mile drive. "How long have you—"

"Will you go—"

They both laughed. Jack held out a hand. "Ladies first."

"How long have you pastored the Cowboy Church?"

Jack clicked his tongue against his teeth. "Various arenas for the last three years. I kind of inherited it from a brother and it stuck. We started at your arena in the spring." He placed his hand on the console. "You're welcome to join us."

Erin shook her head. "Appreciate the offer, but I'm not much on church going." She steered around a pothole.

"No fancy attire or attitude needed." A teasing note sounded in his voice.

"Thanks." Her lips grew in a grim line. No. Church and God and prayer hadn't helped her mom or her dad in the least. Why should she waste her time? But she'd enjoyed this morning, so didn't pour her true feelings out.

"You off to visit your dad today?"

"Yeah." She veered to the right and took an exit toward home. "As soon as I clean up." She hit the blinker and turned toward the ranch house. "Hate to hit the hospital smelling like my deliveries." She parked in front of the barn and settled against the seat, staring out the window. "Again, Jack, let me say thanks."

"You're quite welcome, Erin." Jack touched her arm, and she swiveled to face him.

"Want you to know we'll be praying for you and your dad." His lips tipped up. "Anytime you need help, just holler. You're not alone in your battles, you know." He lifted a finger and pointed heavenward then to his chest. "Just ask."

Outside the window a barn swallow took flight. Didn't Mrs. Stevens, her Sunday school teacher, say God knew about the birds? Erin's throat tightened so she nodded. Tears stung her eyes, and she pinched the bridge of her nose.

Jack leaned forward. "Is there anything else I can do now to help?"

Erin drew in a deep breath. His words seemed to sweeten the air. *Reckon a preacher's prayers might reach heaven better than mine ever did.* She cleared her throat. "Continue to pray for Daddy and add the arena."

Jack lifted an eyebrow. "You mentioned the arena last night. What's going on?"

Since Jack had a congregation meeting at the arena, maybe he deserved to know it would be snatched from him in three months. "The bank has called our note. Seems there is a developer interested in the property, wants to turn it into a strip mall, and the city council thinks it would be good for the economy. We don't have money to hire any fancy attorneys to fight a losing battle." She waved a hand toward the barn. "The ranch is barely making ends meet. Now you tag on Daddy's hospital bill—" She ran her hand around the steering wheel. "But losing that section of our property—" She drew in a deep breath and let it out slowly. "I just can't imagine life without rodeos in the backyard." She drew air quotes around backyard.

Jack's jaw grew tight. "Was that why the guy in the suit appeared?"

"Yep. He was a banker." Erin sniffled.

"I've seen him at two other arenas. Wonder if he's scooping those up, too."

Erin shrugged. "I just wish we made more money so we could get out of debt." She sighed. "Guess that's a pipe dream."

Jack tapped her arm. "Not necessarily. Let's think on it and—"

"You will pray." Erin chuckled. "Bet that was your next sentence." Jack's cheeks grew red. "I didn't mean to embarrass you. I'm sorry." Erin reached for his hand and squeezed it. "I appreciate your thoughtfulness. Truly."

Dusty's heart beat was surely loud enough for Erin to hear. The flush continued until his face and ears burned. What must she think of him? He cleared his throat. "Yep, prayer works." He shifted in the seat. "Brainstorm session needed. Arena Aid. How's that for a title?"

Erin laughed. "AA. Powerless over banks. Might work. But who is the Aid part?"

Trickling through the odors of cattle work was a sweet flowery scent. Dusty drew in a deep breath, hoping to capture the fragrance. Her hair tumbled down her back without a cap to hold it in place, and he longed to run his fingers through it. *Bet it's soft as down.*

"What do you think?" She peered at him.

Dusty realized he'd tuned out. "Repeat please. I was somewhere else." *Thinking of you.*

"Should we do a bake sale or barbecue? That can raise some cash." She turned to look out the window. "Entails lots of work, but I'm up for it." She turned back to him. "Well?"

Desperation tinted her words. Dusty's throat tightened. He longed to pull her in a hug, to ease her worries. She seemed to look past his acne scars. But one as beautiful as Erin would count him as a friend, not anything else. Past experience proved that true.

"Yeah, good ideas." He smiled. "Let's think bigger."

Erin raised an eyebrow. "Bigger? Define that."

"Currently the arena is only used for rodeos on the weekends, right? What if you hosted other events?"

Her eyes brightened. "4H kids used to show animals there years ago. I don't know why they quit." She squeezed his hand once again. "Great idea. I can contact the school and see who is in charge."

"Bigger. 4H is a start. What else?" Dusty ran his hand over his jaw. "Buck outs. You know, just practice riding, not competition. I know a wrangler who could set that up. Just need publicity."

"Oh, Pastor Jack, you've no idea how you've helped." Erin placed a hand on her chest. "I feel a trickle of relief already."

Dusty grinned. "Glad to be of service." He reached for the door handle. "Guess I'll hit the road so you can visit your dad. See you tonight." He slid from the seat.

"At Cowboy Church?" Erin smiled. "I haven't exactly agreed—"

Dusty tipped his hat. "You know you're welcome." His heart jumped into his throat again. *Please come. Please see what the Lord is doing.*

"Maybe. That's the best answer right now. Maybe."

"Good enough." He shut the truck door. He pulled his keys from his pocket and headed to his truck. "Maybe is a start."

CHAPTER 7

Erin threw back the covers and slid from the sofa. The grainy morning sky hung heavy with rain. She hoped the downpour wouldn't happen during rodeo time. She had not slept well as ideas kept popping into her head. She should've had a notebook to capture them. She yawned and ran a hand over her hair. Thoughts of the arena—and Jack.

"Pastor Jack, girl. Don't forget he's a preacher." She scooted toward the bathroom. While brushing her teeth, she eyed herself in the mirror. "You'd be such a great preacher's wife." She grinned a toothpaste smile. "I can see it now, baking casseroles and visiting the sick. Sheesh." Visiting her dad yesterday was hard enough. "Not the life for me. I'll take angry bulls, the heat and smells over that life."

Erin slid on a clean T-shirt and jeans, grabbed a scarf and created a turban for her unruly hair. Pulling on a boot, she whispered, "Okay God, Jack says You are with me, so prove it. I'm off to talk to Conrad, rather plead with him, for an extension. Can't see any other way to save the arena. Please."

To her surprise, tears stung her eyes. The short one-way conversation calmed her. "Strange. Truly strange."

Grabbing her small purse and the truck keys, Erin headed out the back door. Her mouth watered when she thought of the biscuits and gravy at the diner. She'd fill up and be prepared for battle. She hoped.

The diner's tables were full. Ranchers and farmers tucked away biscuits as fast as the waitress could bring them. Erin tapped the server on the shoulder. "Save me some, Ruby."

"Honey, there's plenty, don't you worry none." She pointed to a small booth for two in the corner. "Hop over there, and I'll bring you breakfast."

Erin smiled. She didn't have to place an order with Ruby around. She settled on the cracked vinyl seat, a potted plant towering above her on the ledge. Steven Johns sat to her right, his nose in the newspaper, and a well-dressed stranger sat behind her. No need for conversation which suited Erin fine this morning.

What was she going to say to Conrad? Get on her knees and beg? No, she would explain the circumstances and ask for an extension. By the end of two quarters, surely she'd have enough to pay what was owed. She could make payments for the hospital bill, and they'd tighten their belts at home. She toyed with the water glass Ruby had plunked in front of her. "Glass half full or half empty, Erin?" She shook her head. Her moods swung from full to empty all the time.

Ruby slid a plate of scrambled eggs, hash browns, bacon, biscuits and gravy on the table. "Enjoy, sweetie pie." Her grin filled her face.

Erin dug in. Comfort food. That's what this was. She slathered a biscuit with butter and honey, creating a mess for sticky fingers. She bit into the mixture and closed her eyes. Taste did bring comfort. Brought memories of her Mama and pleasant times at the breakfast table. She chewed and sighed. Sometimes being a grownup stunk.

"So what did you think of the grounds, Conrad?"

Erin started at the sound of Conrad's voice. The man behind her must've faced the banker. She leaned further back behind the plant lest Conrad spot her. She wasn't ready for a discussion with him. The biscuits and gravy rolled around in her stomach. Maybe filling up before a confrontation wasn't the wisest idea.

"Exactly what we want. Plenty of space for a building and parking." He cleared his throat. "I especially like the location. Right by the highway." The man stood and tossed his napkin on his plate. "Let's get out of here and talk strategy. Need to move on this. Get the—"

"Country bumpkins off the property?" Conrad chuckled. He trailed behind the gentleman as he went to pay.

Erin clutched her stomach. Surely she wouldn't be sick in public. She watched out of the corner of her eye as the two left the diner. Country bumpkins? That's what Conrad Butler saw when he looked at her? Anger stirred in her middle and surged into her mouth. She clasped her hands over her lips lest a tirade burst out and overwhelm the entire diner. But then she'd be waging battle for most of the people there. They, too, were country bumpkins.

A vein in her temple began to throb. She gritted her teeth and massaged her head.

"Girlie, you all right?" Ruby placed a hand on her shoulder. "Those biscuits not go down right?"

Erin lifted her head and stared into Ruby's brown eyes. Funny. She'd known Ruby all her life and never noticed her pretty brown eyes. "I'm fine, Ruby. Just have a bit of a headache coming on. Think I'll go home. Won't get the audience I need today."

Ruby frowned. "Baby, I have aspirin if you need it."

"I'm okay. Thanks." Erin tugged a twenty from her pocket and placed it on the table.

"Let me get your change."

"Nope. Hope that makes up for all the times I've been stingy or forgetful." Erin squeezed Ruby's fingers. "You're a true blessing." She turned and walked out of the diner. "Blessing? Preacher's wife words?" The words had popped out without any thought. She climbed in the truck and sat still. Where was life taking her? She felt she was on a slippery slope, going down, down, down with no way to stop. "I'm tired of being alone—"

Jack's words reverberated in her brain. *"You're never alone."* He had pointed toward heaven and himself. Erin tapped the steering wheel. "Wish they were by my side right now." She started the motor and glanced at her cell. A call to Pastor Jack would settle her nerves. No. She'd run errands and see how she felt. If the biscuits settled into place, then she'd face the banker.

Dusty tucked his cell phone in his shirt pocket and skimmed the list on the table. He'd managed to contact five possible vendors for the arena. And a food truck. Erin could rent out space to several trucks with different cuisine because they were always in demand. He eyed the other names with check marks: cutting horse competition, Susan's dog show, a buck out, even a tractor pull. Each person agreed the Higly market was centrally located and could draw a good crowd. Dusty gave them Erin's phone number and encouraged them to get on the arena calendar. He promised to help advertise, even on short notice.

Erin. Freckles on her nose, a mess of hair, tiny when standing next to him. Why, he could tuck her up under his arm, and she'd fit fine. He sighed. "If only." He ran a hand down his face, his fingers tracing acne craters. She hadn't seem to notice Pastor Jack's face. What would she think of a bullfighter's face? What was the difference between the two personas? Pastor Jack was helpful, empathic, kind. But so was Dusty the bullfighter. She just didn't know him.

He propped his chin on his hand. "I think tonight she will meet him." He nodded. "Yeah, the timing is right to shed the mask." He chuckled. "Guess we will see if the lack of grease paint scares people. Including Erin."

Conrad bid Mr. McMillan goodbye and shut his office door. He rubbed his hands together. So far, so good. He just had to convince the Storms to sell.

He settled in the chair behind his desk and rocked back. "What will it take, Erin Storm, for you to give in and convince dear old dad?" He smiled. "Attention. That's a start. Good deeds." He raised a brow and leaned forward to grab the phone's receiver. When his secretary answered he said, "Barbara, order a gift basket for Mr. John Storm. He's in the rehab center by the hospital."

Kindness number one. What could be next? Dinner? Certainly. The new Chez Suzanne. He bet Erin had never eaten there, since she'd have to shed the cowboy boots. And dancing? He pursed his lips—

tasting a kiss? Charming must exude from his demeanor. He had to act quickly. McMillan wasn't the type to wait around.

CHAPTER 8

E rin stared at the door to the rehab center. Just the thought of entering and seeing her dad in pajamas without his jeans and boots made her stomach churn. He only had a few more days of therapy to get everything "back in gear" as he called it, so this should be easy-peasy. Her lips tipped up at the phrase the therapist used when working with him. Sure, when you had good use of all your faculties life was easy-peasy.

"Okay. Happy face. No banking discussions. Just happy-happy-happy to be here." Erin swung down from the truck, straightened her shirt and crossed the parking lot. She entered the sliding glass doors with a swish and circled to her dad's room. He wasn't there.

A nurse walked by pushing a computer on a stand. Erin knew it was used to record everything from blood pressure readings to doling out medicine. "Excuse me." The nurse looked her way. "I'm looking for my dad."

"Check the dry erase board in his room. It lists all his activities for the day." She smiled and continued down the hallway.

Erin turned toward the private restroom by his bed and spotted the board on the door. Her dad was in therapy for the next ten minutes. She settled in the vinyl, very uncomfortable recliner to wait. What information should she give him? She hated to keep him totally in the dark, but then again, she wanted him to focus on getting better. Erin needed Dad back to norm. She needed advice.

She crossed one leg over the other and toyed with a thread on the hem of her jeans. What events could the arena attract? She stared out the window at yellow chrysanthemums bobbing in the wind. She dropped her leg to the floor and shot out of the chair. For years her mother's garden club had hosted flower events at the arena. When did that end? She ran a hand through her hair in an effort to recall. Her mom had gotten sick in the winter and even quit attending her church. She'd stayed home unless it was to go to the doctor. Erin had been in what—she scrunched her eyes shut—seventh grade? Yes. The year she had the choir solo and Mom wasn't there. A tear welled up, and she opened her eyes to swipe it away.

"Crying 'cause you miss your old dad?" Her father's booming voice caught her off guard.

Erin swung around the end of the bed and reached to hug him, then paused. "Okay, where does it hurt? I don't want to cause further damage." She looked into his hazel eyes, so like her own. "You okay?"

Her dad slid into bed and tugged the covers over his bare, white legs. "I'm better now." He huffed and leaned against the pillows. "Promise. Now bend over and plant one here." He patted his cheek.

Erin kissed him and settled against the bed, her hand gripping his. "How's it going?"

"Going." He shifted and groaned a bit. "I'll have a pain pill in a few and take me a nap." He cleared his throat. "Give me an update on life outside these four walls, please."

Erin told him about the Higly and Ridgeley deliveries and the two more scheduled. "All efficiently delivered and invoices collected."

"Money in and money out." Her dad gave her a wan smile. "I'm grateful for your help, Erin." He sighed. "I know I took you from your life in Houston. You had a budding career—"

"I wasn't happy there. This is where I want to be." She squeezed his fingers. "Please let me."

A frown pinched her dad's forehead, and his eyes roved across her face. He squinted. "You sure?"

Erin nodded, her heart beating so loudly she was sure the nurse down the hall could hear it.

Mr. Storm sighed. "Stuart wants to pursue a career in the military." He paused and gave her another assessing look. "I can use the help. So if you're willing—"

"Oh, Daddy." Erin jumped up and leaned over the bed railing about to squash her father in a bear hug. She checked herself. "Thank you," she whispered. She raked a lock of hair from his forehead and kissed him there. "You won't regret it. Promise."

Her dad rested against the pillow and closed his eyes. "Let's talk more about it tomorrow, pumpkin." He smiled. "I love you."

"Love you too, Daddy." Erin straightened the blanket over his shoulders and slipped from the room.

Now, more than ever, she had to save the arena. Because it was hers.

Conrad punched in Erin's number, and she answered on the first ring. "Good afternoon, Miss Storm. I hope this finds you well. How's your father?"

The sound of a clearing throat came through the phone.

He'd caught her off guard. Good. He liked to be in control. He placed his elbows on his desk and glanced around his well-appointed corner office.

"He's coming along nicely. Thank you for asking." Her voice sounded shaky.

"Miss Storm. Wait." He gave a tinge of hesitancy to his next words. "May I presume and call you Erin?"

"Of course."

He had her. "I know we got off on the wrong foot since I had to deliver business news." He waited a beat. "I apologize for the timing." Conrad drew in a deep breath. "However, I was sincere when I said I would like to get to know you. Do you think we could put our business exchange to one side and have dinner one evening? Soon?"

Her breathing sounded rapid through the receiver. Good. She was nervous. "I think I'd like that, Conrad."

Timid mouse. Conrad drew circles on his desk with one finger. The cat was about to pounce. "How about Thursday? Have you been to the new French restaurant in Waco?" A twenty minute drive might soften her up even more.

They negotiated the times and Conrad punched END on his phone. "Ha! Operation Swallow the Storm continues." He reared back in his chair so hard it almost toppled over.

Erin sat in the rehab parking lot and stared out the window. More mums. Yellow and the unusual rust she favored. Conrad Butler had just asked her for a date. And not lunch at the diner. A date. Gussied up and primped to go to a fancy restaurant and pay astronomical prices for a dab of food. She shrugged. What did she care? He was footing the bill. And what better way to get on his good side than follow his lead. He most assuredly was the alpha male type.

She laughed. "Here I was all ready to race to his office and beg on bended knee. And he's being hand delivered to me." A puffy cloud tinged in pink scudded by. "Okay, God. I'll give You props on this one. Remind me to tell Pastor Jack." The words escaped her lips before she gave them any thought. She shoved the truck into gear and headed for the exit. Wonder what Pastor Jack would think about her date? Would he be jealous?

"Erin Storm. Jealous? Why would he be?" She flipped on the blinker and turned toward home. Her lips twitched until a grin formed. "Would be kind of nice for him to be jealous. Just a little."

Dusty scanned the tablet. He had listed as many local events as he could think of and made quite a few more promising phone calls. He couldn't wait until rodeo time to tell Erin. He stared at his cell phone. Why not call her now? He longed to hear her voice. Maybe she wasn't too busy, and he could swing by the office. Watch her face light up as he ticked off ideas, one by one. Bull buck outs, cutting horse, sheep wrangling, auction, antique shows—the list was two pages long. He and Erin could set aside time to discuss a calendar and make call backs. Surely she'd be pleased at his effort to help save the arena. Arena Aid. AA. He chortled. Glad it wasn't the real deal, although meetings could be held there free of charge if the business kept running.

He stood and shook his jeans straight, lifted his right boot and polished it on the back of his left leg then did the same with his left boot on his right leg. His white shirt hung on the room's door handle ready for tonight, so the denim one he wore, wrinkles and all, would have to suffice. Erin would overlook that. He skimmed his hand down the shirt front. He could take it off and iron it, but cheap motels didn't come with irons and ironing boards.

"She'll take me like I am, she's that kind of girl." Dusty grinned in the mirror, plunked his hat on his head and started toward the door. He retraced his steps and grabbed his cell phone. Maybe he should give her a call. A heads-up. Not just show up on the doorstep. He leaned against the door jamb to call, the hot breeze fanning his hat. Four rings and no answer. A lead balloon dropped in his belly. Well, he wasn't busy for the next two hours, he'd make a swing by Storm Contractors' office and look for her rig.

Dusty stomped out and climbed in his truck. "I really wanted to see her, Lord." The morning mist and ever-blowing dust had created mud on his windshield. He flipped the wipers on to clean it off. *Pray for clarity for her.*

Dusty grasped the steering wheel and leaned forward to peer out the window. The voice had been as clear and deep within as though the Lord were standing on the hood of his truck. He pressed his fingers to his eyes. More important than seeing Erin, than being seen by Erin, was Erin seeing and seeking Him. That's where his focus should be. A flush crept up his neck. He'd set himself up as important instead of the Lord. "Father, forgive me." He began to intercede for Erin Storm.

CHAPTER 9

Erin jerked the hem of the black dress lower. Each one she'd tried on in Chrissy's new boutique seemed shorter than the last. She glared at her muscled calves. She looked like some sort of body builder.

"This won't do either, Chrissy." She unzipped the dress and slipped it off. Chrissy's hand appeared above the dressing room door and grabbed the garment.

"You are impossible, Erin Storm." Chrissy huffed then shoved another dress over the top. "If you backtalk me on this one, you're out of here." She chuckled.

Erin laughed. Chrissy was her best friend and almost flipped when she heard about the impending date. Impending doom was Erin's take. Why had she agreed to some fancy-schmancy place out of town? She'd be stuck, unable to walk home if she didn't like how the evening progressed. Ugh.

She slid the next dress over her head. The shimmery blue fabric felt yummy against her skin. The tea length skirt was full—she could twirl in it if she had a mind to. The bodice hugged in just the right places and wasn't low cut. Erin felt like...a woman.

Chrissy tapped on the door. "Open, open. I want to see."

Erin hit the latch and the door swung wide.

Chrissy gasped. "Oh, my stars. That's beautiful on you." She pushed Erin on the shoulder. "Turn. Turn." Erin completed a circle and gave a curtsy. Chrissy clasped her hands in front of her. "That's the one. You have to take this for sure." She tapped a fingernail on her teeth. "Now you'll need shoes."

Erin stared at her reflection. This was the most gorgeous dress she had ever seen, much less worn. She reached under her arm for the price tag, but was met with Chrissy's fingers. "No. We will discuss this later." Chrissy had tears in her eyes. "Oh, honey. Your mama would swoon if she saw you." She chuckled. "And you'd better hope your daddy lets you out of the house." Chrissy bustled toward the front of the store.

Erin nodded and slipped out of the dress. If she were going to charm Conrad Butler, she had to be up to his standards. But to buy a dress for one time wear? She hung the beautiful garment up, sighed, and slid to the dressing room bench. The three way mirror caught her reflection.

Oh boy.

Farmer's tan wouldn't show in that dress. It wasn't so short and clingy she had to wrestle with it. It spoke elegance. She closed her eyes. "God, I like this dress. Any way I can have it?"

When she opened her eyes, three of her peered back from the mirrors. "Jeepers. That's like one prayer for each of you lately." She reached for her jeans and T-shirt then pulled on her Ropers. She stared at the dust encrusted soles. "And new shoes." She wailed. "This will cost way too much." Erin stood, tendrils of defeat starting to wrap around her middle, then recalled a pair of her mother's sling back black pumps. Barely worn. They'd have to do.

Chrissy stood at the counter, the dress hanging in plastic wrap on a hook. She glanced at Erin's face and held up a hand. "Listen to me."

Erin shook her head.

"Listen. To. Me."

Erin propped against the counter, her chin on her elbow. "I'm listening."

"Do you recall spring break our sophomore year in Houston?" Tears brimmed in Chrissy's big blue eyes. "My parents' divorce. My devastation?"

Erin nodded. Such a hard time for her sweet friend.

Chrissy lifted a brow. "What did you do?"

"What do you mean? I didn't do anything." Erin shifted and

planted both boots on the floor, a mental calendar flipping pages, a frown crossing her brow.

"My point exactly." Chrissy lifted the dress from the hook and held it out to Erin. "You didn't do anything. You gave up a spring break trip to share Blue Bell ice cream and watch me wallow in misery. You stayed by my side and wiped my tears. This, my friend, is payment for that particular kindness." She tucked the hook over Erin's finger. "I can never repay all of your kindnesses, but this is a start." She raised a hand when Erin began a protest. "Gift horse."

Erin batted her eyelashes to keep tears from splashing down her cheeks. "Thank you," she whispered.

Chrissy leaned in. "Just go wow him. And make him postpone a closing date." She giggled. "If this doesn't strike his fancy, he's blind."

Erin pirouetted in front of the mirror in her parents' bedroom, memories of twirling with her mom assailing her. A lump formed in her throat. "No crying. No crying." She patted gently under her eyes. Lorena Mery, her hairdresser, had styled her hair and "painted her face" as her dad would say. Erin leaned closer to the mirror to make sure no mascara smudged. Lorena's results were...amazing. She tipped her lips in a smile, making her hazel eyes twinkle. Now if she could erase the words "country bumpkin" from her memory, she might enjoy herself.

Propping the front door open to listen for Conrad's approach, Erin ran possible conversation scenarios through her brain. Would any stick? He was, after all, an amazingly handsome man. And other than the arena property, she couldn't figure out why he would be interested in her.

"Don't fool yourself. That's the reason you're going out with him. The arena." She leaned against the arm of the sofa staring at the pasture out front and the weathered barn. Her whole life. And Daddy wanted her help. Her heart leapt with joy. Another bout of tears began to well up.

"Cut it out. You'll have black stripes by the time he gets here."

Gravel crunched and an engine roared. Butterflies began to beat Erin's ribcage. She picked up her mom's delicate shawl—a symbol of her mom's hugs. A car door slammed and footsteps beat a rhythm up the porch steps.

"Erin?"

She gasped. "Pastor Jack?" She swung the door wider and stared at him. "What are you doing here?" Jack's jaw worked back and forth, his lips moving but no words forming. "Jack?" Erin reached out a hand and touched his elbow. "Is everything okay? Would you like to come in?"

"No. No, I see you're about to leave." He ran a hand over his jaw. "We can talk later." He turned and then spun back around. "You're beautiful." A flush crept across his face, and he bolted for his truck.

"Thank you," Erin called after his retreating form.

Dusty heard her words and lifted a hand in reply. He'd never felt so foolish in all his life. He'd stood there gaping, like a wide-mouth bass on a hook gasping for air. Now he understood the phrase "took my breath away." For Erin Storm had just taken his. He shot a glance in his rearview mirror. A low slung sports car dodged potholes in the ranch road on the way to the house.

"The banker?" Dusty stilled. In just a short while, the banker had wormed his way into Erin's good graces? "Good enough to get all dolled up," he growled. An iron taste coated his tongue. Disgust. "If she needs banker style, then she's certainly not the woman for me."

He reached for the ignition, fired up the engine and peeled out of the driveway. Rocks and debris flew from under his tires. He only hoped some of it reached a sports car.

Chapter 10

Thirty minutes into the evening, and Erin tried to pay attention to Conrad's monologue. Her hairstylist had suggested if she were stuck for conversation to ask about Conrad's life. *"Men love to talk about themselves, sweetie. Give him the opportunity."* Lorena was right. Erin knew more about Conrad Butler than she cared to by the time they arrived at the restaurant.

He wheeled into the parking lot and caused the valet to scramble out of the way, then barely acknowledged the shaking attendant's presence as they exited the car.

When the maître'd asked for the name on the reservation, Conrad bristled. "Conrad Butler. I'm here frequently"—he leaned in to read the man's nametag— "Pierre." He glanced at Erin. "If that's even his real name." A flush burned the tips of Erin's ears. She mouthed an apology to the older gentleman.

Once seated, Erin gasped when Conrad snapped his fingers to summon a waiter. He ordered a bottle of wine, but Erin insisted on iced tea. His mouth quirked in a slight sneer. If only she'd driven her truck and met him here. The fancy French cuisine listed on the menu turned her stomach. If Conrad thought his uppity behavior impressed her, he was wrong. So far she felt nothing but embarrassment. Could she sit through a dinner even to save the arena?

"Excuse me for a moment, please." Erin slid from her chair and made a beeline for the ladies room. She tugged her cell phone from her pocketbook and stared at it. Who could she call to come rescue her? Chrissy didn't drive well at night, her dad was in rehab, Stuart overseas. She ticked off names and excuses until she hit upon—

"J-Jack?" She stammered when he answered. At the sound of

his voice, relief flooded her middle. "I have a huge favor to ask." She gulped. "I need prayer and wisdom." Within a minute she blurted out her dilemma. "I'm so uneasy. What do I do? Frankly, I want to bail."

Pastor Jack cleared his throat and prayed, asking the Lord to guard her heart and give her wisdom. After the *amen*, he added, "You're there to ask about the bank note. Take sight of that. If you fly the coop, he's going to be really upset. Obviously he's trying to impress you." Jack paused. "Take it slow. Smile. Eat what you can. And know I'm continuing to pray."

Erin nodded. "Take one for the team, eh?" She gave a soft laugh. "Think I needed to hear that. Thanks." She tucked her phone into her purse and gazed into the mirror. "Okay, Erin Storm, hitch it up and head out." She flung the door to the restroom open and strode into the dining room much like she entered an arena.

A small basket of bread sat on the table alongside her tea glass. Erin slipped into her chair and smiled. "This smells delicious."

Conrad stood and helped push her chair in. He leaned forward and whispered, "So do you."

She felt his breath on the back of her neck. Erin froze. She didn't have a clue how to respond, so she ignored his remark and reached for a roll. Once he was seated, she proffered the basket.

He shook his head. "Not wasting carbs on that."

Erin ground her teeth.

"I took the liberty and ordered." Conrad sipped from his wine glass. "You look like a chateaubriand kind of woman."

"Thank you," Erin smiled and sipped tea. Who didn't like a great steak?

"So tell me, Erin." Conrad toyed with a fork. "Do you plan to stay in the area after this quarter?"

She raised a brow and gave a half-hearted laugh. "Of course I plan to stay." She chewed the bread slowly, watching him. Swallowed. Sipped tea. *For the team, Erin, for the team.* "On our land." She caught a flash of uncertainty in his eyes. *Our land, mister.*

Conrad tipped his head, muscles in his jaw working. "Do you not see the problem before you and your family?" he hissed. "A great deal of money is due quite soon. And unless a very wealthy uncle has died" —he reared back in his chair— "you won't be able to make the payment. Are you really that obtuse?"

Her cheeks flamed. Did he think her totally uneducated? Each word from his mouth served to stoke the fire in her belly. *Be nice for the team.*

He sipped his wine and watched the waiter set salad plates before them. Conrad leaned forward. "Obviously this has become more than just dinner." He sniggered. "Even in your fancy duds you can see it's become a meeting which isn't going your way. Pioneer Bank will own your property soon. City council seeks areas to expand for jobs." He jabbed a finger toward her. "That is what you don't get. The city," he fairly spit the word, "doesn't want rodeo grounds cluttering up the most marketable corner in the county."

Erin tossed her napkin on the table. "Why are we here?" She waved her hand in a circle. "Why the fancy restaurant in our fancy duds when we could've had this same discussion at the diner?" She shoved her chair from the table. "Did you think wine and a fancy roast would help pave the way for you to take ownership faster?" She propped her hands on the table and leaned in. "Are you that obtuse, you big snob?" She grabbed her purse and shawl and headed for the exit.

The waiter grinned and held the door for her. "Way to go, sister."

Erin ducked her head and stepped into the evening air. She drew in a deep breath. "Yeah. Way to go." A sprinkle of stars made their presence known behind the building. She surveyed the parking lot and sighed. "Guess I wish on a star for a way home." The lump in her throat and brick in her belly hardened. Tears stung her eyes and trailed down her cheeks. So long, mascara.

"Your wish is my command."

She jolted and spun around to face Dusty, the bullfighter.

Erin's eyes widened and her cheeks turned bright pink. "What are you doing here?"

In truth, Dusty wanted to gather her into his arms and never let go. Dare he mention his road flight from Higly to the restaurant in record time? "Heard of a maiden in distress, so thought I'd offer my services."

"How did you know—" Erin stared at him. Perspiration dotted his upper lip, and he felt a roiling in his stomach as he watched the dawning realization. "Pastor Jack?" The whisper caught on the wind. She gripped her elbows and drew herself in. Unshed tears caused her eyes to look black. "Dusty and Pastor Jack. One and the same?"

He stood still under her scrutiny. When she reached out and gently trailed a finger across his grease-painted cheek, he thought his head would explode. Would Erin think he'd tried to deceive her? Had he?

"I've never been so grateful to see a clown in all of my life." Erin launched herself into his arms. Dusty held tightly, her head against his chest. "I've blown it for the team, Jack...er...Dusty." She reared back slightly and looked into his eyes. "What do I call you?"

He shrugged. "Whatever you'd like."

Her delighted laugh floated in the wind. "Dusty. My hero." She hugged him again, then took a step back. Her lips gave a small smile. "But as I said, I've blown it." She pointed behind him.

Dusty turned.

Conrad stood in the harsh light at the entrance watching. "A clown and a washed up rodeo queen." He barked a laugh. "How touching." He turned to the valet and ordered his car. "I will be in touch soon, Miss Storm." He climbed in his sports car and revved the engine. The car fishtailed through the gravel before it gripped the road and sent Conrad on his way.

"Guess I really need that ride now," Erin said.

"At your service, ma'am." Dusty offered his elbow and she slid her hand through the crook. He pulled it tight against his side. How he hoped this would last forever.

Epilogue

M r. Storm, Erin, and Dusty celebrated a good doctor's report with chocolate milkshakes at the diner. Mr. Storm smacked his lips. "Been hankering for this taste since I got out of rehab. Now show me those contracts."

Dusty handed the folder to him. "We have signed agreements for thirteen accounts spread over the next four months. Plus four more yes votes, just not signed." He propped his elbows on the table. "With the cash flow from the last two month's rodeos, the church offering, and donations, the bank note is up to date."

Erin grinned. "Daddy, can you believe it?"

A frown crossed Mr. Storm's brow. "Sounds great, but that's just up to date. We'll need much more to get it through the city permits. Can't beat the finances, true. However, beating city hall is another story."

"Finish up your drink and follow us." Erin and Dusty stood up.

Mr. Storm took one last slurp and joined them. "Okay, pardners," he slapped a hand on Erin's shoulder, "what's next?"

"That." Erin pointed out the window.

Mr. Storm bent and peered through the glass. "A trail ride?" He walked outside and stared at the line of people on horseback, led by Frank Cottrell. "Frank, what's going on? What's this parade for?"

Frank settled his hands on the pommel of his saddle. His horse danced a bit to the side.

"Well, Hank, best ask that rodeo girl of yours."

Erin giggled and propped her hands on her hips. "Yes, Daddy, ask me." She gestured to the riders. "Meet the Riders for the Storms. They called a special city council meeting to block the annexation of the rodeo grounds for a mall, and it passed. Now we're heading to the town hall to let them know we have enough votes and plan on making this the best arena around." She gave her dad a one-armed hug. "What do you think about that?"

Her daddy gazed at her. Erin's heart pounded in her chest so hard she thought it would burst. Dusty gripped one of her hands. She glanced at him and grinned.

Mr. Storm said, "Well, I'll be a monkey's uncle."

"And Daddy..." She stood on tiptoe and kissed his cheek. "Dusty and I want to get married right in the center of that arena."

Mr. Storm eyed them both, threw back his head, and laughed.

Dusty pulled Erin close and leaned her backward to plant a kiss— right in the center of her smiling mouth.

LIBERTY AND LACE

JALANA FRANKLIN

Help Wanted

Inquire within

*Be anxious for nothing, but in everything by prayer
and supplication, with thanksgiving, let your requests
be made known to God; and the peace of God, which
surpasses all understanding, will guard your hearts and
minds through Christ Jesus.*
PHILIPPIANS 4:6-8 NKJV

For Shekeitha, Dana, Lisa, and Penny.
This story came to life because of you. (Snicker)

Chapter 1

Rosemont Plantation, Alabama
March 3, 1841

The beauty of the morning stole Abigail's attention, just like always. Streaks of golden sunlight penetrated the glass panes above the servants' table in the large, airy kitchen, the soft shafts accentuating each line in the rise and fall of large, gray flagstones paving the room's floor. She sighed as she folded the crisp white linens to perfection.

"Miss Abigail, you gonna waste your life away honey. I been sighin' out that winda' goin' on twenty-five years now, and I ain't got nowhere doin' it neitha'." Rhoda's fingers made short work of the large ball of dough. She slid the pans closer to her large belly and pulled the dough apart. "If you ask me, you oughta be pourin' that tea for Miss Julia 'bout now."

Abigail sat up straight and gasped, turning to face the black woman. "Oh my goodness! I forgot. I was doing these linens for Mrs. Allen, and I did it again. Oh, Rhoda, what am I going to do? She'll be furious, and she's always so mean when I mess up." She hurried to put her basket out of the way.

Rhoda wiped her floured hands on her well-worn light blue apron. "I know Miss Julia ain't the one you talkin' 'bout. Why she so sweet an' all. She don't never be mean." Rhoda threw her head back and belly-laughed. "You go on, Miss Abigail. I 'spect you be gettin' a tongue lashin' like you thinkin'. Hey, I know. Maybe you rush in all flustered like, and she might not think so hard." The twinkle in her eye almost made Abigail forget how her tardiness could affect her treatment for the rest of the day.

Rhoda pushed Abigail out into the yard, clucking her tongue the whole time. Abigail fairly ran across the portico and into the back door of the foyer. Thank goodness it was open. Julia might not have heard her approach had she been a little quieter. She tip-toed into the parlor just as Julia glanced toward the door.

"Abigail, please come precisely when I call. You know I expect more from you." A long sigh escaped Julia Allen's lips. She fanned her neck like she thought she was royalty, making a spectacle of herself in front of everyone again. Her long black tresses had been carefully curled to perfection around her porcelain, heart-shaped face. Long lashes swept across her ebony eyes and rosy cheeks. Everyone thought her a beauty, and she knew it. Between the ridiculous sighs, she added, "It's not every day you get to wait on friends like mine."

"Of course, Miss Julia. I'm so sorry. I was helping in the kitchen for your mother." Abigail fluffed the feather pillow propped behind Julia's shoulders with as much enthusiasm as she could muster, unspoken words itching on her lips. Words she shouldn't say. Words she wouldn't say, if she could help it. *Oh, Lord, help me to stay quiet. Help me be humble. Please.*

"And what are you mumbling about? You're not...praying again, are you? Haven't I told you to focus on your work? You can pray at night, beside your bed, like you're supposed to." She patted her neck with a handkerchief. "Now get on with my instructions. Don't let me catch you praying again, or I'll have to tell Papa."

"Yes, Miss Julia. I shall try." Then under her breath she added, "But the Bible does say to pray without ceasing." She blinked a couple of times. She'd learned it was a good way to emphasize her ignorance. Julia usually gave in to her when she did it.

Julia's icy stare sent a trickle of fear down Abigail's spine. She tried to swallow, but her throat chose that moment to close, causing her head to swirl. A sickening panic swooshed through her middle. She'd always argued with Julia, but this time Julia didn't wave her away with her fingers. Some of Julia's more eloquent friends were seated in the parlor with her, and Abigail knew they'd mentioned her attitude before today.

"I will not be spoken to in such a manner. Ever. Again." Julia closed her painted fan and pointed the tip toward Abigail's nose. "Never, ever." She stood quickly and stepped forward, keeping her eyes on Abigail's. "You will apologize to my guests, and I expect Papa will have something to say about the matter, because I will tell him." With the flick of her wrist, the fan opened, and her eyes bored into Abigail's, a wicked gleam looming in them. The fan set in motion once more, and her laugh echoed throughout the room. Most of Julia's friends erupted into laughter as well.

Abigail stood there, unmoving, the brutality of their unmerciful stares creating scars she knew would never heal. Her eyes burned with unshed tears, her ears held a flurry of echoes. *I won't let her see me cry.* She blinked several times, the knot in her throat growing larger. Her fingers clenched into tight fists. This was all her fault. Why couldn't she learn to keep her mouth closed? Oh, how she wanted to run out of the house and find somewhere to hide until it passed. What would she be forced to say? As usual, she'd be expected to wait, in her humiliation, until Julia was ready for her apology. If she could actually speak.

"Well, what are you waiting for? Didn't I tell you to apologize to my guests?" Julia folded her fan and laid it on a marble top table next to the pocket doors. She stood and inched closer, sending chilling fear trickling through Abigail's veins. "Papa? Could you come in here please? I have need of you." Her voice echoed through the expanse of the room, rattling the china tea set atop a rolling cart between parlor chairs. Julia smirked, eyes still boring into Abigail's.

After what seemed like an everlasting length of time, Mr. Allen strode through the opening, a smoky pipe beneath his bushy gray mustache. "Is there a problem, Julia?" He placed a protective arm around his daughter's shoulders, dwarfing her with his height. He didn't speak to the other girls. The room was silent save the sounds of birds chirping through the open window.

Abigail tried to swallow past the thickness in her throat. Perspiration dampened her collar and snaked down her spine, sending tiny chills down to her feet. How she wished she'd held her tongue.

"She did it again, Papa, just like I said she would. I told her to apologize to my guests." Julia flicked a gloved hand in Abigail's direction. "Right here, close to my wedding day, she defies me, knowing how delicate my nerves are. What are you going to do about her, Papa? I want to know." She folded her arms across her middle and pursed her pouty lips.

Julia's father drew his brows together and removed the pipe. "Abigail, you must apologize, and then you may go sit in the chair in front of my desk. Don't dawdle. We don't have all day."

His tone was firm, and Abigail knew she had to find her voice, or face a worse punishment than the last time she'd offended Julia. Her heart lurched at the thought.

"I…" She looked at Mr. Allen through a film of tears. "I am truly sorry for my rudeness. It will not happen again." *I'm not sorry for what I said.*

"There. Now, Julia, aren't you happy with that? I can see the girl is sorry, and I'll deal with her impertinence myself. Go on with your little party." He moved his hands toward her in a shooing motion. "You can have Lester for your errands. Isn't that right, Lester?"

A tall, gray-haired black man with a slight hump in his back emerged from the shadows at that moment and nodded his assent before stepping back to his place beside the large Grandfather clock in the corner.

"I hope you make her pay," Julia snapped. "I'll take Lester over her any old time." She spun on her heel, leaving Abigail to face Mr. Allen alone.

Abigail hung her head for a moment before the thought of freedom crossed her mind. She was just as good as these people. Better. Back home she'd been the belle of the ball. Her friend, Penny, was the only reason she'd signed on to come to this country. Living in America had sounded like something of a dream, whispering promises on the wind, and she'd carelessly flung herself into it. Now there was no Penny. The dreams that had bridged two foreign lands lay in shards, and Abigail had wished a thousand times she'd never visited the spirit who enticed Penny to leave England. The man who was paid well to convince young people to enter agreements of bondage used his wiles on Abigail as well, telling lies, and now both she and Penny had met with ill fate. She sighed, shoulders slumped.

The large, columned foyer loomed before her like a great ocean, threatening to swallow her upon the first hesitant placement of her booted foot. She'd been summoned, and go she must, for her employer wasn't a man to be trifled with. Abigail slowly wiped her fingers over her forehead, sweat dripping into her palm. As she exhaled, she took the first of twenty-two steps across the marbled floor, heart flipping wildly against the walls of her chest, and into Mr. Allen's office. Closing her eyes, she swallowed hard. She might very well explode if she didn't find a place to sit down and calm herself. As she fluttered her lids open, she spied the chair across from his desk. It was small and low to the ground, the only one like it in the whole house. She'd had to sit in it a few times over the last three years.

Only this time, she knew she'd gone too far.

Mr. Allen stood in front of his large, brown leather chair, plopped down in the seat, took up his pen, and dipped it in the inkwell. "I understand you're to leave us in a few short weeks." He didn't look up from the desk top. "It's also my understanding that I can add time to your stay here if you do not perform your duties to our standards." He began to write, his mouth pressed into a firm line.

Abigail opened her mouth to speak but thought better of it. A few short weeks. Surely she could hold her tongue that long. Not that she had a place to go upon her discharge, but she'd accept most anything over her present living arrangements. Mr. Allen had always been kind, but there were others in the house who weren't.

Abigail licked her dry lips, nausea settling in the pit of her stomach. "Are you going to add time to my contract, Sir?"

Mr. Allen glanced up at her then and pursed his lips. He sat like that for a few moments before he leaned back in his chair, and laced his fingers across his middle. "Well, now, young lady, I believe that is entirely up to you."

CHAPTER 2

Mobile, Alabama

York Roberts lifted his gaze to the sign just outside his shop door and sighed. *Expert dressmaker*, it read. Not such an expert if he couldn't find the handmade lace Julia Allen insisted on for her wedding dress. He'd finished the trousseau but had only begun on the dress for the ceremony. Searching for a lace maker with English skills had proven futile for the past eight months. If he'd known it would be this difficult, he'd have sent for the lace from Honiton, England. It would have cost a small fortune, but Julia's family could afford it, he was sure. Now, with so little time left, he'd have to offer other types of lace in place of the Honiton.

His assistant, Clarissa, was out trying one last time to find a suitable lace maker. Would she be successful? Probably about as successful as he'd been finding that beautiful girl from the market. The one who always seemed to slip away before he could get close to her.

The tinkling of the bell on the front door of his shop, snapped York from his thoughts.

"Clarissa, is that you?" He hurried to the front. Julia Allen stood, her mouth turned down at the corners, eyes squinting. Her heady perfume burned his eyes from several feet away, and he reached up to swipe his nose. Swallowing his disappointment, York pasted on a smile. "Well hello, Miss Allen. Is there anything I can do for you today?"

Miss Allen cleared her throat. "Mr. Roberts, you came highly recommended. I've heard nothing but your praises about this shop and your work." She drew in a breath and released it. "That being said, I cannot, for the life of me, understand why my dress, my wedding dress, is not completed. Can you explain this to me? Can you give me one good reason why?" Her jaw shifted slightly, but her gaze never left his.

York's stomach churned and his throat tightened. Where was Clarissa?

She lifted her chin. "I'm waiting, Mr. Roberts."

Miss Allen rubbed a gloved finger along the wooden edge of the hat counter. Thank goodness Clarissa had dusted that morning. The expression on Miss Allen's face did nothing to ease the flutter in York's stomach.

He swallowed hard and cleared his throat. "I haven't been able to locate the Honiton lace required to complete your dress. Perhaps another type of lace will do?" He glanced at the door, willing Clarissa to come back with something. Anything.

Miss Allen's chest rose as her eyelids narrowed into slits. "You knew all this time exactly what I wanted, and you still haven't found it? How could you be so incompetent? My father has paid good money for that dress to be finished. I'm giving you one more week to finish my dress." She raised her eyebrows and gave him a glassy stare. "If it's not ready, I'll take my business to one of your competitors—for everything. Madam Sinclair has already approached me with designs, designs I fancy. I'd think you would hate to lose such a large order. Do I make myself clear?"

Her voice, irritating and vexatious, rattled in York's ears. How on earth anyone had ever fallen in love with a snippet like Julia Allen was beyond his comprehension. Such a shame her attitude didn't compliment her beauty. He pitied the poor chap about to marry her.

"Mr. Roberts, do I make myself clear?"

York tugged at his collar. "Well, Miss Allen, I do have other lace."

"I do not want other lace. I've dreamed of my wedding day my whole life, and it's going to be perfect." She paced the length of the counter, her heels clicking on the hardwood floor. She spun to face him again, the picture of a vixen ready to attack. "I won't take anything else."

York inhaled, then spoke softly. "Miss Allen, you're right. I should have had the dress finished by now. If I don't have the lace by the end of the week, I welcome you to take your business elsewhere." Where the blazes was Clarissa? He couldn't afford to lose this order!

Julia's self-satisfied smirk spoke volumes. "I'm so relieved you've seen your error. I'll expect you at my house for a fitting on Saturday. Be there before noon. If you're late, I'll take off the bonus my father promised." She tightened the fit on each of her gloves as she spoke. "Mr. Roberts, I'm sure you'll have the dress ready."

Relieved, York nodded. "Yes, Miss Allen. I shall do my best to have it ready."

Julia's fiery eyes bore into York's. "I do not want your best. I want the best, and that's exactly what I intend to have, whether it be from you, or someone else. Good day." She spun on her heel and left, slamming the door behind her.

Relieved the glass hadn't shattered, York released a tense breath and slumped against the counter. He pinched the bridge of his nose. There must be someone in this cursed country who could make Honiton lace. And he'd only two more days to find that someone.

Abigail held the lid of the pot and poured the steaming liquid into Mrs. Allen's cup just before Julia burst into the room, red-faced and perspiring.

"The brass of that man! How dare he stand there like that and tell me I can go somewhere else!" Julia jerked one white glove from her hand and started on the other. "Right in front of me. Didn't even flinch. I wanted to smack his face. I should march back in there and give him a tongue lashing he'd never forget." She slapped her gloves against the back of a chair and planted her hands on her hips.

Julia's mother, Corinne Allen, sat on the gold, brocade sofa, intently focused on each stitch of her needlework. Her more mature features mirrored her daughter's in every way. Some would say they'd pass for sisters, especially since the elder Allen wore fashions similar to her daughter's, even though they weren't as becoming on the mother. Abigail scolded herself. She shouldn't even think such things, but they couldn't hurt as long as she kept quiet.

"I'm sure, dear daughter, he will have your dress completed. I've never heard a bad word against him. All the ladies rave about his work. They say he sews better than a woman, although you would never know that to look at him." She looked up, a mischievous smile tugging at one corner of her mouth.

"I gave him until Saturday to have it finished and bring it to me for a fitting. Do you think he'll have it done?"

Something of a frown formed on Mrs. Allen's lips then, followed by a sharp rise of one lone brow. "What on earth provoked you to such a rash decision? You shouldn't have done something so obtuse. You didn't even consult with me or your father." She stood and released a long, heavy breath. "This will have to be mended, and it will have to be done today. There's no time to find another dress maker. He is the best, and he will come through, given time."

"It's the Queen Victoria lace," Julia wailed. "I have to have it, and he can't find it. I won't get married in a dress that doesn't have the Honiton lace. I won't." She stomped her foot on the wooden floor.

Mrs. Allen crossed her arms. "For a woman who is about to say her nuptials, you certainly are being childish. I've never allowed you to act in such a manner in my presence. Your father may allow you to play games with him, but I do not."

Wasn't that the pot calling the kettle black? Abigail thought. Julia was very skilled at playing games with both parents. She'd been watching and listening, and her heart leaped when Julia mentioned Queen Victoria's lace. She knew it well. Most women and some men in her hometown knew how to make the very lace Julia desired, and Abigail had been taught herself. She could make it in her sleep. Should she speak up about the lace, or keep quiet?

"Abigail, might you pour Julia a cup of tea as well?" Mrs. Allen tapped the side of the cup with a fingernail. "Abigail?"

Heart racing so fast she scarcely could breath, Abigail cast her glance away from the pair, wringing her hands once as she did. "Yes, ma'am." Her fingers tingled like fire lit them. She shook her hands, and bumped the cup with her palm, sending it rolling off the tray.

Mrs. Allen eyed her suspiciously, the one brow ever arched. "Is there something wrong, Abigail?"

"Oh no, ma'am. Everything is just fine." Hands shaking, she reached for the displaced cup, then spilled a bit of tea while pouring. "So sorry, ma'am. I'll get that right up." She bit at her bottom lip so hard she tasted a bit of blood.

Mrs. Allen hesitated, then with a victorious lilt in her tone, she asked, "What do you know about Queen Victoria's dress, Abigail?"

Looking from one Allen witch to the next, Abigail swallowed. "I don't know much, ma'am."

"Well, you being from England, I would think you'd have some knowledge of the wardrobe of your matriarch. Surely you know what kind of lace it is." Mrs. Allen seated herself along the edge of the divan and crossed her ankles in a ladylike fashion, then slowly raised her gaze to meet Abigail's.

"Mr. Roberts called it Honiton lace. That's what he said just this morning." Julia just had to add that tidbit.

Abigail's pulse quickened, and she took a deep breath. What were they up to? Did they know she could make the lace? Perspiration trickled down her spine, sending chills to the top of her head, and she wrung her hands once more.

Mrs. Allen, lips pursed, leaned heavily on the velvety roll pillow at the end of her seat. "From what city in England do you come, Abigail?"

Chapter 3

"Well, Clarissa, I suppose we must go out to Rosemont and break the news to the Allens." York slipped his arms into the sleeves of his overcoat and adjusted his collar. "I cannot, for the life of me, understand that girl's insistence upon Honiton lace. I suppose I've failed at being the best in my business." He hesitated. "Clarissa?"

Clarissa folded her arms across her middle. "I don't want to go, Mr. Roberts. I...I don't do well with confrontation, and I have a feeling that Allen girl is going to be full of it." She took a step back.

"I must say, I was counting on your support, but I do understand your reluctance. She's going to be a thorn in my flesh, but there's nothing to be done now. If the lace cannot be found, then it cannot. Don't worry. I've met with far worse. It will simply be a long day. And I'm sure you will be more of a help here at the shop." He snatched his hat from the peg behind the door, and plopped it atop his head before walking out.

He'd known for months this day would come, and now that it had arrived, he loathed the errand he was about to make. The Allens would likely try to destroy his business in this area. Why hadn't he sent for the lace sooner? He'd been so sure he'd find someone in America to make it, but no lace-maker had been found. Admitting defeat wasn't something he wanted to do, but if it was to be done, he'd rather get it over with now.

A fine rain stung his eyes when he looked down the street for a coach. Mr. Dane Bayberry waited at his usual lamp post. York hurried to the carriage, handed the man some change, and opened the door.

"Where to, Mr. York?" The old, bearded driver tipped his hat in York's direction.

"Rosemont Plantation." York sighed heavily, shoulders slumped, nausea settling in his stomach.

"Rosemont, eh? Well, I'd rather pick up rocks in the hot sun, with nothing to drink, than to visit that lot. I've been told there's to be a wedding. Maybe things will soften up when that girl gets gone. They say she's what makes the kinks in the chain, if'n you get my meanin'." He winked and spit over his shoulder. "But if you're set on goin', I guess I can make an exception." This time the edges of his mouth curved upward in a sympathetic grin. Bayberry looked up at the sky and tugged his hat down tighter.

"I appreciate that, Mr. Bayberry. Unfortunately, I have the pleasure of telling the daughter that I can't find the type of lace she wants for her wedding gown."

Mr. Bayberry whistled low. "That's a pity, Mr. Roberts. I'm already feelin' a pain for ya, in my chest, right about where my heart stays." Bayberry patted at his left shoulder. "I should hope the father is home. The mother won't be of a help to ye, they say." He chuckled. "Climb aboard. We'll have ye out there in a jiffy."

What if he decided...not to go? He'd eaten that morning, but his stomach pinched as if he'd gone for days without a bite. This was the right thing to do. Maybe give Julia extra time to get other lace, or get someone else to make the dress. It wouldn't make things easier for her, but it sure would for him. He climbed in and collapsed against the cushions. Then he whispered a prayer of supplication.

The ride went faster than he anticipated, and he found himself standing on the drive in front of a magnificent white structure. His gaze followed the full height of the house to a large cupola about the same size as his shop. Four grand columns adorned the front of the house, and a balcony with a railing hung on the second and third floors. It must have taken years to build such a mansion. York took a deep breath, and stepped up to the double arched doors. Was the inside as beautiful as the outside?

He knocked on the right paneled door, and it opened. York's heart halted for a moment, and his breath caught in his throat. It was her, the girl from the market, standing before him with a long loose braid that hung like tendrils of spun glass, blue eyes the color of the deepest parts of the ocean on a starry night, creamy, flawless skin, and a figure any dressmaker would adore. She had long, curled lashes that were as black as night, and perfectly arched brows to match. Something else about her eyes kept his gaze glued to her. York swallowed and tore his gaze from her, staring instead, at the ground. So that's why he could never find her. She was a servant.

"Are you the dressmaker?" she whispered, leaning so close to his face it seemed like a dream.

"Dressmaker. Yes. That's me. I...I've come to tell Miss Allen I've failed at finding the lace. Is she in?"

She glanced over her shoulder. "How much lace do you require?"

York snapped from the fog that had him spellbound for a moment. "It's useless. She wants—"

"Honiton. I know." She squeezed his arm, sending tingles up to his neck, and he jerked back in alarm.

"I'm not going to tell on you. When you go in there, tell them you have secured the lace. I'll have to work during the night, but I'll have it for you. Please, do not say that it's me. Only tell them you've found it. Do you agree?"

Dressed in a plain calico dress and apron, the girl puzzled him.

"Who are you?"

"It doesn't matter. It matters only that I can make the lace. Here, a small section I made a while back." She pressed a soft folded square into his palm. "Can you keep my secret?"

He stared at the square for a moment before peeling back the folds. The small length was exquisite, perfect in its entirety. He glanced back to her face, tried to read something more. "If you truly made this, only a fool would say no to such a bargain. I can pay double whatever you charge."

Her shoulders tightened, and she pulled back slightly. "I can't take money from other employers until my contract is up here. Simply supply me with thread, and when I'm done in a few weeks, give me a recommendation. That will be all the payment I need."

Perhaps he'd hit his head in the carriage and was now in some kind of dream state, for he only stared at her. Was Clarissa inside, laughing at his expense?

"Mr. Roberts, are you listening?"

"Miss?"

"Abigail. I mean, Gardner. Miss Gardner." A delightful flush appeared on her cheeks as she lowered her gaze. Finally. A name to go with the beautiful face.

He cleared his throat. "I must say, this is all—"

"I know. And I know what you're thinking, Mr. Roberts. I can explain." With another glance over her shoulder, a look of relief passed over her face. "The young Miss Allen came home in a fit over her dress. When I heard her say she wanted Honiton lace, I knew it could be an opportunity for me."

York scratched his head absently. "Then you also know, Miss Gardner, I have no other choice." He sighed heavily. "How am I to get these supplies to you if you don't want them to know?"

She shifted and looked back into the foyer. "I'll need the thread today, different weights, if I'm to make enough for a wedding dress. You'll need to tell me how many yards. If I work diligently, I can make two yards in a night. I know you don't have much time, so you'll have to get it to me today."

"Of course. Make a list while I'm talking to them. Give it to my driver. He won't say anything. And Miss Gardner?" He searched her eyes for something more. "Do you remember me from the market?"

She lowered her gaze, a timid smile edging her lips. "You remember me?"

"Of course. How could I forget?" If she thought him daft, she didn't show it.

"Abigail? Who was at the door?" A strident voice carried from deep inside.

"Oh, no! It's the missus. I've got to bring you to them. Please, don't say it's me who is making the lace." She lowered her voice to a whisper and motioned him in.

Her stricken eyes and desperate pleas were not needed. If she'd asked him to sever his arm and give her the life's blood that dripped from it, he would have been helpless to refuse her. She'd captured him, body and soul. Anything she wished, he would try to see it fulfilled. "As you wish, Miss Gardner."

"Come, quickly." And then in a raised voice she called out, "It's the dressmaker, ma'am."

"Well, don't dawdle. Bring him in here."

She ushered him past countless wall portraits and statues to the back of the marbled foyer and into a large room on the right. Julia Allen and her mother sat across from each other on matching gold brocade sofas. The mother worked on a piece of needlepoint, and her daughter pouted, as he would have expected.

"Missster Roberts. Why, we were just talking about you, weren't we, Julia?" Mrs. Allen set her work aside and hurried over to clasp his hand. "And to what do we owe this pleasure, dear Mister Roberts?" She reeked of the same scent as her daughter, and York sniffed, quenching a sneeze.

He reached in his coat pocket for his handkerchief and dabbed at his nose before addressing her. "Well, I have secured a lace-maker, and I wanted to visit you myself." There. He hadn't told anything false. Pasting on a toothy grin, he acted his part in the scheme, while Miss Gardner's face reflected relief. The pinched lines between her lovely brows had softened. Her shoulders relaxed as they shared a knowing look, and she silently slipped out of the room.

"Oh, Mr. Roberts, I knew you would come through. Didn't I say so, Julia? I only hope that you will forgive Julia for her impatience. She's still a child, and she doesn't realize, sometimes, what she's saying. I'm sure you understand."

Miss Allen folded her arms across her chest and was silent save a dramatic sigh every now and then.

"Mrs. Allen, I've been sewing wedding dresses for a very long time, and I know how special the dress is to every bride." Thank goodness he wasn't marrying her. "Miss Allen, would you still like a fitting on Saturday? The dress won't be finished, but I'll have the lining and the length ready by then."

She batted her lashes with a dramatic flair. "Of course. And I want to see some of the lace on the bottom. I'll know if it's not the right kind. Don't think you can fool me."

"Julia, Mr. Roberts is our guest. Mr. Roberts, please accept my apologies again, on behalf of my daughter. It appears we will have to discuss this matter. Could I offer you some tea and cake? It's the same kind of cake we'll be serving at the wedding. Our cook is skilled as well."

"No, thank you, ma'am. I must get back to the shop. Lots of work to do, so I'd better go." He cleared his throat, excitement fluttering in his chest as he pulled at his cravat nervously.

"Well, you simply must take a piece for later. Abigail?"

"Yes, ma'am," she called from another room.

"Mr. Roberts would like a couple of pieces of cake wrapped up. Have Rhoda do that." Then back to York she said, "Is there anything else I can get you then?"

"No, thank you, Mrs. Allen." He glanced toward the open doorway. "But on Saturday, I'm going to need a girl to help me with the fitting. My usual assistant won't be available. Do you have a girl who can assist?"

The lace-making girl entered the room with a wrapped parcel.

"Abigail will be glad to help. Isn't that right, Abigail?"

"Yes, ma'am. I can help wherever I'm needed."

"See, Mr. Roberts? Everything is under control. Abigail will help you with the fitting on Saturday, and she will see you to the door. You have my deepest thanks for coming all the way out here to bring us the good news. And I'm so glad you were able to find the lace. I never doubted you for a moment. We'll look forward to your visit on Saturday."

York nodded his assent to the older woman, and then followed Miss Gardner into the foyer. Was there anything of merit he could say to her? "So you're indentured here?" he whispered to her back when they'd walked a little ways. So much for merit.

"Yes," she whispered over her shoulder, her long, chestnut hair sliding like silk over that same lovely shoulder.

"And are you from Honiton, England?"

"Shhh. Yes, I was. But now I live here, in America."

"Well, I believe that is obvious," he said, and she snickered. "I was an indentured servant as well."

Abigail whirled to face him. "You? And now you have a fine shop and good reputation as well."

"Yes. Well, I worked for a family in Virginia. They were very kind to me, and gave me excellent recommendations when I left. I'm very fortunate. You mentioned a few weeks for your contract. How many weeks? If I may ask." He fingered the brim of his hat.

"Only five, if I can hold my tongue that long." Her eyes flashed with regret. "I'm sorry, I shouldn't have said that. It's just sometimes, I can't help myself." She rubbed at her eyes absently, dark circles under them signaling fatigue.

"And how on earth do you think you're going to make this lace and keep up with your household duties?"

"Never mind how I'm going to do it. I'm just going to. They can never know it was me. I'm afraid they'd lengthen my contract just to make money from the lace, and I'd never get away from here."

York's chest tightened. His heart hammered against his ribs. "So you're moving away when you're done here?"

"As far away as I can." Her shoulders shuddered as she drew her arms around herself. "The sooner, the better."

"I understand." He regretted the comment. Somehow, he had to change her mind.

"No, you don't. No one does. I need your oath, Mr. Roberts. Spit in your hand and show me your palm."

York recalled his father doing the same thing, many times, when he was a child, so he turned his palm out, facing her.

She spit in her hand, then he spit in his, and they held their palms out again. She grabbed his hand and squeezed.

"It's done then. You've given me your oath. So, now I need the supplies. I took the list to your man out there right after I showed you to the parlor. Will you be bringing them to the bridge then? Tonight?"

"Bridge?"

"Your man. He knows about the bridge. I'll have a boy there by the name of Marcus. He'll get it to me." She patted his arm lightly. "You're a godsend, Mr. Roberts. I was praying last night, and God has heard my prayers."

York's gaze went to her hand, so small but so strong. How did she manage in this big country all alone? Or was she? "Do you have any family here, Miss Gardner?"

Her chin lowered. "Only my friends at Rosemont, workers on this place. My parents would love to come to this country, but I don't want them to make that voyage across the sea. I'm afraid they wouldn't survive the journey."

"Yes. I see." After a short pause, York added, "So you'll be assisting me with the fitting on Saturday. Will this Marcus deliver your work to me before then? I can't wait four days." Not that he wanted to wait even four hours to see her again. She was a breath of fresh air in this polluted environment. No wonder she didn't want them to know her secret. Leaving Rosemont would be the best thing for her, and he intended to help in any way he could.

"I'll have to bring it to you myself. There's a certain place it must be attached so it won't tear easily. I always go to town with Neely and Rhoda on the fifth day of the week. I'll try to have enough for the hem of the lining by then. I'll start tonight after supper dishes are done, if you can get the thread. There may be a need to send it with Marcus. I don't know yet. Please don't hold it against me if that happens."

Her eyes had filled with tears, and York's gut wrenched for the girl. "Here now, what's the matter? I'm going to keep your secret. They don't have to know where it came from."

She sniffed and blinked. "Mr. Roberts, you don't know what this means to me. I only hope my work is satisfactory. And I hope I'm not putting you in an imposition."

"No, no. On the contrary, you are saving me and my business."

She looked up at him then, chin quivering. "I shall do my very best work."

York stood there, captivated by her, but knew he must get back to the shop. Miss Gardner had work to do herself, and he was keeping her from it. "I'll gather some tools and thread and send them with Mr. Bayberry. If there's anything else you need, don't hesitate to send word with him. He'll let me know. I'll let you tend to your other obligations." York placed his hat back on his head and slowly descended the steep steps.

"Mr. Roberts?"

He turned to face her. "Yes, Miss Gardner?"

"Thank you. Thank you so very much."

"My pleasure, Miss Gardner. Until Thursday." He nodded in her direction, then continued to the carriage. "I'm ready to go, Bayberry."

"Yes sir, Mr. Roberts."

The carriage rumbled across the graveled drive, down a long, sleepy path, lined with pecan trees, moss hanging in long tendrils from their branches, a pink sun just above the horizon. It was a beautiful view, but not nearly as beautiful as the one he'd just left behind.

CHAPTER 4

A bigail closed the door. A rough hand grabbed her arm and shoved her back against the cold, brass handle. She let out a small cry before he covered her mouth with his greasy fingers. The door handle pressed into the tender flesh along her spine, sending shooting pains to every inch of her body.

Jamison, the Allens' son. The stench of liquor and smoke followed him wherever he went.

"Don't you make another sound. I saw you talkin' to that highfalutin' fella'. Who was it?" He pressed hard on her mouth and pulled her arm tighter behind her back then loosened his hand enough for her to get a few words out.

"You're hurting me," she hissed through his fingers, fear rising like a flood. Where were the other servants? Her gaze darted from one door to the next.

"You're gonna hurt if you don't tell me. I saw the way he was lookin' at you."

His breath smelled as if he'd eaten the outhouse, and Abigail gagged, tasting bile in the back of her throat. *God help me.* Her eyes closed, tremors violating every muscle in her arms and legs. Was this the day she'd dreaded for almost three years, so close to her release?

"Master Jamison, that you?" Lester appeared a few feet away.

Abigail's eyes opened and a renewed vigor came over her. She raised her boot and crushed the heel into Jamison's toe, as hard as she could. He cried out and released her, hopping on one foot, curses spewing from his mouth.

"You'll pay for that, you little wretch! Mark my words!"

"Jamison! What on earth is going on out here?" Corinne Allen

145

came running, teacup in hand, Julia close behind.

For a moment they all stood there, gawking at Jamison, then at Abigail. Dare she tell what he did? Was it her place, or Lester's, and what if Jamison denied all of it?

"Lester, can you tell us what's going on here?" Shame flooded Abigail as Mrs. Allen's searching look took in the swollen, red marks on Abigail's arm, as well as the undignified close proximity of her son to a servant girl. "Jamison?"

Taking a step away from Jamison, Abigail sucked in a deep breath. "It was me, ma'am. I stepped on his foot."

Mrs. Allen pursed her lips and passed her teacup over to Julia. "Jamison, is this true?"

Jamison squinted at Abigail before turning to his mother. "I stepped up behind her. It was an accident." His tone was laced with sarcasm. He turned to face Abigail, mouth turned up, brows drawn together. "I don't hold it against Abigail. In fact, I'll be glad to apologize. I'm sorry. Next time, I'll be more cautious." His wicked smile did nothing to sooth the fears gathered in Abigail's middle.

Mrs. Allen looked to the last of the lot. "Lester, is that what you saw?"

"I saw Miss Abigail step on Master Jamison's foot, ma'am."

The black man's eyes shadowed his fear in their depths, and the moment Abigail saw it, she realized she wasn't the only one in danger. Lester had actually walked in at the wrong time, even though it had saved her from Jamison's evil intentions. He'd be a target until she was gone. What had she done?

Mrs. Allen certainly did not look convinced, but she turned abruptly on her heel, and strolled back to her sitting room without another word.

Once she'd disappeared into the doorway, Jamison sneered at Abigail. "Don't get any ideas about leaving here. I've got a plan to keep you. Just in case you were making plans." He hobbled off, muttering the same curses he'd yelled out earlier.

How could she have been so careless? All this time, four months, to be exact, she'd avoided him at all costs. Now this. And Lester, too. If only she could tell the master, and if only he'd listen. She turned as cold as if she'd suddenly taken ill. A deep-seated chill coursed through her veins, down to the bone. What was happening? Her shoulders shook and her teeth chattered. Abigail knew she wasn't feverish. Her surprise at the shaking must have been evident, because Lester noticed.

"It yo' nerves, miss. They gettin' to you. Best go sit by the fire in the kitchen and eat some warm soup. Always work for my missus when she get like that."

"Your ...wife... has... chills?" Abigail struggled to say the words, chin quivering.

"Yes, ma'am. They come 'cause you upset. Take a little bit to get over. My wife get like that when the Master come around lookin' for runaways. 'Cause she scared. You gonna be fine, miss. Let's get you to the kitchen.

Lester guided Abigail out the back door and into the winter kitchen. Rhoda worked over an open fire, tending to something that smelled delicious. Spoon in hand, she clucked her tongue when Lester came in, Abigail in tow.

"I know what's wrong, chile. You got a case of nerves. Don't you worry none. Ol' Rhoda, she gonna fix you right up."

Abigail tried to raise her hand to her face, but it was useless. Her fingers trembled so, she scarcely could hold to Lester's arm much less rub her face. Such a strange feeling. She wasn't even cold.

Rhoda guided her to a chair close to the large hearth and draped a warm quilt around her shoulders. "There now. I'll come back with soup. You gonna be fine, Miss Abigail. Don't you worry none."

She did worry. Her chores. What if Julia tattled again? Would Mr. Allen lengthen her contract like he said? The same field she'd stared at through the window a few days before caught her attention. What she wouldn't do to leave this place. Jamison had made his intentions clear the last time. He wanted her, and not in a good way. But how could she protect herself from the likes of him, especially when he stayed drunk all the time?

Abigail closed her eyes. *God in Heaven, please hear me, Lord. Please keep me safe, and help me leave this place at Your appointed time. I am Your servant first, Lord. Please help me.* She opened her eyes when Rhoda touched her hand.

"Here go, Miss Abigail. You jest open yo' mouth, and Rhoda gonna feed you. You be back to normal in no time." She held a spoonful of broth in front of Abigail's nose. Its enticing aroma teased as the steam rising from its warmth tickled her upper lip. Penny's face appeared before her, like a dream. She'd been holding on to somewhat of an unfounded hope that somehow Penny would come walking up the drive when her contract was up, telling Abigail how she, too, was now free to live life in America the way she chose. Shaking her head, Abigail knew the truth all too well. She'd seen Penny's lifeless form lying on the deck of the ship, watched as her lovely face sunk beneath the waves of the sea, and cried herself to sleep night after night. *Oh, Penny, why couldn't you have fought harder to live?*

"Miss Abigail? You's got to open up you mouth, darlin'. Can't catch nothin' if you don't."

Numbed and weak, Abigail forced her lips to part enough to sip from the spoon. It was hard to swallow past the tightness in her throat, and harder still to swallow the blow she'd just been dealt. She had to tell someone, anyone. If she didn't, the earth might as well reclaim her for its own. The power of words could release her from the prison encompassing her soul, if she could only speak them.

"He grabbed me." Her voice rasped. "He... he pushed me against the door, and I smelled his rancid breath. I saw his yellow teeth, and I could almost feel his putrid lips on my face." A lone tear escaped, and dripped onto the spoon. "I thought, I thought..."

"There now, baby. Don't you worry no more 'bout that. He gone now. We gonna take care of you." Rhoda patted Abigail's knee as a mother would her child. "He been like that his whole life. He spoilt, that's what."

"But he said..."

"I know. Lester heard what he said too. We gonna watch out for you, Miss Abigail. We gonna make sure Mr. Jamison leave you be."

If only Rhoda could be right. Jamison had threatened. And he was twice her size. Abigail closed her eyes and swallowed hard, more chills invading. "What if he catches me again, and no one is there to save me?"

After stopping by his shop to inform Clarissa of their good fortune, York instructed Bayberry to visit the best thread-maker he knew. The old woman greeted him with a kiss on each cheek. She didn't speak a word of English, but communication came easily. She showed him many spools of finery, but York showed particular interest in a soft, white thread. It was perfect for the lace, and Miss Gardner would surely approve.

How many spools should he purchase? If the old woman agreed to sell all of it, he'd not go wrong to take the lot. He placed all twelve spools in a wooden box he'd brought along, and her eyes twinkled as she held up three fingers. York placed three coins into her withered palm, and she closed her gnarled fingers around the money, muttering something in her native Gaelic tongue. It didn't matter what she said as long as they understood each other. She appeared to be satisfied, as was he.

Now to get the spools to Marcus at the bridge. Another two hour carriage ride, but wasn't it worth it for the lace?

"Bayberry, are you familiar with a young man named Marcus?"

"Aye, sir. A good lad, he is. Have you got business with young Master Marcus?" Bayberry scratched his scruffy chin, eyes full of curiosity.

"That I do. Miss Gardner, the one who gave you the list at Rosemont, says you know him, and that you should give this thread to him at the bridge. Do you know where this bridge is located?"

"Aye, I know it well. The bridge is common meeting ground for folks like me. I'll be glad to take it, sir, but we'll have to hurry. Meeting time is the eighth hour. To be sure, if Marcus knows he's to get this, he'll wait, but not for long."

"Let's be off then. I'm ready."

Relief flooded York as the carriage bounced along on the open highway. With the thread safely tucked under his seat, nothing could dampen his spirits now. If only he were delivering the crate to Miss Gardner himself.

CHAPTER 5

The next few days were a whirlwind of cutting fabric, stitching seams, and worrying about the lace. York still pondered on the validity of communication arrangements with Miss Gardner. What if, in fact, he needed her for last minute adjustments? How on earth was he to secure her services if she continued to remain silent about her identity?

Spatters of rain pummeled the town, creating puddles at the edges of the cobblestone streets. Bad weather meant bad business. The rain couldn't last much longer or York wouldn't get the lace delivery, and he'd have to postpone the dress fitting. Julia Allen might as well go ahead and release him if he had to delay her plans any longer. He didn't know if he could tolerate the torture anyway.

Clarissa called from the sewing area in the back. "Mr. Roberts, Marcus is at the back door."

York hurried to the back and found the lad waiting with a parcel in his hands.

"It's the lace, sir. She won't be able to make it to town tomorrow, but she said to tell you she was able to make an extra yard. She mentioned you might give me a bit of a wage for my services too, sir."

"She did, did she?" He crossed his arms over his chest, and tried to hide his amusement. He was disappointed she didn't come herself.

"Yes, sir. She did indeed." Marcus cleared his throat, looking away, clearly convincing York that she did nothing of the sort. The boy was fishing.

"Well, lad, what kind of a wage would you be expecting?"

Swallowing hard, Marcus paused before answering. "I'm not quite sure, sir, but I trust that you will do right by me." His fingers fidgeted along the buttons of his top coat and a considerably large tear in the fabric.

A pang of sorrow stabbed York in the gut, and he decided quickly on a plan. "How about the two of us strike a bargain?"

"A bargain, sir?" Marcus shrugged one shoulder.

"Precisely." York touched the rip in Marcus's coat, and the boy's gaze followed. "I'll mend your coat, and I'll give you one gold dollar, but it will also be payment for any future deliveries. You must tell no one, and you must always do a good job, no matter what. Agreed?"

The child's eyes widened, and he grasped the package tighter, fingers turning slightly pale. "Truly, sir? Do you mean it?"

"Of course I do. But if you fail me. I'm afraid I'll have no more errands for you to run. A good name is rather to be chosen than great riches. That's in the good book."

"Aye, sir. I will." His head bobbed up and down excitedly. "I'm a good worker, sir. You can rely on me."

Marcus would probably never keep the money. York was certain his mother would need the wage for their family. Bayberry had said there were several mouths to feed, and not much in the way of income, as Marcus was without a father. York held the coin out, and the boy opened his palm for it. "Do a good job and there may be other jobs as well."

"Oh, yes, sir, Mr. Roberts," he said, head nodding again. Then his head lowered. "Mr. Roberts, I can't take this money. I told a falsehood. Miss Gardner, she—"

"It's no matter, Marcus. All is forgiven." He patted the boy's head.

Marcus beamed. "Truly, sir. You are a man of God, just like they say."

Poor thing. He couldn't be more than ten and two, and already shouldering more responsibility than he should. York only wished he could do something more, but this was a start.

He took the package from the boy, and patted his shoulder lightly. "Give me your coat so I can mend that hole."

Marcus did as instructed and looked on eagerly as York stitched.

Once finished, he held the coat out for the boy.

"Off with you now. And when I need you again, I'll send word with Bayberry."

The boy nodded his reply, still staring at the gold piece between his fingers.

"And put that in your pocket before you go out. I wouldn't want someone to snatch it from you."

"Yes, sir." He slid the coin into his jacket pocket and walked back out into the drizzling rain, face beaming.

Miss Gardner had said she went to town every fifth day of the week. What could have prevented her from her usual Thursday trip? Whatever it was had ruined the day for him, but made for a very happy Marcus.

The package. He had to see the lace. Pulling the string lightly, the brown paper unfolded, and the lace lay, exposed in all its elegant beauty. His breath caught in his throat. He'd never seen such an example of Honiton finery. Each thread meticulously stitched in a luxurious pattern, matching the lace of Queen Victoria's dress to the last detail. Miss Gardner must be secured as a lace maker, at least, even if he could not garner her affection. He brushed his fingertips across the texture of her work, relishing thoughts of their mutual appreciation for quality in workmanship. A beautiful woman with so much to offer a man like him. Perhaps he could convince her to allow him to call when her contract was up. His mind wandered to all of those stolen glances from the market, and the one time she'd actually spoken to him, and then disappeared. How his heart had longed for a chance like this.

She was just clearing the breakfast dishes on Saturday morning when Julia entered the dining room.

"Stop that immediately. I have need of you in my room. Did you forget my fitting this morning?"

Must she always be put in these situations? "Of course, miss, but your mother told me to attend to this regardless of what anyone else in the house told me to do."

Julia stomped her foot and clenched her fists, a deep frown forming. "I'll have you know, my dress is much more important than dishes, and if you know your place, you'll do as I say."

"No, she won't, Julia. She takes orders from me, as do you." Mrs. Allen stood in the doorway, a scowl pasted on her face, hands clasped in front of her. She'd already dressed for the visitor this morning, in her second Sunday best satin dress, no doubt. "I'd be careful if I were you, Julia. You wouldn't want to lose any of your precious wedding plans."

Julia's mouth dropped open.

"No, I didn't suppose you would." Her one eyebrow rose on her left side, as did the corner of her mouth. "Now, Abigail, carry on with your work. Julia, go upstairs. There is plenty of time for everything to be done. Abigail can come up when she's finished here." Without another word, or even another glance, she turned and exited the room.

Abigail shuddered, remembering the conversation she'd had with Mrs. Allen in the kitchen a few days before. And the most terrible thing about it was the fact that there was no one she could tell, no one with whom she could share her feelings. The woman had practically accused Abigail of flaunting herself in front of Jamison, and she'd never done anything of the like. Abigail recalled Mrs. Allen's words with confusion. *"You may have high aspirations with regards to my son, but you will never reach the potential that I have. I will personally see to it myself."* Having no aspirations in regard to the Allens at all, Abigail struggled to find an answer.

Julia stomped her foot and huffed. "I hate how Mother treats me like a child just to suit herself. Papa will certainly hear about this." She clenched her fists and squinted at Abigail. "Don't think I don't see how this benefits you. I can tell Papa of your part in this little farce as well, and he will not think so little of it." She walked out, leaving Abigail speechless with dirty dishes stacked in her hands.

At least there was one rainbow in the dark clouds. Mr. Roberts was bringing part of the dress for a fitting today. Abigail's middle swam wildly at the thought of the man. He looked anything but a tailor, what with his rugged good looks and muscular build. He'd fit in much better at a blacksmith shop or working on a ship. But as it stood, Abigail was thrilled he was neither of those, glad for the chance to work on the dress with him. Perhaps he could truly help her when her contract ended.

She finished clearing the table and headed up to Julia's room, nerves a-flutter. He'd be here soon, and Julia was already being her usual self. Maybe things weren't looking up after all.

"Abigail? Is that you? Come straight in here. I need you to lace up my stays. I have to be ready when he gets here, and that could be any minute. I'm really looking forward to this fitting, because he says he has my Queen Victoria lace, and I can't wait to see it."

"Yes, miss." She began the arduous task of lacing, not caring one whit about Julia's babblings. The only thing on her mind was York Roberts and what he might say to her during his visit.

When she finished tying the last of the laces, Julia sent her to fetch some ice cold lemonade. But as fate would have it, Abigail came face to face with a very disheveled, very intimidating Jamison on the stairs. He grabbed her forearm, squeezing hard, then forced her against the wall.

"Your little dressmaker is in the drive." His low voice was laced with sarcasm, and his breath reeked.

Abigail's heart leaped at his words, but she merely looked down at the pattern on the carpeted stairs and wriggled her arm in an attempt to free herself.

"Yes, just as I thought. You think you have a chance with him. But you don't."

Her gaze flew to Jamison's face, and she attempted to swallow, but it was futile. Nothing could break through the icy fear lodged in her throat. Jamison's evil chuckle did nothing to calm her either, nor the constant pressure of his fingers on her skin.

"That's right. I've taken every precaution to keep you here as long as it takes to have my way with you." Closer to her ear, he said under his breath, "Mark my words. When you least expect it, I'll be waiting, and you will be mine." With that, he released her and resumed his stair climbing, staggering and mumbling under his breath.

Heat coursed through Abigail's veins, heart pounding. She remained on the stairs willing herself to move, but her feet refused to budge. From where she stood, the front door was clearly in view, and she watched as Lester opened it, allowing Mr. Roberts inside with his packages. In a dream like state, Abigail saw their lips moving, but heard no sound, save the ringing in her own ears.

CHAPTER 6

"**M**iss Abigail, you all right?"

She sniffed, and realized her eyes watered with unshed tears, so she blinked several times to abate them. "I'm fine. I...was just fetching some lemonade for Miss Julia." She sniffed again. Where was a handkerchief and a wardrobe to hide in when a body needed them?

"I'll fetch the drink," Lester soothed. "You take Mr. Roberts on up to Miss Julia."

"Yes. Yes, of course." Abigail turned on the stair, careful to avoid eye contact with Mr. Roberts, and slowly ascended to the top while Lester went down hurriedly.

Mr. Roberts whispered as they moved upward. "I was able to make a little more than just the slip. The lace was more than enough to make the first layer of the dress as well. I must say, in all my years I've never seen such workmanship as yours."

Though she knew he couldn't see her face, she smiled her appreciation. "I'm glad you found the work to your liking."

"Liking? I assure you, Miss Gardner, I—"

She touched his wrist, then placed a finger over her lips. "Please..." Abigail's palm tingled where she'd touched him as a herd of galloping ponies pranced in her belly.

He nodded silently, and her eyes locked in on his until Abigail was sure her legs would no longer hold her up.

Mr. Roberts was dressed in his usual blue topcoat and tan breeches, but today his cravat was made of lace. A bit of the lace she'd made. How magnificent he looked, with his rich coffee-colored hair curled at the ends and his clean-shaven face reflecting the sunlight from the front windows. It was impossible not to stare at the cravat, although she tried vehemently to tear her gaze away.

"I see you've noticed." He glanced down at his chest. "I hope you're not upset with me. I wanted just a bit of it for myself." He stared at her intently with eyes so blue they sparkled, as if stars dwelt in their depths. And his voice. It made the hair on the back of her neck tingle up into her scalp.

What was she doing? This was supposed to be a dress fitting, not a suitor coming to call. Or was it? She cleared her throat. "Mr. Roberts, I'm sure Miss Allen is waiting for us."

He reached for her hand and gave it a quick squeeze. "Yes, I'm sure she is." Then he released her fingers as quickly as he'd picked them up.

What torture. To have the pleasure of his touch for only a moment. She released a long sigh before adding, "Mr. Roberts, I am a servant here."

"And as much as I respect that, it means nothing to me."

He inhaled a long breath before looking to the top of the stairs and then began climbing, glancing back at her with a silly grin on his face every now and then, and every time he did, Abigail was struck with the inability to breathe. Mr. Roberts possessed an uncanny talent for stealing her breath, silly grin or not.

The door was open, and Julia motioned for him to go in. He entered the room first, Abigail trailing just behind, trying to gather her wits, and not look like a schoolgirl with her first suitor.

"Mr. Roberts. How delightful. I've been so looking forward to your visit." Julia beamed at him. "I simply cannot wait to see what you've done."

Mr. Roberts lay his packages on the bed as Corinne Allen silently entered from another chamber. He made quick work of the brown paper wrapping and pulled the dress up by a thick wooden hanger, spreading the skirt as he did.

Abigail had always considered pride a hideous attribute, but at that moment, her whole being swelled to overflowing. York Roberts was not a tailor. He was a master. He'd taken her lace and made it into art. The dress was stunning, even in its unfinished state.

The room was silent, save the gasps from the three women present. Abigail so wanted to lavish Mr. Roberts with compliments, but she knew her place, and it wasn't proper for her to speak unless spoken to.

"Wherever did you find a lace-maker, Mr. Roberts?" Mrs. Allen cooed through her fake smile.

"Ah, Mrs. Allen, I did not find the lace-maker. But the lace-maker found me. It was a fortunate mishap that led me to such a skilled craftsman. I daresay, I fully intend to hire them to work for me exclusively." Julia and her mother bent over to examine the lace, and he gave a slight wink in Abigail's direction. Her belly ponies pranced again.

"Yes. Such fine work. I'm sure our Julia will be the envy of every bride in the South. Montgomery will be abuzz for months." Mrs. Allen clasped her hands dramatically in front of her bosom.

"Oh, Mama, it's just what I dreamed of." She turned a pouty face to Mr. Roberts. "I won't share the lace with anyone else. I wanted this lace, and I will be the only bride to wear it."

Mr. Roberts shrugged casually, as if her words didn't bother him in the least. "My dear Miss Allen, this is merely one style of lace. The lace-maker has hundreds of other styles. It's perfectly safe, and you shall be the only one wearing it this season, I'm sure. I'll step out, and you ladies can assist with the fitting. I'll be just outside the door, and you can let me know when to come back in for adjustments."

He did as he said, and Abigail felt sorry for it. Not only would she not be able to see him, but she'd have to deal with Julia and her mother alone, for Rhoda had returned to the kitchen after delivering the lemonade.

The dress was a perfect fit, which didn't surprise Abigail in the least. And it actually was quite becoming to Julia's figure. Mr. Roberts came back in and marked a couple of spots with pins, squinting as he did.

Her heart swelled with admiration as Mr. Roberts rewrapped the dress later, taking great pains with tissue paper, so as not to wrinkle it any more than necessary.

He turned with the largest package in hand. "The other two smaller packages are a couple of extra garments I stitched just for you, Miss Allen. I hope you'll consider them retribution for the delay in finding your special lace."

Julia squealed her delight and tore into the first package, completely ignoring everyone else in the room, and Abigail's heart ached with jealousy for a moment. She'd worn the same four dresses for the past three years.

"Might Miss Gardner show me to the kitchen, where I could find a cold drink of water before my departure?"

Abigail's heart pounded in her chest at his mention of her name, and all thoughts of jealousy vanished. Heat crept up her neck, and she feared the red blotches that always came. Why was she reacting in such a manner?

Julia held the first garment, a light pink dress made of silk, trimmed with large pearls for buttons along the sleeves. She admired herself in the mirror and, apparently, gave no thought to Mr. Robert's request. She merely waved her hand in their direction. She and her mother made all kinds of noises over the dresses while Abigail led Mr. Roberts down the stairs to the kitchen.

"Miss Gardner, I hope I wasn't being too forward about you coming to work for me. I know you'll have to wait until you are released from your contract, but I want you to know that my offer stands, whenever that may be." He spoke in hushed tones, staring at her all the while.

"I have only these four weeks left, just before Julia's wedding. It cannot come fast enough for me, though. Sometimes I fear it will never come." She sighed.

"Come now, don't be negative. Remember, I too was once in your place. It will come faster than you think. God know the ways of the righteous. He'll go before you to prepare the way."

Abigail stopped walking and looked up into his eyes, mouth agape. "Mr. Roberts, is it possible that you are a believer?"

"I gave my heart to Christ when I came to this country. I was but a boy, really, and the people I worked for were devout Christians. They showed me how to accept the gift of salvation and how to strive to live a life pleasing to Christ. Had it not been for them, I would still be living as a destitute. They taught me my trade, and how to pay attention to details, just as someone has taught you. I admire your work, Miss Gardner. Truly I do." He paused for a moment. "And you? Are you a believer?"

Abigail could scarcely believe her ears. Here, standing in front of her was a man who professed Christ as his Savior, who took pride in his workmanship, and who also showed a genuine interest in her as no one else had ever done. Perhaps the way was already being prepared.

"Miss Gardner?"

Abigail snapped from her thoughts and smiled her best smile, the one her papa always liked. "I most certainly am, Mr. Roberts. And I can't tell you how refreshing it is to meet another of the faith."

CHAPTER 7

The last three weeks had gone by in a blur for York. Julia Allen's dress took up most of his time, and he'd allowed Clarissa to take on more of the regular work. Undoubtedly, this dress would be his crowning glory. Mr. Allen was paying enough for it. And Mrs. Allen was right. Julia would be the talk of the South, as would his shop.

Even though he'd kept himself busy, he'd thought of nothing else but the dress…and the lace-maker. Marcus continued to deliver the lace every four days. Much as he appreciated the delivery, he couldn't help but worry about Miss Gardner. When did she sleep? As demanding as the Allen family was, she'd be working for them from sunup to sundown. How on earth could she complete her work and make lace for him? And get enough rest?

He decided to send word to Abigail that he had enough lace for the dress, but he wanted one more thing: a proper Honiton veil. If Julia Allen was so set on having her dress match Queen Victoria's, the veil was something she'd want. He was sure Miss Gardner could be trusted with the design and the style. He needed only to give her a length. But would she have enough time to complete it before the wedding? He had to try, so he jotted a note with proper measurements should the veil be needed.

York stopped working, a picture of Abigail Gardner forming in his mind. He longed to speak with her, hear her voice, brush her fingers with his own. Could one woman completely occupy the thoughts of a man to the point of madness? If he didn't at least get a glimpse of her, he was sure it would be so. With the completion of Julia's instructions for the dress so near, he settled on stealing away to

Rosemont that evening to deliver it. But for the moment, he needed to keep working, even if it meant not stopping to eat.

"Julia, have you seen my mother's string of pearls? I distinctly remember putting them out on your armoire so you could try them on with the dress."

Mrs. Allen's look of concern rattled Abigail's nerves although she hadn't seen the necklace. Anytime something in the house was amiss, every servant and slave was automatically on trial even if they hadn't been anywhere near. It was not a good sign for her, or anyone for that matter. She sent up a silent prayer that the necklace would be found.

"I did try them on with the dress, and I put them back where I found them. I'm not a child, Mother. I know how to put things in a proper place."

Julia rolled her eyes toward the wall, away from her mother's watchful gaze. Abigail's chest tightened. Fingers of dread crept up around her throat, making it hard to breathe.

"Abigail? Have you seen the necklace?"

Mrs. Allen's sharp tone sent icy chills up Abigail's spine, and she sputtered before finally answering. "N-no, ma'am. I saw Miss Julia try them on, but I never saw them after that."

"Yes. Just as I thought. Julia, gather the servants, and we'll find out what happened. I'll check the armoire one more time, and my room as well. I'm not happy about this. Those pearls belonged to my grandmother, a gift on her wedding day." Mrs. Allen strode to the stairs and began climbing, shaking her head.

Julia started barking orders the moment her mother was out of sight. Within minutes the entire household staff was lined up along the walls of the foyer, confused expressions on their faces, waiting for the worst.

Abigail stood at the beginning of the line, near the front door. As they waited for Mrs. Allen to come back, none other than Jamison waltzed through the front door. Abigail inhaled only a shallow breath, then struggled for another. A ringing noise filled her ears, and her fingers trembled. She couldn't look at him. Wouldn't look at him.

"Whoa, what's all this, Julia?"

Julia spun to face him. "Mother's pearls are missing."

"And this is how you expect to find them? The servants?" He laughed a loud, maniacal guffaw, and staggered back into the door.

He was drunk. Again. She rubbed her arm in the spot he'd pressed earlier, taking great pains to wipe the feel of his fingers from her skin. Tonight she'd scrub the spot with soap and the hottest water she could stand.

"I'm doing what Mama told me to do. This is her idea, not mine." Julia placed one hand on her hip before walking toward the back door.

Jamison inched closer to Abigail, and leaned near her left ear before he whispered, "See... I told you I had a plan."

Her stomach lurched in a nauseating whirl, but she didn't give him the satisfaction of looking at him. How could she when even the curve of his lips represented something so sickening and brash because of the nasty gestures he'd mouthed when no one else was around. Every time she looked at him, the same haunting words echoed in her ears. *And you'll be mine.* The room spun round and round, and she tried to swallow, eyes closed, arms trembling. How could she have been so dense? He'd threatened, and with only a week left, he intended to make good on his promises. Now she needed a miracle. *God, are You still up there?*

The carriage rolled to a bumpy stop along the circle drive in front of Rosemont's long, covered porch. York emerged and inhaled the fresh scent of the pink roses that completely encircled the entire house. He assumed the large garden had something to do with the name of the plantation, but one could never be sure. It could always be used as a topic of conversation should the need arise.

Before he could ascend the steps, he noticed Lester standing outside the door, holding it open. "Good evening, Lester."

"Evening, sir. Would you like some help with your packages?"

"I only have the one today. This is Miss Allen's wedding dress. It's finally finished, and I took the liberty to bring it out. I hope she's at home."

"Yes, sir. I believe she in the drawing room. I'll show you to her, if you'll come this way."

York followed him down the long foyer, past countless oil paintings of people the Allens probably didn't even know. The dress tugged heavily on York's arms. It must weigh at least twenty pounds, if not more. So many layers and so much lace made for a cumbersome garment, but he'd given her fair warning before the first stitch was ever made, so Miss Julia Allen knew what she'd be dragging to the altar, and she still insisted on this dress. His arms ached from the weight of the load. Could the old servant walk any slower?

Lester announced him, and he heard a squeal from the bride. She came running from her place beside the spinet. "Oh, it's my dress, isn't it? I can't wait to try it on! It is finished?"

"Yes, Miss Allen. All finished. And I also wondered if you'll be needing a veil. I have a wonderful idea for one, but I wanted to make sure you were in need of one before I got started." He raised his brows.

She looked back at her mother sheepishly. "Well, Mama wanted me to wear hers, but I'd entertain the notion of having my own."

Corinne Allen stood, hands clenched into fists at her sides. "Julia, I believe we already had this settled. My mother wore that veil, and her mother before her. You cannot possibly think to discard such a tradition. Mr. Roberts, we will not be needing a veil. Ours will do nicely."

"By all means, Mrs. Allen, I hope your daughter will wear the heirloom headpiece. I'm sure that anything else would never be a substitute. Might I see it?" He shifted from one foot to the other.

Mrs. Allen's lips actually turned up at the corners the tiniest of bits. Her expression could have almost passed for a smile, and York suppressed a bubble of laughter, turning his face away for a moment. He excused his action by forcing a dry cough.

"I'd absolutely love for you to see it. It really is a sight to behold." She paused and seemed deep in thought for a moment, forefinger at her chin. "Even as much as I love it just the way it is, I wouldn't be opposed to you adding some matching lace to it...for Julia."

"What?" Julia ran to her mother and showered her cheeks with kisses. "Oh, Mama! You're a saint, an absolute saint!"

"Oh hush." She playfully pushed her daughter away, the traces of a smile still playing at her lips. "Go and get the thing. Let him see it, and he'll tell us if he can work a bit of magic."

"Thank you, Mama." Julia dashed from the room.

York nibbled nervously on the inside of his bottom lip until he tasted blood. Where was Miss Gardner? Should he ask for her or not mention her at all? He really could use her help for the final fitting. He sucked in a breath and decided to ask. "Might I use the servant girl to assist me again?"

"No. You may not."

York whirled around. The voice came from Miss Allen's older and much less dignified brother who had been seated on the divan with a plate of pastries in his lap when he'd entered.

"I beg your pardon, Mr. Allen?"

"You heard me. I said you may not have her to assist you." He stared at the morsel between his fingers then popped it into his mouth.

"Jamison! Where are your manners?"

Mrs. Allen's alarmed expression sent off warning bells in York's head, but he ignored them. Jamison gave him a cold, hard stare. Unmoving.

"I might have a few questions of my own, for you." His eyes narrowed.

Mrs. Allen looked on, gasping as if she were having some kind of attack, until York and a servant ran to her. They led her to the divan, and the servant placed some type of yellow powder in her palm. She tossed the powder back into her throat and swallowed a long gulp of water. Then she lay her head back on a cushion while Lester and Rhoda fanned her.

York gaped at the young man. "Do you see your mother? Are you not concerned?"

With a flick of his wrist in his mother's direction, Jamison said, "Not in the least. She does it all the time. Just so happens, Tailor, there was a robbery the last time you were here."

"It's Roberts, and I don't have any idea what you're talking about."

"Oh, I think you do. I think you do. And I've invited the sheriff out here to get to the bottom of it." Jamison crossed his legs and smirked.

York stiffened. "Well, it has nothing to do with me, or the fact that your mother is ill."

Jamison licked his dry, crackled lips. "It has nothing and everything to do with it." His tone was nothing less than sarcastic.

Why did he keep talking in riddles?

"In fact, right now the sheriff has his men searching your store. I'll be anxious to see what they find." Gaze hard, cold, he added, "Won't you?"

Confused and offended, York walked toward the doorway. He had to get to his shop and sort this out.

"Not so fast, Pretty Boy." Jamison stood and clutched his lapels. "You may have everyone else fooled, but not me. I knew what you were up to all along. You'll stay right here until the sheriff arrives." He closed the gap between them and grabbed York's arm, then jerked him back.

"Mr. Allen, I'll thank you to take your hand off of me." York tugged at the hem of his shirt.

"I'll take it from here, Jamison." The sheriff stepped through the open doorway with a few of his men. "We appreciate the tip. You were right. It was all there." He held up a half full flour sack. "All of it." The sheriff turned toward York. "Mr. Roberts, I'm going to have to ask you to come with us."

CHAPTER 8

Only two more days. Two more days, and she would be free! Abigail pranced into the kitchen, raised her arms over her head, and squealed. The sound echoed throughout the high ceilinged room and out into the courtyard.

"Hold on now, girl. What you be gettin' all excited about?" Rhoda peered at her, a stern expression on her face, eyes ablaze with anger. "How you be so excited when Mr. Roberts held up down at that jail? Him, with eyes for you and all. I'm 'shamed of you, that's what."

"Mr. Roberts? Jail? Rhoda, whatever are you talking about? Why is Mr. Roberts at the jail?"

A sharp gasp came from the large black woman. "Miss Abigail, you didn't know. I forgots all about you bein' gone to market yesterday with Neely."

Abigail ran to Rhoda, grabbed her shoulders. "Know what? Tell me, Rhoda. Tell me now."

Rhoda sniffed as her eyes pooled with tears. "I'm sorry, child. I'm so sorry."

Abigail thought of Penny, how no one told her then either. She swallowed hard and fought the nausea building in her throat then gritted her teeth before she spat out, "I don't care how sorry you are. Tell me what happened."

Full blown crying erupted and Rhoda's whole body trembled, despite the heat. "They got him. The sheriff took him to jail last night. I thought you heard by now. Came and got him right here. Said he been stealin' stuff from other folks. Said they gonna send him back."

"Send him back? What on earth are you talking about? Send him back to where?" Abigail knew where. But she couldn't admit it, not even to herself. "What did they say he stole?"

"Back to England, miss. And they say he stole jewelry and the like. Mrs. Allen's pearls, a ruby ring from Nora Whitfield's mother, diamond ring, and other stuff. They found all of it at Mr. Roberts's store. He gone when they do it, so he don't know they comin'."

"Rhoda, you don't actually think Mr. Roberts capable of doing such a thing, do you?" Abigail raked her hand across her face and battled wailing.

Rhoda's chin lowered. "I don't know, Miss Abigail. I don't wanna think it, but they found all them jewels in his place. They say that all they need to send him back."

The room twisted into an abyss of darkness, and Abigail clutched at the edge of the table for support. York Roberts sat in a cold, dark jail cell because of her. Jamison's threats had come to fruition. He was probably sitting out there on the porch in one of those polished white rockers right that very moment, impatiently waiting for her to come and beg for Mr. Robert's release. Could fate have dealt her a harder blow? Two days and her freedom would have been assured, and now it sailed as far away as the country she'd left behind. Maybe the ties that bind couldn't be severed after all.

Well, she wouldn't do it. He could wait all he wanted. In forty-eight hours she'd be able to walk out of Rosemont a free woman. She could visit Mr. Roberts at the jail herself, and perhaps gain her footing about the situation, even though she was sure she knew most of it already. Couldn't she play Jamison's game, too? Apparently, he'd never met the real Abigail, and she needed to introduce them.

The stone walls of York's cell felt damp to the touch, as did the packed dirt floor, and everything was cold. With nothing but a small wool blanket for cover, the nights had been more than uncomfortable. He'd gotten very little sleep, for he dare not lie down. The floor reeked of urine, and he'd seen hundreds of cockroaches scuttling across. So when he did try sleeping, he sat up, propped against the wall, on a small stone ledge. It was the only place he could relax enough to actually sleep, though it be minute fractions of time.

He'd just gagged down a few bites of tasteless, watery porridge when the jailer approached his cell on rather wobbly legs. Probably from the ale he'd seen him downing the night before.

"Mr. Roberts, there's a young woman here to see you. Says it's urgent that she speak with you." He overemphasized each word as if he could hardly believe it himself.

York's spirits rose. Could it be Abigail Gardner? "Did the young woman give a name?"

The jailer scratched his ear with the edge of one of his keys. "I don't recall. It's not my job to secure information for prisoners. Do you want to see her or not? I can only give you a few minutes." He edged toward the door he'd come through.

"Then, yes." York lunged to his feet. "I'll see anyone who wants to see me." Except Jamison Allen. What had he ever done to deserve this treatment from the man? He sensed it had something to do with Abigail, but what?

"Right." He winked. "I'll bring 'er on in then. She's a purty one. Might wanna freshen yourself up a bit, heh-heh-heh."

He'd been wearing the same dirty clothes for the past four days in this same filthy cell. The only form of hygiene he'd been able to practice was wiping his teeth with the corner of his shirt, and he'd sacrificed some of his rancid smelling drinking water to meagerly wash his hands. Nothing would wash this experience from his memory though. As long as he lived, he would remember the rotting smell of this jail cell. Nausea had set in his gut the moment he'd heard the click of the lock.

The jailer came hobbling down the long, dark corridor once more, a shadowy figure following just behind. York's heart pounded so hard in his chest, he feared it may burst. He prayed it was Abigail. He could not endure the disappointment of another.

As they approached, he gripped the bars in front of him. York pulled his face into the opening between two bars, and struggled to focus in the dim light. The jailer stepped aside, giving York a full view of his visitor.

"Hello, Mr. Roberts."

Dressed in an exquisite blue gown, customary braid transformed into a lovely updo, wearing gloves like a proper lady, and carrying a matching reticule, Miss Gardner took his breath away. Even though he couldn't see the alluring hue of her eyes in the darkness, he knew the color of the dress matched perfectly.

"Miss Gardner."

They stood staring at one another for several moments. Laughter erupted from the other end of the hallway before a door was slammed, and the laughter turned to snickers. One voice sounded like that of a female. He scratched the side of his nose, but it sounded more like a blade along a length of wood. Even when she licked her rosy colored lips, it rumbled in his ears.

Miss Gardner had taken a few long breaths. Should he speak?

The jail worker had said they wouldn't have much time, so he asked, "Did I make that dress?"

She glanced down at her skirt and smoothed at it with her gloved hand. "Er, um, yes? Clarissa said you would insist on it, I mean, since I made all that lace."

"And she was entirely right. It would appear I owe you much more than a dress." He placed both hands through the bars, and she responded by grasping them. His breath caught in his throat. "You don't know how much your visit means to me." He squeezed her fingers, then drew circles on the backs of her hands with his thumbs.

"I simply cannot bear the thought of you being in here another day. I came as soon as I could." Her hands trembled in his.

Her contract. "So you're free now…"

She nodded, but a sadness still covered her features. "Now we have to free you. I've spoken with the jailer. He says the only way you can get out is if we prove your innocence. Otherwise, you'll be on a ship bound for England at the end of the week. That only gives us a few days to get the proof. And I know who did this."

"Jamison Allen."

Her sharp intake of breath told him she knew more than just a name. "Miss Gardner..."

"Abigail. Call me Abigail." A compassionate, yet endearing smile followed, and she squeezed his hands tighter.

"Abigail, I need you to tell me what Jamison is holding over your head." She abruptly tried to release his hands, but he gripped her tighter. "I know he's using me to get to you. It's all I've thought about since I've been in here. He was so angry when I asked for your assistance again, he refused my request, and that's when everything went askew." Fearing the worst, York tipped Abigail's chin until their eyes met once more. "Did he try to...take advantage of you?"

She tensed for a moment. York saw the dark circles rimming her lovely blue eyes and wished with everything in him that he could pull her into his embrace, to show her some measure of protection. It wasn't fair for her to bear this alone.

"No, no. He...he kept threatening, but I avoided him. Now I think his plan is to get rid of you because he knows how much I..." Her gaze dropped again.

"You what, Abigail?"

She cleared her throat. "I know that's what he's up to. Jamison is waiting for me to beg for your release, or at least to beg for some mercy. He knows how I...feel about you." The last declaration emerged in a whisper.

"And how do you feel about me?" He pulled her closer to the bars, closer to him.

"Mr. Roberts..."

"It's York. If I'm to call you Abigail, then you should call me by my given name. Isn't that the right way to make things equal?" He felt her breath, so soft, along his neck and chin, and he wanted nothing more than to kiss her, but after being incarcerated for days, it wouldn't be right to insist on such a gesture. That would come, given time. For now, having her close was more than he could have hoped for. "Could you ever care for me, Abigail?"

Her chin raised at the question, eyes alight with emotion, and he saw his answer in their depths.

"I thought, perhaps, we..." She paused, as if waiting for an answer he didn't give right away. He waited too long and her gaze turned stony. "I won't trouble you anymore." She pulled at her hands, but he held fast.

"Something passed between us at that first visit when you offered to make the lace. It's been your face haunting my dreams, your voice I hear, telling me not to give up in this wretched place, the scent of your hair I imagine when I close my eyes. You have captivated my heart, Abigail Gardner. If it weren't for my untimely departure, I would have asked for a chance " His gut wrenched at the thought of losing her already.

"Don't. Don't say it. You'll have a chance. We're going to work this out."

"And how do you think we can do that with me, a convicted man in a jail cell, bound for England?"

She looked up at him with confidence, a knowing smile playing at her lips. "Well, York, I think I have a plan to stop him."

CHAPTER 9

"**I** know it's hard to believe, but it's true, sheriff. I know it is. He loves to brag. If you'll only give him a chance, he will tell everything, especially to Mr. Roberts. I can do this. Please let me try."

Abigail, surprising herself at how fearless she'd become, had decided she was not leaving the sheriff's office until he agreed to at least part of her plan. She knew the truth, and it had to be told.

The skeletal, hollow-cheeked old lawman with a pointy beak-like nose sat in his chair, much to her surprise, for her entire tale, long as it was, with his fingers laced, and hadn't said one word. Once she gave a lengthy pause though, he sat a little straighter in his seat, and cleared his throat.

"Miss Gardner, is it?"

His loud nasally voice matched his looks perfectly, and she had to cover her mouth to stifle a chuckle.

"Yes, sir."

"It's a well-known fact, in this office, that Jamison Allen is a thief and a liar."

She gasped and covered her mouth.

"And as bad as it is, well, your Mr. Roberts is just a pawn in a very clever game. Look around you, Miss Gardner. What do you see?"

Abigail's gaze traveled the length of the room, confidence sinking into the murky depths of the Mississippi by the second. A thief and a liar and the sheriff knew it. Her breathing came more rapidly, and she resisted a strong urge to chew on her bottom lip. What was he prompting her to say? What did he expect her to say? "Sheriff, I—"

"What you see, Miss Gardner, is an office supported by wealth.

What you see is a sheriff who will retire with a good sum of money to live on. What you see is peace, tranquility, and the like. I aim to keep it that way, Miss Gardner. Now, you were saying?" He faked a terrible smile and waved a bony hand toward the door.

"Wh-What are you saying? Are you telling me I need money to get justice?"

"Miss Gardner, I'm not trying to say anything except that everything is as it should be. The law was broken, and a perpetrator is behind bars. Now, I suggest you find your place. It's my understanding that you've just earned your freedom. Be a smart girl and go on your way. It'd be a pity to have to go back. If I were you, I'd leave things be."

Even though her blood boiled at the very sight of the man, Abigail held her tongue. The sheriff would be of no help to York whatsoever. Best to lick her wounds and find another way to prove York's innocence. She turned and walked toward the door, dreams trampled, ideas forming in her mind.

"Could you answer just one more question?"

"I suppose I could, Miss Gardner." He'd picked up a pipe and poured tobacco into its bowl.

"How long will it be before Mr. Roberts is shipped back to Britain?"

The old man thumped the pipe with his finger a few times, didn't look up. "Ship leaves Friday morning, bright and early."

"Bright and early. Thank you." She made her way out of the office and into the street. What an unlikely turn of events. He was in on it. Probably the whole town knew of Jamison Allen's deeds and did nothing about it. People with money thought they could get away with anything and everything, but she was about to change all that. She'd learned a thing or two about those clever games, too.

Jamison Allen's favorite haunts were places Abigail should never think of visiting, but being a desperate woman had forced her to do things she shouldn't do before, so she headed in the direction of one of the local brothels. If Jamison wasn't there, someone could probably tell her where else to look.

The building was aptly named The Palace, and was known to hold a queen and many a princess. Jamison had been delivered home from the place countless times in a golden carriage, complete with red velvet seats and curtains. His pockets were always empty, and his father would smack him in the face sometimes. He always went back though. Rhoda had said Jamison was searching for a semblance of love he never found at home.

As Abigail approached the door, her heart began beating wildly in her chest. What if they tried to lure her into service with them? How would she escape? Just as her knuckles touched the ornately carved wooden door to knock, it opened, and a small, round-faced Asian woman motioned for her to enter.

Abigail shook her head. "No, I just need some information."

The woman smiled and motioned her in again, but Abigail's feet remained planted in place.

"I don't want to come in. I'm just looking for someone." She crossed her arms over her middle.

But the little woman only stood there, smiling her wooden smile, unwavering.

Abigail's patience had worn fairly thin when another woman with painted red lips and long black, ringlet curls peered over the head of the smaller one. "Can I help you, miss? This one, she don't speak English."

"Yes. I'm looking for Jamison Allen." She heaved a sigh. "I'm told he visits here."

"That he does." She cocked her head and thrust out her ample chest. "I daresay, this house is more of a home to him than Rosemont." Her tone was laced with sarcasm. She would be of no help whatsoever.

"Is he here?"

"No. He's not. Anybody else you looking for?" The woman scratched beside her nose. Abigail remembered Penny doing the same thing when she told a lie.

"Please. I really need to speak with him." She clenched her jaw and gritted her teeth.

The woman eyed her, clearly rattled. "I know who you are. You're

Abigail. His description of you was perfect."

Mouth agape, Abigail said nothing, waiting for the woman to continue.

"He's mine, and I don't share, so you'll have to get your—"

Jamison, a little disheveled in appearance and smelling of perfume, pushed in front of the woman. "Well, well, well. Abigail. So nice of you to look me up." He straightened the lapels of his jacket and smoothed the sides of his hair.

Jamison's glare unnerved her, but she forced a watery smile, despite the shakiness in her limbs.

"Leave us, Juanita. Abigail and I have some catching up to do, don't we, darling?"

The girl, Juanita, rolled her eyes and disappeared, swallowed up by the huge house.

"I take it you've found my little present."

The horror of that moment didn't really sink in until Jamison parted his lips and she saw his wicked smile. He was actually proud of what he'd done to York.

"I'm here to strike a bargain, Jamison." Even though Abigail had a plan and she'd gone over the conversation in her mind, she still wasn't really prepared for the role she was about to play. A bead of sweat rolled between her shoulder blades and she flinched.

"Oh, it's a bargain you're looking for, is it? Well, do speak up, for I love a bargain."

His sneer caused her heart to beat faster, so she started walking toward the street. He matched her stride, and even tried to link arms with her, but she pulled her arm away and shuddered inwardly. Finding him at the brothel made her like him even less. "Could we find a place to sit, away from here?"

"Keep walking. We'll have tea at the Village Inn. We'll look like a regular couple. Won't that be nice?" He looked back toward the brothel and muttered something under his breath.

"I'm not looking for nice, and we're not a couple, although I'm open to listening to your terms, and then you can listen to mine." She took in a deep breath and released it.

"Oooh, feisty and beautiful. I like that. I've always liked that about you. Come now, Abigail, can't we play nice together?" He fingered her sleeve lightly.

"I assure you, Mr. Allen, I don't play nice." She pulled her arm away. "I have other appointments to attend to. Let's start talking."

Jamison reached out and took a strand of her hair between his fingers. "I don't need to talk. I know what I want. And I think you might be ready to give it to me. Am I right?"

Abigail jerked her head just enough so her hair fell from his grasp. "Mr. Allen, I'm not going to give you anything. We're talking about some kind of a trade. That's the only reason I'm here."

She pulled on her collar in an effort to cool herself. The sun was past hot, and she'd worn too many layers. Thank goodness she'd allowed herself that. At least she didn't feel so self-conscious with all that padding. With Jamison's roving eye, one could never be too cautious.

"Abigail, we're old friends. You can stop calling me Mr. Allen. I'm just Jamison to you. I could be more than that though. You and me, we could have something special."

"Mr. Allen—"

"Jamison."

She forced a cough. "Mr. Allen, I am willing to entertain the notion of spending some time with you." The words left a bad taste on her tongue. "But I do have some reservations. What can you do to help Mr. Roberts? I'm sure with the weight you pull in this town, you could change his circumstances."

A deep scowl formed on Jamison's face. "What? So you can run to him when I'm done with you? No." He stopped, grabbed her arm and jerked her toward his chest. "See here, Missy. I've waited long enough for you. I intend to marry you. You'll be mine forever. I won't have another man's filthy hands on you, ever."

At a momentary loss for words, Abigail struggled to find her voice. Every fiber of her being screamed inside her, but her throat had a mind of its own. After what seemed like an eternity, she finally breathed out, "You can't be serious."

"Serious? Of course I am. Why do you think my father paid for you to come here in the first place?" He sneered. "Why do you think you've never been whipped for talking back to my sister? I owed a debt to my father. Naturally, I couldn't work in my own household. You were already there. I simply told my father to extend your contract. He reluctantly did so, and your service has relinquished my debt." The lines between his brows softened. "Your own debt was paid after only one year. But now the contract is settled. You're free, and I'm free. We can leave here, get a fresh start somewhere else, maybe in the Carolinas."

So he'd used her for his own gain. Jamison rattled on about his plans for a few more moments, a softness touching his features, something Abigail had never witnessed before. Perhaps he really did wish to change, but even if she didn't love York... What a thought to cross her mind. Did she love York? Was this what love did to a woman? Make her toss everything else to the wind? Well, she could never actually give Jamison a chance. He'd used her to pay his debt. What woman, in her right mind, would fall for that? Abigail gripped the sides of her head as if to cover her ears.

"Abigail, can't you see I've done all this for us? I hand-picked you myself. From all the dozens of girls, I picked you. It's what my father did, too. He picked my mother, and look how great they are together." Jamison squirmed in anticipation of her answer.

So that was what Mrs. Allen meant when she said something about never living up to her potential. *Think fast, Abigail.* How could she shift the odds in her own favor? If she could only persuade Jamison to confess somehow. Maybe if he were drunk? No, it had to be something subtle.

"I think I might like a fresh start," she blurted out.

Jamison stilled, and stared at her. "What are you saying? That you'll marry me?"

Chapter 10

Abigail fumbled with her reticule for a moment before she came up with an answer. "Jamison, I must admit that this has all come as quite a shock to me. I didn't realize the extent of your, um, devotion. At the same time, I cannot overlook the unfair treatment of Mr. Roberts, and I feel totally responsible for his predicament. With that said, I don't see how I could start any kind of new life with his fate on my conscience." There. No lies, and still a little inviting. Her heart pounded a wild rhythm in her chest.

They'd reached the Village Inn. Without a word, Jamison opened the door, and allowed her to go first. Odd behavior for someone who'd taunted her mercilessly for the past three years. He led her to a small table with only two chairs. The smell of scorched coffee hung thick in the air. How many other girls had he brought to this same table? A feeling of shame crept over her, and she wanted to run, but that wouldn't help York at all. She had to see this through.

They sat down across from each other. Jamison blew out a long breath, clearly unnerved.

"I think I may have a solution to your problem." He laced his fingers together on the table. "What if the tailor got to stay, keep his business, and all of this just goes away?" His brows rose at the last word.

"In exchange for what?" She tried to swallow, but her throat was as dry as powder.

"Well, now that's the tricky part." The muscles in his jaw tightened. "You'd have to marry me. We'd leave just as soon as the nuptials have been performed, and your tailor can resume his life, just like nothing ever happened."

"You can do that?" Not really all that surprising, considering how he had gotten York in trouble in the first place.

"Of course I can. Money can be a very influential tool. My father has promised to give me my portion of the estate when I leave, but I have to be married. And that, my dear, is where you come in." He flashed her a toothy grin, so full of himself.

"I couldn't marry you until Mr. Roberts's name is clear. And even at that, a loveless marriage is not at all what I had in mind for myself. There's got to be something for me, too." Keep playing the game. Something was bound to give.

He softened again. "It wouldn't be a loveless marriage. You'll learn to love me. I know you will." His hand slid across to cover hers.

The waiter placed two cups of steaming tea on the table beside their arms.

Something pricked at her conscience, but only for a moment, and she pulled her hand away. "Tomorrow. Give me until tomorrow, and I'll do it, but you have to clear Mr. Roberts first. If he walks out of the prison tomorrow, I'll marry you."

Jamison shifted in his chair. "Tomorrow then. Say noon? I'll have everything ready." He reached for his cup and then raised it in a toast. "To Mrs. Abigail Allen."

Abigail couldn't drink anything lest it come back up, so she just sat there with a pasted grin, biding her time, thinking. What had she just done? Wouldn't it be just as well to go back to England to be with York? But she couldn't do that. It would cost hundreds of dollars she didn't have. Another thought came to her. "I have another appointment, Mr. Allen."

"As do I. I have many preparations to make. You've made the right choice, Abigail." He winked and lay his napkin beside his cup. "Shall we?" They rose and walked to the door, where he took her hand. "Until tomorrow." The hard lines reappeared around his eyes, and he squeezed her hand harder than necessary. "I will break you if you cross me. Don't try anything foolish. I have connections all over this town."

"I have no intention of doing anything foolish." She did intend to cross him, though, in any way she could.

They went in opposite directions, Abigail toward town and he back to the brothel, no doubt. She had one last chance to help York before tomorrow and very little time to do it. There was one more person in law enforcement who might not be persuaded by the wiles of money, and she had to see him. She walked with a determined stride for nearly a half hour before she reached the moderate white house with four tall columns in front. This was it, she was sure. Abigail went to the front door of the house and knocked. When the door opened, a sweet-faced gray haired lady stood, peering around the edge.

"Come in, dear. What can we help you with today?"

"Is this the home of the constable?"

"Yes, it is. Would you like to come in? My husband is reading in the library, but I'm sure he'll have time to see you."

Abigail's stomach fluttered as she stepped over the threshold. The house smelled of fresh baked bread and was tastefully furnished in such a way, Abigail was sure there were no children about. So many things that would break. It reminded her of her aunt's cottage back in England. No children there, either. Would the constable be as harsh as her aunt?

"Right this way. I'll introduce you. What's your name, dear?" She hobbled away from the door.

"Abigail Gardner, ma'am." She followed the little hump-backed lady down the corridor.

They entered the library where another face greeted her with a kind, sweet smile. The lady introduced her and motioned for her to sit across from the white-haired gentleman who reclined with his feet propped up.

"What can I do for you, Miss Gardner?"

"Well, sir, I have a big problem I'm hoping you can help me with."

"Yes, well, tell me all about it, and we'll see." He'd laid his pipe beside him on a small table when she'd entered, and he reached to retrieve it then.

"I suppose I should ask you if you and the sheriff are really good friends."

He took a puff of the pipe and blew out rings of white, puffy smoke. "As friends go, no, we are not. Why do you ask?"

"Mr. Collier, I have reason to believe the sheriff is taking bribes. I have a friend who is incarcerated right now for crimes that were committed by someone else. The sheriff knows this, but refuses to do anything about it because of the money he receives from wealthy people in town."

The constable removed his pipe once more and spoke. "Miss Gardner, you're going to have to be straightforward with me. Don't speak in riddles. I've got to have names. Tell me everything."

"Yes, sir. My friend in jail is York Roberts." She lifted her chin in an attempt to look confident.

"The tailor?" The constable sat forward and put his feet on the floor. "He does excellent work. I believe he made this shirt I'm wearing." He looked down at his shirt and back up at her.

"Yes, sir." She shifted from one foot to the other. "And he was accused of stealing jewelry from clients' homes. And then the sheriff sentenced him to go back to England on a boat this Friday. He didn't steal the jewelry though. Jamison Allen did. And he says he can clear it all up if I marry him."

"Jamison Allen, you say? Now that's interesting. I've been trying to catch him for years. And I suppose you're in love with Roberts? Am I right? It's been my experience that any woman fighting for the rights of a man has got to be in love."

The flutters returned and the room suddenly felt hot. "Well, um... yes, sir."

He chuckled. "Yes, I remember the first flames of love. Very powerful. Makes you do things you never thought you could. As for the stealing and the boat, well, that cannot be done legally without a trial. Did he have one? If he did, I'm not aware of it, for this is the first I've heard of it."

"No, sir. The sheriff told him it was his sentence. And he told me, just this morning, that the ship leaves Friday." Abigail twisted her reticule strings around her fingers.

"Young lady, let me change out of my house slippers and I'll accompany you to the courthouse myself." He stood and laid his pipe back on the table. "I'll take a look at his indictment and see how all of this came about."

He left the room in a hurry and came back ready to leave. "I've just told the missus that we've gone. We'll have to go fast, or the courthouse will close." Hat in hand, he walked toward the corridor.

"Mr. Collier?" She trotted after him. "There's one more thing."

"Yes, child, what is it?" He stopped and turned toward her, eyes wide.

"Jamison said that if I crossed him, he'd break me."

"Oh, that's not good. Not good at all. Yes, well, we'll take care of that, too. We'll have no harm come to you in this. An innocent bystander and all." He waved a hand toward the exit, and they continued on. "Don't worry, sweet girl. I may be old, but I'm still a good shot. I can protect you from the likes of Jamison Allen should the need arise."

Abigail breathed a sigh of relief. If only she could shake the nasty taste in the back of her throat when she remembered Jamison's breath in her face.

They hurried out and down the street into the busiest part of town. The old man was winded, but he kept going. By the time they reached the courthouse, there was only a few minutes left before it closed. Mr. Collier led the way to a room where records were kept. He approached a tall, wiry man, who was standing at the front of the room.

"I need to see an indictment against one Mr. York Roberts, please."

The man nodded and began looking through papers. After several minutes, he turned to the constable. "There are no indictments here against anyone with the name Roberts."

"Check again, man. A lot is at stake here. A man's livelihood." He patted the counter a few times, his chubby red fingers creating quite the sound.

The man did as he was told, and still came up with nothing. So, they left that room and Abigail followed him to another, on the second floor. The sign on the door read Judge Tucker, and Abigail gasped.

"What's wrong, child? Don't you want to see your man freed?" He tried the door, but it was locked. "Drat! Just as I feared. He's already gone home for the day. I'll have to ride out there. Tell me where you live, and I'll bring you the news as soon as I find out something."

"What's going to happen? If you do anything tonight, I'm afraid Jamison will come after me." She tightened her hands into fists and loosened them, perspiration dampening her gloves.

"Nonsense. He won't know a thing until tomorrow. Now, what's the address?"

Abigail told him of her address with a heavy heart. What if the judge didn't listen to the constable's tale? And what if the constable was wrong, and Jamison did come after her tonight?

"Now you go on home, and I'll do my job. I love to see justice done, and I believe if we can get this straightened out, it will be." He patted her shoulder reassuringly.

"Mr. Collier, I'm depending on you. Please, make the judge understand."

"I'll do my best. It's all I can do." He smiled the same sweet smile she'd seen when they'd met. Then she walked toward Clarissa's house, but wished herself a thousand miles away.

A few hours later, a knock sounded on the door. Had the constable come with news of the judge's decision? She unlocked the door, and it opened with so much force she staggered back into the wall. Rough hands grabbed her, twisting her backward with her hands behind her. She tried to scream for Clarissa, but the only sound she could make was a muffled cry, like that of a child. She knew she was no match for the likes of Jamison.

"I warned you not to cross me," Jamison's drunken voice growled.

Just as she'd feared. Now she'd never see York again. Jamison had said he'd break her, and he would. She knew it as well as she knew the sun would rise the next day. He bound her wrists so tight her arms and hands throbbed with every beat of her heart. "You don't want to do this, Jamison."

"What happened to Mr. Allen? You know, Abigail. I really believed you today. I thought you were willing to try. But you can't let that tailor go. He's nothing. And you could have had everything with me. You couldn't let me show you how much I love you." He touched her face with the pad of his thumb.

"You don't love me, Jamison. You don't treat people you love like this." Abigail squeezed her eyes shut and opened them again. "You've never shown me any kind of affection. All you've ever done is belittle me and tried to scare me."

"What?" He slammed her to the wall, his forearm under her chin. "I've never belittled you. All boys try to steal kisses and favors from girls. I was just being a boy. I've shown you affection. You've never returned it. And that's where you went wrong." He jerked her through the door and pushed her toward his horse. "You're going to pay for what you've done. When I'm finished with you, Roberts won't want you either. When you left me today, I followed you." His eyes narrowed. "I know exactly what you're up to."

Nausea flooded Abigail's stomach. Could this really be happening to her? "Please, please, Jamison! Don't do this! Let me explain."

"Explain? There's nothing to explain. You had a chance. Now it's gone." He went around her and grabbed her hair, giving it a jerk toward the horse. "Put your foot in the stirrup!"

"I can't." She went limp. "I need my arms. Jamison. Please!"

"Shut-up!" He struck her hard in the jaw, sending her plummeting to the ground. "I don't want to hear your voice. Now, get up, or I'll put you on the horse myself."

Tears flowed freely down her cheeks. Her dusty hair hung in tendrils over her eyes. *Oh, God, please help me.* Abigail tried to roll to her knees, but every time she moved, an excruciating pain shot through the side of her head.

"Didn't you hear me? I said get up!"

His boot made contact with her ribs more than once. With every blow, pain coursed throughout her entire body. Was this how she would end? *God, are You there?* Horses were approaching and she felt herself being dragged to her feet, the world spinning and turning gray. Then something cold and hard touched her cheek.

"Make one move, and I'll end it right here," he rasped near her ear. "Don't come any closer, Roberts. I'll shoot her. I'll do it."

York slowed his horse, and slid to the ground a good thirty feet away, as Jamison lifted Abigail's seemingly lifeless body up into his grasp.

To his right, the constable held up his pistol. "Judge Tucker has his gun, too, Jamison. Might as well give it up. You can't win this."

Abigail's head hung limp as an uprooted violet over Jamison's arm, hair a tangled mess. Had Jamison's blows killed her? A cold sweat broke out across York's forehead. His heart pounded like a drum. For a second, he thought he saw her move, but it was just his imagination. The darkness shadowed the pair, and York had a hard time distinguishing. This was supposed to be a wonderful moment between the two of them, a moment that might not ever happen. Her life hung in the balance, all because of him.

"Abigail! Abigail, I'm here!" York called, the cold sweat enveloping him, legs trembling.

"Shut up, Roberts. You can't have her," Jamison sneered through clenched teeth.

Her head raised a few inches. "York?"

Jamison gave her a squeeze. She moaned and flinched.

Thank God she was alive. York wanted to run to her, but the worry that Jamison would discharge his pistol on her kept his feet rooted to the spot. The pain in his chest hurt as much as if he'd been dealt the blows himself. How could he have let this happen to her? He should have known Jamison would go to any length to win. He eyed Jamison, his breath coming out in shallow gasps.

The constable spoke again. "We've talked to the sheriff, Jamison, and we've got paperwork. You're going to jail. Your own father is willing to testify against you, as well as one of your neighbors who saw you break into a house. Let Miss Gardner go. Let her go, or I'll shoot." He pointed his gun in Jamison's direction.

"No, Mr. Collier!" York extended his arm toward Collier's hand. "You might hit Abigail." Desperation clutched at his heart along with a sick swirl in his stomach. He'd never let himself care for anyone enough to make himself sick, yet here he stood. "He can have me instead."

Mr. Collier kept his eyes trained on Jamison, but answered York through pinched lips. "I assure you, Mr. Roberts, I am an expert marksman. I've won the regional championship seven years running. I think I can handle this."

"Go ahead and shoot. I've got nothing to lose." Jamison pulled back the hammer of his pistol, but the constable fired before anything else could be done. Jamison's body flung backwards, as did Abigail's. She dropped to the ground in a heap, with him just behind her.

York took one step forward but his legs suddenly wouldn't hold him up. An extreme pain jabbed through his chest, and he clutched at the spot. Blood on his hands. Must...get to Abigail.

Bile rose in his throat. Then he collapsed in front of his horse, and everything went black.

CHAPTER 11

For three days she sat by his bed, anguished, willing him to wake. Doc Woods said Jamison's wild bullet couldn't have taken a better aim. Doc was surprised York had made it this long, he'd lost so much blood already. If only her faith had been stronger, none of this would have happened.

"God, why couldn't I have trusted You more? You know everything before it happens, and yet You still allow us to make our own mistakes. I feel so helpless. Please, God. Show me what to do. Tell me how to pray for York."

The old constable patted her shoulder. He had come for a little while the past three days. "You know, Abigail, sometimes God allows us to go through things to test us. Perhaps that is the case here as well."

Abigail looked up at him.

"I'm sure you're in need of rest. Doc says you haven't eaten much, and he says you need to be giving your ribs some special attention."

She shook her head. "I'm fine."

He frowned. "Why don't you let me stay for a bit while you get some rest in the next room? I can come over and get you should he awaken."

"No. I can't leave him. This is all my fault. I should be the one lying here. It was me that made Jamison mad, not York." She couldn't just leave York alone in this dreary place. He'd become as necessary to her as breath. She didn't want anyone else watching him. What if he woke up and she wasn't there? Her chest ached, and she longed to be alone with York once more. "I never should have come to this country..."

The old constable sighed. "Listen to yourself then, child. You keep blaming yourself, when it's really no one's fault. The devil comes to seek, find, and destroy. If you keep blaming yourself and not Satan, then you've fallen into his snare. God can't use people when all they want to do is feel sorry for themselves."

"How can you say that? God doesn't want to use me. I'm nothing special to Him." Grief hemmed the framework of her life, and he said God could use her. She didn't want to think about the future, not one that might be without York. Bitterness made her reluctant to listen to him or to anyone else for that matter.

Mr. Collier sighed and shook his head. "That's where you're wrong. As long as you allow yourself to be a vessel, God can use you. He can use anyone as long as they are willing. Perhaps God brought the two of you to this country so that He can use your talents together for Him."

Her chin quivered, and her eyes stung. She wanted to scream at someone. "No, you're wrong. Look at York. How can God use this? How can I even trust God again if—"

"No." He raised his hand. "Don't even say that. We know all things work together for good to them that love the Lord. God is working. Even though we can't see Him working, we will see the fruit of His works. God is a gentleman. He won't force himself on anyone. He allows us to choose. You can be happy with the fact that you belong to Him and go on your merry way, or you can choose more. God gives more to those who diligently seek Him."

"I...I want what God has for me. But I want what God has for York, too. I'm not ready to give him up. I just realized a few days ago how much he means to me." She looked down into the face on the pillow, tears pooling.

He sat down in a chair on the other side of the bed. "Get some rest in the next room. I promise I'll watch him carefully. I've got to. He makes my clothes, and I'm sure I'm in need of a new pair of trousers." He chuckled softly, then shooed her toward the door. "Go. And talk to God while you're in there. He's always listening." The old man lay his head back against the wall and laced his fingers together across his round stomach.

She trudged into the next room and sat on the edge of the tiny resting bed. "God, I need a miracle," she whispered.

Everything she knew about the world had changed. What if God chose to take York? Could He still use her in some capacity to the glory of His kingdom? Would she even care? For the next hour, Abigail poured her heart out to God, asking Him to give her some semblance of contentment, asking Him to spare York's life. And if He chose not to spare him, she asked Him to help her cope. She finally drifted into a restful sleep, peace flooding her soul.

A soft stirring near her arm alarmed her, and she opened her eyes. "York?"

"No, Abigail. It's Constable Collier. I just wanted to let you know it's time for me to go home. You've slept a good four hours, and I want you to feel free to get some more rest, but I'll be making my way back to Mrs. Collier. She gets antsy if I'm not home by supper time." He patted his belly.

She sat up and rubbed her sleepy eyes. "Goodness, I didn't mean to sleep so long."

"I'm glad you could get in a few winks." He turned his hat round and round. "Did you, perhaps, get a chance to speak with the Almighty again?"

She took a few slow and easy breaths. Her heartbeat was steady, and she'd decided she wanted some reassurance. "Thank you, Mr. Collier, for allowing me the rest, and I'm sure you were right." She looked down, fiddled with the cuff of her sleeve, and noticed a stain that hadn't been there before. What was the right thing to say? "I think...I've come to an understanding with Him. And I think I'm ready for whatever He chooses for me."

The constable's eyebrows rose, and he smiled. "That's my girl. You can't go wrong when you rely on the power of God's almighty grace. Of that you can be sure. He always knows what is best for us." He patted her hand. "I'll be back tomorrow. Perhaps there will be a visible change."

"Yes. Perhaps." She looked up into his kind, warm eyes. "Mr. Collier?"

He turned. "Yes, child?"

"I want you to know that God has used you to be of a help to me."

He chuckled. "I know. I've been praying that He would do just that. He always comes through, one way or another. Be blessed, young Abigail." And he toddled out the door, perhaps taking a bit of her childhood with him, for she felt older, and somehow wiser.

Abigail walked back into the dimly lit room where York lay, chest tightly bandaged. He looked almost ethereal lying there, and she imagined him smiling down from Heaven. Was his soul already there, and only his body clinging to the life it once knew? She sat down in the closest chair and placed her hand over his. It felt warm in her palm. She remembered his beautiful blue eyes, and what she'd give if he could look at her once more. He had such an easy manner, and he never seemed to get mad at anyone, always the gentleman. The unremitting ache in her chest had dulled somewhat, and she began to think about the future.

Leaning over, she kissed the back of his hand, the hand that had so tenderly fashioned the dress she had on. "Oh, York, if only you could wake up."

"I could kiss you back if you'd come a little closer, love."

Abigail jerked her head up and raked the unruly locks from her eyes. "York?"

"Have my looks changed that you don't even recognize me?"

She held her breath for a moment, tears stinging behind her eyes. Her chest tingled and her heart began racing. "No. No. Your looks haven't changed at all." She squeezed hard on his hand. "In fact, you look as handsome as I've ever seen you."

His lazy smile and closed eyes told her the opium he'd been given was working. Maybe it was working so well he didn't realize what he was saying.

"Well then, bring those lips closer to my face. I can't kiss you back if you don't." His lids fluttered a few times, and he tried to raise his head.

Abigail jumped from her perch and ran from the room, arms flailing wildly. "Doc! Come quick! He's awake."

He came running down the hallway. The tears flowed freely now, and she fought the urge to laugh. Her breath came in spurts and she started feeling light-headed, laughing and crying at the same time, with no way to stop herself.

Doc Woods ordered her to sit down. Nothing, even the nausea that set in, could dampen her spirits at that moment. Prayers had been answered by the One who set the universe into motion. Abigail breathed her thanks to Him over and over.

Doc finished his examination of York. "Well now, young man, it's nice to see you plucked back from the brink of death. You gave us all quite a scare."

York looked from the doc to Abigail and back to the doc. "Near death? How long have I been here?"

Doc Woods breathed on his stethoscope and placed it on York's chest. "About three days. Breathe in deep."

York's gaze settled on Abigail.

Doc said, "Took quite a while to get that bullet out."

"How did I get shot?"

"Jamison's gun went off when he was hit. The bullet got you in the side. You lost a lot of blood. Your girl here stayed the whole time. Never left your side. I'd say you'd better snatch that one up before someone else does." Doc patted him on the leg. "I'll be back in a while to check on you again." He walked out.

Heat crept into her cheeks as soon as the doc started talking. Red blotches always appeared when that happened, so she pulled some unruly hair around to cover it.

York reached out a hand, and she took it. "You stayed the whole time?" His eyes searched hers.

Abigail pulled back on her hand, but he held fast.

"Did you?" he asked.

She swallowed hard. "Yes." He probably thought her a dunce.

His brows rose. "So when were you planning to lean closer? Now would be a good time."

Her prancing belly ponies had sprouted wings and were now fluttering all around in her middle. York pulled her hand toward him. She tried to swallow again. Mesmerized, she found herself only inches from his face. His hand slid to the back of Abigail's head, and he pulled her into a kiss, full on the lips, a soft kiss that lingered long after their lips parted.

She licked her lips. It was now or never. She had to ask. "So...you love me?"

His eyes widened. "What?"

"Do you love me? You've called me love twice."

His eyes crinkled in the corners, a smile daring to emerge. "Didn't that give you your answer?"

"No. That tells me you are very good at kissing. I asked if you love me." She raised her hand to his cheek. "Do you?" She couldn't believe her own audacity.

His lips turned up in a hint of a smile. She knew, almost word for word, what he would say next, for he'd said it over and over in his sleep.

"I do love you, beautiful lace-maker."

THE HANGMAN

RALPH VOGEL

"For we are his workmanship,
created in Christ Jesus for good works,
which God prepared beforehand
so that we would walk in them."
EPHESIANS 2:10

Dedicated to my wife, Helen,
who is the epitome of Sara in love and forgiveness

CHAPTER 1

Lyona, Kansas
July 1, 1870

"**G**od is the ultimate jury and judge on the sins of mankind!" Luke Stone sat in respectful silence as Reverend Bartholomew's thunderous voice rang out, reverberating through the rafters of the Methodist Church. Years of accumulated dust slowly rained down like an invisible powder of white flour. Sunbeams streaming through the slightly smudged windows illuminated the powder and gave the interior an impression of an early morning fog.

"Who is man that he should be the decider of the fate of God's creation? Who is man that gives him the powers of the Almighty?"

Sweat trickled down Luke's neck and back. Across the sanctuary, fans waved in ever increasing speed, keeping up with the drenched speaker's fiery rhetoric.

"God in His grace has overlooked the growing sins of man, but a time will come when that grace will end and man will forever be condemned to burn in the hell fires already kindled for him!"

For Luke, the stifling heat in the wooden building already felt like the hell fires Reverend Bartholomew was shouting about. Beside him, his small son shivered. He softly patted Josh's back and whispered, "Don't be afraid, that is for bad people. You and your brother, James, are not bad people."

With eyes wide, Josh asked, "Is Hanna like us, Dad? I mean, is she considered not bad like us? She is a girl." Hanna, who sat on the other side of Josh, questioningly stared at both of them.

"Shhh. The preacher will hear you, and I don't want his attention."

"Every man should fear for his life if he decides against God's will. None will be spared in that day of final judgment when Satan and his mob of evil angels will burn in everlasting torment. Neither killer, gambler nor drunkard will escape the wrath of the Almighty for they will be sent down to Hell along with the Evil One!"

James tugged on Luke's sleeve. "Dad, I'm scared."

"Don't be. He's not talking about you."

"I'm also tired and the bench is so hard. Can we go now?"

After an hour and fifteen minutes the congregation was thoroughly wet. Hair hung on foreheads and arms glistened with perspiration. Ladies dropped their fans in their laps, their muscles too tired to wield the paper fans.

"Everyone in Lyona will stand before God and plea for his life if he be found in opposition to the Lord's direction and will. Perdition will be filled with those who profess innocence but lack justification." The preacher repeatedly struck the feeble pulpit with his fist, the blows echoing. "Now is the time for recognition of wrong doing and evil intents. Now is the time for all to admit sin and receive the sweet grace of salvation. Now!"

A new batch of powder was loosed with the pounding of the pulpit, and Reverend Bartholomew glared at the captive listeners who sat melting before his gaze and the stifling heat of the building. "Who—I say, who is able to say they meet God's standards today? Many of you are killers, killers of the soul either by gun or by deed. I say to you today, God will not let you into Heaven with blood on your hands or guilt in your soul."

Bartholomew held his fist in the air. "Who among you has the power of life and death in your hands?"

A hush fell over the crowd. Silence hung in the stale air like a closed envelope. Then a soft voice suddenly wafted over the stillness of the moment. "The hangman does."

The quiet in the room gave way to the creaks and groans of wooden benches as bodies turned, moving as one, and people stared at the man in the back row.

Seated in a relaxed manner, dressed in well faded and worn clothing sat a man with long grey hair that hung about his bent shoulders. Dark eyes peered out over a scruffy white beard flecked with black.

Caught in mid stride, Reverend Bartholomew stared, swallowed loudly, and cleared his throat. "What did you say? Were you being blasphemous in this house of the Lord!?"

The aged man slowly stood, resting both of his gnarled hands on the back of the pew in front of him. "No, sir. I rightly gave an honest answer to your question you were asking. I am to understand that you asked who had the right and power to decide if a man should live or die. I only answered you honestly. The hangman has that kind of power over a man's life. I know, because I'm a hangman, have been for a right many years now. I must say, though, that the job is not for anybody, takes a special kind of person to be a hangman. You might say that I am doing the Lord's work by carrying out justice according to what the law says. You say that God is the one who decides the rightness and wrongness of man. Well, so do the courts. I only fulfill on this good earth what God does in Heaven."

Having said his piece, he slowly let go of the pew and sat down with deliberate motion. All eyes of the worshipers remained on him. Quietness reigned. Ever so slowly, one by one, the people turned back to the front, staring at the reverend.

Luke suspected that the good reverend had been taken by surprise. After several silent minutes, he found his voice again. "Man's decision making is often flawed and not of a spiritual nature. God is perfect and does not make mistakes. I would take God over a hangman anytime, and so should you!" He offered a closing prayer and everyone filed out of the sweltering room.

Luke followed the crowd, listening to their confused whispers. Out in the fresh air, he guided his children away from the wagons and buggies others were boarding. He was in no hurry to leave, and he was certain that Josh, James, and Hanna were going to ask questions. Somehow he needed to be ready with answers. The only problem was that he wasn't too sure he had any. The close of the church meeting was rather unusual to say the least.

Where was the good-natured chatter? Why hadn't the reverend stood at the door to shake hands? He hadn't moved from the behind the pulpit yet. The hangman had captured everyone's attention even better than Reverend Bartholomew.

He led the children to his farm wagon, hoisted them up, and climbed aboard. Gently slapping the reins over the pair of geldings, he encouraged the horses to strain forward. The wagon jerked, and they made their way home.

The children huddled together in the back, talking quietly to each other. Luke sat alone on the wagon seat under the sun. It was times like this that he missed his wife. If only Doctor Crawford had been able to see her sooner, maybe she would not have died. Appendicitis the doc had said. It took her so quickly. She hardly seemed sick, but Luke acknowledged that she was one who rarely complained. If only she had, things would be different. Now the children had no mother, and they needed one. He was a lousy cook, and the small farm took all of his time to keep it running. He couldn't see how he could keep being both father and mother to three children who, at this time, really had neither.

He needed to find someone to care for his kids. If he couldn't hire anyone, and money was a consideration, he would just have to try and find a new mother for them. The children must come first in his mind. He would never find another wife like Rose. What a kind and tender woman she was. The memories of what used to be brought tears to his eyes. Not wanting to frighten the children, he fought them back, wiping his cheeks with the back of a fist.

Back at the cabin, he sent the children inside while he went to the barn to care for the horses. His children's calls for him to hurry and fix their dinner carried across the ground. Luke shook his head.

Without a helpmeet, keeping the farm going would be impossible. Perhaps he should stop farming and find a job in town. At least it would be a steady income, but what of the children? Who would be there to watch them? And could he even pay for help if someone could be found? He hung his head and sighed. How could losing someone change a person's life so drastically?

"Dad!"

He headed for the house. Tomorrow he would go to town and look for work. Surely one of the businesses could use some help. His thoughts became a prayer. *Lord, if You see my needs please act on them. Not for my sake alone, but for the little souls you have entrusted me with. That's all I ask. Please, Lord, please.*

CHAPTER 2

After a restless night and a breakfast of fried bacon and potatoes, Luke hitched up the team, loaded the three children aboard, and started the four-mile trip to Lyona. As the horses steadily plodded along Luke ran the number of businesses through his mind. There was the bank, grocer, pool hall, stables, saloon, clothing store, harness shop, blacksmith, butcher, and various other small businesses that he could explore for a job. The question was, which one would offer the best chance for employment? Perhaps, a better question would be, which one was he most suitable for?

He had spent most of his life helping his dad around the farm, and when both parents died without warning, the entire task of the farm fell to him. Although unprepared, he managed to muddle through the seasons that followed, never profiting much, but surviving. When things began to stabilize, he found Rose during a summer church revival meeting. He'd instantly fallen in love with her soft yellow hair and dimpled smiles, and later she'd told him she found his muscular build, jet black hair that hung carelessly over his forehead, and clear blue eyes appealing. He'd scoffed at her description, and then she told him she admired his perseverance and the kind, unhurried manner that set him apart from the other brash young men who came to call on her. He sniffed. Ah, Rose, she'd been meant for him, and him for her.

Fighting back tears, he brought the wagon up to the town's bank, tied the team to the rail out front, and pointed at the children. "Stay in the wagon. I won't be long in the bank. There are some things I need to talk over with Mr. Belcourt." They nodded their agreement, and he entered the shaded building, blinking until his eyes adjusted to the darkness.

"May I help you, Luke?" The teller, Mr. Peester, greeted Luke the way he greeted everyone, politely.

"Yes, I would like to speak to Mr. Belcourt, if I may."

"Wait here, sir, and I will see if he will see you."

After a few moments the banker ushered Luke into his office. "What can I do for you, Mr. Stone? Do you need a short term loan until harvest, or is this a social visit?"

Holding his hat loosely by his side Luke, battled shyness. "No, sir, I don't need a loan, I need work. You see, I can't keep the farm operating and still see to the needs of my children. What I need is steady employment."

"I see. And you were wondering if I had an opening for someone like you at this bank?"

"Yes, sir, I'm a good worker and honest. Ask anyone." Small trickles of sweat began to crawl down his chest. The urge to turn around and walk out of the office hounded him.

"Luke, I know you to be an upright person and a hard worker, but can you cipher numbers rapidly and accurately? Have you had any experience handling my—er, someone else's money?"

"Well, no, sir, I have not had the opportunity, but I can learn. I did complete the eighth grade and passed with good grades." Having to defend himself as a capable person made him uneasy. "I have kept the farm running without too much debt and always paid off my seed loans."

Shifting in his large roller chair, Mr. Belcourt stared at the top of his desk.

"Mr. Stone, I do not doubt for one second that you are an honest and capable person. You also appear to be a fine father to your three children. It is with great remorse that I cannot use you. You see, it's not you, it's the lack of experience with large funds. I hope you can understand."

Shame and embarrassment fell over Luke. Slowly, he replaced his dusty hat and ambled toward the door. "I understand. You need a more experienced person than I am. Thank you anyway."

He returned to the wagon and caressed the necks of the horses, allowing the humiliation of the event to slowly ebb out of him.

"Daddy, did you get done what you wanted? Can we get down now?" Josh sent a pleading look over the top of the wagon's side.

"No, children, I need to visit another store. Stay there. I'll be back shortly." His feet carried him along the boardwalk to the mercantile. The sound of the tinkling bell above the door brought the store keeper from the back room.

Wiping his hands on a soiled apron, he scooted behind the main counter. "Now, what can I get for you, Luke?"

"What you can get me is a job." Still feeling the sting of refusal, the words almost stuck in his throat, making it difficult to speak without croaking. "Do you have any work for me? I would do anything. Stock shelves, load wagons, wait on customers…anything."

"Luke, I truly would like to help you out, but at this time I cannot. You see, business has been a tad slow of late and I have to watch my pennies, too. I am honestly sorry. Perhaps you can try again later when the hot months of summer are gone and harvest is done."

Anger pricked. He retreated to the door, stopped, and turned around. "Do you know of anyone who could use my help?"

"I'm awfully sorry, Luke. It seems everyone is having a somewhat hard time at this part of summer. Really sorry. Wish I could help you, but I can't."

Luke visited every store in town, except the saloon, and every shopkeeper gave him the same answer. There were no jobs to be had. Defeated, he returned to the wagon, his heels dragging and his head low.

"Daddy, we're tired of sitting here. You were gone so long." Hanna's plaintive voice pierced his ears and conscience. "Sara came and sat with us. She even sang to us and told a few stories. She's nice."

Looking into the back of the wagon, he gave a start. A petite, pretty woman sat with the children. Her calico dress sparkled in the bright sunlight, as did her friendly smile.

"Hello, Mr. Stone. My name is Sara Daniels. I noticed the children were getting lonely and restless, and since I didn't have anything special to do I invited myself to keep them company. Do you mind?"

Her effervescence struck him like a bolt out of the blue. "Why, no, that was quite all right. I intended to not be gone so long, time just got away. Thank you for being with them. It's nice for them to be around a woman since they lost their mom last year."

"Yes, I heard of that. I am so sorry for the loss. If I could be of any help to them I would be willing to do so."

Gazing into her kind face, he almost forgot the details of his upsetting morning. "It was nice of you to spend time with them. I hope you don't think that I was being a neglectful parent. I mean, you were nice to be here…"

The more he spoke, the harder it was for him to make sense. But why? He'd seen pretty women before. Why did this one cause his words to stumble? Perhaps he was tired. But he didn't have time to worry about it. He had to find work.

Reaching up, he helped Sara down from the wagon. "Thank you again for being nice to the children and for understanding."

"I enjoyed the time with them. Remember what I said, if I can help them let me know. Just ask for Sara. Most people know me in town."

As he boarded the wagon he watched her walk down the boardwalk, her calico dress waving in the slight breeze. For the first time in a long time he felt an emotion that was not all depression or sadness. But what was it?

CHAPTER 3

Days melted into weeks. Taking care of the children, maintaining the farm, and being a cook, clothes-washer, and house-cleaner made time go fast, but he didn't think he did any job as well as it should be done. One person could do it all but not well. More times than he could count the picture of Sara Daniels in her bright calico dress hove into his mind's eye. Each remembrance stung his conscience. He owed his allegiance to Rose, his first love. After all, Rose was the one who gave him Joshua, James, and Hanna.

But Rose wasn't with him anymore as his wife or helper. And Sara did say, *"If I can be of any help with the children, ask."* The problem was what and how to ask. And where could he find her? She didn't give him an address, and he couldn't recall seeing her in church or around town. She had to belong to some family, but which one? She'd told him, *"Ask for Sara. Everyone knows me."*

Asking for a young lady he did not know didn't seem at all proper. Townspeople might reach incorrect conclusions because of his inquiries. But if asking for her was the only way to find her, then he would gather inner strength and ask, for he must find someone to help with the children.

On a Saturday afternoon in mid-August, Luke took the children to town and visited the mercantile to stock up on a few provisions. He instructed the children to stay in the wagon and he entered the store. The mercantile was crowded with other families also looking over food items or bolts of cloth, and the owner, Mr. Hatcher, was busy trading farm eggs, cream, and milk for items off the shelves. Luke had to wait quite a while for his turn, but eventually Mr. Hatcher approached him.

Wiping his hands on his soiled apron, he smiled. "Howdy, Luke, haven't seen you around of late. Any luck in finding work?"

Luke shook his head. "I need these things." He handed over his list of supplies, sucked in a breath of courage, and forced himself to ask the question that had pestered him for weeks. "Who is Sara Daniels, and where does she live?"

Everyone in the busy store stopped what they were doing and the room fell deathly quiet. Only the ticking of the clock on the wall could be heard.

Luke looked around in confusion. "Did I say something wrong?"

Hatcher cleared his throat. "Why are you looking for her?"

Aware that everyone was listening, Luke fidgeted. "Well, I met her the last time I was in town. She was in my wagon tending to my kids because I had taken so much time trying to find someone who would hire me. She just appeared out of nowhere. I hadn't seen her before."

Hatcher put Luke's list on the counter and began moving it in slow circles on the wood surface. He gave a wry smile. "There was a good reason for that, Luke."

"Why do you say that? Where has she been?" To his relief, others returned to their shopping, although they sent curious or disapproving looks in his direction from time to time. He kept his voice low as he addressed the storekeeper. "She is a rather handsome lady and a friendly one, to boot. She apparently liked my children, and they took a shine to her, too. Is that so bad?"

"No, I don't mean to imply that she is a...well, shall we say, a bad lady. It's just that some folks don't hanker to someone who is a little different than they think themselves."

Placing his weight on one foot, Luke looked directly at Hatcher. "And what do you mean by that?"

Hatcher scratched his chin and shrugged. "Well, it's just that some folks set their sights a little higher than they should when it comes to others. Actually, don't most of us think more highly of our own selves than we do of others around us?" Little beads of perspiration began to form on his creased brow.

"I guess if you mean that some people are greater snobs than others, I reckon you're right. Never did think it proper for anybody to judge others more harshly than they do themselves. When that happens, that person is in for a fall, and when they fall they get a tad nasty because they don't like to be reminded how wrong they've been."

Raising his apron to wipe the sweat from his brow, Hatcher nodded. "I suppose you're right, but rightness don't make changes when it comes to self-correction, does it? I mean, if a person has to admit they're wrong, it takes a slice of pride out of their hide and they get sullen and defensive."

"Hatcher, you're beginning to sound like Reverend Bartholomew when he's fixin' to lay a slab of truth on us in one of his fiery sermons. Now, why don't you just up and say what you've been jawing around?"

"If you can stand the truth of the matter as everyone knows it, then I guess I can lay it out straight." Hatcher sent a quick glance around as if making sure no one would overhear. "It's like this... Sara Daniels comes from a right and proper family. They lived near three miles west of town. Ain't nobody living there now as far as I can tell. Anyway, one Saturday night they all came to town like all of the other farm folks, and Sara was with them. To make a rather long story short, she came to be with child and her folks near had a fit. They stopped coming to town and no one ever saw Sara again. That is, until a few months ago. Suddenly, out of nowhere, she appears. No one knows where she lives or what she does, but the good town folks of Lyona have speculated about all of that."

Genuine concern struck Luke. "Where is the child she is supposed to have had?"

"No one knows." Stepping back from the counter, Hatcher wiped his face with his stained apron. "Truth be told, no one rightly knows if she had a child or even how the child came to be if there was one. But that don't matter to the good townsfolk. They have righteously judged her and found her guilty of being a loose woman."

"I see."

"Do you? Looking for her does you no good in the sight of those who live here and know her. If you associate with her, you might as well hang a sign around your neck declaring you are willing to associate with an unrighteous and soiled dove."

Luke absorbed Hatcher's tale. He didn't understand how a person who seemed so lively and concerned with the needs of another could be as evil as Hatcher presented her to be. But then again, did they really know the truth, or were they only speculating?

He stayed quiet while he waited for Hatcher to fill his list, then he slowly walked out of the store. He put his supplies in the back of the wagon, smiling at his children who'd fallen asleep on the hay filling the bottom of the bed. They resembled angels lying in a manger. A lump filled his throat. Rose would be so proud of what she created.

On the way home, Luke sorted through what Hatcher had told him about Sara Daniels, speaking to the horses' rumps. "Is what I heard the truth or only what others want to believe? Has anyone ever sought out what actually happened, if indeed she did have a child, and has anyone reached out to her in kindness to help heal what must have been a frightening experience? How long must a person have to pay for a mistake, if there was one, when even God in His mercy forgives?"

As much as it pained him, he worried about what people would think of him if he asked Sara to help care for Josh, James, and Hanna. Sara must be hurting inside and needed a friend, but what if people turned their backs on him and his children for befriending her? Was it worth the risk? He would have to pray about it.

CHAPTER 4

A week of doubts and conscience-searching finally took Luke to a decision. He needed the truth about Sara, and the best person to ask was the town's sheriff. The sheriff wasn't a tale-bearer, and he'd likely know where to find Sara, too. So he loaded the children in the wagon and made the drive to town.

He parked the wagon in a shady spot a short distance from the sheriff's office. Then he dismounted and admonished the children to stay put. He stepped onto the boardwalk and ambled along to the stone building that housed the sheriff's office. There he encountered an elderly man, apparently sleeping with his chair tipped back on two legs against the wall. Long grey hair fell from under his pulled-low hat. As Luke eased past, the chair suddenly landed on all four legs and the man tipped up his hat. Luke recognized him as Jeremiah West, the hangman.

"Howdy, Luke. You looking for the sheriff?"

Luke jolted in surprise. The hangman knew him? "Why, yes, matter of fact I am. Is he in?"

"Can't say that he is. Ain't seen him all this morning. I'm to guess that he either overslept or decided to not come by the office today. What you need him for?"

Luke fiddled with his hat. "Oh, nothing important. I...I just wanted to see if he knew of any work to be had around town. I need to take care of my children." He hadn't told the whole truth, but he did not want to share that he was looking for Sara Daniels. In fact, he didn't want to talk to Jeremiah West at all. What did he have in common with a hangman?

"Ain't no work available that I know of. Hasn't been for some time now. Things have been slow around town of late, but I know where you might find a bit of work if you was to decide to accept it."

Luke's pulse picked up. "Who do I need to see?"

"Me."

Luke's eagerness faded in an instant. What could a hangman offer a farmer? "Why you?"

"Son, I'm getting a tad long of tooth and don't hanker to ride so far these days. I'd be obliged if you would consider learning to take my place."

A cold chill traveled throughout his body. "Me, a hangman? You better look for another person. I couldn't do that."

"I figured the same thing when the chance came to me, but I begin to see that what I was doing was what the law wanted done." Jeremiah West spoke softly and slowly. Puckering up, he spat a brackish wad into the dusty street beyond the board walk. "You need work, and here is work to be done. You wouldn't do anything that doesn't need doing. The pay is not too bad, and it's lawful. How can you beat that?" Taking a wad of tobacco out of his shirt pocket, he bit off a corner and began to chew.

Luke held his arms wide. "But I couldn't just up and hang somebody I didn't know!"

"You mean you could hang only those you do know? Now that would be a bit harder, I am to think."

"But...but I don't have the expertise, let alone the will, to do such a thing. My conscience wouldn't let me."

West shrugged. "You get over that. It's like painting a fence. Once you do it over and over, you can do it without thinking. It comes easier each time."

Luke backed up a step. "Mr. West, I don't think I'm interested."

West settled the tobacco in his cheek. "Didn't you say you needed work so that your younguns can be taken care of properly? Here's your opportunity. You might want to reconsider. What do you make a month now? Sometimes nothing I vow, and nothing is somewhat hard to live on, especially with little ones depending on you."

The old man pointed a gnarled finger at Luke. "Do you know what the territory of Kansas pays for a hanging? Up to two hundred silver dollars. Even a soldier boy gets only sixteen dollars a month, and that's if he's lucky. You figure it out and see what you come up with."

Silver dollars flashed in Luke's mind, and he pushed back the image. Taking a life was not what God wanted man to do. It wasn't what he wanted to do, but where did a man draw the line between personal beliefs and what the world had to offer? Could it be that this offer was God's way of meeting his needs? God worked in strange and mysterious ways. Could this be one of them?

He shifted his weight from foot to foot, uncomfortable with his thoughts. "I don't know. It seems wrong to take a life, even if it's condoned by law."

"You think on it Mr. Stone, and let me know what you decide. I'm generally here unless I get a call to practice my trade. If you choose to become an enforcer of the law, I would be willing to train you. You may not know it, but there's more to hanging a man than just hanging a man. Much more."

Luke returned to his wagon, his mind spinning. This was a job offer and it did pay well, but could he do it? What would his children think of their father becoming an executioner of men? Would he ever be able to enter a church again after taking a life? He shuddered at the thought. With his mind in a cloud, he untied the horses and climbed up onto the wagon seat. As he picked up the reins, a familiar voice called from the bed.

"Hello. You were gone for quite a while. I spent the time with your children again. I hope you don't mind. I really don't have much to do these days, and they seemed to need someone around."

Sara! Luke spun around on the seat to face her, hardly able to change his thought from the hangman to the lovely young woman. "I—I was looking for work. And for you."

A smile brightened her face. "Me? Why were you looking for me?" Her smile dimmed. "No one seems to want me around, why should you?"

"Sara, this may or may not be the time or place to say this, but I need someone to watch over my children while I work the fields and take care of the animals. You said you'd help, and that you didn't have anything else to do. So it may be a good solution for both of us. They apparently like you, and you seem to like them."

She glanced at the children, worry wrinkling her brow. "Have you thought of what the town folks will think and say?"

"Yes, I have, and I'm sure there will be many tongues wagging and heads shaking, but I have to think of what is best for my family. What about you?"

She hung her head. "I'm already considered a hussy so it won't bother me none, but it could damage you in the sight of all those good folks."

"I'm aware of that, and I'm also aware that you could serve a good purpose for my children. They need someone more than me to meet their needs. I can't pay much but I can offer room and food. It will have to be that way for a while until I can get on my feet again. Tell you what, if you're willing, get your things and I'll take you out to the farm right now. By the way, where are you staying?"

"At Widow Smallwood's boarding house. She was a good friend of my parents and she lets me live there free of charge. I help her around the house on occasion for the bed and food."

"Very well then, go and pack your things. I'll drive around and pick you up." Turning to the six little ears in the back of the wagon, he asked, "Is that all right with you?"

They chorused, "Yes!"

CHAPTER 5

Sara sat in the back of the wagon with the children on the drive from town to the Stone farm. Was she doing the right thing, going off with a man who didn't have a wife? The children needed her, and she longed to become their friend. But there was no chaperone for them at the farm. Folks already spoke ill of her, and she couldn't change it. She hated to see these children hurt by gossipers.

When they reached a grassy lane leading to a simple cabin, Luke stopped the team and lifted out the children one by one. "Go on up to the house." They scampered off, and he turned to Sara. "If you've changed your mind, I will take you back to town. People who do not understand what is in the heart of a person often create a truth to fill the gap of ignorance, and there will be a lot of truth-creating going on when word gets out that you are living in my house."

Had he read her mind? Sara gave him a sad smile. "It doesn't bother me, but if you are worried I will go back. The townsfolk have labeled me as a loose woman and one to be shunned without knowing the truth."

He frowned. "What is the truth, Sara? If you don't want to tell me that's fine. It's your life and your business. But maybe if I knew what the situation is, I could come to a better understanding of our current position."

She swallowed a laugh. "My, but you sound like one of those lawyer type men who are always trying to figure things out. Well, maybe I do owe you that much seeing as you have not judged me at will. The truth is, I came to be with child and my parents sent me off to St. Louis to stay with my aunt until the baby was born. They said

I should give it to someone else and pretend that it never existed. People don't know this, but a person cannot pretend that something that happened didn't happen."

A single, sad tear rolled down her cheek and dripped off of her chin. "My baby died at birth. When I was healthy enough to return to Lyona, I came back only to find out that my parents had moved and didn't leave word where they went. So now I'm alone."

Luke shook his head. Sympathy glowed in his eyes. "I didn't mean to bring up bad memories for you. I don't need to know anything else. The past cannot be changed because it's gone, but the present and future can be. Perhaps it would be best for you, and for me, to focus on what can be rather than what was."

His kindness gave her courage to share her thoughts. "No, you're wrong. I won't fool myself into believing that bad events in life never affect the future, because they do."

Looking at Sara with a small grin on his face, Luke chuckled. "Now who's sounding like a lawyer?"

"I'm sorry, but I have to get things out in the open. If I don't they will always haunt me, never freeing me from the pain of rejection. Oh, I've tried to pretend that anything said or done to me didn't matter, but it did and still does."

Luke stood helplessly while tears made their way down Sara's face and dripped onto her calico dress. He dragged his bandana out of his back pocket and handed it to her, resisting a strong urge to take her in his arms and comfort her like a child who had stubbed her toe. He knew the pain that came from loss. He felt it when Rose died, and he still did.

Luke reached into the bed and gave her shoulder a little pat. "You don't need to say more, Sara. I understand."

She gazed at him with watery eyes. "Do you? Do you know what it's like to have someone you don't know or care about force himself on you and then have your parents and the whole town blame you? The drummer could leave town, but I couldn't!"

His children's laughter carried from the yard outside the cabin. Their happy sounds didn't match the feelings coursing through him. "Sara, you and me have some healing to do. I think yours will take longer, but it will happen. We'll both make sure of that in the days to come."

She didn't answer, so he climbed back on the seat and flicked the reins over the horses' backs. As he pulled the wagon in front of the cabin, the structure suddenly seemed very small. He turned to face her again.

"Sara, this cabin has two bedrooms, one a little larger than the other. We can do this one of two ways. The boys can sleep in the bigger room with me since they need their own bed, and Hanna can sleep with you in the smaller room. Or, if you're uncomfortable with me in the house, I can sleep in the barn. Summer will be no problem, and in the winter I can use blankets and hay. Which way do you want it to be?"

She chewed her lower lip for a moment and stared at him. Finally she sighed. "If there are doors on the rooms, I think you could stay in the cabin. This is your house and you should not have to leave it."

He nodded. "It's settled then. I think we can work out a schedule to both of our satisfaction and make changes as we see the need. Your main job will be to take care of Josh, James, and little Hanna while I'm gone. That includes fixing meals for them, too. If you want to do more, like cleaning and washing clothes, that's up to you. I don't think anybody will bother you here. When you need supplies we will both go into town and get them." He offered a wry grin. "That way the town will have something to gossip about."

That night, lying in bed and listening to the small sleeping sounds of his sons in the next bed, worries attacked Luke. When word spread that Sara was living in the house with him, what would Reverend Bartholomew say? He should visit the good pastor as soon as possible and tell the true situation before others had a chance to create a false tale. The decision soothed him, and he closed his eyes and waited for sleep to come. When it did, it was restless.

His dreams took events and churned them into a patchwork of confusing semi-truths. Rose's face and the image of a hangman's noose, surrounded by the cries and accusations of unidentifiable faces in the small town of Lyona, taunted him. Even in a state of half-sleep, he recognized that the morrow with its bright sun and dewy grass would be welcome.

Chapter 6

Morning came early with a hint of rain as the clouds hung low over the western horizon. A slight breeze stirred the cottonwood trees that shaded the small cabin. With the animals tended and breakfast finished, Luke prepared to harness the team and make his way to Reverend Bartholomew, hoping against hope that no one else had visited before he did.

The trip to town did not take long for the horses were rested and eager to pull. Upon entering town, he headed for the small, white building with an unpainted cross on top of a short spire. He knew Reverend Bartholomew's habits, and he was sure he would find him in the church performing his morning prayers.

The reverend was at his usual spot in the front pew reading from his well-worn Bible. Luke tiptoed up the aisle and paused as he neared the front of the church.

Without turning around or lifting his head, the Reverend spoke. "Good morning, Luke. I've been waiting for you."

He drew back, surprised. "How did you know it was me?"

Shifting to rest one arm on the back of the pew, the preacher chuckled low in his throat. "How long have I known you? Most of your life I would venture. Now do you think I wouldn't recognize your step and your problems? I can pretty well tell who is approaching by how they walk. I also listen very well. Maybe that makes you think I have magical powers, but no such thing exists. Now, you came to talk to me about Sara Daniels—or is the topic going to be more about Jeremiah West?"

Luke stood open-mouthed. No magical powers? He scarcely believed it. Regaining his composure, he plopped onto the bench near

Reverend Bartholomew. "I thought I would get here before others did with their biased opinions and false concerns. I guess I was wrong."

"And what would those be?"

"Well, you apparently already know that Miss Daniels is living at my place and that Mr. West has asked me to train to become a hangman. I suppose it makes me look like a fool or a very unethical person. Maybe both."

The preacher shook his head. "Not at all, Luke. It makes you look like a person who has to make some very hard choices, and that is the way of life. I will ask you, though, have you thought out the consequences of what decisions you may make? Too many times people make choices without analyzing what the cost or outcome may be, and then they end up blaming others for the mistakes they made. Human nature, I guess, or the lack of prayer to find the right answers to life's perplexing problems."

He closed his Bible and set it aside. "Now, I think I understand what you are facing. Correct me if I am wrong, but you need a helpmeet for your children and an income to provide for their needs. Is that close?"

Luke nodded. "That sounds fairly right."

"And does that need include you?"

Wrinkling his brow, Luke frowned. "What do you mean?"

"Come, Luke. You know what I mean. How do you feel about Sara? Is she only a child caretaker or is she a bit more than that in your mind? She is a beautiful woman, you know, and is obviously looking for a little meaning to her life. Are you willing to bring fulfillment to her search? I think by the look on your face that there is more to Sara Daniels than a person to care for your children. Am I right?"

Luke didn't know how to respond to the blunt question so aptly proffered. "I...I haven't let myself really think about it. I have been so concerned for the welfare of the boys and Hanna that I haven't stopped to think through my feelings."

"If the children were not there, would you still be thinking about Sara?"

The question caught him off guard. He needed to answer honestly, so he gave it some serious thought. Eventually he lifted his head and looked directly at Reverend Bartholomew. "Yes, I would."

"I thought so."

Even though the reverend wasn't surprised by Luke's answer, Luke reeled at the realization that he did care for Sara. When had he crossed the threshold that separated his love for Rose and what he felt for Sara? "B-but should I?"

"Why shouldn't you?" The Reverend put his hand on Luke's shoulder. "Rose is not coming back. She is now in a much better place than Lyona. It is all right for you to have feelings for another. You don't have to stop loving Rose to make room in your heart to love again. People who live in the past never have space for love in the present. Don't let that happen to you."

Luke nodded slowly. "But...what will people say?"

"Don't concern yourself with the townsfolk. They do not have to live your life. Only you can do that, which means only you can decide the correct thing to do. But never leave God out of the decision-making, for He knows what is best for you."

Luke hung his head. "I'm not yet sure what is best."

"Then pray. With prayer and a clear conscience, you will choose wisely."

Luke appreciated the preacher's wisdom. The fiery Reverend Bartholomew possessed a fatherly, gentle side that increased Luke's respect for him.

"Are we ready for the other problem, Luke, the one involving Jeremiah West?"

He forced himself to transfer his thoughts about Sara to the other plaguing issue. "That is a tough one, Reverend. I don't condone killing, and I see hanging as a form of killing no matter how the law looks at it."

"I understand your feelings. I know you have a tender heart and a tender heart feels the pain of others more than most. What you have been offered is a service that the territorial laws of Kansas have endorsed. There's no doubt it is a severe form of punishment. What you are struggling with is the legality of law with the law of God as you see it. Be happy that you have this struggle, for if you did not you would be a hard person indeed with little conscience to guide you."

"Am I seeing it wrongly?" Earning such a wage would benefit his family, but at what cost to his soul?

"I cannot answer this. You must look at your inner being and see what your heart tells you, taking into consideration your children and, yes, Sara. Pray about it, Luke, and God will give you peace."

CHAPTER 7

By the time Luke left the church, clouds had completely covered the sky and droplets of rain began to dance on the backs of the team and on Luke's hat. Small rivulets made their way around his brim, cascaded over his nose, and dampened his lap. He didn't care. More important things were on his mind than getting wet.

Questions ran their long fingers through his mind. How should he approach Sara? He didn't even know if she cared for him, and if she did, would she trust a man again? How would the children react to a new mother? They liked Sara, but would they like her enough to allow her to take their mother's place? In his mind, that could never happen. In his mind, one person could never take the place of another. They could only fill in the empty spot that was left by the departed one. At least, that's the way he saw it. He wondered how Sara would see it.

The sky took on a darker tone during the drive. As he reached the barn, patches of lightening lit the sky in the distance. He unhitched the team and led them into the dark, open space to their stalls. Pitching hay to them allowed him to delay going into the cabin. Why did he hesitate? Was he not so sure after all? Maybe what he was feeling was not love at all but only a desire to find someone for the children. Why was it so hard to be certain? A rumble of thunder rolled in the distance as if warning of an ominous omen.

He secured the barn doors to the sound of the horses' content nickering. They liked their warm stall and sweet hay. At least they had no doubts about what they wanted. He entered the cabin, removed his wet hat, and hung it on a peg near the door. Then he remained in place. What should he do next? Approach Sara or wait until she expressed feelings for him? He'd never felt so clumsy and uncertain in his own home.

Sara stepped from the kitchen. Her gaze found him and she and came to an abrupt stop, surprise on her face. "Oh, I didn't know you were back. Supper is almost ready. We're having beef stew tonight. I hope you're hungry because there is a lot of it."

At that moment Joshua, James, and Hanna sprinted from their rooms. They grabbed Luke around his waist and knees, squeezing as hard as they could.

Luke laughed. "Whoa there, you're going to knock me off my feet."

Sara smiled, such fondness in her eyes it made Luke's heart catch. "They're glad to see you. This was one time you didn't take them along with you into town. Did you get done what you wanted to do?"

Still standing in the same spot, hands resting on the top of the boys' heads, he could only muster a small reply. "Yes." Then other words poured out of him without effort. "Sara, I have spent a long time visiting with Reverend Bartholomew, and he helped me understand some things." Seeing her standing near the table with a look of trusting anticipation on her face left him slightly in awe of the moment. "I am ready to face the future instead of lamenting the past."

Sara placed one hand on the back of a chair. "What do you mean?"

"The first time I saw you, my heart jumped a little. I didn't want it to, but it did. I wasn't sure what that meant, but I think I do now." Heat flooded his face. Looking down at his feet, he struggled for the next words. "Do you...do you like me?"

Whatever she'd expected him to say, that wasn't it. Sara drew a startled breath, then she giggled. "Is this your way of proposing to me, Luke Stone? If it is, you're doing a very poor job of it. But if that's the best you can do, I guess I'll have to live with it."

He jolted his head up. His hands reached for some unseen object to hold. His Adam's apple jumped and then he blurted, "Yes, it is. I have come to realize that you are what I need. You are what the children need. The question is, do you need us?"

Sara wanted more than to be needed. She moved across the floor and took hold of his hands. "Needs can be met and the reason for them is then over. But love goes on forever. Do you love me, Luke?"

His fingers tightened on her hands. "I think I loved you the first time I saw you sitting in the wagon in that wonderful calico dress. And when I saw how the children responded to you, I knew. Even though my mind didn't want to admit it, I knew. It took Reverend Bartholomew to get me to recognize it. I am so glad that I went to see him." He looked deep into her eyes. "Do you love me?"

She nodded, very sure. "The first time you helped me out of the wagon, I knew. I loved your heart, and still do. It's kind and considerate. I understand how much Rose must have loved you. If we marry, I promise not to try and take her place. I cannot, but what I can do is continue where she left off, loving you and being the best partner possible." She paused for a moment, gathering her courage. "There are two more things to consider before we make any definite plans, though. How do your children feel? And what about the town of Lyona?"

He snorted. "Who cares about Lyona? I'm not marrying a town. They'll have to find their own bride. As to the children, they've been standing here. Let's ask them."

Turning to the three small listeners, Sara kneeled down to their level. "What would you think if I became your mother? Would that be all right with all of you?"

The answer came not with words but with a unified rush, almost knocking her backward.

Luke smiled down at them. "I think you have your answer, Sara, and it's a resounding affirmation."

Extracting herself from the six arms hugging her waist and knees, she stood and turned a serious look on him. "Luke we must keep ourselves separate until we are married. That is the only proper thing to do. I am aware of what the town people think of me, but it isn't true. I want things to be right from the beginning, and I think you do, too."

Looking a little bashful, Luke stepped forward, "Is hugging okay? I have a powerful lot of hugs to give. Been saving up for some time now."

She swallowed a giggle. "I think hugging would be fine. You can see the children have no trouble with it."

"We'll need to talk to Reverend Bartholomew about a wedding date. I don't think we need to make a special thing about it. Most of the town folks would probably not come anyway. Besides, like I said, I'm not marrying the town, I'm marrying a pretty gal in a calico dress!"

CHAPTER 8

With the issue of Sara behind Luke, the problem of Jeremiah West still faced him. Now that he would have a wife again, funds would be more of a necessity than ever before. As he readied himself for bed, he weighed the things he knew. Despite consistent seeking, he had not been successful finding work anywhere in or around town. Mr. West still needed someone to take his place. Apparently no one wanted the job. But did Luke? It would mean having the money he needed to take care of his family. But what was right? He spent many hours in prayer before going to bed.

Rising before the sun came up he was delighted to find fresh coffee, biscuits, and fried eggs waiting for him. Also waiting was Sara, clad in her calico dress, a radiant smile on her face.

"I couldn't sleep either, so I decided to get up early and be useful. I knew you would want to go into Lyona today, and I figured you would do it as early as possible. How's that for knowing you?"

He sat at the table and picked up his fork. "Well, if you had the kind of night I did, I'm sure I can understand the reason for being an early bird. I have to settle a problem that has developed over my looking for work. Truth be told, I have been offered a job, but it's not one that I want or feel comfortable with. I'm fixing to go into town and turn the job offer down. At least I think I'm going to reject the offer."

She sat across from him. "What is it? What could be so bad that you would not even consider it?"

Would telling her about the offer to become a hangman be the right thing to do, or would he be better off not mentioning it at all since he had no intention of accepting it? He lowered the fork and gave her his full attention.

"Last night, after you accepted to be my wife, I was very happy and was sure I would have the most restful night in a long time. Even the gentle rumbling of thunder and the soft drops of rain falling on the roof gave hint that it would be so. I was wrong. The thing that has plagued my conscience came back in my dreams. I must go to town today and take care of that problem."

"What is it that bothers you so? Maybe I can help."

Her offer made him smile in spite of his worry. "You know that I've been trying to find work in Lyona, only there isn't any, at least none that I could find. When I was ready to give up I stumbled upon Jeremiah West sitting in front of the sheriff's office. To make a long story short, he offered me a job that I think I cannot take."

"What kind of work did he offer you? Is it one that is not legal or safe?

"Oh, it's legal all right, and I reckon it probably is safe enough. But it's one that requires a person to be hard of conscience and not caring for others." His appetite fled. He pushed the plate aside. "Sara, he wants me to take his place. Do you know what he does for a living? He is a hangman."

He waited for her reply, but she sat in stunned silence. He almost thought he heard the beat of her heart. Breaking the silence, Luke pushed back his chair and crossed to the door. Before stepping outside, he sent a pleading look at Sara's blank expression. "I'll see you later today."

Sally, his only riding horse, carried him over the slightly muddy road. He took his time, sending up prayer after prayer for wisdom and guidance.

The street of Lyona was quiet with few people stirring about. Outside the sheriff's office, where he'd been before, Jeremiah West sat with his chair leaning back against the wall, peering out from under his drawn down hat. He smiled as Luke dismounted and looped the horse's reins over the hitching rail.

"Howdy, wondered when you'd be coming a-calling. Jobs still open if'n you want it."

Luke clomped up on the boardwalk and stood in front of the old man's chair. "That's what I came to talk to you about, Mr. West. I don't think I can accept the job, but I thank you for the offer."

"Did you find a different job?"

"No, but I don't think I have it in me to hang somebody."

West chuckled. "Yep, I felt the same way myself years ago, but the money helps a heap. Don't you need the money?"

Luke sighed. "Sure I do. I have my children, and I will be getting remarried soon. But I don't think my new wife would be thrilled with me if I took the work." He turned to leave.

West's chair hit all four legs and the man rose. "Tell you what, son, why don't you go with me to Brookville. It's a new settlement not too far from here. Seems a gentleman from the underside of the law tried to make a hasty withdrawal from the bank there and killed a teller in the process. Got hisself caught and sentenced to hang. You can watch and see how things are done."

Nausea attacked. "I don't think so, Mr. West. I don't think I'd have the stomach for it."

"Would you have the stomach for an extra hundred silver coins? I'd be willing to share half of the pay if'n you kept me company there and back." He coughed into his fist. "Been ailing a bit lately an' I would feel more comfortable if'n I had company along."

One hundred dollars was more than he could make in many weeks of back breaking work. Temptation nibbled at him.

West wheedled, "You won't have to do a thing. Just travel over with me, be there, see how things go."

"I don't know." Luke scratched his chin. "I could use the money all right, and I'd hate to leave without help if you really need it, but the hanging part is not to my liking."

West scuffed to Luke. "Tell you what, you come along, and if you decide that you don't have the stomach for it, you can walk away. The money's yours anyway. Is it a deal?"

Luke processed what a hundred dollars would mean for him and

Sara now that they were to be married. The money would allow him time to look for a better job without rushing. But salving one's conscience wasn't easy. The ointment only covered the pain so other wouldn't see it, but the sufferer still knew it was there. Even so, the hundred silver coins drew like a magnet. He swallowed the bile rising in his throat. "When is the hanging?"

"Day after tomorrow at sun-up. They pick the early time so's not so many people will be there to watch. That means we need to leave tomorrow, spend the night on the trail, and be ready when they bring him out to see the sun rise for the last time. Scaffold's already been built according to the telegram. Won't take long. I reckon we'll be back to Lyona by evening and I doubt that anyone will know you've even been gone."

"And you're saying the money is mine even though I don't take your place?"

"That's right, son. You can't beat that offer, can you?"

"All right, I'll go." He pointed at the man. "But this is no guarantee that I will become a hangman after this is over."

Remounting Sally, he aimed the horse for home. As he passed the little white church building, he wondered what Reverend Bartholomew would think. Would his reputation be tarnished by participating in a hanging? He tried to tell himself he didn't care what the townsfolk thought, but deep down it did. No man wanted to be thought of in negative ways. What would Sara think? He could still see the look on her face when he mentioned Jeremiah West and the hangman job. It was a bad time to bring roadblocks into a marriage not yet fulfilled. He would have to be careful.

Keeping the mare to a slow pace, he let his mind drift to the boys and Hanna. How would they feel knowing their father took lives at the end of a rope? His mind spun. The struggle between maintaining his efforts to be upright and in good standing with God and the offer to make his family more secure was a hard fight to wage.

He aimed an anguished look skyward. "Dear God, help me to do right. Please guide my way because I'm confused and only You can show me the right path to take."

CHAPTER 9

That night the restlessness returned. There was no soft patter of rain drops or the slow rumble of wet thunder to ease his troubled mind. The recurring stab in his conscience kept repeating, "You're no killer, Luke. You're no killer." Finally he surrendered to the enemy of rest and got up.

Making his way to the main room and the coffee pot waiting on the warm stove, he poured a cup and sat down at the table. His mind continued to wrestle with the decision he had made to accompany Jeremiah West to the hanging in Brookville. Was he doing the right thing? His family needed the money, but was it worth it?

A soft hand landed on his shoulder, it was Sara. "I can't sleep either. I know you're struggling with your decision, and so am I. Luke, I have to be honest with you. I don't know if I can marry a man who deliberately takes another man's life." A hint of tears accompanied the statement. "I love you, but this matter will always be a silent ghost between us. I cannot be what I should be to you with that specter always there." Before he could answer, she disappeared back into her bedroom.

He laid his head on the table. Now he faced the possibility that he may lose a love that he finally allowed himself to find. Was trying to secure a little freedom from want worth the loss of that love? He thought not. He resisted the urge to burst into her bedroom, hold her, and tell her that he had changed his mind, that he would not go to Brookville with West. He started to rise, and then he remembered he gave his word. Jeremiah would be waiting for him in the morning. A man's word was sometimes all that a man had, and it was to be as good as gold. Sitting back down he decided to wait for sunrise, and then he would go to Lyona and meet West. He prayed Sara would be there when he returned.

Luke rode Sally solemnly through a morning bathed with freshness and promise. He found Jeremiah waiting at his usual spot. Suddenly the morning sunlight didn't seem as bright.

The old man slowly got up and spit a wad of tobacco into the street. "Got here, huh? Wasn't at all too sure you'd come."

"I gave you my word, so I'm here, but it might cost me a future wife." The words came out bitter and short.

West shrugged. "When she sees the silver she might be a little more forgiving. Most women I know would not have a problem with silver." He mounted his horse and reined away from the rail. "We best be tracking so's not to have to hurry so much. By the looks of your old mare we won't be able to hurry. Will she make it?"

"She'll make it. I'm not so sure I will."

When the sun began to shine its last rays, West reined in near a stand of cottonwood trees. "This 'pears to be a good place to spend the night. Brookville is just over that rise up yonder, won't take long to get there and prepare for the event. Speaking of which, after we eat, I'm set to show you how to tie a proper hangman's noose."

The promise of the lesson almost stole Luke's appetite, but he washed down a supper of cold beans and jerky with strong coffee. When they'd finished eating, the old hangman took a rope out of his saddle bag and fingered it lovingly.

"Yes, sir, a good rope is the promise of a good job and continued employment."

Luke held his empty coffee cup between his palms. "Jeremiah, I've been thinking. I'm not sure I want to go into Brookville. I don't know if I can stand the sight of a man dangling on the end of a rope, slowly choking to death."

West snorted. "Shoot, son. That ain't the way it is at all. You got it all wrong. They don't choke a nary bit, least ways not if the hangman does his job right. You see, they break their neck and never feel a thing. You watch tomorrow and you'll see I'm right."

He shoved the rope toward Luke. "Here, you feel this here rope. It won't feel like anything you've ever felt before."

Luke took it and pulled it through his cupped hand.

"See? It's smooth, slightly oily, and bendable. It don't get that way by accident. You have to make it that way, and that takes time." West sat cross-legged beside the dying fire. "You got to find a good rope made of strong hemp, about three quarters of an inch thick. You wash it with a mild soap, let it dry, and wash her again, only this time you don't use any soap. After that you put it in an iron pot full of water and boil it for about nine hours. After that you have to let it dry." He chuckled. "That might take a mite of time."

Luke didn't want to listen, but he couldn't seem to help himself. The old man spoke about making a hangman's rope the way others might talk about the weather. No emotion. Something didn't set right.

"After it's dry you pull it over a piece of iron or strong board. You see, that breaks the little fibers in the rope which softens the outside. When that's done you make you a little fire and carefully singe the rope, being careful not to burn it. That takes away all of the fuzz and straw pieces that are in it. Once again, you wash it thoroughly, dry it and pull it over the board good and hard to take the stretch out of it. When that's done, you oil it with mink oil. You keep doing that until the rope is soft, supple, and slides through your hand like a slippery pig. Then you'll have a good hangman's rope that will do the job."

Luke stroked the rope, amazed at how much work went into creating it. "What about the noose. Is that special?"

"Not necessarily. Most any child can tie a hangman's knot. It's where you put the knot that's important." West squinted at him in the waning light. "The knot has to be on the side of the neck so when a person drops, it quickly breaks the neck. That is, if it's done right.

Put the knot in front or back of the neck and the person'll just hang there, strangling for air. 'Course, he won't get any, so death'll come, but it's better to break the neck."

Luke shuddered. "You make it sound so easy."

"It ain't easy. It takes some savvy." West stretched out on his side, propped up on one elbow. "You have to judge the weight of the person. You don't want a large man to drop too far or his head might come off. Most people in the crowd don't like to see that. If the man is too light, he has to drop farther in order for the neck to snap. Takes some judgment. That's why a good hangman makes a few practice drops with a sack filled with grain or sand about the same weight of the man."

Dread settled over Luke. How he wished he had not promised to come, but it was too late now to back out. Was it too late to salvage the bond between him and Sara? He prayed not.

In the morning they met the man Jeremiah West had come to hang. He was slight of build and seemed young, but there was such a look of hardness about him. The local preacher took Luke and West aside and explained how he'd tried to talk to the murdering thief about where he was to spend eternity, but to no avail. West seemed unmoved, but Luke's heart ached for the hopeless situation.

After the preacher left, Jeremiah claimed he'd forego a practice drop so the event could take place quicker. By the time the sun marked nine o'clock, a crowd had gathered at the foot of the scaffold. The condemned man, hands tied behind his back, was encouraged up the thirteen steps to the platform by the local sheriff. They positioned him on a trap door. The lever, which the hangman would pull, would send the man plummeting to his death.

The sheriff asked the prisoner if wanted to be hooded, and the man shook his head. The preacher offered last rites and an opportunity to repent, but the man rejected both offers with a string of oaths directed at everyone in general.

At the front of the crowd, a middle-aged woman with two boys clinging to her wept as she watched the process unfold. Luke guessed these were the wife and children of the murdered teller. Luke watched the crowd instead of Jeremiah West. He didn't want to see the carefully placed noose around the head or its knot to the left side.

Suddenly the condemned man stopped swearing and began to beg and plead, mentioning his love for his sainted mother. Then Luke heard the lever's squeak-thump, followed by a whoosh and a soft snap. Gasps erupted from the crowd. Luke peeked out of the corner of his eye and glimpsed a swinging shadow. He turned sharply away. Moments later West clapped him on the back and said, "A job well done."

L uke broke out in a cold sweat. He ran into the shaded gap between the jail and a store, fighting to keep down his breakfast. Why had he come? He had no business taking a life, even if it was deserved according to law. He stayed between the buildings, hiding, until he was convinced the crowd had cleared and the sheriff's officials carried away the condemned man's body. Then he returned to the front of the jail.

Jeremiah West had gathered his rope and was lovingly placing it in his saddle bag. "Well, what do you think?" Pride showed in the radiant smile on his wrinkled face. "Everything went as it should have. Now all we have to do is collect our money and be on our way home. If'n we leave now we could make it home by the evening hours, that is if'n your old mare can keep a decent pace."

Luke stayed with the horses while West ambled into the sheriff's office. A few minutes later he returned with a small leather pouch. "Look here, we done been paid. Wasn't too bad of a day if'n I say so myself, and you have a share in it like I promised."

Still feeling queasy, Luke stared at the ground. "I don't want it."

"Don't want it? Look, boy, we done made an agreement. If'n you came with me we would share in the reward of the work. You kept your part of the bargain and I intend to keep mine. Don't want anyone to say that I'm a coldhearted man that doesn't keep his word." He opened the pouch, counted out a hundred silver coins, and slid them in Luke's shirt pocket. The weight seemed heavier than it should have. Maybe the weight of his conscience gave it heft.

Mounting old Sally, Luke set his face east toward Lyona. Jeremiah tried to joke with Luke, but Luke remained solemn. Finally West blasted a snort.

"I can't for the life of me understand why a person who has just been given one hundred dollars can be so quiet and unhappy. Now you can breathe a tad and buy something nice for those little younguns you have."

Pulling on Sally's reins, Luke stopped the mare and stared at Jeremiah. "In my way of thinking, the Bible says that a man should not take the life of another man. It is God's job to judge and carry out what sentence He wills."

"Just how do you know that this was not God's will for us to carry out a just judgment on a criminal? 'Pears to me God is not bothered by justice. Isn't that what He is all about, justice?"

"Justice, yes. Vengeance, no." Gently spurring Sally, he continued up the trail, followed by Jeremiah West, who continued to mutter in disbelief.

All the way back to Lyona, one thought plagued him. Would Sara still be there? She made it clear that she did not approve of his going with Jeremiah. If only he hadn't placed so much importance on the money. After all, which was more important to him, silver or Sara? He worried the entire ride home.

They reached the outskirts of Lyona at dusk. West veered off to wherever he lived leaving Luke to finish his trip back to the cabin and whatever awaited him. The sun was a mere slit on the horizon when he rode into the yard, the last rays glancing off of the barn siding and gleaming like small candles set in a row. He dismounted and led Sally into the barn, grained her, and brushed her coat lightly. She responded to his soft talk and attention with an acknowledged grunt.

At last he left the barn and closed the doors behind him. He looked toward the house. No one had come out to greet him when he rode up. and no light shone through the windows. A cold fear crawled up his back. A sudden urge to shout at the sky brought him to his knees, a prayer borne of fright forming on his lips.

"Dear God, I don't deserve the goodness You have given me. I know I have probably disappointed You this day. Can You forgive me?" The future that seemed so bright only a day ago evaporate into nothingness. Everything that seemed to be going so well for him and the children was whisked away by his foolishness. He truly loved Sara, and now it appeared that she left and took the children with her. Sadness filled his being and a sense of total failure and defeat tugged at his heart.

Sitting there in the dust, he wanted to pour the ashes of misery over his head. Is this how Job felt when all things fell apart? Could he still trust in God when He, by all appearances, abandoned him? Job continued to trust. Maybe Job was stronger than Luke Stone.

He pushed to his feet and forced himself to approach the house. He entered the cold, empty room, sat heavily at the silent table, and rested his head in his hands. Suddenly a flickering light appeared. A candle? He stared hard as the little light neared and then six small arms encircled his waist. Soft giggles filled the air. He wrapped his arms around his children, his heart rejoicing. They weren't gone after all. But why had there been no light when he rode up? And where was Sara?

Then someone touched the candle to a lantern, and light glowed over a woman clad in a calico dress. Sara! Jumping to his feet, he rushed to her and wrapped her in a tight embrace while tears of relief cascaded past his stubble of a beard. "I thought you had gone and taken the children with you. There was no light when I rode up. No one was here to greet me like the children usually did."

Gently pushing him away, Sara gave a sly smile and pointed to the table and chairs. "Sit down and I'll tell you all about it.

"When you left I was ready to leave, too. I was going to take the children to Reverend Bartholomew and return to the boarding house. But I didn't. If we are to be married, I need to trust you to do the right thing. I must have faith in you. Isn't that what marriage is all about—trust and faith?"

Luke caught her hands and held them. "I almost lost you in my haste to make things better. When I left the barn I realized that life is more than security and wealth, it is companionship and the love that others have for you and you for them. I think we can have both here in this house with each other and the children."

He squeezed her hands, eagerness filling him. "Let's not wait. Let's go into Lyona tomorrow morning and have Reverend Bartholomew marry us. I don't care if the town talks or if I never see Jeremiah West again, all I want is you and the love of Joshua, James, and Hanna."

Epilogue

The church bell rang at nine o'clock in the morning, drawing curious people from the street to the church. The bell had never rung before at such an unheard of hour. As they entered, they found Reverend Bartholomew standing at the front of the church with a man and woman before him. Three children, holding bouquets of wild flowers, surrounded the couple.

The preacher smiled and invited everyone to take a seat. "I called you all here to witness the marriage of Sara Daniels to Luke Stone." A stern frown formed on his face. "Don't any of you forget this is the house of God, so sit down, be quiet and respectful, and be mindful that the good Lord is watching over all of you right now!"

The wedding flowed smoothly, and when it was over the happy couple and their children returned to their farm. The preacher shooed everyone out to attend to their own activities, and as he closed the church doors behind the last straggler, he muttered, "This will be a wedding to remember. No one got hanged!"

The Karussell Painter

Help
Wanted

Inquire
within

Kim Vogel Sawyer

*"...endurance produces proven character,
and proven character produces hope."*
ROMANS 5:4 HCSB

For Mom and Daddy, who persevere

CHAPTER 1

Early February
Shadybrook, Missouri

"Dad, are you really going to keep this place forever?" Jessa Matthews couldn't recall ever speaking so forthrightly to her father, but somebody had to say something. If her suppositions were correct, he was teetering on the brink of bankruptcy, and what kind of daughter would she be if she stood by and let him fall over the edge?

Dad looked up from the gears on the decades old, gas-powered engine and wiped his hand across his forehead. A streak of grease marred his brow, hiding the worry lines. He chuckled, but Jessa heard sadness in the release. "Now, if I didn't have the park, what would I do with myself?"

She let her gaze rove across the amusement park grounds, every ride and brightly painted building as familiar as her own reflection. Her mind tripped through the suggestions she could give Dad—travel with Mom, read a good book, visit Mom's family in South Dakota. But she bit down on the end of her tongue and prevented the ideas from escaping. Dad had to keep his hands busy. Otherwise he wasn't happy. Mom understood him, and Jessa did, too, but she wished he would busy himself somewhere other than this time-consuming park. If something didn't change, the place would suck the heart out of her father. And now he'd borrowed against his retirement account to purchase a rusty, paint-chipped carousel. What was he thinking?

She crouched next to him, grimacing as her overall straps bit through her bulky layers of sweatshirt and thermal long-sleeved T into her shoulders. "Dad, about Joy Land..."

"My granddad named it for my grandmother—her name was Joy, you know."

Jessa knew. She'd heard the story a hundred times about how her great-grandfather purchased the land and built the amusement park during the heart of the Great Depression and, despite the financial challenges of the times, kept his family sheltered, clothed, and well-fed.

"I started working here during the summer of 1975. I was just thirteen." Dad aimed a wry grin at Jessa. "Felt like a big-shot, too, in Granddad's trademark red-and-white striped vest and straw hat with the red brim. Of course, when Dad took over from Granddad in '79, he got rid of the vests and hats. Too old-fashioned, he said." He heaved a sigh and gazed outward, seeming to drift away. "This'll be my fortieth summer."

Jessa touched his arm and waited until he looked at her. "Not many people can claim to have worked four decades at the same place. There'd be no shame in letting it go. Neither Great-granddad nor Grandpa would hold it against you. You've more than paid your dues to Joy Land."

Dad's brows pinched. "Paid my dues? Jessa..." He released a sigh that formed a wispy cloud of condensation, his expression so sad it pierced her heart. "My dad might have viewed this place as a duty rather than a delight, but my years here have been a labor of love. Just as Granddad's were."

He tapped the dusty knee of Jessa's worn insulated overalls. "Have you forgotten? When you were little, you thought Joy Land was a magical place. Mom and I worried so much over you. You were the shyest kid around. But when we brought you here, you lit up. Joy Land brought out the unreserved exuberance you seemed to lack everywhere else. When you started working at the park you blossomed, each year a bit more of your timidity dropping away and bold confidence replacing it. I can't tell you how many times your mother and I thanked God for the change Joy Land brought to you."

He rose, his joints popping, and gazed down at her with hurt glimmering in his pale blue eyes. "I thought that's why you chose business administration instead of something arts related for your degree—so you'd be prepared to take over the reins at Joy Land when I retire. Was I wrong?"

Jessa slowly straightened. A few strands of her long hair had escaped her stocking cap, and a chilly breeze tossed the strands across her face. She pushed them behind her ears with trembling fingers. Dad wasn't going to like her answer, but she had to be honest with him. Maybe if he knew the truth he'd finally realize Joy Land had served its purpose in their family and it was time to let the park go.

She drew on the boldness he'd claimed Joy Land had given her and forced the answer past her dry throat. "I'm sorry, Dad. I love you, and I don't want to disappoint you, but I...I don't think I want to be the fourth generation of Matthews to operate Joy Land."

Max Behrend stopped several yards away from the overall-clad man and lovely young woman conversing next to an old, grease-covered engine. Obviously he'd arrived at an awkward moment. Even though he couldn't hear what they were saying, their tense frames and unsmiling faces told him they were engaged in a serious discussion.

He glanced at his wristwatch. Ten past two. The owner of Joy Land didn't expect him until two-thirty. Good. He had time to let them finish their talk while he explored. Familiar tremors of excitement needled his flesh as he eased around to the opposite side of the *karussell*. Such a sad-looking conveyance. It could very well be the most run-down carousel he'd ever seen, and he'd seen plenty of carousels in his twenty-seven years of life. Even so, just touching the chipped paint on the wooden waving mane of the horse frozen in a galloping position gave him a thrill.

Many carousels had a variety of animals—wild cats, giant birds, bears, and sea creatures—but this was an old one. So old only carved horses two deep were mounted on the iron frames. So old the movements gave each horse a rocking motion rather than carrying the steeds up and down on a pole. He tapped his chin, trying to recall the American manufacturer who had specialized in the rocking model. The name escaped him, but he'd ask his father. Papa would know. Gunther Behrend knew everything about *karussells*.

And little about his son.

Max pushed the sad thought aside and ran his hand over the horse's hindquarters. By the age of the wood and the simplicity of the carving, he guessed the carousel to be from the mid- to late-1800s, manufactured no later than 1905. Well over a hundred years old. A smile tugged his lips upward. Ah, such a treasure.

He knelt and examined the chain and iron wheel system that carried the wooden platform in a circle and rocked the horses. He shook his head, marveling. Rusty in some places but, with the exception of the train rail needed to secure the carousel in place, all intact. A treasure for sure.

"Dad, I'm not trying to be disrespectful, but this merry-go-'round is nothing but junk. How can you be sure you didn't waste your money on it?"

Max cringed. The woman didn't see this beautiful piece of history as a treasure? Such a pity. The need to enlighten her overwhelmed him. He pushed upright and rounded the wooden platform with wide, determined strides. "Miss, this is not junk. The *karussell* is very, very valuable."

She drew back at his approach, her eyes of pale gray with darker blue rims widening. "Who are you?"

He extended his hand. "I am Max Behrend. And you are...?"

"Jessa Matthews."

According to the emails he'd received, Joy Land's owner was a Matthews. Since she'd called the man *Dad*, she must be the owner's daughter. She didn't accept his hand, so Max turned to the man instead. "Then you are Stan Matthews?"

He gave Max a firm handshake. "That's right."

Max bounced a smile over both father and daughter. "It is very nice to meet both of you."

The woman scowled. "What are you doing here? Joy Land isn't open for business."

Mr. Matthews stepped beside his daughter and slung his arm across her shoulders. "Jessa, Max is here at my invitation. Both his father and grandfather are renowned carousel refurbishers in Germany. When I discovered Max was in the U.S. on a work visa, I contacted him and asked him to look at the carousel and give me an estimate on bringing it up to snuff."

Max frowned. He'd picked up more than a fair amount of English and he knew the meaning of "snuff," but sometimes words used as slang tripped him. "What is meant by 'up to snuff'?"

The man laughed. Max enjoyed the sound of it. The hearty laugh seemed to take some of the tension from the air, too, which was also nice. He hated to see a father and child in turmoil with each other. His father had been very upset when Max left for America a year ago, and their communications were still stilted and uncomfortable.

Mr. Matthews' grin stayed in place when he answered. "Maybe I should say making it appeal to the public so they all want to take a ride. Does that make more sense?"

It did, and Max was eager to see it happen. Old gems like this deserved to shine and to be enjoyed. "Yes. And may I tell you the *karussell* is a rare piece of history. Although I have read about them, I had never seen one with the rocking mechanism until now." He turned his fervent gaze on the daughter. "I know it looks very sad and *ungebflegt*—"

She scowled.

Max sought the English word. "I mean unkempt."

Her expression cleared.

"But it has the potential to be very *schön*—beautiful—again." Just as this woman must be beautiful when she allowed herself to smile. The lines of worry marching across her brow didn't belong on the face of someone so young.

"I'm glad to hear that," Mr. Matthews said. "I bought it sight unseen from an estate sale in southwest Kansas and had it shipped here. According to the previous owners, it's been in pieces in a barn for more than forty years. It took me three days to put it together. I'm no expert but I'm pretty sure all the parts are there."

Max nodded. "I have given it only a cursory examination, but I agree it appears to be complete. Of course, you will not know until it is placed on a track and connected to a power source whether it is in working order." He glanced past the pair in their matching grease-stained overalls to the rusty engine. Did they intend to actually use the outdated equipment? He held back the query and fixed his attention on the daughter. He longed to erase the consternation from her pretty face. "But for its age, it is in very good condition. You wait and see. A good scrubbing and a new coat of paint on each of the horses, and this *karussell* will be more than up to snuff."

Mr. Matthews laughed again, but to Max's disappointment the daughter didn't even smile. She said, her voice timorous, "So it's worth salvaging?"

Max looked directly into Jessa Matthews' eyes. "Very much worth salvaging, Miss Matthews."

She looked aside. He'd disappointed her. And even though he wasn't sure why it bothered him, the realization stung.

CHAPTER 2

M ax followed Mr. and Mrs. Matthews—or Stan and Kathy, as they insisted he call them—into a charming little house at the edge of Joy Land's property. Stan carried Max's suitcase, Max carried his laptop case, and Kathy carried a casserole dish with wonderful aromas sneaking from beneath the foil cover.

"This was my grandparents' place." Stan led Max up a short hallway past an old-fashioned bathroom to a small bedroom. "Granddad was a construction worker. He built the house with the help of a half dozen men from his church, using materials salvaged from other jobs."

"Resourceful," Max said.

Stan smiled. "Very." He flopped Max's suitcase on the tall iron bed's mattress.

Max slipped his laptop from its case and followed Stan back to the living area.

The man kept up a steady flow of talk. "It's not a fancy house. Few could afford a fancy house in those days. But it was built right. The roof won't cave in on you."

Max glanced around in wonder at the plaster ceiling, wallpapered walls, and simple, sturdy furnishings. He felt as though he'd moved backward in time. "And it sits here empty with all these things inside? No one bothers it?"

Stan chuckled. He slipped his hands into the pockets of his trousers and rocked on his heels. "To be honest, a caretaker usually stays here. It's wise to have someone close by the park at all times. But our caretaker resigned and moved to Florida two weeks ago and I haven't hired a new one yet. So now the house can be yours for as long as you need it. Providential, yes?"

He smiled. It certainly was.

The man scratched his cheek, his expression turning sheepish. "If you don't mind, while you're here, would you keep an eye on the park? I'd be glad to pay you for the extra duty."

Max shook his head. "No need for that. When I accepted your invitation to come to Missouri and look at your *karussell*, I expected to stay in a hotel and eat fast food dinners. This cozy little house built by hardworking hands is much nicer. And if your wife keeps bringing casseroles that smell as good as the one she has with her tonight, that will be payment enough."

Stan laughed and clapped Max on the shoulder. "Deal."

Kathy stepped into the wide doorway between the living area and kitchen. She placed her fists on her hips and raised her eyebrows. "Why aren't you two at the table? The food's growing cold."

"We're talking, dear," Stan said, a smile toying on his mouth.

"Of course you are." The woman sighed and shook her head, but she smiled, too. "You can talk while we eat."

Max joined the pair in light laughter. He liked both of the Matthews and their easy way with each other. In his travels he'd discovered not all American couples were so relaxed and happy together. And not all German ones were, either.

The three of them settled around a square, wooden table in the middle of the kitchen. The lone empty chair stole a bit of his contentedness. Too bad the daughter hadn't come, too. According to Kathy, Jessa was a college senior and needed to study. He hoped she wouldn't have to study every evening. He wouldn't mind getting better acquainted with her. He put his laptop where her plate would be and the spot didn't look quite so lonely.

Stan offered a prayer, and then Kathy ladled noodles, beef, peas, and mushrooms swimming in a thick, creamy sauce onto their plates.

As Max chewed and swallowed the first bite of the savory casserole, he opened his laptop. "Do you mind if I research while we eat? Your *karussell* has me curious."

Stan waved his hand. "Feel free. I'm curious about it, too. The people who sold it said it belonged to the husband's grandfather. They knew little about it."

"If the time wasn't the middle of the night in Germany, I would call and ask my father. He would know more than any Internet site." With a few clicks, Max brought up a search engine and typed in *Carousel + 1800s + rocking mechanism*. He continued forking up bites and engaging in conversation while scrolling through the hits. He chose one that seemed promising and opened a page from a museum website in Kansas.

He scanned the information and his heart leaped with excitement. Stan was talking about how to obtain railroad ties for the carousel, but Max couldn't resist interrupting with an exultant cry. "Yes! I knew it!"

Both of the Matthews jumped.

"Please excuse my rudeness." Max held back a chuckle at their stunned expressions. "But when I first looked at the carousel's unique mechanism, I suspected it was special. It seems this article confirms it. Stan and Kathy, listen to this."

Jessa pushed the textbook aside and flopped back in her chair. She needed to prepare for Monday morning's economics test, but she couldn't stay focused. Images of the dilapidated carousel laid out on the park's grounds and the handsome face of the blond-haired German man kept intruding.

She rose and paced the narrow room. Normally she liked the solitude of her efficiency apartment in the upper floor of a flower shop on Main Street. Why did the walls seem to press in on her tonight? Maybe she should have gone with Mom and Dad to take supper to Max. Hadn't Grandpa always said the way to get rid of an itch was to scratch it? Of course, Grandma always countered that the more you scratch, the deeper the itch becomes. Grandma and Grandpa spent a lot of time contradicting each other. Maybe that's why Dad so studiously avoided engaging in disagreements.

Her conversation with Dad that afternoon could certainly be classified as a disagreement—a painful one. She never fought with her parents. Not like some of her friends did. She loved Mom and Dad too much to be disrespectful of their feelings. But she'd hurt Dad today with her scornful comments about the old carousel and her lack of interest in taking over the park.

Her chest went tight. Had she really told Dad she didn't want Joy Land? And did she really mean it? She paused at the window and stared out at the street below, letting her mind drift through childhood memories of Great-granddad Matthews, a big, cheerful man who always smelled like cherry tobacco. She was only eight when he died but she had dozens of remembrances filed away, each of them entangled with Joy Land and each of them laced with happiness. She deliberately examined every reflection of her great-grandfather, and the fuzzy wisps of memory brought a smile along with a sting of loss.

She had a lot more memories of Grandpa Matthews, who'd passed away only a year ago. Sadly, they didn't raise the same warmth and affection as the ones of Great-granddad. She loved her grandfather, but Grandpa had always seemed tense, dissatisfied, making her want to keep a distance between them. As Dad had said, Joy Land was Grandpa's duty, and he hadn't relished honoring it. She sighed. Maybe the joy of owning Joy Land skipped generations and she was more like Grandpa than Dad or Great-granddad. The idea didn't set very well.

Turning from the window, she started for the desk where her economics textbook waited, open. But then she changed direction and snagged her puffy jacket from the hall tree beside the apartment door. Evening, when the lights on the rides shone brighter than a thousand Christmas trees and music filled the air, was her favorite time at Joy Land. With the park not yet open for the season, it would be dark and quiet on this night, but she still needed to go there, to walk the grounds, to remember and reflect and examine herself. Thanks to Dad's motion detector lights all over the grounds, she'd be safe.

The decision made, she slipped on her jacket, grabbed her car keys, and headed out the door. She drove, tapping her gloved fingers impatiently on the steering wheel, to the edge of the park. As she passed Great-granddad's little house, she noted the yellow glow of lights behind the curtains. So Dad had hired a new caretaker already. Why hadn't he told her? She snorted under her breath. Probably because he thought she wouldn't be interested after her outburst at the park earlier that day.

She pulled her car next to the gate, shut off the ignition, and hopped out. As usual for this time of year, the gate was locked, but she'd climbed over it before and she could do it again. The iron was cold and slippery, but the rubber soles of her hiking style boots caught hold. Within seconds, she landed lightly on the opposite side and strode toward the center of the park.

As she passed the ticket building, a floodlight ignited. She squinted against the glaring light and continued onward, other lights blazing to life along the way. By the time she reached the carousel, which Dad had laid out in the center of Joy Land's "town square," the area was as almost as bright as if the park was open for business.

She stepped onto the carousel's platform, grimacing when the old wood creaked in protest, and eased between the first pair of horses. She rested her palms on their paint-chipped saddles. A chill breeze eased through the empty park, and the first of the motion-detector lights went out. She shivered. If she wanted light, she'd have to keep moving. Slowly she circled the platform, lightly tapping each of the horses as she went and scooting around the edge of the rotted sleighs. She reached the fourth sleigh, the only one that appeared solid enough to hold her, and she slipped into the warped seat. Closing her eyes, she rested her head against the rolled back and inhaled, trying to recall the wonder and joy she'd experienced as a child. Only dust and the slight scent of decaying wood filled her nostrils. Sadness attacked.

She whispered, "Why can't I feel what my father feels for this place?"

"I wonder that myself."

The male voice came from near her right. Jessa released a shriek and bolted from the seat. On the ground beside the carousel, an unlit flashlight in his hand and a scowl on his face, stood the carousel painter.

CHAPTER 3

"What are you doing here?" They asked the question at the same time, her voice filled with aggravation and his with curiosity.

Jessa huffed. She clambered out of the creaky sleigh and stepped onto the ground. "You nearly scared me to death. No one's supposed to be in the park when it isn't open."

"So why are you here?"

What a silly question. "I can be here anytime I like. My family owns the park."

He shrugged, the movement slow and somehow masculine. "This is true. But at dark, by yourself? And climbing the gate?"

She jolted. How had he seen her?

"I feared someone with foul intentions had entered the park."

His formal speech pattern laden with warmth—very different from the college students beside whom she sat in classes—removed some of her irritation. But he still hadn't told her why he was here. "I didn't expect anyone to be on the grounds. Why are you still here? Is Dad around, too?"

Max cupped her elbow and guided her back onto the carousel's platform. They sat side by side in the sleigh. The wood groaned like an anguished ghost, but it held. "Your father and mother left an hour ago. Your father allowed me to stay in the little house built by your great-grandfather and asked me to keep watch over the park. So..." A beguiling smile curved his lips. "When I saw a car pull up and stop, and then someone went over the gate as easily as a monkey climbing in trees, I decided I should investigate."

Heat filled her face. She'd never been compared to a monkey

before. "Well, as you can see, I'm not up to mischief."

"No, but I am curious why you came at night all alone. Is something troubling you? The bitter words you had with your father, perhaps?"

She gawked at him. Was he clairvoyant? "What makes you ask that?"

The slow shrug that bunched his suede jacket and emphasized the breadth of his shoulders happened again, making her stomach tremble in an odd way. "I gathered from comments your parents made at dinner this evening that you are uncertain about your future vocation. Even a fool would discern how much this park means to your father. Your uncertainty and his desire to see the park remain in the family's control would create conflict between any child and father."

The automatic lights flickered and went out, leaving them in deep shadows. She hugged herself. Now more than ever she wished she'd gone to dinner with her parents and Max so she'd know what Dad said. "It isn't that I dislike Joy Land. It's a part of my family history, even a part of who I am. I'm just not sure I want it to be my whole life, the way it was for Great-granddad or Grandpa. The way it is now for Dad."

"Ah."

That was all—*ah*, as if it held a meaning Jessa should understand. She frowned at him. "You should know what it's like to be expected to carry on the family business. After all, your father and grandfather are carousel painters and you've become one, too. Did you feel coerced into the career?"

He flicked on the flashlight and held it so the beam flowed upward, highlighting his startled features. "Coerced? Do you mean forced?"

She nodded.

"Not at all."

He spoke with such staunchness Jessa experienced a prick of jealousy.

"I grew up watching *Vater* and *Opa* create beauty out of what once was plain or even dilapidated. From the time I was old enough to hold a paintbrush I wanted to make the same kind of beauty. It has always been my desire."

So the joy hadn't skipped generations in his family. The prick of jealousy became a throbbing pang. She sighed. "Then I'm happy for you, I suppose."

His lips twitched with a grin. "Thank you."

He didn't need to make fun of her. She cleared her throat. "But I can't understand why Dad bought this old merry-go-'round. Joy Land has lots of other rides. Including a merry-go-'round on the side of the park dedicated to the youngest visitors." Hadn't she learned the importance of return-on-investment in her business classes? Dad needed to take the same classes. She slapped the wood seat. "This thing is nothing but an eye-sore and a waste of money."

"A waste—" He aimed the flashlight at her face.

"Hey!" She put up both hands to block the onslaught of light.

He left it there. "Do you mean what you just said?"

Eyes squinted shut, hands in front of her face, she nodded.

He lowered the beam.

She looked at him. The sadness she'd witnessed on Dad's face earlier that day now showed clearly in Max's crestfallen expression. She stifled a self-deprecating snort. Wasn't she a ray of sunshine today? "What's wrong?"

"What would you say if I told you this Carry-Us-All is of more value than all the rest of the park's rides put together?"

Jessa released a short laugh. "I'd say you're exaggerating. I happen to know how much the wooden roller-coaster is worth." She couldn't resist bragging a bit. "Great-granddad named it Montezuma's Revenge. It was the first roller-coaster built in Missouri, and it's the only remaining wooden roller-coaster in the whole state. Dad has a separate insurance policy for that ride alone."

"Impressive." He raised his eyebrows briefly. "Even so, I hold to my previous statement. Because, Jessa Matthews—"

The flowing way her name emerged with his German accent turned her bones to liquid.

"—I believe we are sitting on an original Parker Carry-Us-All."

She suddenly realized his dialect wasn't the reason the word "carousel" sounded different. "What do you mean, a 'carry-us-all'?"

Max shifted in the seat to face her, his blue eyes shining in the slanting beam of the flashlight. "I researched your *karussell*, and I believe it was built at the C.W. Parker Factory in Abilene, Kansas. Do you know about C.W. Parker?"

They hadn't covered factories that built carousels in her business classes. Jessa shook her head.

"Mr. Parker was entranced by a merry-go-'round on which his little daughter took a ride, and he purchased one for his family's use. Then he decided to build them for others. He thought the name merry-go-'round sounded too much like a child's entertainment, and since people of all ages rode the conveyances, he called the ones built in his factory Carry-Us-Alls instead. Some credit him to the evolution of the word we use today, carousel."

He bounced the light beam across the horses. "Look at the horses, at their manes and saddles and tails. Simplistically carved, yes?"

Jessa examined them although she'd already taken note of their lack of elaborate details, especially when compared to the animals on the park's newer carousel. Their simplicity was one of the reasons she didn't think they were worth much. She nodded.

"The horses on Parker's first Carry-us-alls were very simply carved, becoming more ornate with each year of production. This leads me to believe this carousel could be one of the very first produced."

A shiver worked its way up Jessa's spine—a shiver unrelated to the chilly evening air.

Max went on, his voice fervent. "There are only three known early Carry-Us-Alls in the United States, all housed at museums. If we discover this truly is an original Parker Carry-Us-All, it will be the only one still in operation at an amusement park."

His exuberance was contagious. Jessa battled tremors of excitement. But Max had forgotten something. "But this one isn't in operation. We don't even know if it will function. If Dad can't get it running, will it still be worth what he paid for it?" She'd almost fainted when she saw the cancelled check.

"Even in disrepair, it is a piece of your country's history. That, Jessa, makes it invaluable."

She flipped her wrist, dismissing his words. She'd learned the importance of supply and demand. A supply was worth as much as demand dictated, and demand was powered by desire to obtain. Who, besides a museum curator or someone like Max, would see the value of the Carry-Us-All? "That doesn't answer my question. Dollars, Max. What is it worth in dollars?"

"Let us imagine it is not a Parker early Carry-Us-All but only an old *karussell*. Just in case my suppositions are incorrect, yes?"

Jessa wouldn't argue.

"So, this *karussell* as is..." He chewed his lip a moment, his gaze angled skyward where stars winked far overhead. "Twenty-four horses—twelve jumpers, twelve prancers—circa 1895. Being conservative, I would estimate twenty-five hundred dollars each. Take that amount times four when they have been restored, and the horses alone would bring a sale price of at least two hundred forty thousand on the collector's market."

Dizziness attacked. She gripped the sleigh seat. Had she misunderstood? "Two...two hundred forty *thousand*?"

"Minimum. And that does not include the sleighs, which are also prized by many collectors." He met her gaze fully. "Now, consider if it is a fully intact Parker Carry-Us-All, and..." A slow smile grew, tugging the corners of his lips upward. "What are you thinking, Jessa?"

She owed her father an apology. She rose as unsteadily as if the carousel was turning circles. "Excuse me, Max. I...I need to..." She took off at a trot for her car.

CHAPTER 4

Max enjoyed attending church service with the Matthews Sunday morning, and he enjoyed the dinner afterward in Stan and Kathy's simple ranch style home even more. Apparently Jessa and Stan had set aside their disagreement, because daughter and father were smiling, laughing, at ease with each other. It gave his heart a lift. Especially when he juxtaposed their relaxed exchanges with the one he'd suffered through early that morning.

His father's exasperated tone still echoed in Max's head, and even though he was a grown man, his heart ached to be at odds with Papa. Would they ever come to agreement on Max's desire to become a U.S. citizen?

"Max, would you like more?" Kathy held the serving platter with a half dozen pieces of baked chicken toward him.

He shook his head and wiped his mouth with his napkin. "No, thank you, ma'am. I have had more than enough. Everything was very good." He wouldn't call the meal a fancy one like his mother always prepared for guests, but he'd enjoyed every bite of the herb-flecked chicken, sliced potatoes in a cheesy sauce, and green beans he suspected had been grown in a garden out back.

"Well, I hope you've left room for dessert. Jessa brought a pecan pie." The mother aimed a warm smile at her daughter.

Max raised his eyebrows. "You baked a pie?" She'd been industrious last night after fleeing the Carry-Us-All.

The girl's cheeks went pink. "I didn't bake it. I bought it. At the grocery store bakery." The pink deepened to red. "I can bake. I mean, I'm able to bake a pie. But I had studies to finish last night, so..."

For some reason her confession and the embarrassment staining her face tickled him. He couldn't resist a light chuckle. "You accomplished much more than I did last night, then. I didn't go pie-shopping. I only studied."

Kathy and Jessa began clearing the table. Kathy said, "We'll be right back with the pie."

Stan stacked his arms on the edge of the table and turned an eager look on Max. "I assume you were studying the carousel."

Max imitated Stan's pose. "Yes, sir. I researched the Parker carousels and was fortunate to find descriptions of the earliest ones. I spoke with my *Vater* this morning"—he hoped evidence of the terse exchange didn't show on his face—"and he advised that it would be best to make your Carry-Us-All as close to original as possible. Not a renovation, but a true restoration. Therefore, I suggest keeping to a simple, primary color palette."

Stan shrugged. "You're the expert. I will bow to your discretion."

"*Vater* also advised housing the Carry-Us-All in a structure that will protect it from excessive sunlight and weather changes. Your carousel is an investment and warrants extra care to preserve its value. Having a protected environment will also allow me, or whatever painter you choose to hire, to work without dust sticking in the paint." He smiled. "The wind does blow here."

The women, each carrying two dessert plates holding good-sized wedges of pecan pie, entered the dining room while Max spoke.

Jessa set a plate in front of Max and slid into her chair, tipping her head in an inquisitive gesture he found endearing. "We could probably use the horse barn as a protected environment for the carousel while you work."

Max frowned. "You aren't using it for revenue now?"

Stan picked up his fork. "For years we rented out the building for wedding receptions and other gatherings, but changes in state laws about accessibility forced us to turn it into a storage space instead. But Jessa's right about it giving you a protected place to work. It's plenty big enough. And we might even be able to renovate the barn and leave the carousel inside when we get it operational."

Max liked Stan's positive outlook—always "when," not "if."

Jessa chewed her lower lip for a moment. "Max, do you have an idea how much it will cost to restore the carousel?"

Worry pinched her brow again, stirring Max's sympathy. He and *Vater* had prepared a bid. He wished he could tell the Matthews that the cost would be minimal, but misleading them wouldn't do any good. His honesty might chase the plan of restoring the old Carry-Us-All far away. They might even throw him out of the house. But he would tell them the truth. He drew in a deep breath and began.

Jessa forgot about the tempting pie in front of her and sat, slack jawed, while Max outlined the length of time he would need to work on the carousel and how much it would cost. Dad sat with his lips tight, a line of white around his mouth indicating his shock. A restored carousel was worth a great deal–she didn't doubt Max's estimates because he spoke so knowledgeably–but could her family truly afford to invest in the piece of history, as Max called it?

She waved her hands. "Wait, wait. A year of work? That means we won't be able to offer it to visitors this season. That means money will be going toward it but not flowing back from it."

Understanding glimmered in Max's blue eyes. "That is often the case for investments, Jessa. Surely you know that from your studies."

Jessa dismissed his gentle words. "Textbook examples aren't the same as real life. Where are we supposed to get another hundred thousand dollars to invest in this thing?"

When Max and Dad both grimaced, guilt struck. She shouldn't speak so flippantly of the old carousel. She would destroy the peace she'd restored with Dad. She tempered her tone and spoke again. "I guess I didn't realize the carou–the Carry-Us-All would take so long to fix. I thought people would be able to ride it when we open on Memorial Day weekend."

Dad chopped a tiny bite from his pie but he didn't carry it to his mouth. "I figured we might not be able to use the ride this year. So that doesn't surprise me. But I'll be honest, the cost of restoration worries me a bit. I hadn't expected to put so much forward." He pushed the little piece of pie around the edge of his plate, his head low. "Max, I hope I didn't bring you here for no reason."

Jessa couldn't bear her father's despondence. Dad was always positive, always seeing the bright side of every situation. She gave the table a light thump with her fist. "Don't give up yet, Dad. Maybe you could get a grant or something to help with the cost of renovation. I mean, if this really is a Parker Carry-Us-All, won't there be historical groups interested in seeing it restored?"

Dad looked up, hope igniting on his face. "That's a good thought."

Max swallowed a huge bite of pie and grinned. "There are other ways to raise money, too—ways that let the community invest in the project."

Investment was something she understood. "Like what?"

He finished his last bite of pie before answering. "There are twenty-four horses on the Carry-Us-All. What if you invited businesses to pay a fee—anywhere from fifteen hundred to three thousand dollars—for the privilege of naming a horse. Then you put a small plaque beside the horse showing its name and the name of the business sponsoring it."

Dad laughed, the sound so joyful Jessa couldn't help smiling. "What a great idea! The businesses could write it off as an advertising expense, and we would receive revenue toward the renovation."

An excited quiver traveled up Jenna's spine. "Their feeling of ownership might even bring them and their customers to the park to visit 'their' horse."

Max grinned, his eyes shining, and Jessa got the feeling he was happier about her enthusiasm than the fact his idea held merit. He raised one eyebrow, the gesture impish. "Would you like to hear more ways to raise money for your Carry-Us-All renovation?"

His deep, melodic voice drew Jessa in. She nodded, her hair bouncing on her shoulders. She pushed the strands behind her ears and gave Max her full attention. "All right, we're listening. What else you got?"

CHAPTER 5

During the month of February it took every bit of Jessa's self-control to focus on her studies and stay away from Joy Land. Knowing carpenters were installing large Plexiglas windows in Great-granddad's massive barn to allow people to observe the Carry-Us-All's transformation, knowing Max was already at work behind those windows, made her want to visit Joy Land every day and watch the progress. But graduation was only a few months away. Final exams and interviews with professors required her on campus. So she satisfied herself by making Saturday visits to the barn.

Max firmly insisted on no visitors in his work area—visitors stirred dust and, worse, stole his concentration. But he never complained when Jessa popped in on Saturday afternoons. Sometimes she sat quietly and watched him work, content to merely admire the serious pinch of his brow and the steadiness of his hand as he applied a filling compound to cracks in the wood or whisked a block of sandpaper over old paint. He tended to whistle or hum while he worked, usually hymns, and often she caught herself adding harmony to his tunes, which always made him smile.

She liked his smile. She liked him. Maybe too much considering he was her father's employee and would only be in the U.S. a short time. But still she made it a point to visit every Saturday and spend a few hours watching him work and then joining him and her parents for dinner in the evening. Of course, Mom and Dad picked him up for church on Sunday mornings, which meant Jessa got to sit beside him and listen to his baritone during song-singing and observe his attentiveness during the sermon.

Almost against her will, she found herself pondering what it would be like to share more than a few hours on the weekends with Max. She'd dated several boys in high school and a few in college, but no boy had ever captured her attention the way Max had. She sensed he felt the same way about her. She read his interest in the tenderness in his eyes, the careful way he listened when she talked, even his smile, which always seemed softer and full of secrets when he aimed it her direction.

Her infatuation led her to share her feelings with Amy, her best friend from school, over a cup of coffee in the college's snack bar on the last Friday in February. Amy listened, and to Jessa's surprise her friend didn't express a word of elation that Jessa had found someone she cared about. Instead, she said, "You better be careful."

Jessa drew back, her spine connecting with the padded backrest of the booth's bench seat. "What's that supposed to mean?"

Amy leaned close, her dark eyes sparking. "Foreign men come to the states on work or student visas in the hopes of snagging the affection of some desperate girl."

Jessa bristled. "Are you calling me desperate?"

Amy rolled her eyes. "No, of course not. I know better. You'd never throw yourself at some guy just so you could be in a relationship. But this painter doesn't know that. He could be buttering you up because he sees you as his ticket."

Frowning, Jessa shook her head. "His ticket to what?"

"To remain in the United States." Amy sat back and nodded, her expression smug. "It happens all the time. As a matter of fact, there have been three situations on this very campus in the past two years with foreign students romancing an American citizen so they can stay here."

Jessa gaped at Amy. "That's not true."

"It is true." Amy nodded emphatically. "One student was from Europe, another from Southeast Asia, and yet another one from South America. If a U.S. citizen marries a non-resident, the non-resident's place here is secure." She leaned in again and lowered her voice. "Be careful, Jessa. You don't want to end up being his means of staying in this country. I'd hate to see you get used that way."

Although she wanted to ignore Amy's warning, Jessa couldn't set her friend's ominous words aside. The worry was still rolling in the back of Jessa's mind when she arrived at Joy Land the next afternoon and let herself into the barn where Max crouched on the dirt floor, studiously carving out a section on one of the sleighs. She pulled up her stool a few feet away and perched on it, observing him. Could someone who appeared so honest and friendly harbor underhanded intentions? She didn't want to believe it.

He paused in his task and shot her a smile. "Good afternoon. How were your classes this week?"

He always asked about her classes, as if he truly cared. She swallowed the warm rise of affection and forced herself to answer nonchalantly. "Fine." She glanced around. "You got a lot done this week. Two horses look ready for paint." Pointing at the sleigh, she tipped her head and squinted. "But that thing's a mess. Why'd you decide to tackle it instead of continuing with the horses?"

Max tapped one area on the sleigh's side, which curved like a slippery slide's bed. "Lots of rotted wood. The longer I leave it, the more the rotting can spread. I decided it needed my attention worse than the horses do."

Jessa pressed her palms together and clamped her hands between her knees. "Max, may I ask you something?"

He went back to carving, his brow puckered. "Mm-hm."

"When your work visa is up, do you plan to stay in the U.S.?"

His head bounced up as quickly as if a piece of string gave it a yank. He gawked at her, his blue eyes round and innocent. "How did you know?"

A sick feeling flooded her stomach. "I didn't. I just...guessed."

Max sat back on his heels, his hands still on the sleigh, and smiled at her. A sweet smile. A mesmerizing smile. "We must be what you would call kindred spirits for you to guess such a thing without me ever saying a word. But, yes, it is my dream to live in America. I love my homeland, but there are so many more opportunities here.

Whatever it takes to remain, I will do it."

Amy's warning clanged in Jessa's memory. She blurted, "Even marrying someone?"

Had she also guessed his fondness for her? Heat flooded Max's face, and he wanted to look anywhere but into her eyes. Yet he couldn't turn away. Her blue-eyed gaze held him as effectively as an eight-inch bolt held the two halves of a *karussell* horse together.

They'd only known each other a month with few hours together. But the time they shared held importance to him. He liked her. He liked her parents. He admired their Christian faith and their love and respect for each other. Although only a short amount of time had passed, he felt as though their friendship was years long already, and he wanted it to continue to for years to come. He wanted it to deepen to something more.

But he couldn't tell Jessa his feelings so soon. She needed to finish school. He needed to complete this project. Neither of them had time for romance. Besides, before he wooed an American woman, he wanted to be an American himself. Citizenship took time, but it would be time well spent.

"Max?"

He'd gone too long without answering her question. He gathered his thoughts and repeated his earlier statement. "I will do whatever is necessary to remain in America."

A hint of distrust glimmered in her eyes. He'd frightened her somehow. Should he have admitted his attraction to her? He started to rise and approach her, but she leaped off the stool and picked it up, holding in front of her like a shield. He remained in place, unwilling to alarm her any further than he already had.

She backed up a dozen paces, settled the stool on the ground, and climbed up again. "Well, just so you know, I'm not in the market for a husband."

Did she know how petulant she looked there on the wooden stool with her arms crossed and her lips pulled into a pout? He battled a chortle. He nodded slowly. "That is fine with me. I'm not in the market for a wife." Yet.

Her eyes narrowed to slits. "Really?"

He raised both palms as if surrendering. "Really."

She seemed to examine him for several seconds, and then she relaxed, her shoulders wilting. "Dad said you had another idea for bringing in some revenue to put toward the restoration."

If she was willing to change the topic, he wouldn't argue. He returned to the sleigh and picked up his awl. "The men who installed the windows had pieces of Plexiglas left over. I asked them to use the pieces and create a hinged box that can be secured with a small padlock. I intend to drill a slit in the top of the box and mount it beneath the center window so people who watch the renovation can make donations to go toward the project." He shrugged. "It might not bring in much, but sometimes people are generous. Especially if they like what they see."

She sighed. "They'll like what they see." Her cheeks blazed pink.

And his face heated. He turned his attention to the sleigh and kept it there.

CHAPTER 6

March blew in, some days carried on a cool breeze, other days balmy and offering a promise of warmer days to come. Max was grateful for the sturdy old barn that blocked the wind and allowed him to work in a comfortable space. Stan intended to update the barn with a better heating and cooling system as soon as grant money from a historical preservation group arrived so the old Parker Carry-Us-All would always be in a temperature controlled environment. Max appreciated Stan's dedication to protecting the irreplaceable *karussell*, and he spent hours each evening investigating other ways of helping offset the costs of renovation.

With the arrival of April, Max and Stan were no longer the only workers at the park. A crew arrived daily and scattered across the grounds, readying rides for operation, touching up the buildings with paint, and making other repairs. Every day the air of festivity heightened as opening day steadily neared. Frequently Max looked up from his activity to find faces on the other side of the Plexiglas windows—friendly faces, interested faces. Twice he discovered crumpled bills and a spattering of coins in the bottom of the mounted box.

The donations, although hardly enough to purchase a quality paintbrush, thrilled him. If the workers were willing to contribute, surely patrons of the park would be even more generous. But he needed to show people the Carry-Us-All's potential. So he dedicated the first two weeks of April to one horse, a jumper, its graceful legs caught in a perpetual, delicate leap. The horse bore no elaborate carvings to limit his creativity, so he looked at the wooden horse as a blank canvas.

He decided to create an American horse—snow white with blue eyes and a gray mane and tail streaked with dark blue to give the illusion of movement. He chose not to shadow muscles. Shadow lines would intrude upon the clean white expanse. He shaped a brown saddle on the horse's back and decorated the saddle with a gold border and featherlike swirls. When Stan saw it, he commended Max for his detailed work, and Max hid his smile. If Stan liked it so far, what would he think when he saw the finished project?

Max spent days creating a patriotic saddle blanket in bold red with a blue stripe that circled the horse's neck. He marched white stars through the path of blue and added a slim border of silver to make the stars sparkle. Gold braiding and fringe on the blanket's edges required an entire day of careful work, but he didn't mind. Such joy he found in using his paintbrushes and paint to bring the animal to life again, giving it color and personality and pride.

To finish the blanket, he painstakingly painted a bald eagle in flight with the pole of a waving American flag gripped in its talons. Three stars—a larger one and a smaller one on the left of the eagle, and a medium-sized one on the right—balanced the design. Finally, he added a red harness with more white stars and a blue and gold conch, and the horse's transformation was complete.

After applying three treatments of protective clear coating, he was ready to mount the horse in front of one of the windows where everyone could enjoy it. He dug his cell phone from his pocket to call Stan. He would need help securing the horse on the base he'd built. Before he could push the buttons, a call came through. Jessa's number flashed on the screen, and his heart gave a leap that competed with the horse's fanciful lunge. For reasons he couldn't understand, she'd stopped her habit of coming by on Saturdays, and he'd missed her.

He eagerly pushed the "accept" button and held the phone to his ear. "Jessa, hello." He sounded as breathless as if he'd run a race. He pressed his palm to his stomach and forced a calmer tone. "How are you?"

"I'm fine, thank you." She sounded so formal, unlike the Jessa he'd first known. "I wondered if it would be an inconvenience for me to come by and bring someone with me."

He would never consider her an inconvenience. "Of course not. As you pointed out to me on the first night of our acquaintance, the park belongs to your family. You're welcome here any time." He chuckled softly, remembering the stunned expression on her pretty face when he'd come upon her in the sleigh.

The sound of a clearing throat came through the phone. Then her voice again, soft and tremulous, making him wonder if she, too, was recalling details of their time in the shadowed park. "Yes, well, one of my friends told a newspaper reporter about the Parker Carry-Us-All"—which intimated she'd been talking about the project to others, an encouraging realization—"and the reporter would like to come to the park, maybe take some pictures if you're open to it, and interview you. That is, if you're available."

Max sent up a silent thank-you prayer that he'd finished one horse. It would make a wonderful photograph for the paper. "Please, come over," he said, unable to squelch a smile. "I will be ready."

Jessa listened with half an ear to the reporter's questions and Max's concise, thoughtful replies. She couldn't take her eyes off the horse painted in traditional red, white, and blue. She itched to touch the braided trim or the eagle's feathers. The painting was so realistic, she was certain her fingertips would feel the bumps in the braid or the softness of the down. She propped her hands on her knees and bent close, examining the tracings of silver that made each white star become a tiny pillow against the red blanket.

The circus animals on their newer carousel had elaborate colors, too, but the paint had been applied to carved flowers or swirled designs. This horse was simply carved, only a smooth shape. How had he managed to turn it into a three dimensional work of art?

A flash of light behind her shoulder startled her, and she jerked upright.

The reporter grinned at her. "Sorry to scare you, but you didn't give me much choice. You were so engrossed, you didn't even respond when I asked if you'd mind stepping aside."

Her face flaming, Jessa scuttled away from the carousel horse.

The man circled the horse, snapping photos from every angle, and then invited Max to stand behind it. "Can you hold a couple of your paintbrushes, cross your arms, and give me an artistic stance?"

Max laughed. "If you say so."

Jessa caught herself transfixed by his confident pose, his ease in front of the camera. He displayed such charisma and poise, yet without a hint of arrogance. He really was a very appealing man.

The reporter snapped two pictures and then let the camera hang from its strap against his chest. "I've got everything I need." He strode forward and shook Max's hand over the horse's back. Then his gaze roved the horse, and he whistled through his teeth. "That's really something. I'll look forward to seeing the whole carousel—"

"Carry-Us-All," Max and Jessa chorused.

He grinned. "Excuse me—Carry-Us-All complete. And I'll encourage the newspaper owner to sponsor one of these steeds. I might sponsor one on my own for my part-time photography business."

Jessa hugged herself to hold back a crow of delight.

Max beamed at the man. "If you decide to sponsor a horse, you tell me your favorite colors or your wife's favorite flowers. I will make it special for you."

With another grin, the reporter waved goodbye to both Jessa and Max and strode from the barn.

Jessa whirled on Max. "Did you hear that? Maybe two sponsors already! And the article hasn't even been released!" Her admiration for him, her amazement at his artistic ability, and even a rush of happiness at seeing him again after holding herself aloof for so long spilled over.

Impulsively, she threw her arms wide and launched herself into his arms.

CHAPTER 7

The moment his arms closed around her, she wriggled free. What was she doing, throwing herself at him like some kind of groupie? She tugged the hem of her shirt over her hips and smoothed her hair into place, studiously avoiding meeting his gaze.

"Jessa, what is the matter?" Genuine confusion colored his tone.

He must think she was a real ninny. She bit her lip, angled her head low, and refused to answer.

His heels scuffed on the floor, and then his hand cupped her chin, forcing her to lift her face. The tenderness she'd witnessed on previous occasions shone in his blue eyes. A smile gently curved his lips. "You need not feel embarrassed."

She swallowed. Embarrassed was only half what she felt. She was too afraid to explore the other half.

"There is nothing wrong with friends sharing a hug of success. That's what it was, yes? A moment of celebration for our plans coming together?"

A celebration was taking place beneath her breast bone. Her heart bounced around in her chest as if it had lost its hold. She offered a hesitant nod.

The corners of his eyes crinkled. He brushed her cheek with his thumb—one quick, almost impersonal caress—and lowered his hand. He crossed to the horse painted in America's colors and gave its saddle a pat. "What do you think of this? I wanted to have one horse all done for people to see when the park opens and they make use of the observation windows. It will be good for them to have an idea of how the Carry-Us-All will look when it is fully restored. Then they'll be more likely to contribute toward it, do you agree?"

She moved to the opposite side of the horse and let her gaze rove from the nose to the tip of the tail. She shook her head, amazed. "Max, the horse is beautiful. I had no idea it could look like this. I thought you'd just paint it a solid color, maybe paint the mane, tail, and hooves, and that would be it. What you've done is spectacular. Now I understand why it will be a full year to finish the Carry-Us-All."

She finally looked at him, her face growing warm under his steadfast gaze. "How long did it take you to paint this?"

He frowned. "Hmm, two days for the application of primer, then one day for each color, a full day for each layer of marine varnish..." He flicked his fingers upward one by one, lips pursed. "Ten—no, eleven days."

Jessa's mouth fell open. "Just to finish one horse?"

He chuckled softly. "That doesn't include the days I spent stripping the old paint, filling cracks, sanding it smooth as silk, and making sure it was very clean to receive the new paint." He shrugged. "It takes much time, but if it is done right, this horse will still be bright and colorful twenty years from now. It's important to me that all is done correctly."

She slid her fingers over the horse's sleek nose. "So much work..."

"Yes, it is. It takes focus and perseverance." His expression turned serious. "But I won't complain about the length of time or the difficulty of the tasks set before me. You see, Jessa, *Opa* and *Vater* taught me the benefit of endurance. Endurance builds character. It is important to me to be a man of strong, dependable character."

Most young people she knew didn't have the patience to spend days on a project. They wanted to click a few buttons and enjoy instant gratification. She'd admired Max before, but her esteem for him multiplied in that moment. "Your *Vater* and *Opa*"—the German words tripped on her tongue—"taught you well. I'm sure they're very proud of you."

An odd, pained look crossed his face, but a smile chased it away so quickly Jessa thought she might have imagined it. He plucked the paintbrushes from his shirt pocket and ran his thumb over the bristles. "Yes, well, they did teach me well, and I'm grateful for their teaching. Were it not for my ability as a painter, I wouldn't be here in America at your family's amusement park, working on this project, and..." He flicked a glance at her, warmth in his gaze. "I wouldn't have met you."

Be careful. Amy's admonition snapped in Jessa's mind. He was pulling her in. Or was he? He'd claimed he wanted to be man of strong character, and a man of strong character wouldn't deliberately use people for selfish gain. Jessa couldn't make sense of her jumbled emotions concerning Max.

She pulled in a fortifying breath and chose her words carefully. "I'm glad Dad hired you. You obviously know what you're doing, and I'm confident your work on the Carry-Us-All will assure its secondary market value. I trust you not to waste Dad's money."

She said she trusted him, but clearly she didn't. Or she wouldn't be slowly backing away from him. She wouldn't become stiff and uncertain in his presence. After their weeks of only seeing each other at Sunday church services and lunch afterward, he'd missed her. The way she hugged him made him think she'd missed him, too, but now he didn't know what to think. Jessa Matthews was a very confusing young lady. Or maybe she was only confused. He would be patient with her. Perseverance worked well when applying paint. Perhaps it was equally applicable to relationships.

He forced a smile, hoping it appeared genuine. "I promise I won't waste your father's money. And I will pray that the newspaper article brings businessmen out to the park to see what we're up to in here." He deliberately used *we* instead of *I* hoping she would envision them as a team. According to Stan and Kathy, she hadn't found a place to work after graduation. Maybe this Carry-Us-All would entice her to give Joy Land an opportunity to truly become *her* park.

"It would be a blessing if all twenty-four horses received

sponsorship." Worry eased into her voice. "It also helps that you're letting Dad pay you a monthly salary the same way he does his other employees instead of asking for the entire bid up front."

Max's father wasn't happy about the arrangement. Never had *Vater* allowed incremental payments. He claimed Stan could run out of money and cease paying Max. But *Vater* needed to learn to trust Max's judgment about payments, and about where he would live. Max gave Jessa a smile. "If I could do this project for no charge, I would—that's how special I think the Parker Carry-Us-All is, how wonderful the opportunity to bring it back to life again."

Jessa shook her head. "No, Dad wouldn't even consider letting you do this project for the chance to restore an original Parker Carry-Us-All. He always says a workman is worthy of his hire, and he's always rewarded hard work with fair wages. You're a qualified restoration expert well worth what you've asked. I confess, I was a little shocked by your bid, but now that I've seen what goes into the restoration and the end result..." Her gaze slid to the American horse. "I can't be anything except grateful that you're available."

He liked this relaxed Jessa, and he liked hearing her speak openly. The reporter had gone, and she probably had studies waiting, so he needed to let her go. But he wasn't ready. It might be weeks again before they had time together. He would stretch these minutes as long as possible. As if giving a cue, her stomach growled.

Jessa's eyebrows rose and she flattened her palms on her stomach. Max burst out laughing. "Did you skip breakfast?"

A sheepish grin lifted the corners of her lips. "Yeah, I guess I did. And it is after one. Maybe I should—"

"You should come sit over here and share my lunch with me." Max caught her elbow and guided her to the corner of the barn, where his insulated lunch box and jug of iced tea waited. "I always bring plenty because sometimes I stay and work past the supper hour. So there is enough for both of us." He gestured to the cleared spot on the floor. "Go ahead. Sit down."

She remained in place, her hands gripped over her belly. "I

shouldn't eat your food."

Max chuckled. "It's your mother's food. She delivers bags of groceries every week to your great-grandfather's house for me to eat. So sit. Share it with me." He held his breath. If she scurried away, he would see it as a sign that she didn't want to have a friendship with him. It would hurt, but he would survive. And it was better to know now than later when he'd allowed himself to grow more firmly attached to Stan and Kathy and their pretty daughter.

She gazed at him, uncertainty in her light blue eyes, and then without warning she plopped down and criss-crossed her legs. She stuck out her hands. "All right. One sandwich."

Max blew out his air and sat down near her. He opened the box and pulled out two thick ham and cheese sandwiches wrapped in plastic. As he handed one of the sandwiches to her, she spoke again.

"And then I've got to get back to my apartment and practice for Monday's interview with a firm in Kansas City. It's a great opportunity. I don't want to mess it up."

CHAPTER 8

The first Saturday in April, Stan and Jessa asked to meet with Max in the evening at the caretaker's cottage. Although he wondered what the meeting would involve, he eagerly accepted. Any opportunity to spend time with Jessa should be seized and seized cheerfully.

They arrived at six thirty, Jessa carrying a laptop case over her shoulder and Stan balancing two pizza boxes on his palms. They sat at the kitchen table, Stan offered a prayer, and before any of them had removed a slice of pizza from a box, Jessa dove into the purpose of the meeting.

"Traditionally Joy Land opens its gates to visitors the Saturday before Memorial Day, but what do you think about having a 'sneak preview' a week ahead of the regular opening—a special event by invitation only—with proceeds going toward the restoration of the rare Parker Carry-Us-All?"

Stan chewed and swallowed. "Who would we invite?"

Jessa slid a slice of ham and mushroom pizza onto her paper plate. "I'd limit the reach to Wyandotte, Johnson, and Leavenworth Counties, but I'd send invitations to business owners, librarians, museum curators, educators, newspaper reporters, and radio station hosts."

"That's a lot of people."

She shrugged, making a face. "I estimate only twenty-five percent will accept the invitation. But even at that, we'd have a sizable turn-out. I thought about making it a costume event and suggest they dress in early 1900s fashion."

Stan whistled through his teeth. "I don't know, Jessa. Would grown men participate in something like that?"

She looked at Max. "What do you think? Would you be willing to wear a 1900s suit and hat to the event?"

Max patted his mouth with his napkin. "It would add to the air of festivity for us to be costumed, and it would help transport people back to the time when the Parker Carry-Us-All was being built. I suppose you could make costuming optional and let those invited decided how they wanted to dress."

"But you'd wear a costume?"

If it would please her, he would stand on stilts and pass out balloon animals. "Of course."

Jessa sent a triumphant grin her father's direction. "See? And if we invite the families of those invited, then you've got kids clamoring for an excuse to play dress-up. It could really be fun."

Stan chuckled. "All right, all right, I concede defeat. I'll visit the costume shop with you and Max and rent outfits for your mother and me."

"Great!" Jessa took a bite, washed it down with ice water, and went on with enthusiasm. "I'm still toying with a name for the event, but I'm thinking something like 'Capturing the Past' or 'Bridging Yesterday With Tomorrow' or—"

Max interrupted, "'Carry-Us-All to Yesteryear.'"

She grinned. "That's not half bad." She held up her hand, and Max high-fived her. She swiped her hand on her jeans leg and picked up her pizza again. "We can set up an *hors d'ouerves* table—nothing real fancy, just miniature servings of things you'd see at an old-time carnival or county fair. For our program, Dad, you could give a brief overview about Parker Carry-Us-Alls in general and their significance to Kansas history—after all Kansas, is our across-the-river neighbor—and Max could do a Q-and-A about the work involved in restoring the carousel."

Stan raised one eyebrow. "And just what is your role in all of this?"

She shrugged, suddenly turning shy. "Well, to close the program, I'll share how each of them can contribute toward this amazing piece of history by sponsoring a horse, making a donation toward the project, or purchasing a ticket bundle to share with employees, friends, or family." She dropped the half-eaten slice of pizza and rested her elbows on the edge of the table, her eyes sparkling. "I saw a steam organ listed for sale at an antique auction in Missouri, and I thought it would be a great addition to the over-all experience of stepping back in time. Maybe you and I could—"

"I don't have time for auctions at this time of year, Jessa."

"Oh. Well then..."

Stan's obvious disappointment stung Max, as did Jessa's crestfallen expression. He said, "When is the auction?"

She sighed. "Next Saturday."

If he put in extra hours Monday through Friday, he could be away from the park for a Saturday expedition. "I'll go with you."

Her eyes flew wide. "You will?"

He nodded.

Delight burst over her face and ignited joy in Max's chest. She turned to her father. "What do you think, Dad? Should Max and I go see it, make sure it's operable, and place a bid? I mean, how can we have a turn-of-the-century event without turn-of-the-century music?"

Max added his thoughts. "A steam organ would have been used to enhance the ride's experience, so its inclusion would be historically accurate. You could showcase it with the *karussell* and make it part of the ride."

Stan laughed. "I don't suppose I have much choice in the matter, do I? It's either find something to provide music or be forced to break out my old accordion."

Jessa groaned, but her eyes glittered with mischief, and Max couldn't stop a grin from pulling on his lips. He liked seeing her bubbly and enthusiastic and joy-filled. He also thrilled at her enthusiasm about the event. Did her change in attitude mean she wouldn't take the job in Kansas City and would, instead, take over the management of Joy Land?

Stan put his hand over Jessa's. "All right, go to the auction. Take Max, and both of you give the steam organ a thorough look-over. Ask for the auctioneer to play it for you. Don't place a bid unless you know for sure it plays. I'll send you with the business checkbook, and I'll trust you not to go over the amount I designate." He leaned back and shook his head. "Let's hope the organ works and that we're the only ones interested in it. My budget can't take a bidding war."

Jessa couldn't stop grinning. When was the last time she'd had so much fun? Memory failed her. She rolled down the passenger side window of Dad's truck, rested her elbow on the ledge, and let the spring air wash over her face.

Behind the steering wheel, Max handled the truck like a pro. At first she'd been nervous about letting him drive. She'd heard they drove like race car drivers on the *Autobahn*. But handling Dad's tricky stick-shift scared her even more than the thought of someone from Germany taking control. She shouldn't have worried. He followed the speed limit signs religiously. And he had no trouble getting them to the auction, maneuvering the crowded field designated as a parking area, and then returning to the highway for the drive home. He seemed relaxed, and his casual pose relaxed her.

Plus he'd been a great companion the entire excursion from their fast-food breakfast, to speaking with the auction organizer about the steam organ, to wandering the grounds and examining the other items for sale. Then, when the steam organ came up for auction, he maneuvered her to front of the crowd where the auctioneer couldn't help but see her flash the card with her number on it. Only one other person bid against her, and that man dropped out before she reached Dad's ceiling. When the auctioneer announced her number as the winning bidder, she turned and jammed both palms in the air for a double high-five. Max had responded without a moment's hesitation, his smile rivaling the brightness of the sun. They'd had so much fun.

She angled her face toward him, still grinning. "Thanks, Max."

He glanced her way, curiosity on his face. "For what?"

"For going along. For helping. I could have never wrangled that organ into the back of the pickup on my own."

He flipped his hand as if shooing away her words. "The auction people would have helped you."

"Yeah, but they wouldn't have celebrated with me the way you did." He'd turned the entire day into a celebration just by being his cheerful, supportive, cooperative self. She liked being with him. "It was a good day."

He smiled a thank-you and turned his gaze forward. They rode in silence for several miles, and then he gave a little jerk. "Jessa, may I ask you something?"

She angled herself sideways as best she could with the seatbelt restricting her movement. Ah, yes, better to observe his profile and the way his sunshine colored hair lifted in the wind. "Sure."

"It has made me happy to see your excitement about the Carry-Us-All and the fundraising event." He sent a quick look at her, his brow furrowing. "But I am curious why you suddenly have enthusiasm instead of apprehension?"

Jessa released a short laugh. "I'd be pretty foolish not to exhibit enthusiasm considering the project will benefit me so much."

A slow smile lifted the corners of his mouth and brought his dimples into view. "You mean as the future owner of Joy Land?"

"I mean as a graduate with good grades. The fundraiser is my final project for my business applications class."

His smile disappeared and a frown replaced it. He gripped the steering wheel as tightly as if he wanted to choke the plastic circle. "You...your final project? You are doing it all for a grade? Instead of to help your father?"

She frowned, too. "You don't need to sound accusatory. You know I'm working toward a degree in business administration. Projects are part of the senior year." She shrugged. "So I came up with a project that benefits Dad and Joy Land as well as myself. There's nothing wrong with that, is there?"

He nodded, the motion adamant. He pushed the buttons that raised both of their windows. The wind noise abruptly stopped, and her ears began to ring. He aimed a disappointed look in her direction. "It's wrong because it is sending the wrong message to your father. He thinks your involvement means your interest in the park."

She gaped at him. They'd had such a wonderful day, a day of laughter and camaraderie. Where had his friendly countenance gone? A hint of defensiveness pinched her chest. "Well, of course I'm interested in the park. For heaven's sake, it's been in my family for years. I don't want to see it collapse. Dad's investing hundreds of thousands of dollars into the Carry-Us-All. I want to see him receive a return on his investment. What kind of daughter would I be if I just stood back and let him go under, financially?"

"What kind of daughter would you be to build his hopes up and then knock him down?"

She shook her head. "You aren't making any sense, Max. How is planning an event to bring needed revenue into the park's bank account knocking him down?"

"Because he interprets your involvement as more than interest in his bank account. He sees it as interest in helping him run the park. He sees it as—"

She waved both hands in the air. "Wait a minute, wait a minute. Is this Dad talking, or is this you?"

Red streaked his clean-shaven cheeks.

Awareness dawned. She slumped against the seat. "Why do you care so much if I take over Joy Land from Dad or not?"

For long minutes he sat with his lips pressed together, his narrowed gaze aimed at the road. Then he flicked a sheepish look at her and sighed. "Because I don't want to see you disappoint your father the way I have disappointed mine. And because I don't want you to be...far from"—he gulped—"me."

CHAPTER 10

He'd been too forthright. Her stunned expression and the blotches of pink on her face told Max he should have stayed quiet. But since he'd started talking, he might as well finish. But not while he was driving. He needed to look into her eyes when he shared his heart with her.

Just ahead, an exit led to a gas station with an ice cream shop built at one end. He hit the turn signal, angled the truck onto the off ramp, and pulled into the station. He parked directly in front of the plate glass window of the ice cream shop where they'd be able to keep an eye on the steam organ from inside.

Without a word, they disconnected their seatbelts and got out. Max met her at the hood of the truck. Temptation to reach for her hand pulled hard, but she slipped her hands into her jacket pockets, as if fearful he would do that very thing. Holding back a sigh, he opened the door for her and gestured her in.

He ordered a banana split, and she requested a small chocolate shake. He paid for their order and took the little plastic number from the cashier, and then they slid into a booth in front of the window. He placed the number at the edge of the table. Sunshine bounced off the truck hood, reflected from the building's tin eave, and splashed patches of light on the table. He placed his linked hands in the middle of one splash and met Jessa's somber gaze.

"Have I frightened you?"

She licked her lips, her eyes shifting away briefly and then settling on him again. "Maybe. A little."

"Because I have moved too quickly?"

She hugged herself and hunkered against the red vinyl seatback.

"Yeah, partly."

Max lightly tapped the pads of thumbs together, unable to sit completely still. "What is the other part?"

She leaned forward, arms still crossed over her middle, and scowled. "I guess I'm confused. Why does it matter to you if I take over Joy Land or not?"

One of the ice cream shop workers hurried to their table. "Here you are!"

Jessa leaned back, and Max shifted his hands out of the way. The girl placed their order in front of them, told them to enjoy their treats, and bustled off. As soon as she moved away, he stretched his hand across the table, palm up. She sent him a startled look. He bobbed his hand. "Let me pray before our ice cream melts."

Surprise appeared on her face. She probably wondered why he would pray for ice cream—it wasn't a meal. But he needed the connection with his heavenly Father before he finished his conversation with her. She gently placed her hand in his, and he closed his fingers around it. Then he bowed his head and offered a short prayer expressing thanks for their safety during travel, gratitude for the acquisition of the steam organ, and a request for God to bless the food. When he opened his eyes, Jessa seemed less tense.

Max slid his spoon through the mound of whipped cream and answered Jessa's question as if they'd had no interruption. "It matters to me because it matters so much to your father. I admire him. Respect him. I know how much he cares about you. I see it in the way he talks to you and about you. You are his pride and joy."

She ducked her head, a pretty blush forming on her cheeks. She took a long sip from her straw, and the color in her face faded. "You don't have to tell me that Dad loves me. Or Mom either, for that matter. I already know. And I love them, too. But Dad's real pride and joy is Joy Land. I'll do what I can to help him keep it because I know how much it matters to him. But he's going to have to understand that it isn't my pride and joy."

"Are you sure?"

She pushed the sweating paper cup aside. "Again, why is this so important to you? I get that you like my folks. Most people do. They're very likable. But why do you want me to stay in Shadybrook and help Dad operate Joy Land? Why are you trying to prevent me from going out and...and seeking my own fortune?"

"Because I think you are seeking something else for the wrong reason."

She frowned. "And you think this because...?"

"Do you remember the night I found you on the Carry-Us-All sleigh?"

She nodded.

"That night, you told me you didn't want Joy Land to become your whole life, the way it is your father's whole life. But you were wrong about him. Joy Land is not his whole life. You and your mother, you're more important to him than Joy Land. And even more important than you and your mother to him is his love for his Savior. I've seen evidence of his love for God in the things he says, the things he does, the way he treats people. You've seen it, too, haven't you?"

Tears pooled in Jessa's pale eyes, deepening the dark rims around her irises. "My whole life."

He smiled. "You see, Jessa, Joy Land gives him a place to serve, but the people—his employees, those who visit the park—the people God puts in his pathway are what is important to him. That's why Joy Land is 'joy' to him. It puts him in contact with others and gives him a place to shine the light of God's love." He tipped his head and fixed her with a steady gaze. "I think maybe you have some misplaced jealousy that makes you want to go away and form a life apart from Joy Land. But unless it is God Himself leading you away, you will never be happy." Knowing he was in a land where God led him gave him peace even though *Vater* still grumbled about the choice. "You must serve where God wills, not where you will. Do you understand?"

"I...I think so." She blinked several times and took a few more sips of her shake.

His ice cream was rapidly melting and creating tiny waterfalls over the edge of the boat shaped bowl. He slurped up bites and let her think. He hadn't wanted to offend her, but she'd said a good daughter would do what she could to keep her father's business from collapsing. A good friend would try to keep her from making a grave mistake. He wanted to be a good friend to her.

"Max?"

He looked up with the spoon between his lips.

"In the truck, you said you didn't want me to go far away from... you."

He pulled the spoon free and swallowed. "Yes. I said that."

"Does that mean you...like me?"

He chuckled. He couldn't help it. She looked so apprehensive. "If I said yes, would you run from the restaurant screaming?"

A smile appeared on her face, then she lowered her head, and the smile went away. "It depends on why you like me."

He began listing the reasons in his head, ready to share.

She lifted her face. "Do you see me as your means of staying in the United States?"

His jaw dropped. All reasons dissipated like a puff of smoke. He jammed the spoon into the mushy mess and reared back. "I spent a year in the U.S. as a foreign exchange student when I was sixteen. I had to go back to Germany after I graduated from high school, but after my nineteenth birthday, I returned to America with a work visa. For the last seven years, I have applied my hand to different occupations in order to prove I can be a useful, productive member of this country. Every evening I study in preparation for the citizenship examination, and as soon as possible, I will take the exam and pledge my allegiance to this country. So to answer your question, no, I do not need you to remain in the United States. My attraction for you gave me another reason to want to be here, but I would never use you for such selfish purposes."

The banana split no longer held any appeal. She could finish her shake in the truck. He pushed out of the booth and dropped a dollar on the table. "Let's go, Jessa. Your father will be eager to see the steam organ."

Jessa sat quiet and miserable on her side of the truck the rest of the drive to Shadybrook. The happiness of the outing had shattered, and it was all her fault. Why had she listened to Amy? She should have trusted her own heart. Hadn't her weeks with him showed her Max was a man of character? She'd hurt him by questioning his motives, and she feared she'd spoiled any chance for them to continue their friendship.

She held the soggy milkshake cup between her palms and stared out the window at the passing landscape. Maybe it was for the best. After all, when he finished the Carry-Us-All, he would move on. After graduation she'd be taking a job...somewhere else. Or maybe not. He'd made some good points, and she needed to spend time in prayer for discernment. She knew the importance of seeking and following God's will, and if it was God's will for her to continue the Matthews' legacy at Joy Land, then she needed to be obedient.

When they reached town, Max drove to her parents' home and pulled into the driveway. Jessa's car waited at the curb. She'd planned to give him a ride to her great-grandparents' cottage, but she wondered now if he'd go with her. He hadn't said a word since they left the ice cream shop.

He shut off the engine and opened his door. As he slid out, Mom stepped onto the front porch and braced her hands on the iron railing. She smiled, seemingly unaware of the frost surrounding Jessa and Max.

"Max, I dropped Stan off at Joy Land a couple of hours ago. He asked if you would take the steam organ there so he can put it in the barn with the Carry-Us-All, then he'll drive the truck home later."

Max nodded. Mom waved and returned to the house. Max climbed back in behind the wheel. Jessa was still seatbelted in. He paused with the key near the ignition.

"Are you getting out here, or are you going to Joy Land?"

She really wanted to witness Dad's face when he saw the steam organ, but Dad was intuitive. They'd ruin his delight if they showed up with this cloud of tension over them. She had to restore their ease first.

She tentatively touched Max's arm. "Max, I'm really sorry. I shouldn't have asked what I did."

He turned a sad look on her. "I'm sorry, too, that you think so little of me."

The gentle statement stung worse than if he'd railed at her. "It isn't you. It's...one of my friends told me about foreign students who try to woo American girls so they can stay in the U.S. I just worried... I thought..." She hung her head. "I was wrong."

He didn't say anything.

She sighed and unsnapped the belt. "I better head to my apartment. I've got work to do on the Carry-Us-All to Yesteryear event."

"All right. I will see you in church tomorrow."

His tone emerged stilted. Lacking warmth. UnMax-like. But a tiny flicker of hope followed her from the pickup. At least he intended to see her again.

CHAPTER 11

Sunday after church Max chose to take a sandwich to Joy Land and work on the Carry-Us-All instead of going to lunch with Jessa and her parents. He said it was because he'd been gone on Saturday, but Jessa knew better. He was avoiding her. She understood why, but it hurt. More than she'd expected. The hurt lingered through the remaining weeks in April.

Between attending classes, studying for examinations, and working on the fundraising event, she had little time to spare. Even so, she often found herself staring into space, thinking about Max or stewing about her future. Her interview with the Kansas City firm had gone well, but they intended to interview other candidates, too. It could be close to graduation before she heard from them. Mom always preached that worry accomplished nothing more than ulcers and forehead wrinkles, so Jessa did her best not to worry. Instead, each time questions or concerns entered her mind, she prayed for God to still her anxiety and whisper His peace to her soul. It worked concerning the job. About Max? Not so much.

Because the fundraising event would take place at Joy Land, she had to visit the barn frequently to hang banners or measure for table placements or other pre-party preparations. So she couldn't avoid seeing Max. Nor did she want to. Each time their paths crossed he was very polite, even friendly, but he seemed to hold a piece of himself away from her. The part he withheld—the open, warm, tender part— was the part she liked the most, and she mourned its loss. How much her foolishness had cost her.

The Thursday before the event, Jessa arranged to be away from the college campus and intended to spend the entire day at the barn.

Max kept the area nearly dust-free to protect his work, so she had little cleaning to do, but she wanted to get chairs and tables set up in readiness for Friday's decorating. By Saturday at 6:30, she needed to turn the barn into a carnival scene that would rival the movie *Mary Poppins.*

She borrowed her dad's pickup and a flat trailer from a man from church and used it to haul the rented chairs, tables, striped tent canopies, and serving carts to Joy Land. The workers at the rental company loaded everything for her, but when she arrived at the barn she faced the daunting task of unloading everything herself. Unless Max would take time away from the Carry-Us-All and help her.

He didn't even hesitate when she asked, which sent a rush of appreciation through her, and it spilled from her lips. "Thank you so much, Max. I knew I could count on you."

He smiled, but he didn't verbally acknowledge her comment, robbing her of the chance to hear his smooth, deep voice. They worked in silence, carrying in the hundred chairs, dozen round soda-fountain type tables, and everything else. Then he helped her place them according to the floorplan she'd drawn out. When they were done, they were both sweaty and panting, but Jessa didn't mind. Even without decorations, the area took on an air of festivity with the carousel pieces organized neatly at one end, the colorful steam organ standing proudly in the corner, and the curved iron tables ready for guests.

Max swiped his hand over his forehead then jammed his fingers through his hair, leaving the blond strands standing in damp spikes. "Have you received many RSVPs from families? I confess I am concerned about curious children trying to climb on the unfinished horses and sleighs."

Her heart thrilled to converse with him even though it was an impersonal topic. But then again, maybe not. The renovation of the carousel was very personal to him. "I've ordered posts and yellow rope, which I'll string across this part of the barn so people won't go into your work area. If you could leave the American horse there in front of the window, though, for people to closely examine, I would appreciate it."

He crossed to the horse and put his hand on its mane. "The frame holding it is very secure. If the children would take turns, they could sit on it and have a picture taken. Of course, that is if it isn't too late to add one more idea to your celebration."

She melted. He finally sounded like the old Max, the one who wanted to help defray the costs of bringing the Carry-Us-All to life. She bounded over and put her hand near his on the horse's head. "That's a great idea. I have a digital camera. If I bring my printer, we could print them right here and let the people take them home right away."

"You will be busy in other ways, so I will take responsibility for photographing. Yes?"

He'd also be able to make sure the horse was handled gently, which would ease his mind. She nodded. "Yes. Thank you. I appreciate the help."

With a slight bob of his head, he stepped away from the horse and put his hands in his pockets. His smile remained intact, but the slight separation felt like a lash. "Then I will leave you to your work, and I will return to mine."

"Max, wait."

He paused and sent her a questioning look.

She chewed the inside of her cheek. Wait for what? She didn't know what she intended to say. She only knew she couldn't bear this distance between them any longer. She blew her bangs upward and held her hands wide. "I'm hot, thirsty, and hungry. Do you wanna go to a drive-in with me and get something? Get away from here for a little while?"

"Thank you, but I brought my lunch."

She held her breath. Would he offer to share it?

"And I have a great deal of work to do. You go ahead."

Jessa stifled a frustrated sigh. She'd asked a stupid question, but she'd apologized. Did he have to be so...so stubborn? She stomped a winding path between the tables to the door. She slammed it good and hard behind her, too.

Max cringed as the door's slam echoed through the barn. He hadn't meant to make her mad, but he'd spent a lot of time thinking over the past weeks, and the only way he knew to prove he wasn't interested in her for the sake of citizenship was to stay away until he held his prized citizenship document in his hands.

It wasn't easy to keep his distance. Everything within him longed to spend time with her, to engage in lengthy conversations, to get to know her better and better. As difficult as he found holding himself aloof, he knew it was the right thing to do. For him, and for her, too. She was young, would receive her college diploma soon, and she had plans for her future. Those plans might take her away even before he finished the Carry-Us-All. Pursuing her could pull her away from what God wanted for her. He wouldn't intrude upon God's plan. But he would continue to pray for God to reveal His plan for Jessa, for him when he finished the Carry-Us-All, and—maybe—for the two of them together.

All day Friday Jessa and a team of caterers worked as busily as ants collecting food for winter. Somehow they transformed a seventy-year-old barn into a 1900 turn-of-the-century county fair. He caught himself pausing frequently to admire the candy-striped awnings, the bright colored buntings, and the strings of what appeared to be canning jars hanging from the ceiling beams. When they plugged in the light strings, the little LED bulbs inside the jars resembled fireflies trapped behind glass. He shook his head, amazed at the details. She'd done an incredible job in planning the décor, and he looked forward to telling her so when the caterers and others cleared out.

But when the workers gathered armfuls of trash and empty boxes and headed for the door, Jessa followed them out and didn't return. So Max stood in the middle of the barn beneath the swags and unlit jars, loneliness weighing heavily on his shoulders.

CHAPTER 12

Dad had missed his calling. He should have been a politician. Jessa stood at the edge of the room with Mom, a lace parasol resting on her shoulder, and watched her father. Attired in a dapper pinstriped suit complete with vest, flat-brimmed straw hat, and white-tipped patent shoes, he paced, gestured with his cane, and smiled at all the right times during his brief lecture about W.C. Parker and the creation of the Carry-Us-All. His interjections of humor were perfectly timed, and the laughter and nods and smiles from the crowd made her chest swell with pride in him.

A lump filled her throat. Dad personified joy. He personified Joy Land. She wanted the same deep delight and sense of fulfillment Dad possessed when she entered her vocation. And in that moment, all the prayers she'd been sending up for God to give her guidance returned an unwavering, unequivocal, unmistakable reply. She knew where she belonged.

Dad finished his speech to rousing applause, then he introduced Max and opened the floor for questions. Jessa listened with half an ear, inwardly reeling at the confirmation she'd received and wishing she could shout it from the rooftops. But it would have to wait until the Carry-Us-All to Yesteryear event was over.

She had penciled in thirty minutes for Max's Q&A, but she allowed it to go a little longer rather than squelch the attendees' enthusiasm. However, when forty-five minutes had slipped by and it showed no signs of slowing, she decided she better intrude or they might lose everyone's attention before she made her presentation. Since hers involved how the attendees could give, she needed to catch them when they were still attentive and interested rather than tired and ready to put their children to bed.

She moved away from Mom and Dad and slowly ambled up next to Max, waiting for him to finish his explanation about using paint absent of turpentine but splashed with milk so the color would bear luster. As soon as she finished, she touched his elbow and smiled at the crowd.

"I'm sure you're as eager as I am to see the Carry-Us-All completed and operational. It will be beautiful thanks to this artist's amazing God-given abilities with a paintbrush. Please feel free to talk to Max later this evening. For now, can we give Max Behrend one more round of applause?"

Max bowed twice and then slipped off to the side of the room while the applause died down. Jessa set her parasol aside and linked her hands, resting them against the full skirt of her pale pink dress.

"Thank you, all of you, for coming this evening and sharing our joy with us. Yes, joy. In 1936 my great-grandfather built this park with his imagination, determination, and his own two hardworking hands. He named it Joy Land in honor of his wife, Joy, and the perseverance of three generations of Matthews men has insured the park remained open so families can come and enjoy an afternoon of fun and relaxation." She caught Dad's eye, noted the slight pinch of his brow, and momentarily lost her place in her planned speech. Nervousness attacked. But then her gaze flitted to Max, who smiled and gave her a thumbs-up sign, and her confidence returned.

Facing the crowd again, she explained the various ways businessmen could partner with Joy Land in restoring the Carry-Us-All. She found it hard to stand still when murmurs of eagerness swept through the room. She invited everyone to have their photo taken with the completed horse, swallowing giggles at children bouncing in their chairs and pulling at their parents' arms.

Then she drew in a deep breath and launched into the impromptu portion of her presentation. "I told you earlier that three generations of Matthews men have served at the helm of Joy Land. First my great-grandfather, then my grandfather, and finally my father, Stan

Matthews." She paused as a spattering of applause broke out, several people smiling at Dad. "As Joy Land enters its eighth decade of service to Shadybrook and the surrounding communities, a change is coming. A shift in leadership. No longer will a Matthews man bear the title Manager."

She risked a glance at Dad. The glimmer of tears in his blue eyes and his grip on Mom's arm nearly stopped her, but she knew he would understand and support her decision. She sniffed, lifted her chin, and finished. "Because a Matthews daughter is stepping into that position. It is my great pleasure and privilege to share with you my intention to continue the Matthews tradition of providing a place of joy, relaxation, and laughter to our community. With God's help and the inherited perseverance of the Matthews men who preceded me, I pray I will see Joy Land flourish for another generation."

Max smiled so much while taking pictures of people on the American horse, his cheeks hurt by the time ten o'clock rolled around and the last visitors finally filed out the door. But it was a good kind of hurt. A happy hurt. And now that everyone was leaving, he would be able to tell Jessa how proud he was of her decision.

But first he would have to pull her away from her father. If Stan ever decided to stop hugging her.

Max stood nearby on crumpled crepe paper and broken popcorn kernels, unable to wipe the smile from his face. The joy radiating from Stan Matthews was contagious. If Max was still a boy instead of a grown man, he would whoop and gallop around the room with glee. But all he could do was hook his thumbs in his borrowed striped suspenders and rock on his heels, waiting for his chance to congratulate Jessa.

Finally she turned, and the pretty face that had captured his heart the February night on the Carry-Us-All sleigh sent a smile in his direction. Automatically he opened his arms, and to his delight she scampered directly into his embrace. He hugged her hard, finding her a perfect fit in his arms. He kept the hug short, aware that her parents were watching, but short didn't seem to matter. By the time she stepped away from him, his pulse was thrumming as rapidly as the steam organ's most rousing tune.

"Thank you for helping me find where I belong," she said, smiling up at him with pink cheeks and tear-damp eyes.

"I've always known where you belonged." In his arms. But she probably meant Joy Land. He laughed and scratched his chin. "I am glad my few words of advice helped you."

She tipped her head, and a strand of hair slipped from the pouf in which she'd fashioned it to cup her rosy cheek. "And your prayers?"

He nodded. "And of course, my prayers. You have had those, too." Even during their disagreement, he hadn't stopped praying for her. He and *Vater* had not yet found their peace with Max's desire to be an American citizen, but God had honored the prayers for peace between the Matthews father and daughter. The realization gave Max hope for himself and his own father.

Stan gave Max a clap on the shoulder. "How about we leave this mess for another day and go home? I don't know about you, but I'm exhausted."

Kathy placed her palms against Stan's striped suit placket and laughed. "No, not yet. I'm not ready to see you change out of this costume. You look so..."

"Dapper." Jessa contributed the word.

"Yes, dapper. It's a shame people don't dress up this way anymore. It was such a dignified gathering, didn't you think?"

"Indeed." Stan puffed out his chest. "I thought people would find it childish, but nearly everyone came dressed in costume. They all seemed to enjoy the opportunity to truly take a step back in time."

"To a simpler place," Kathy said on a sigh.

Max's heart skipped a beat. He opened his mouth to share his idea.

But Jessa spoke. "Why not do it again sometime? Not a get-together like this one, but a special day when those who come in costume would receive free admission and one complimentary ticket to ride the Carry-Us-All."

Max burst out laughing. "I was going to say that."

She gawked at him. "You were?"

He nodded, smiling. "And I thought I would say make the first step-back-to-yesteryear day the same day the Parker Carry-Us-All is available for the public to ride."

Stan chuckled and shook his head. "You two make a dandy team. It's a good idea, and I will let Joy Land's up-and-coming manager make all the arrangements. But for now..." He yawned and draped his arm over his wife's shoulders. "Take me home, my dear. This dapper man is about to collapse."

The two of them sauntered off, arm in arm, leaving Max with Jessa. He looked after the happy couple. A smile pulled at his lips. He settled the smile on Jessa and extended his elbow in gentlemanly fashion. "Shall we go, too?"

She giggled and curled her slender fingers through the bend of his arm. "Let's."

EPILOGUE

Where had the year gone? Her first season as co-manager was past, along with the winter months which she spent planning park special events and hanging out in the barn with Max while he finished the Carry-Us-All. Now, from across the park, she heard the steam organ's happy tunes playing, setting the mood of celebration.

Jessa waited with Dad and Max inside Joy Land's entry ticket station for the town square's clock to chime nine o'clock. A long line of visitors waited to enter the park. And more than half of them wore 19th century costumes. Jessa gaped at her father. "Have we ever had this many show up for an opening day?"

Dad grinned. "Not that I can recall. I guess the new manager knows what she's doing." He hugged her shoulders and laughed.

Jessa shifted her attention to Max, who stood with his thumbs caught beneath the straps of his suspenders and his face shaded by the brim of a flat-brimmed straw hat identical to the ones worn by every park employee. With Dad's blessing, she'd reinstated the red vests and straw hats, and the attire added to the festivity. Everyone needed an escape from time to time, and Joy Land would offer it for as long as God allowed their business to flourish.

Bong! Bong! Bong!

The crowd momentarily fell silent, then people began counting the tolls. "Six...seven...eight...nine!" A cheer rose.

Dad grinned. "Time to open the gates." He pressed a button, and the iron gates swung slowly inward.

While the ticket-takers assisted the eager attendees, Jessa gripped Max's arm with both hands, almost bouncing in excitement.

"Look at this, Max. It's wonderful! Have you ever seen anything so wonderful?"

"Yes, I have."

She looked up at him in surprise, and the glimmer in his eyes temporarily stole her ability to breathe.

Slowly he reached inside his vest and removed a folded sheet of paper. He held it out to her. "There is this."

Her fingers trembling, she unfolded it, then gasped. She clapped her hand to her face. "Oh, Max..." She held his official citizenship document.

He plucked the paper from her hand and set it aside. His hands raised to cup her cheeks and he lifted her face to him. "And there is you." A smile curved his lips. "Now that I am an American, I can ask you...would you be willing to spend the rest of your life with a *karussell* painter?"

Jessa rose up on tiptoe and answered with a kiss.

DOCTOR KAT

JULANE HIEBERT

Whatsoever ye do, do it heartily,
as to the Lord, and not unto men;
knowing that of the Lord ye shall receive
the reward of the inheritance:
for ye serve the Lord Christ.
COLOSSIANS 3:23

Chapter 1

Chicago
Mid June, 1905

"This is the most ridiculous scheme you've ever invented, Kathleen. I only wish your father were here to tell you, since you seem to translate everything I say into some kind of threat or debate or—"

"Father would shake my hand and tell me how proud he was of me, Mother." Kathleen Weston took a deep breath. "And it's not a scheme. It's a well thought out choice."

Her mother lowered herself to the rose brocade settee and fanned herself with a lace handkerchief. "A well thought out choice, you say? I suppose this whole idea of your becoming some kind of...of animal doctor was a well thought out choice as well. You've no idea the angst your chosen occupation has caused me. You've made me the laughing stock of my friends. If only you'd have followed in your father's footsteps and become a real doctor."

Kathleen lowered herself to the settee and gripped her mother's hands. "I am a real doctor. My diploma from McKillip reads Kathleen Olivia Weston, Doctor of Veterinary Medicine. Perhaps if you emphasize the doctor title, they'll overlook the rest of it."

"And then they'll wonder why you didn't stay in Chicago. And must I tell you, yet once again, I have the same question? After all, we do have horses in Chicago." She dabbed her nose with the bit of lace in her hand. "Why Kansas? How could that possibly be a well thought out choice? There's nothing west of Kansas City except wind, snakes, and uncouth cowboys. Hardly a place for a refined young lady to take up residence, let alone a career that's still considered too dangerous and un…un—"

"Sophisticated? Is that the word you're searching for, Mother? You know how Papa hated that description of our life. I think he'd much rather have taken care of animals than some of the whiney women he encountered all those years as a doctor."

Her mother stood. "That is quite enough, Kathleen. I haven't the strength to argue, and I'll not defend our social status. It's those whiney women, as you call them, who've made our very comfortable life here possible. The first time one of your animals pays you and sings the praises of your skill, please let me know." She dabbed her eyes. "Oh, my dear…I do love you. Even after these ugly words, I do love you."

Kathleen wrapped her arms around her mother. "And I love you, too. I know this isn't what you wanted for me. But I'll never be able to thank you enough for allowing me to pursue my dreams. I'll write as soon as I'm settled. And yes, they do have a post office in Lyndale."

Something that resembled a smile twitched her mother's lips. "How could you possibly know, my dear? If I remember correctly, you chose Lyndale by closing your eyes and making circles above a map before you finally pointed to a specific location."

"And if I remember correctly, you gave my hand a bump, hoping, I'm sure, my finger would land on Chicago."

"It was me who bumped you, Kate. Not Mama."

Mother turned a mild frown on the freckled face of Kathleen's six-year-old brother. "It's Kathleen, Andrew, not Kate. If I had wanted her called Kate that's what I would I would have named her."

Kathleen tapped Andrew's nose with her finger. "You can call me, Kate. Mama scolds, but that was Papa's name for me, too."

His chubby cheeks puffed with a grin. "I don't want you to leave, but I made you something." He handed her a crudely wrapped package. "Will you open it, please? I want to see you be surprised. I made it all by myself."

"Of course I'll open it. I love surprises." She slid to the floor and pulled him down beside her. "You made this all by yourself?" She untied the knot in the string, then bit the side of her cheek when the prized gift was revealed. At the top, DOKTR KAT sprawled across an oblong board and underneath the title it read VETNARY. A hank of red yarn was attached to the top corners to make a hangar, the nails holding it bent and uneven. A lump swelled in her throat, and she willed her mother to not say a word.

"You have to turn it over to see the rest. I ran out of room on the front and couldn't put your whole name. Will you still like it?"

She turned the sign over, and one lone E swam before her tear-filled eyes. "Oh, Andy, I love it. And you know what? I'm going to hang it right outside my office and tell everyone in Lyndale, Kansas, that the best little brother in the whole world made it special for me."

"Really? Will you tell them my name, too?"

She pulled him to her. "I will, for certain."

He squirmed away and his chin wobbled. "I'll miss you. I wish you didn't have to go away to be a vet'nary."

"She doesn't have to go away, Andrew. She's choosing to leave us."

"You make it sound as though I'm never coming back, Mother." She stood then pulled her brother to his feet and tweaked his nose. "I'll miss you, too, squirt. But I promise to write and tell you all about Kansas. And I'll bring you something special when I come home at Christmas."

He gave her a crooked grin. "A cowboy hat, Kate. Bring me a cowboy hat."

"I would hope you could find something more suitable for the boy, Kathleen."

"I'll only bring him a cowboy hat if there's a cowboy wearing it." She winked at her.

"That's disgusting, Kathleen, both the silly proclamation and the unladylike gesture with your eye. I do think you enjoy my discomfort." She cradled Kathleen's face in her hands. "But then, you're so very much like your father, I suppose I should expect it." Her voice softened and her eyes swam with tears.

"That's the nicest compliment you could give me, you know. I love you, Mother. I'm glad I won't have to tell you goodbye at the train station. It's easier this way."

Her mother grasped her shoulders. "My dear daughter, you've never done anything the easy way. However, this time I must agree with you. I'm not at all sure I could stand watching that train roll away from us."

Kathleen swallowed. "I know." She kissed Mother's cheek, then placed her brother's gift in the trunk with her treasured books and ran her fingers along the inscription before she closed the lid.

DOKTR KAT, VETNARY. It didn't matter how it was spelled, the sound of it pleased her.

"Are you telling me there are no trains traveling west of Kansas City?" Kathleen eyed the man at the ticket counter. This was not a fact she'd want her mother to know.

"No, ma'am. I'm not saying there are no trains traveling west of Kansas City. What I'm saying is, there's no rail service to Lyndale, Kansas. I can get you close, but you'll have to rent a buggy to go the rest of the way in."

"Exactly what do you consider close?" Why hadn't she checked on this before now? Because who would believe there were still places inaccessible by rail, that's why. What if her mother was right, and there was nothing but wind, snakes, and uncouth cowboys in her scientifically chosen place of practice?

"Well, let me see now." He went to a map on the wall and tapped his finger on a spot west of Topeka. "I can get you here—Junction City. From there, Lyndale's about half-a-day buggy ride."

"Then I need a ticket to this Junction City place." She counted her money and handed it to him. "I guess the people in Chicago don't know train service is still limited in some areas."

The man laughed. "People in Chicago don't think there's anything west of here except tornadoes, rattle snakes, and ill-mannered cowboys."

She smiled at him. "And they must have gotten their information from my mother."

"You must not have people there, since you don't know how to get there and all."

"No, no family. I'm Doctor Kathleen Weston, and I'm going to Lyndale to set up my practice."

One long wrinkle snaked across the man's forehead. "They have a doctor in Lyndale, ma'am. I know because he's been through here. That town isn't more than a hundred people on the Fourth of July. Can't imagine them needing another doctor."

"Oh, I'm not a medical doctor. I'm a doctor of veterinary medicine, sir."

"A veter— An animal doctor? But you're a woman."

"And this is 1905, not the Dark Ages." At least he acknowledged her gender.

"I don't mean any disrespect, but what's a woman like you going to do when one of them rancher's cows need..."

"First I'll pray that I'll remember everything I've been taught. I'll roll up my sleeves, do what I have to do, and then I'll ask for a good strong cup of coffee. Does that answer your question?" Oh, it did her good to see him turn red.

"You don't mean you'd actually..." He grimaced.

"That's exactly what I mean. Now, may I have my ticket, please?"

The train ride to Junction City gave her time to reflect on her years of schooling. The same kind of derision had been a daily occurrence. Only by proving herself, over and over again, had she been able to gain the respect of her fellow students—and those were few. She knew it would be hard. Papa had warned her. She expected no special treatment, and she got none. And while she suspicioned she'd been given tasks and assignments not required of her male colleagues, there was no way to prove her theory. Only one thing, one seemingly small thing, had kept her going—Papa's words.

"Remember this, Kathleen. Colossians 3:23 says 'Whatsoever ye do, do it heartily, as to the Lord, and not unto men; knowing that of the Lord ye shall receive the reward of the inheritance: for ye serve the Lord Christ.'"

Chapter 2

The sky wore the pink blush of dusk when Kathleen arrived in Lyndale. While she'd managed to rent a horse and buggy for the journey from Junction City, the livery owner would not allow her to leave so late in the day—said he wouldn't send a young woman alone across the prairie at night.

In retrospect, she shouldn't have flaunted her doctor status. It meant nothing more to the man than a reason to give her what was obviously the poorest specimen of a horse in the livery. She had obliged him, and taken a room in the hotel until early morning. She could almost see the glee in the man's eye as he took her money and handed her the reins of the swayback creature he'd hooked to an even sorrier appearing buggy.

One wheel had shimmied and wobbled like a circus contortionist the entire way. She'd prayed it wouldn't fall off, and it hadn't. She didn't savor the idea of being stranded with a broken buggy wheel in the middle of nowhere, and the dread of predicted snakes shivered across her shoulders as she'd made her way across grass that was belly high to the poor horse. It didn't help that the south wind had blown so hard her eyes were nearly matted shut from the dust. Now, all she needed was an uncouth cowboy to finish the dismal picture of Kansas her mother had painted.

A welcome splay of light emanated from a large glass window with HOTEL painted in large black letters. Similar buildings adjoined on either side. The one on the left was dark, but she could make out the sign—CONNER'S DRY GOODS. A sliver of light peeked from behind closed shades on the windows of the one on the right. Perhaps a private residence? It didn't matter. She was dusty, hungry, and tired.

All she wanted now was a place to stable the horse, a hot meal, an even hotter bath, and a soft bed. In the morning she'd find a suitable place for her practice. *Her practice.* Just thinking those words gave her fresh motivation.

She tied the horse to the railing in front of the hotel, though she doubted the pitiful animal would have taken a step without her urging. Tomorrow she'd give the poor thing a good exam, though she doubted Trembley would be interested in her diagnosis. Other than a dog barking in the distance, the town was quiet and the street deserted. That was fine with her. She didn't relish drawing the curiosity of a crowd before she was ready to make her presence known in a more dignified manner.

Two large ferns graced either side of the wide double doors of the hotel lobby. A worn blue and gold carpet edged with scrolls of red was anchored to the scuffed plank floor by several brown leather chairs. It wasn't Chicago, but it was clean.

An older woman stood behind the desk, her once-blond graying hair was wadded into a loose bun, of sorts, on the very top of her head and held in place with a silver comb and a yellow pencil. She looked up when Kathleen reached the counter, and a smile brightened her heavily powdered face. "Well, goodness me. Look at you, dearie. What's a young lady like you doing coming into Lyndale, Kansas, this hot and windy June night?" Her blue eyes twinkled. "My name's Maggie, by the way."

Kathleen returned the woman's smile. "I'm Kathleen Weston and I hope to make Lyndale my home. Would you perhaps have a room available until I can find a suitable place to live?"

The woman crossed her arms on the counter and leaned toward her. "You mean you aim to stay more than one night? You know, sweetheart, there's not a lot of people who wander in here stating they plan to stay. Normally I'd ask questions that weren't none of my howdy-do, but you don't appear to be one who'd up and cause mischief of any kind. If you're going to stay around there'll be plenty of time later. I tell you what—I not only have a room available, I also have a bath, can get you a hot meal, and I know where I can get the key to a home I think might suit you just fine."

She sucked in a deep breath, grateful the woman hadn't pried. "Would you also have a place I might stable a rather sorry looking horse? I need to make sure the poor animal is settled before I do another thing."

The lady opened a large book, gave it a twist, and pushed it to her "Sign here. You don't have to tell me...got the critter from Trembley's Livery in Junction City, didn't you? Small black horse with a back so swayed you could build a bridge across it?"

Kathleen signed her name. K.O. Weston, her official signature, but chose to omit the prized DVM behind it. "You know the man?"

"I know the horse. Poor thing has made more trips between Junction and here than I can count. Trembley sends him our way, and Doc Finley takes pity on the old mare. He brushes her down, feeds her good for a few days, then finally trails her back to the livery. He threatened to keep her the last time. This might just be the trip to seal his threat."

Kathleen perused her surroundings. "You mentioned a hot meal. Is there a restaurant close by?"

The woman chuckled and walked to a closed door at the side of the room. She winked at her and then opened the door, put two fingers in her mouth, and let out a whistle the likes of which Kathleen had never heard. At least not coming from a woman. "Hey Doc! Got a hungry one here. Still have some steak and taters?"

She was not at all prepared for the cook who emerged. Of course she'd seen handsome men before tonight. There'd been plenty to choose from in college, had she so desired. Many, in fact, who'd suggested marriage, but always with a condition—give up her foolish notion of becoming a veterinarian and become a wife and mother like God intended a woman in the first place. Her reply to all had become repetitive thanks, but no thanks. But...oh, my!

She was not a small person herself, standing five feet nine inches, but this...this specimen filled the doorway clear to the top. He had an apron, of sorts, tied around his middle, and a gun belt slung low on his hips. And his rolled-up sleeves revealed tan arms with muscles she'd be at a lack to identify. There was strip of cloth tied to keep his hair out of his eyes, but didn't hide the thick, black locks that hung to his shoulders. His eyes were...were...well... She'd bet her diploma those blue eyes could see right through her, and she crossed her arms across her waist just in case.

"Got taters, Maggie. Had a nice chunk of steak but threw it to Daisy a few minutes ago. She's a bit off her feed, though. Probably hasn't touched it. I can rinse it off if you'd like."

Kathleen's hand involuntarily flew to her mouth.

"Don't you pay him nary one minutes notice, dearie. He's just trying to get a rise out of both of us. Kyle Finley, you behave yourself. This is"—she turned to look at the book—"Miss K.O. Weston. It is Miss isn't it?"

She nodded. This was the Doc Finley the woman mentioned earlier?

"Miss Weston plans to make Lyndale her home, then you up and pull some fool trick like this. I oughta turn you over my knee."

He laughed. "Who're you going to get to help you, Maggie?" He stepped from the doorway and gave her a hug, then bowed to Kathleen. "I'm sorry, ma'am. Maggie here would think something was wrong with me if I didn't tease her. I have plenty of steak and potatoes, if you care to dine."

"Give her time to catch her breath, you big hunk of nothin'." Maggie took her arm. "You come with me, sweetheart. I'll show you to your room and even draw your bath for you."

"Sure you don't need my help drawing that bath?" He winked at Kathleen.

"Stop it, Kyle. Have you no manners whatsoever?" Maggie steered her toward the steps. "And you can bring that food to her room. No need of her sitting in there with all those ruffians gaping at her while she eats. Don't think you can pull any shenanigans. I'll be in the next room and you know how thin these walls are. And while you're waiting, you can bed down the old mare Trembley pawned off on her. You know where to put her."

"Is he always so...so uncouth?" Mother's warning had proved true. Kyle Finley wasn't a cowboy, but if he was a sample of the men around here she was in big trouble.

Maggie patted her hand. "Not always. I think he was as surprised to lay eyes on you as you were, no doubt, on him. Kyle has every female in these parts wishin' he'd notice them. He pays them no mind. Says he has no time or room in his life for a woman. Then you come along and he acts like a schoolboy."

"Does he own the restaurant, or whatever business is behind those closed doors?"

"Oh, it's a restaurant all right. My place, in fact, but I can't be in two places at the same time, and Kyle likes to cook. Comes from good Finley stock, but wants no part of their penchant for fame and fortune. His family all moved to Kansas City years ago. Guess they outgrew the likes of Lyndale. We're just glad Kyle decided to come back here after he finished his schooling. Good man. Don't come any better, even though you saw the rascal side of him a little while ago." She took a lamp from the shelves behind the counter, lit it, crooked her finger and beckoned her to follow. "That room and bath I promised are upstairs. You need your trunk? I can holler for Kyle to fetch it."

She lifted her valise from the floor. "I have nightclothes in here, but I could use the small trunk in the back of the buggy so I'll have fresh clothing for tomorrow."

Maggie turned and cupped her hands around her mouth. "Listen up, Kyle. This little gal needs the small trunk from her buggy. Did ya hear me?"

"The whole town heard you, Maggie. I'll bring it right up."

She patted Kathleen on the shoulder. "Don't worry, I won't let him in your room. Watch your step. These stairs are steep."

Kathleen paused on the bottom step. "Ma'am, do you mind if I address you as Maggie? I don't remember hearing your last name."

The woman laughed. "Last names aren't important around here, dearie. Some would call us uncivilized, but we'll grow on you."

"So...what about the gentleman?"

"Kyle?" She giggled. "He'd get a real kick out of being called a gentleman."

"You called him Doc. Is that a nickname?"

"Guess you could call it that, only it's the nickname of every true medicine man I've ever known. Kyle's the only doctor for miles around."

"And he also cooks? What happens if he is called away while he's fixing food?"

"He washes his hands, gives me a holler and I finish whatever he started. You're not from a small town, are you?"

She shook her head. "Chicago."

Maggie led the way to the end of the hall. "Here it is. Room 6. I call it our honeymoon suite. Mostly because it's the only room in this hotel with just one bed. Usually put as many as I can in a room, but keep this one special. If Kyle pays a call to a couple he thinks might be fussin' or just in need of a night away, he sends them my way. We fix 'em up with the honeymoon suite and, sure enough, they leave happy the next morning. Doc says it's good for both our businesses. He delivers a little one nine months later, they pay him in whatever they have to spare. He won't take money from nobody. Barters for his pay, shares the spoils and it keeps us both happy."

She put the lamp on the marble top dresser. "The bathing tub is down the hall two doors. Has its own separate room. Course, that's nothing new for a city gal like you, but it's downright special out here. Towels are hanging on the hooks, soap in the dish, and there's even some rosewater on the shelf. You take your time. I'll knock twice when I have the water ready for you, and will knock three times when I bring the food so you know it's me."

"Are there other guests? Is there...am I in any kind of...I guess I'm wondering why this Kyle, or Doc, carries a gun."

Maggie shrugged. "I'm not sure the silly thing is even loaded. You saw him. Now you tell me, if you were someone bent on mischief and you encountered a man like him wearing a gun, would you still try something foolish?"

"But isn't there a sheriff or someone in town to handle such matters?"

"Uh-huh. Kyle."

"You mean Mr. Finley is a doctor, a cook and the sheriff?" Was there nothing this man couldn't do?

"All those things you mentioned, plus the undertaker. He has a sign in his office that says *If I can't cure you, I'll bury you for free.*"

"That's terrible." Oh, how her mother would gloat if she could hear this conversation.

"Ain't it though?" Maggie patted her arm. "You best commence with your ablutions or you'll end up having to eat a cold supper."

She waited until the woman left, then sat on the edge of the bed. So this was the honeymoon suite. Maggie wasn't kidding. One single bed, and the tub was in a separate room down the hall two doors. She flopped backwards and put the pillow over her face. She'd allow herself a good long laugh before commencing with her ablutions. She could always cry later.

CHAPTER 3

Kathleen stopped at the bottom of the stairs and squinted against the sunlight streaming through the big window. She wouldn't tell her hostess, but the honeymoon bed had a sway in the middle as bad as Trembley's old mare.

"I was wondering if you were alive up there, dearie. Kyle said if you didn't come down by 7:30 I was to check and see if you'd died in your sleep. Wanted me to be sure and tell you about that sign in his office." Maggie emptied a jug of water onto one of the ferns then set the container on the floor and brushed her hands along her black taffeta skirt. "Kyle hitched up your buggy for you before he left." She pulled a ribbon from around her neck and retrieved a key from her ample bosom. "Left the key to your house, though."

"The key to my house? Do I not have a choice where to live?"

"This ain't Chicago, dearie. Here in Lyndale your choice of houses is take this one or stay on here. I don't think you'll be disappointed, but if you decide to stay here Kyle will drag your things back and I'll be glad for the company."

"But what about furniture. Is there somewhere—"

"Furnished."

"And maybe I could have a bite—"

"Kyle took breakfast. It's in the warming oven of your stove."

"How much—"

"Rent? You needn't worry your pretty little red head about that one bit. You see, it's the old Finley place. Like I told you, they moved back east, all the way to Kansas City, and left the house like they was comin' back. Only everyone here knows they won't. Kyle says he'd rattle around like a marble in a tin can all by his lonesome, so he's glad to see someone come along who'll put a light in the window again." Maggie motioned to the door. "You best get going before word gets around there's a new unmarried gal in town. Just take the street in front of the hotel and follow it clear to the end. That'll be the place."

Kathleen grabbed the woman's arm. "Wait, Maggie. You told me last night that Mr. Finley barters for his pay. If he won't take rent what will he expect from me?"

Maggie plunked her hands on her plump hips. "Not one thing more than you're willing to give, 'cept perhaps a cup of coffee now and then. He'd never call himself a gentleman, but I'm here to tell you he is...through and through. So don't go thinking you're in any kind of danger. Now, you better run along. That poor horse has stood hitched to that buggy long enough. Oh, and by the way, Kyle says he's not going to return the deprived thing this time. Says since she's a female, all she needs is someone to tell her how pretty she is, give her a good back rub every day, make sure she's fed, and she'll come around and be a good steady work horse in no time."

She bit her tongue. Just as she was beginning to think Kyle Finley might have some good character qualities, his comparison of a female to the poor excuse of an animal only proved her mother was right. Did he really think sweet talk, a back rub, and food would make a woman a good steady work horse?

"You'll find a barn behind the house. Said to tell you to put the little lady in there and he'll see to her when he gets back into town."

"And when might that be?" She intended to look after the horse first thing. In retrospect, she should have taken care of it last night. *Your patient first, Miss Weston, before personal comfort.* How many times had she heard that proclamation?

Maggie shrugged. "Have no idea. He went out to the Clements farm. Seems Theodore's old milk cow has a plugged spigot."

The man made house calls for animals, too? "I had no idea this Doctor Finley was a veterinarian. I assumed his was a regular medical practice."

"A veter...oh, you mean one of them fancy animal doctors? No,

Kyle's a real doc, if that's what you mean. People around here don't much care about the initials behind a name. Most of 'em figure if Doc is smart enough to treat a person, he's smart enough to fix their animals as well."

She wanted to argue the point but doubted Maggie would understand. She'd take her things to the house appointed for her, tend to Trembley's mare, and wait for the surprised look on Kyle Finley's face when she asked how he fixed the plugged spigot. Did he bury animals free, too?

Her first impression of the house chosen for her punched holes in her wildest imagination of what she might call home in Kansas. The last dwelling before the open prairie, the two-story house sat well back from the street and was surrounded by a white picket fence. The yard was fenced in such a manner that a large box was created, its open side allowing ample room for a horse and buggy without encroaching onto the street. From her vantage point, she could also make out a wide gate that opened from the prairie side of the house. She made a mental note of its convenience for future patients. Though she would have rather been closer to the other businesses, she didn't suppose it would take long for people to find her. After all, how could they miss the old Finley place?

Going through the side gate revealed a whole new world, and she caught her breath. This was as lovely as anything she'd ever seen in her affluent Chicago neighborhood. Why would Kyle Finley not want to call this place home? Not only was there the barn Maggie mentioned, but several other outbuildings as well, all painted white with dark green trim. Even the paths leading to them looked as though they had been freshly swept clean of debris. A large weeping willow tree spread her branches over a manicured section of the north lawn, a backdrop for the white willow furniture arranged in front of it. She blinked. Mother would give up her Flinch parties to receive guests in such a setting.

"You must be Miss Weston."

Kathleen whirled toward the voice. An elderly, gray-haired man stood not ten feet from her, a hoe in one hand.

"Sorry if I frightened you. I'm Leonard. Maggie said she'd send you this way, but I don't suppose she remembered to tell you I'd be here. She said I was to carry your trunks into the house and show you around since Kyle is busy this morning."

"You did frighten me. Do you...do you live here, Mr. Leonard?"

He chuckled. "There's no mister in front of my name, and no back name, either. Just Leonard will do. And to answer your question— yes, I live here."

"I'm so sorry to intrude. I understood the home was empty."

"Well, the inside is full of furniture and the like, but there's no one living in it. But then, even when the Finleys were here it might as well have been empty. It takes more than warm bodies and things to make a home, you know. Kyle invited me to live in the big house, but I didn't take him up on it, so he fixed me up a real good place out in that little building." He pointed to a small shed not far from the house. "Snug as can be in the winter. Catches the breeze from all sides in the summer. Couldn't ask for anything more, except maybe a pretty little lady living in this place."

She smiled at him. He seemed harmless enough. "Are you the caretaker, then? It's beautiful back here."

"Isn't it, though? I'm not sure who takes care of who, ma'am. It does my old bones good to see things all done up. Reckon it doesn't hurt the trees and bushes, either. Kyle doesn't care much about highfalutin' stuff, but he does have a special liking for what God makes." He nodded toward the horse and buggy. "Old Trembley got your money, I see. Kyle says I'm to keep her here. Fancies himself as much a veterinarian as a medical doctor. Fact is, sometimes I think he'd rather doctor the likes of that old mare than he would people. Well, I best be cartin' them trunks into the house, or Maggie will give me a tongue lashing for sure."

"Thank you. If you'll just take them into the house, I can manage from there. I'll go put the horse in the barn like Mr. Finley wanted, then I'll come in. Oh..." She dug in her pocket. "Maggie gave me the key."

He chuckled. "Everyone in this town knows the place hasn't been locked since the Finleys moved. They could've helped themselves over and over if they didn't think so highly of Kyle. Maggie just feels important when she digs that key from the front of her dress. No, you keep it. You might feel safer if you was to lock up at night."

"But you'll always be here, right?"

"Always here, unless and until the Lord calls me home." He unloaded the buggy and set the trunks on the ground. "You know how to unhitch this buggy once you get to the barn?

"As a matter of fact, I do."

"That's good. That's good. I've been praying the Lord would send some good woman for Kyle. I've made a whole list of gotta haves."

"Gotta haves?" She didn't much like the idea this Leonard thought she might be an answer to his prayers. But she was curious about his list.

"You know—gotta have more than a pretty face. Gotta have enough stomach to not faint at the sight of blood. Gotta have sense enough to let Kyle think he's the boss. Gotta have—"

She raised her hand. "And because I can unhitch a buggy, you think I fit somewhere on that list?"

He nodded "Unhitching a buggy shows me you have more than a pretty face. Time will reveal the other things."

Well, she might as well put a stop to this before it went one more *gotta have* further. "Would it help you mark me off the list if you knew I was not, in any way, in the market for a husband? Not now, and nowhere in the foreseeable future."

"You got something against being a wife and mother?"

"No. Not at all. It just doesn't fit with my plans."

Leonard smiled and shook his head. "Your plans, huh?" He picked up a trunk and hefted it to his shoulder. "I'll carry these things in for you while you go take care of the horse and buggy. If you need me, all you have to do is holler. I'm never far."

She slipped her hand through the cheek piece of the bridle. She'd walk the horse to the barn then decide what to do with her. "Come on, pretty lady. Let's get you rubbed down and fed then..." She snorted. She was doing just what Kyle Finley said he'd do—tell her she's pretty, rub her back, and feed her.

"Wait a minute, missy." Leonard trotted up behind her. He probably had one more *gotta have* to add to his list.

"I almost forgot to tell you. You might want to be careful when you open the barn door. Daphne will do most anything to escape, and it's like threading a needle with a rope to get her back into the barn."

"Daphne?"

"Kyle's goat. Got her when he delivered the last Hamilton baby. Oh, and there's Prudence."

She rolled her lips. "Who, or what, is Prudence?"

"Prudence is a gilt. That's a girl pig that hasn't—"

"I know what a gilt is, Leonard."

"You know what a gilt is?" He grinned at her. "Missy, you surely are more than a pretty face."

"Is there anything else I should know before I venture into the barn?"

"Well..." He took a deep breath. "There's Rufus the rooster and Ruby his hen. Then there's Gwendolyn. She's a goose." He frowned and twisted his mouth to one side. "You want me to name them all?"

"All? There's more, and they all have names?"

He nodded. "Kyle's an old softie, but he wouldn't like it if he heard me tell you. Says we humans aren't all lumped together. We've got names, so why shouldn't animals be given the same respect?"

"So I suppose if he had an entire herd of cattle, he'd name them all?"

"It's not likely that will ever happen, Miss Weston. You see, the animals in that barn represent a family to Kyle. Take Daphne, for example. For the Hamiltons to give a nanny was like them giving money away. They have seven little ones, and they need every drop of milk their goats can give. Kyle doesn't need the money. Doesn't need the animals, either, but he knows how proud these people are so takes them with a smile, brings them here, names them, and says they're probably the best Finleys this country has ever known."

"I suppose if I'm to live here, I'll learn to tell them apart with or without names. I'll be careful opening the door, but please don't tell me he keeps them penned up all the time. Animals are like people— they need to have fresh air and be allowed to run and climb and root. If the door was opened of a morning so they could come and go as they pleased, they'd likely put themselves in the barn at night."

He cocked his head. "You don't say? Yes, ma'am. You surely are more than a pretty face. You be sure and give me a holler if you need help, now, you hear?"

"Thank you, Leonard. I will." Oh, how her peers at the college would laugh if they knew people named the likes of goats and gilts. At least they weren't called Kathleen.

CHAPTER 4

Theodore Clements wiped a frayed bandana across his forehead. "Surely do thank ya, Doc. Tried ever'thing I knew before askin' ya to come all the way out here for a…well, reckon you know why 'tis you're here. Wished I woulda thought to tie one leg like that. Crazy cow busted my knee when I yanked on her…when I pulled on… doggone it, Doc. I'm right grateful."

The man's obvious discomfort never failed to amuse Kyle. He often found men much more reticent to talk about what ailed them, and it seemed even more difficult when they tried to explain what bothered one of their animals. "No need to thank me, my good man. I'm grateful for the trust you show me."

Clements pointed to the house. "You best come sit a spell. Hilda would never forgive me if I didn't bring you in for a cup of coffee and a biscuit. Besides, we gotta surprise for you this time, seein' as how you won't take money.

Kyle grinned at the burly man. "Sure wouldn't want to miss one of Hilda's flaky biscuits. I don't suppose you might have a drop or two of your sweet clover honey, would you?"

"Lands, Doc. Hilda's got a jar with your name on it sittin' right on the kitchen table just waitin' for ya." Theodore seemed pleased he'd asked.

"Is that my surprise? Can't think of anything I'd like better, or could use more. I do have a liking for Hilda's biscuits and honey."

The beefy farmer plunged his hands in his pockets and stirred the dust with the toe of one boot. "Not the surprise. Hope you ain't disappointed. Hate it terrible we ain't got cash."

Kyle gripped the man's shoulder. "I wouldn't take cash if you had it. You know that, don't you? Folks around here don't owe me more than what you already pay me. A good friend is all I ask."

"Won't call ya again if ya won't take somethin' for your trouble. But right glad to know you don't look down your nose at us poor folk. I reckon what we've got for ya today will be somethin' you can use right off. Don't have to wait for it to lay eggs, or get fat enough to butcher, and don't have to milk it ever' day."

"You got my curiosity hopping, Theodore. How long you gonna keep me in suspense?"

The big man grinned and cupped his hands around his mouth. "Hildaaa! You can come out now." He turned to Kyle. "It was her idea so I'll let her show ya."

Kyle admired Hilda Clements. Big with their first child, due—by his estimate, though she'd been reluctant to answer some of his questions—in late July, she stood as tall as her husband and had a normal stride that could keep up with most men. Wheat colored braids crossed in the back and were pinned in place on top of her head. Always pink-cheeked, as though she'd been out in the sun without a bonnet, her smile was genuine and her voice soft as a summer breeze.

"*Komm mit mir.*" She pointed to a lilac bush near the water pump and beckoned him to follow her.

"No, Hilda, English. Speak English to the doctor."

She shrugged. "Too often I forget. Excuse, please. Come with me." She stepped to the bush, then beckoned him to come closer.

Theodore chuckled. "You'll have to get on your knees, Doc. Hilda don't bend so good these days."

He dropped to his knees and parted the lower branches. Four little fur balls lay in a heap, one gray, one yellow, one black, and one calico. "Mama cat was obviously a popular lady."

"You choose. *Ja?*"

The kittens stirred, and the calico opened its eyes and tottered away from its siblings.

Kyle picked it up and cuddled it in his hand. "Are they ready to leave their mama? I could use a good mouser, but this one seems awful small."

Hilda cupped one hand and held the other one a little bit above it. "*Ja, kleines Miezekätzchen.*" She blushed. "Little. Little pussycat.

The kitten curled into a ball in the palm of his hand, and its purr vibrated against the base of his thumb. He eyed Theodore. "You sure they're ready to be weaned?"

The big man tipped his head back and laughed. "Better be. You still got that sign up in your office?"

Hilda slapped at him. "*Nein, nein,* Teeodore."

He put his arm around her shoulders and pulled her to him. "Don't worry, my *liebling.* He winked at Kyle. "They're as ready as they're gonna get, I reckon, Don't know what's happened to the mama. Always came to the barn with the other cats when I was milking, but haven't seen her for a few days. Hilda's been feeding these cow's milk and they've started swatting at flies and grasshoppers. When they get a little bigger they'll chase most anything that moves."

"I've not had much experience with cats. You think it'll live without milk?"

Theodore gave Hilda a squeeze. "Will it live without milk?"

"*Ja.* But water it will need. And love. Much *lieben.*"

He wouldn't tell Theodore, but the reason he hadn't much experience with cats is they always made him sneeze. However, now with Miss Weston on the premises, it would get the *lieben* it required without his involvement. He cradled the kitten in one hand while he climbed into his buggy. "Let me know if that cow needs more attention. You know where to find me."

"*Warten*—wait! The biscuits I bake for you." Hilda brushed past him, her long strides propelling her to the house. She may not bend so good, but even large with child she moved with ease and grace.

"Can't leave without the biscuits and honey, Doc." Theodore beamed. "My Hilda...she's a good hearted woman, isn't she?"

Kyle nodded. "She is at that, Theodore. You're a lucky man."

"You could be so lucky. Just take a good look around the next Sunday meeting. You could have your pick, you know—eeny, meeny, miny, moe."

Kyle shrugged. "That's not how I want to choose a wife. Truth is, Theodore—for me it's not so much a matter of what woman I can live with as it is what woman I can't live without."

Hilda returned before her husband responded. She handed Kyle a paper bag. "For you. *Tausend danke!*"

"And a thousand thanks to you, too, Hilda. I'd come in the middle of the night for your biscuits and honey."

He leaned from his buggy to shake hands with Theodore. "You come get me when that little one decides to make an appearance."

"Sure, sure. When Hilda says it's time, I'll come."

"Just make sure there's plenty of hot coffee."

"*Und* biscuits." Hilda smiled at him.

"And biscuits. Lots of biscuits."

Kathleen used her shoulder to slide the heavy barn door open with caution. She'd unhitched the buggy while still outside, a tedious task made more uncomfortable from the hot sun trying to melt the top of her head. But the time it would take to get both horse and buggy inside would give anything close by ample time to escape through the opening.

Beams of light from a row of windows on the back wall illuminated the spacious interior. Barn swallows dipped low above her, then winged their way to their mud nests high in the beams. Two pigeons balanced on a wire that stretched across the wide alley between a long row of stalls, but they seemed content to watch. She tugged the door shut, and it was as if she'd given some sort of signal. A flutter of wings, and Rufus perched himself on a near stall partition and crowed. Numerous hens cackled, clucked, and scratched in dust and straw below him, though which one was Ruby was not apparent. The fattest pig she'd ever seen grunted, snuffed, and waddled from one of the stalls. And out of the corner of her eye Kathleen caught movement that soon made itself known as the heretofore illusive

Daphne. The animal raised on its hind legs, planted its front legs on Kathleen's midsection, and promptly nibbled two buttons from her blouse before she could react.

"Why, you...you goat, you." She shoved her away then grabbed at her blouse. They were strategic buttons, to say the least. She'd dropped the horse's bridle when Daphne attacked, but the animal had put itself in a stall and stood, head down, with the two pigeons now perched along the sway of her back, as though they'd found a new nesting site.

Prudence waddled to Kathleen's side and rubbed against her legs with such force it knocked her feet from under her and she landed on her bottom. Dust flew, she sneezed, and the pig proceeded to root around until at last, with a groan, it plopped its fat body across her legs. It hurt, but try as she might she wasn't able to dislodge the animal.

Daphne must have recognized the advantage, and moved behind Kathleen. At least she didn't have buttons down her back. However, she did have combs holding her hair in place, but that revelation came too late.

Oh, if only Mother could see her now, sitting in a heap on a dusty barn floor with a pig draped across her legs, trying to keep decent by holding her blouse shut, while a goat proceeded to slobber on her neck and slurp the combs from her hair. She battled dissolving into hysterical laughter. Or tears.

The creak of the barn door opening gave her hope Leonard had missed her and was coming to her rescue. But that hope was short-lived when Kyle Finley stood above her, hands on hips, and a grin splattered from ear to ear.

"Leonard said I'd find you here." He gave the pig a nudge with the toe of his boot "Move, little girl." The animal grunted and lumbered to its feet. "Are you hurt? I see you met the family. All except this one." He pulled a calico kitten from inside his shirt and set it on Kathleen's lap. "My earnings for the day. She'll be a good mouser."

"She'll also be a good mother." She freed one hand so she could hand him back the kitten. "Hold this little one for a bit. Would you mind helping me off the floor?" Maybe he wouldn't notice she had a fistful of blouse.

"Not at all." He grasped her hand. "Something wrong with your other arm?"

So much for hoping he wouldn't notice. "Your goat welcomed me by chewing off two buttons, Mr. Finley."

He cocked his head. "And, perhaps a comb, too?"

She closed her eyes. How disheveled she must appear. Add one more *told you so* to mother's arguments. "And a comb. She'd have gotten my earbobs, too, had they not been hooked into my ears."

"I'll make it right somehow. I imagine Maggie has a button box."

"You needn't bother. I have my own."

He shrugged. "No bother." He set the kitten on the dirt floor. "What did you mean this little one would be a good mother?"

"All calicos are female, Mr. Finley." She brushed at her skirt.

"Experience, or guesswork, Miss Weston?"

She tapped her temple with one finger. "Education."

One side of his nose wrinkled. "Education? They teach you such things in finishing school, do they?" He slapped Prudence on the rump. "Move, little girl." He bent and used both hands to push the pig away, and the animal responded with a squeal.

"I didn't go to finishing school, Mr. Finley. Please be gentle with her."

"I didn't hurt her. She's female and thinks if she squeals I'll feel sorry for her."

She plunked one hand on her hip. "Spoken like a true gentleman— presume you know what a woman's thinking. And how do you know it didn't hurt? For what it's worth, I suspect she's going to be a mother, also."

His heretofore friendly countenance darkened. "Exactly what kind of education did you receive, Miss Weston? Please don't tell me you fancy yourself some kind of animal expert. Maggie says you hail from Chicago. I doubt you encountered goats or pigs in the city. I will accept your fascinating information concerning Miss Calico's future, but I know for a fact it takes two pigs to make piglets, and since there's no other such animal in this barn I'll dismiss your suspicion regarding Prudence."

She gulped. This isn't at all how she planned to make her services known, but she'd not shy from the telling. All the harassment she'd endured with her schooling had toughened her resolve. She didn't faint at the sight of blood, and she didn't allow ridicule to bother her. "I don't fancy myself an expert, kind sir. However, I am in fact a doctor of veterinary medicine. And as far as your gilt's impending motherhood, was she never exposed to a boar while on the farm from whence she came?"

His scowl, silence and abrupt departure bothered her more than all the scorn she'd ever endured.

CHAPTER 5

If Kyle could have slammed the barn door, he would have. He did give it an extra hard tug and a kick on his way out. With any luck at all, she noticed. "Doctor of veterinary medicine. Of all the crazy ideas. Who does she think she is? There isn't room enough for both of us in the entire state of Kansas, and I was here first. I suppose she would've known what to do with the plugged spigot."

"You talking to me, Kyle?"

He stopped, inches away from Leonard. "Did you know?"

"Know what?"

He pointed to the barn. "Did you know she claims to be a veterinarian? A woman veterinarian at that."

Leonard chuckled. "Can't deny the fact she's a woman, now can you? About the veterinarian part...no, I didn't know. Is that what has you so upset?"

"I'm not upset. She just caught me by surprise, that's all." He gritted his teeth. "Thinks she's going to come here and set up her business, charge these good people an arm and a leg to take care of what I've been doing for them all along. They can't afford her, and I don't need her help."

"Well, I'm glad you're not upset." Leonard winked. "Did she tell you all this?" He crossed his hands on top of the hoe handle. "You weren't in there more than five minutes. She must've talked fast."

"Did you know all calico cats are female?"

"Yes, but I suspect you didn't."

"So, you were the one who told her. I bet you told her Prudence is going to have piglets, too."

Leonard straightened and met his gaze with a frown. "Now hold

332

on, Kyle. I did tell the young lady about your menagerie but nothing more. And why would I tell her anything at all about a calico cat? You don't even have a cat."

He ran his hand through his hair. "Hilda Clements gave me the pick of a litter for my help this morning."

"I see. So of course I'd know you would bring home a calico kitten and feel it important to apprise Miss Weston of that fact. I'll admit to recognizing Prudence's impending motherhood, but you're the doctor. I didn't figure you needed my keen observation. Nor did I discuss it with the young lady."

Kyle crouched and made circles in the dirt with his finger. "What I don't need is some female marching in here all high and mighty, charging these dear folk, and—"

"What you do need is a good swift kick on that part of your anatomy most padded. What are you afraid of, Kyle? I don't think you're nearly as concerned about her charging your patients as you are befuddled by the fact she's a very attractive, obviously intelligent woman. She threatens you, and you're jealous."

He stood. "I'll concede the fact she's an attractive woman, but that's as far as I'll go. She doesn't threaten me, and I'm not jealous. But a woman, attractive or not, has no business giving these good folk information and advice on how to care for their animals."

Leonard laughed. "Or giving the good Doctor Finley information he didn't already know." He laid his hand on Kyle's arm. "Why not give her a chance. What could it hurt? Take her with you the next time one of your patients needs help with an animal. See how she handles it before you tar and feather her."

Kyle jerked his arm away. "I don't have time for this argument. It's dinner time and I need to get back to the restaurant."

"Did you take a look at Trembley's old mare?"

"No need. We have a resident veterinarian. Remember?"

His old friend shook his head. "I must say your true Finley colors are showing right now. And it breaks my heart." He turned and shuffled toward the barn.

Kyle hung his head. Didn't the man realize how hard he'd worked to distance himself from the Finley moniker? He'd chosen to return to Lyndale after his training so he could prove he wasn't like the others. It hadn't been easy. He'd worked hard to prove to the community that he wasn't like his family. And intended to work just as hard to keep some fancy woman from exploiting their occasional need for an animal doctor. Their livestock was their living. Lose a cow and they also lost the source of milk for their babes or meat for their table. The same for goats or pigs or chickens. They all represented wealth in a manner unknown to the Finley ancestors. People laughed at the sign in his office declaring a free burial if a patient didn't live. But it wasn't intended to be a joke.

When he returned to the hotel, Maggie greeted him with a scowl. "About time you got here. Don't tell me it took all morning to unplug one spigot."

"What would you know about plugged spigots? I suppose you're one of them, too."

She slammed her hand on the counter. "One of them what? You want to back up and rephrase that mouthful? I don't like the way it sounds."

"Veterinarian, Maggie, that's what." He turned the guest register so he wouldn't have to read upside down. "Well, that explains it." He rapped his knuckles on the counter. "Look at this, Maggie. See how she signed her name? K.O. Weston. I bet she laughed all night."

"What in all of heaven's stars are you talking about?"

"That...that person you sent to live in my house."

"You mean Miss Weston? Why would she laugh at how she signed her name? And where else would you have her live?"

"Just take a look. K.O.W." He jabbed his finger on each letter. "What's that spell? Huh? I'll tell you. Cow. It spells cow. That should have been a dead giveaway. And the Hutton place is empty. Why didn't you put her there?"

"Cow? Giveaway?" She put her hand on his forehead. "Do you have a fever? You're talking plumb crazy. And the Hutton place is five miles out of town."

He pushed her hand away. "It's well suited for her. I bet you knew it all along."

"Knew what? In the first place, Kyle, K.O.W does not spell cow. I don't think it spells anything so why should that be a giveaway? For your information, cow is spelled with a C. And here's one more little tidbit for you to chew—I never laid eyes on the girl until she came in here last night. You had no problem with me putting her at your place this morning, so why're you in such a frazzle now? Besides that, how's she supposed to get there? Trembley's old mare isn't reliable."

"Why, that's no problem for the likes of someone like her. And don't tell me you didn't know she was a veterinarian. A lady animal doctor. And by the way, I know how to spell cow, but K O W and C O W sound alike, so you should have figured it out. No doubt she thought it quite clever."

"A lady veterinarian?" Maggie shook her head. "So that's what's got your britches all bunched? What bothers you the most...the fact that she's a woman or that she's a veterinarian?"

He held up two fingers. "Both. She doesn't have any right to come marching in here and taking over a man's job. Everybody with any sense at all knows a woman's place is in the home. Take this morning for instance. Poor Theodore couldn't even tell me what was wrong with his cow. How do you think he'd feel trying to explain it to a woman? Where's my apron? I have dinner to fix."

"How do you think Violet Hamilton feels, or Lucille Thomas, or...or me? In case you haven't noticed, we're all women who find it necessary to tell a man what's ailing us. And you're nosey enough to ask questions."

"That's different. I'm a doctor."

"And so is Miss Weston."

He plunged his hands in his pockets. "She's not a real doctor."

Maggie swept a straggly strand of hair off her neck and tucked it into the comb on the top of her head. "And you're not a real animal doctor."

He should know better than to argue with the woman. But she was wrong and he'd prove it. "Come with me." He motioned for her to follow him into the restaurant. There were only three men in there, but that would be enough to prove his point.

"Where you been, Doc?" John Henry Carlisle shoved his empty cup across the table. "Sure could use a refill."

"I'll get you one as soon as you answer a question for me."

"We gotta start taking a test before you'll feed us?" All three men laughed. "What if we fail?"

"If you fail, you have to drink Maggie's coffee. But I can almost guarantee you'll pass this one. Now, let's say a new lady came to town."

"Married?" A silly grin plastered on each face.

"No. Unmarried. And let's say this so-called lady says she's a doctor."

Maggie pulled on his arm. "Kyle, this is unfair."

William Townsend scratched his head. "But you're the doc. You tellin' us some woman is moving in on you?"

"Not on me so much as on you. What if this new unmarried lady in town says she's a veterinarian?"

"A what? There's ain't no such things is there?"

He grinned at Maggie. "See...what'd I tell you?" He turned back to the men. "There must be. At least that's what she says. You might want to ask her yourself. Maggie, here, put her up at my old place. I'm sure the new woman animal doctor would appreciate a welcome. Oh, but you need to know her name, don't you? Well, all I can tell you is her initials are K O W."

William scowled. "Cow? Her initials say cow?"

He nodded. "See, Maggie? And you thought I was wrong." He nodded at the men. "Kinda explains it, doesn't it?"

Maggie shook her head. "All that explains is that none of you can spell. And her name is Kathleen."

Ralph Connor pulled on his goatee. "You mean she's h-h-here? In Lyndale? Where's her h-h-husband? Why don't he keep her at h-h-hhome where a woman belongs, like the Good Lord intended?"

John Henry wrapped his fat hands around the lapels of his coat and puffed his chest. "Well, I can tell you one thing for sure. That... that woman won't be treating any of our animals. I'll make sure of that. And by the time I get through, she'll be ready to pack up and move on. You're the only doc this place needs."

William rapped his knuckles on the table. "Amen!" He turned to John Henry. "What do you mean *by the time I get through*? She's a woman. Not like you can just up and run her out of town."

John Henry leaned his forearms on the table. "Think about it, fellas. What is it a woman needs most?"

Ralph gasped. "B-b-but we're already m-m-married."

Kyle waited for the laughter to die down. "Now that Ralph has squelched that idea, maybe you should tell us what else you think a woman needs most?"

John Henry shrugged one shoulder. "Nothing else. We all know just how helpless a woman is without a good man. Goodness knows I don't need to be reminded. Victoria doesn't make a move without asking my advice. But there are plenty of single men around Lyndale... including you, Finley. Surely one of you could be convinced to help her out of her single, look-at-me-I-can-do-a-man's-job status."

Kyle held up both hands. "Leave me out of this one, fellas. But you might just be on to a plan, John Henry. All we'd have to do is make sure the news gets around there's a new unmarried lady in town, and she'll be too busy warding off suitors to establish herself as a veterinarian. Some young man will get a wife, our women will stay at home where they belong, and our animals will be safe."

"Our women, and our animals? How convenient to lump us all together." Maggie hooked her fingers through the handles of all three cups and gave a yank. What little coffee was left in the cups puddled on the table in front of each man. "For shame. Shame on all of you for such talk."

"We weren't talking about you, Maggie." William pointed to the cups. "I hope you're going to refill those, and maybe mop up what spilled."

She crossed her arms across her bosom. "Do you, now? Have you forgotten the good doctor runs this place? A man in a kitchen. Imagine that. And I've never heard a word of complaint out of the likes of any of you. And you know why?" She marched to the front window and pulled the blind, then released it so hard it spun when it reached the top. "You think because I'm a woman I don't know what goes on here after you put the closed sign in the window?" She pointed at the banker. "What do you tell Victoria, William, after you've eaten the meal she spent her day preparing for you? Do you say you have books to balance? And must I remind you that your head teller's name is Rebecca? A married woman you pay to do what others might deem a man's job?"

He scowled. "Now, Maggie..."

"And you, John Henry Carlisle. You're the head of the schoolboard, and who do you have teaching both girls and boys?" She scratched her head. "Oh, yes. I do believe her name is Tamara Hubert. You don't seem to mind taking her out of the kitchen. But I do wonder how her husband feels about it?"

"But, Maggie..."

Ralph squirmed, and Kyle couldn't blame him. The way it was going, none of them were going to escape unscathed.

Maggie shook her head. "I came from your store not one hour ago, Ralph Connor. Your own sweet Abigail had one babe on a hip and one pulling on her skirt the entire time. In fact, I distinctly remember her telling the older one to 'run find Papa to help.' You know what that itty bitty girl told her mama? 'Papa gone.'" She reached behind her and grabbed a towel from the counter. "One of you men mop up the spills. And, Ralph, you hightail it next door so your wife can go back in the kitchen where God intended a woman to be—if you can call *home* four cramped rooms behind a curtain."

Kyle squared his shoulders. "Come on, Maggie. You know we weren't lumping you into this conversation. It's not like you even have a—"

She whirled to face him. He expected her to finish her rant with gusto. But he wasn't prepared to gaze into eyes so full of pain. "Don't you even try to finish that sentence. Do you think I need to be reminded my husband is dead? Do you need reminding?"

He gripped her shoulder. "Maggie, please..."

She slapped him away. "Don't you *Maggie, please* me, Kyle. You were the one who told me after Wilmer passed that no one person could be expected to be in two places at once. Remember? 'I like to cook,' you said. 'Let me run the restaurant and you take care of the hotel. Wilmer would want it that way.' you said. And I listened because I needed help as much as you needed to help. But no more. This town doesn't need a hotel. And it doesn't need a restaurant either—not if all the women in Lyndale stay at home like the Good Lord intended."

"Are you s-s-saying you w-won't refill our cups?"

Maggie leaned across the table to address Ralph. "That's exactly what I'm saying." She straightened, walked to the front, pulled down the shade, and put the CLOSED sign in the window. "Good day, gentlemen. Games are over. My deed to this place trumps your four-of-a-kind. This establishment is out of business." She glared at Kyle. "And you can move your things out of the hotel."

He raised his arms. "What? You're kicking me out. Why?"

"Why, you ask? Because the hotel is my home. I'll no longer be receiving guests, and it wouldn't be proper for an unmarried man to stay here with an unmarried woman."

"That's crazy. Everyone knows you're old enough to—"

"Old enough to do what I've threatened to do for a long time, young man? Old enough to do what your own parents should have done years ago?" Her eyes welled with tears. "I must say, Kyle Finley, you're done your father proud. If someone dared disagree with him, he'd garner the opinion of a few faithful and they'd soon become the majority. 'If at first you don't succeed, do whatever it takes to win.' That was his motto."

Her words cut deep. He wasn't anything like his father. This wasn't an issue that concerned his own well-being. A woman veterinarian, with one misguided procedure, or one missed diagnosis, could mean a family losing their livelihood.

"You don't understand, Maggie. Where am I to go? I can't go to my place for the same reason you won't allow me to stay on at the hotel."

"I hear the Hutton place is empty."

"But that's five miles—"

"Yes, I know. But if you start now you should be able to get there before dark."

He looked at the men around the table. Men he'd known since he was a child. Men he trusted to come to his aid should the need arise. But now they were all busy staring at the ceiling, the floor, their laps. "You all going to just sit there? Don't you have anything to say?" He shook his finger at the banker. "Tell you what, William, next time you have one of those carbuncles you...you can just...just sit on it. That's what."

CHAPTER 6

Kathleen propped herself against the splintery wall between stalls and made a nest of her skirt to accommodate the kitten. If only Finley would have made some comment. Even a snide remark would've allowed her to defend herself. Though she doubted he'd be interested in any argument she'd present.

The metal pulley on the door screeched against its glide as it slid open, and her heart thumped until she ascertained it wasn't the real doctor who'd entered. She smiled at the older man as he approached. "You've seen Dr. Finley, I presume."

Leonard chuckled. "Heard him before I saw him."

"I can only imagine. Believe me, this entire scenario is not at all how I planned to make myself known. You know how they say hindsight is always so wise? Well, I should have signed the prized DVM after my name in the first place." She gave her hair a twist and pushed it behind one ear. She had a button box, but she'd need a visit to Connor's Dry Goods to purchase more combs.

Leonard overturned a bucket and lowered himself onto it. "Why didn't you?"

She rubbed the back of her neck. "I was too tired and too defensive to take the chance, I suppose. I fought disgust and derision from men peers all through my schooling. My mother has made it very plain that I've chosen a most unlikely—and unladylike—pursuit. My father was a doctor. A real doctor, as Kyle Finley describes himself. The man at the depot in Kansas City warned me Lyndale already had a doctor and couldn't imagine anyone ever needing the services of a woman, especially a fancy woman veterinarian. I never intended to be deceiving, but I did want to be a bit more prepared for the ridicule

I imagined would come."

"Did Kyle ridicule you?"

The kitten had escaped the confines of her nest, and Kathleen scooped it up again. "He didn't actually speak, but the expression on his face shouted contempt and scorn the like of which I've never experienced. I can spit words with the best of them, but the good Doctor Finley shut me up with his own silence." She shook her head. "I won't be welcomed or accepted here, will I?"

He rested his elbows on his knees and peered into her face. "Be honest with me. Did you think you would? You've already stated you imagined there would be ridicule. My thought is you caught Kyle off guard. He's seldom challenged. However, I do believe you embarrassed him, and it somersaulted into jealousy—though he adamantly denied my accusation."

She leaned her head against the rough stall. "I've chosen a profession best suited to a man, Leonard, but I've not forgotten how to be a lady. Until today, that is. My upbringing forbade me to knowingly humiliate anyone for any reason. Even while in school I sought only to be recognized as someone with equal intelligence, while my fellow colleagues derived great pleasure from what they supposed to be my discomfort when called on to name a part of the anatomy or present an oral report on reproduction. I learned to distance myself from their derision and state the facts as though I were one of them. I didn't expect a doctor to be offended."

Leonard stretched his legs in front of him. "Tell me this, if you will. I'm not going to argue the fact you're a woman veterinarian. I don't reckon I could say anything you haven't already heard. But why did you choose Lyndale, Kansas, of all places?"

The kitten was now snuggled between her shoulder and her chin, and she stroked its silky soft head. "There's no logical answer as to the why. Perhaps your question should have been how I managed to choose this place. The truth is, I circled my hand above a map and let my finger do the deciding." She smiled. "Scientific, wasn't it?"

He laughed. "Then I'll phrase my next question with that in mind.

How did you choose to pursue veterinary medicine? I'm sure you must have been aware of the odds stacked against you."

"Very aware. From the moment I first stepped through the doors of McKillip Veterinary college in Chicago. I became more mindful of that fact every single day of my schooling. My mother has not hidden her disapproval of my choice. But I think Dr. Finley's reaction has been the most painful. I have every argument, every defense, every line of battle down pat. But it's very difficult for a woman to reason with silence."

He nodded. "Ah, yes. The fine-honed Finley approach to anything that doesn't meet their approval. Though I must say, I honestly thought Kyle was above all that. Some roots go very deep."

"How far do those roots extend, Leonard? Is every family tree in this community somehow connected?"

A frown settled between Leonard's eyebrows. "Kyle Finley represents all that the people for miles around consider good. He's respected not only as a doctor but as a man. But it hasn't always been like that. Kyle fought long and hard to gain his own place apart from the Finley name. At first folks thought he wouldn't accept money because he considered them poor. People around here are proud, Miss Weston. And they don't expect handouts. But Kyle was smart enough to ask for what they could give. Things like Daphne and Prudence. Then came the time he no longer had to ask. They offered."

She pulled the kitten from her shoulder and held her nose to nose. "Like this little girl." She cuddled the kitten next to her cheek. "Do I stand a chance here, Leonard?"

A crooked smile wrinkled across his face. "People around here are good people, but they're very loyal. I hate to say it, but I'm afraid as Kyle Finley goes, so goes Lyndale, Kansas."

She plopped her hands on her hips, then remembered the two missing buttons. If he noticed, he gave no indication and she attempted to regain her modesty without drawing more attention to herself, albeit most certainly too late given the way she'd been playing with the kitten. "I see. However, I don't play games, Leonard.

If I can't make it on my own merit, then I'll admit defeat and leave. But you must know...I have yet to be routed by a man."

Kathleen hung the last piece of clothing in the ornately carved walnut armoire and leaned against the closed door to gaze at her surroundings. Mother would be surprised and, perhaps, a bit jealous to know her new dwelling rivaled that of her Chicago upbringing though, judging by Doctor Finley's reaction to her announcement that she was, indeed, a woman veterinarian, she might not be staying long.

As thy days, so shall the strength be. Papa's ever-present reminder whispered to her. *One day at a time, Kathleen. Use the gift of today and refrain from the temptation of unwrapping tomorrow.* But she was a planner. And she'd never found a way to devise a plan that didn't include the tomorrows.

One trunk remained to be unpacked, then she could call it a day. While Kyle had left food for her, as Maggie advised, that was a long time ago, and he must think ladies ate like birds. One biscuit and one slice of ham hadn't filled her. Had Ruby failed to provide eggs for the good doctor? Perhaps this would be a good time to venture into town. The days had grown longer and there would be plenty of daylight. She'd walk, eat at the restaurant, visit with Maggie, and see if she could determine the depth of Kyle Finley's disdain. But first, she'd check on the animals. She wanted to keep a close eye on Prudence should she decide to start her nesting.

She'd saved the heaviest trunk for last, the one containing her prized veterinary books— Hill's *Atlas of Veterinary Clinical Anatomy*, Schaefer's *New Manual of Homeopathic Veterinary Medicine*, and Chawner's *Diseases of the Horse and How To Treat Them*. They had become both her best friends and her worst enemies. They represented long hours of study, long hours of soul searching, and many long hours of heated debate. They were like a Bible to a preacher, or Merck's Manual to a physician. More than a reference.

They epitomized Kathleen Olivia Weston. All of who she was, all of who she wanted to become.

She knelt and opened the trunk with her eyes closed, wanting to savor this moment. And when she allowed herself a peek, the first thing she observed was her little brother's homemade sign. She lifted it from its wrapping and clutched it to her breast. Sweet Andy-boy. The sign was crude. Others would laugh. But it, too, embodied her ambition, her dreams...and her fears.

There. She admitted it. She was afraid. Not of the dark or what animals might do to her. Scorn and contempt didn't frighten her— she'd already weathered those storms. Even failure didn't cause the anxiety that caused her heart to thrum. One could always start over again.

No, what terrified her—the one thing that would make her curl up and want to die—was if she were ever to disappoint those who put so much trust in her. Those who encouraged her, believed in her, prayed for her. Oh, her mother fretted and scolded and looked down her very aristocratic nose. But never, not even for one minute, had she stopped loving her daughter, and Kathleen knew it. Knew it down deep. Knew it the way a daughter knows. Knew it because she, too, was a woman and understood another woman's own fears.

She lowered the lid of the trunk. The books could wait until another day, and she'd not take the time to walk to the restaurant. Tomorrow she would get supplies from the mercantile. But for now, there was a more urgent endeavor to accomplish before sunset.

CHAPTER 7

Kathleen hung the treasured sign over a post on the front fence then stepped back to examine its effect.

"I know a better place for your shingle, if you care to hear about it."

She shivered and twirled toward the voice. "Oh, Maggie." She put her hands to her throat. "You scared me. I didn't know you were there."

"I just got here. Thought maybe you could use a friend."

She dropped her hands to her side. "Doctor Finley told you, didn't he?"

"Me, and the three biggest mouths in Lyndale. That's why I'm here. I don't suppose you by chance have a good strong cup of coffee, do you?"

She laughed. "I don't have a thing in the kitchen to eat. In fact, I'd planned earlier to walk to the restaurant. But then I got sidetracked."

Maggie bent to read the sign, then chuckled. "Kyle tried to convince himself, and anyone else who'd listen, that your initials spelled cow. Wait until he sees that you announce yourself as Doctor Kat."

Kathleen turned the sign around to show her the lone E. "My little brother calls me Kate. There wasn't room on the front for all the letters. But I promised him I'd hang it outside my office, and I won't break that promise."

"You do know what you're up against, don't you?"

"I do, but it's nothing I haven't faced before. Given time, I can prove myself. Would you like to come in? I do have water, and you're right—I could use a friend."

The older woman smiled. "I was hoping you'd ask. A lot has

happened this afternoon, and I want you to hear it first from me. But I also have a plan. Would you mind if Leonard joined us?"

"I think perhaps he's already gone in for the evening, but we could see." She pulled against Maggie's arm. "I take it you know him well enough to trust him?"

Maggie patted her hand. "Oh, my dear. Everyone trusts Leonard. You needn't worry about a thing. And unless I miss my most learned guess, I have a feeling he can furnish us both with a good strong cup of coffee."

Kathleen's heart warmed at the greeting between the two obvious old friends. And by the second cup of coffee, along with sandwiches and cookies Leonard insisted they share with him, she no longer felt like an extra thumb. She'd not forged many friendships in Chicago. While other girls curled, powdered, rouged and giggled their way through their teen years and the coveted debut, she had begged, whined and threatened to run away until she was allowed to travel to New York City to volunteer at a rescue shelter for dogs and cats. Her mother told her bridge club Kathleen was visiting relatives. To be included in conversation now, and not seem an oddity, was pleasant. More pleasing than she'd ever imagined.

"Ladies, keep your cups. I have a feeling we'll need more coffee before the evening is over. Find a comfortable seat and I'll join you shortly."

"May I help with the dishes?" Kathleen carried her own plate to the cupboard while Leonard stacked the rest.

"No, I never allow my guests to help. The house is always so quiet after company leaves, and I've found the best antidote for loneliness is to reflect on the joys of friendships. I relive the evening as I do the dishes. By the time the last dish is put away I've had a good time of reflection and am ready to retire." He pulled a chair opposite the small settee where the two ladies sat. "Now, Miss Maggie, I know you're dying to tell us what took place at your fine establishment that was so important you took the chance my fine young Doctor Finley would not be called out in the midst of the supper hour." He crossed his legs and leaned back in his chair. "Talk away, my good friend."

By the time Maggie finished, the wrinkles in Leonard's forehead had deepened, and a weight had settled on Kathleen's shoulders.

Maggie put her arm around Kathleen's shoulders. "I see that look of frustration, my dear. But this is not over. Not by a long shot. You still have not heard my plan."

"How can any plan work against the wiles of these men? All influential, I must say. At least in school I was given a chance to prove myself, albeit my colleagues didn't have much choice but to grant me that opportunity."

"Just listen. I say you move back to the hotel. I have my living quarters there and you can choose any room, or as many rooms, as you want. We'll share the kitchen."

"But I need an office."

"I know. You didn't let me finish. We'll turn the restaurant into an office for you. It's right on Main Street. You can hang your sign where everyone passing can see it. And in the meantime, I'll take you with me and introduce you to every woman in Lyndale."

She shook her head. "I doubt they'll be impressed."

Leonard stood and brought the pot of coffee to refill their cups. "Don't underestimate Maggie and her friends, Miss Weston. I think you'll find them a bit more progressive than their menfolk."

"All I want is a chance to practice my calling. I don't want to cause family problems. My father lived by God's Word, and he made sure I understood that a person's ultimate goal should be to do everything as unto the Lord and not to please man. He encouraged me to pursue my dream of becoming a veterinarian. But he would never want me to cause discord in an entire community."

"I can imagine Elizabeth Blackwell faced the same kind of prejudice. But she paved the way and today female physicians are slowly becoming more accepted and even admired among their colleagues. Perhaps you, too, will pave the way." Leonard leaned forward in his chair. "Your father left you a code to live by that is to be envied. Unfortunately, Kyle's family also left him a legacy. He's tried very, very hard to rid himself of that heritage. He wants no part of what he understands all too well to be snobbery. Yet, try as he might, there is within him an ingrained response to anything that threatens the reputation he's worked so hard to gain—and sadly that includes the favor of man."

"But how does my being here threaten him? I know my limits. I would never attempt to treat a human being. I'm not trained in that capacity, and frankly it would frighten me."

"We're not a community of scholars. We're a simple people. Not ignorant, but simple. Most see Kyle Finley as the doctor, and it doesn't much matter whether it's their child or their cow." He shrugged. "I know that sounds very crude to your Chicago ears. I cringe at the illustration myself. But you see, Kyle has chosen a lifestyle opposite of his upbringing, and at the same time has allowed pride of that choice to motivate him."

Kathleen ran her finger around the rim of her cup. "Papa had a lot to say about pride, too."

"I imagine he did if God's Word was important to him. But I'm quite sure Kyle doesn't recognize it as pride." Leonard reached for Maggie's hand. "You, my fine lady friend, are the only one I know who can nail the boy's feet to the ground."

Maggie shook her head. "And you hold the hammer to do it. But I pray that will never be necessary." She stood and put her cup on the table. "Do you agree to go along with the plan, Kathleen? We'll not force you."

"I just got unpacked, but I would be more comfortable in the hotel knowing how Doctor Finley feels about me."

"Let's get what you need to spend tonight at the hotel, and we'll come back tomorrow to get the rest. Would you be willing to help load her trunks again, Leonard?"

He put his arm around Maggie's shoulders. "Do I have a choice?" He winked at Kathleen. "You will find, Miss Weston, that when this lady speaks, most of Lyndale trembles."

"*Pfft*. Don't you listen to him. He's just grumpy because I wouldn't marry him."

Kathleen laughed. "He proposed?"

"I propose every time I see her, and she always turns me down."

Maggie tapped his chin. "And won't you be surprised the day I say yes?"

The look that passed between them caused Kathleen's stomach to tighten. There was much more there than the words spoken. It was the same expression she'd observed between her parents when they didn't know she was anywhere near.

Now she did feel like the extra thumb.

Kyle leaned his back against the hotel desk and crossed his arms. "I didn't expect to see you back here, Miss Weston. Leaving so soon?"

Maggie's eyes clouded. "No, Kyle. She's staying. I'm going to see to that. She'll pack the rest of her things in the morning. Leonard has agreed to bring her trunks here to the hotel, then the house will once again be yours. You needn't go to the Hutton place after all."

"I thought the hotel was closed."

Maggie grasped his folded arms. "Why are you doing this, Kyle? This isn't like you at all. I would never have believed I'd see you so...so cruel. I live here. This hotel is my home, and I'm free to share it with whomever I please. And right now, Doctor Kathleen Weston pleases me."

He pushed away from the desk and lifted a box and his black bag from the floor. "I think I have everything. My supplies are still in the room I used as my office. If anyone needs me in the night, you'll just have to keep them here and send for me. I'll be in the barn. I only hope any delay in my being notified will not cause further problems for a patient."

Miss Weston stepped forward, her hands clenched together at her waist. "It's your home, Doctor Finley. You needn't stay in the barn. There's nothing of mine that should pose an obstacle to you staying in the house tonight."

"I'm aware of that, Miss Weston. However, the distance between my home and my barn is not the issue, ma'am. It's the amount of time wasted between this hotel and my home that's the concern. People around here are used to finding me at the hotel. They know which one is my room. They call out their name, knock three times and I know it's an emergency."

"And does this apply to both man and beast?"

"I took an oath, Miss Weston."

"As did I, Dr. Finley. However, I am very aware that man was given dominion over animals. I would never usurp your authority or expertise in the treatment of your patients. I would only hope you would extend to me the same courtesy."

"I've worked hard to gain the trust and respect of this community, Miss Weston."

She nodded. "And I will do no less...if given the opportunity."

He shouldered past the women, then turned for one last parting shot. "I'm not completely ignorant of the Bible, you understand. God not only gave man dominion over the animals, he formed man first. Women were made to be helpers, keepers of the home, child-bearers. You'll have plenty opportunities to prove yourself a faithful wife and mother once the young bucks around here realize you're unmarried. I suggest you avail yourself of such prospects and leave the doctoring to me."

"Oh, my dear, dear boy." Maggie put her arm around the younger woman's shoulders. "Unnecessary hurtful words spoken with such Finley eloquence. I suggest you go home and do some deep soul searching. Your oath is to relieve pain, not cause it."

The click of the door as it closed behind him echoed like a gunshot through the empty street. The very traits he'd worked so hard to deny, the attitude of superiority he loathed, the pride of name and station he'd used as accusations crowded around him like an angry mob, and it made him so sick to his stomach he leaned against the corner of the building and retched.

It was going to be a long, long night.

CHAPTER 8

Kathleen had kept a smile plastered across her face so long her top lip twitched. So these were the women of Lyndale? Maggie had invited the Ladies Missionary Society of Lyndale Community Church to meet at the hotel and, by way of introduction, had held little brother Andrew's sign for all to see. Now she waited for Maggie to hush the murmuring.

Such a varied gathering. Some were dressed in silk or taffeta, while others wore dresses of cotton. Yet all, she surmised, wore their best for the occasion. And while there was not the feeling of animosity, there was a great deal of curiosity manifested by shy smiles and conversations held behind gloved hands. She understood. She had just as many questions. Only one woman in particular caught her attention. A tall woman, her blond braids pinned to the top of her head like a crown, sat in the back row. She was obviously very pregnant and seemed to be quite uncomfortable. Kathleen was able to make eye contact with her and received a sweet smile. Were her cheeks always so flushed? She'd ask Maggie later.

"Okay, ladies. Now that you've whispered and tittered, I make a motion we allow this newcomer in our midst an opportunity to tell us about herself. And for you ladies who've already had an earful from your husbands, please keep an open mind...and heart."

"I second the motion." The lady with a rose print dress and pearls raised her hand, and smiled at Kathleen.

"Thank you, Victoria." Maggie turned to Kathleen and lowered her voice. "She's the banker's wife. You ready?"

She nodded. "May I stand? I think you will all be able to hear me better if I stand."

"You do whatever is the most comfortable for you."

She stood, took a deep breath, and willed her lip to stop twitching. "Good afternoon ladies, and thank you for giving me this opportunity." When she explained the reasons for the sign, their faces softened and they responded with smiles and a few oohs. The lady with the pink cheeks even wiped at tears.

She told of her father's encouragement and his daily reminder to follow God's Word. She shared her mother's angst, and there were numerous nods of understanding, perhaps even agreement. She compared her struggle to be accepted into a man's world with that of Doctor Elizabeth Blackwell. Then she took a deep breath. Would she be able to convey her heart?

"You want to know how I chose Lyndale, Kansas?" She smiled and demonstrated, then waited for the laughter and chatter to subside. "I had no idea Kyle Finley even existed. But I'm not sure that even had I known it would have kept me from coming. Because, you see, I don't see myself in competition with him. I think we could learn to work together. I'm sure there are things he could teach me, and equally sure I could do the same for him. I don't know any of you, but I hope to become acquainted. And the very last thing I want to do is cause friction in your homes. All I ask is for a chance to prove myself. I graduated at the top of my class, even above my male colleagues. But that doesn't mean anything unless I can earn the trust of your husbands. I want to be your friend."

At first there was silence, then a roar of applause greeted her. Smiles replaced furrowed brows. Eye contact replaced furtive glances. Except for the pink-cheeked woman in back, who sat on the edge of her seat, one hand kneading the small of her back. They probably weren't the most comfortable chairs. If only she hadn't talked so long, but no one else seemed to mind.

Maggie clapped her hands for attention. "If you have questions, now's the time to ask them, ladies. But stand up and give her your name. She won't remember them all, but give her time."

The lady in the rose print dress stood. "Hello, Kathleen. My name is Victoria Thomas and my husband is the banker. He's also one who believes all women should be tied to the house by their apron strings." Victoria waited for the laughter to die down. "I think I can speak for most of us here this afternoon. None of us want our homes interrupted, and no one chooses discord. However, neither do we agree that you should be shunned. So I'm going to make a motion— if I'm allowed to do that, Maggie—that we step out of our kitchens every morning, say at 9:00, ladies, and pray for Miss Weston."

The motion warmed Kathleen. "Thank you, Mrs. Thomas. I can certainly use your prayers."

Victoria nodded. "I'm not finished, dear." She turned to the ladies. "And I say we keep track of the minutes we pray. Not to gain favor from God, but rather for every minute we pray we set supper on the table those minutes late. And if questioned, we'll tell them why."

There was an audible gasp.

Maggie stood. "You mean, if we pray for ten minutes, supper is ten minutes late? Oh, Victoria, the digestive system of every man in Lyndale is going to tie in knots."

"Yes, I know. But we'll be at home, in our kitchens, and who can argue against prayer?"

The room erupted in laughter and animated conversation.

The tall lady with the blond braids raised her hand.

Maggie nodded. "You have a question, Hilda?"

"*Ja.*" She grimaced.

"Hilda?" Maggie clapped her hands again. "Ladies, please. Hilda, dear, is something wrong?"

"*Ja.*" As she pushed herself to a standing position her eyes widened, and she slowly sank back to her chair. "Too early, *das* baby comes."

Kathleen pushed through the crowd of women, and the puddle of water on the floor by Hilda's chair confirmed her suspicions. She gripped the woman's hands. "Are you having pains?"

Hilda nodded.

"How long ago did they start?"

"Since breakfast we eat."

Maggie shook her head. "Oh, Hilda. Why did you come here if you were having pains?"

"*Sei so lieb.*" She rolled her lips tight, but didn't make another sound.

"What did she say, Maggie?"

"I'm not sure. Something about a friend, I think."

Kathleen knelt by her side. "Hilda, can I ask you to please speak English? I can't understand your German and we need to communicate...to talk. You understand."

She nodded and gave the hint of a smile. "*Ja.*"

"Good. Now, is your husband at home?"

She nodded. "Doctor Finley come check our *milch* cow."

Maggie rolled her eyes "Well, Doctor Weston, until we can get Kyle away from the plugged spigot, it looks like you're in charge."

Kathleen pulled on Maggie's sleeve. "What do you mean I'm in charge? I've never delivered a baby. At least not a human one."

"Well, there's a first time for everything. Let's get her to a bedroom." She turned to the group of ladies. "One of you, I don't care who, fetch Dr. Finley. He's out at the Clements farm. And bring Theodore back with you, too."

"I'll go. My buggy is right outside." Victoria Thomas pulled her skirt from her ankles. "Maybe you should dismiss the meeting, Maggie."

"I'll do no such thing." She stood and clapped again for attention. "You ladies want to pray, now's a good time to start. Can't think of a better reason for supper to be late than to welcome a new Lyndale babe."

Kathleen wiped perspiration from Hilda's forehead. "Do you think you can walk?"

She nodded.

"Is there a bed in Kyle's old office?"

"There's a bed, and he still has most of his supplies here. Just down the hall, maybe twenty to thirty steps."

"Then help me, Maggie." She put placed her hand under Hilda's elbow. "And you better be praying."

355

"You say a woman comes to doctor our animals? And John Henry Carlisle plans to run her out of town?" Theodore Clements hitched his foot on the bottom rung of the fence.

"Not run her out of town so much as make sure she ends up married and at home where the Good Lord intended a woman to stay in the first place. Tell me, friend. What would you tell this lady doctor is wrong with your milk cow?" Kyle rested one elbow on the top rail. If only that woman was present to hear it for herself.

Theodore shrugged. "I tell her my cow's..." He made a squeezing and pulling motion with his hand, and turned bright red with the demonstration. "No, I'd tell her my cow kicked when I..." He plunged his hands into his pockets. "I wouldn't tell her nothing. I'd ask Hilda do it."

"Aha!" Kyle slapped the top rail. "That's what I thought. But what if you didn't have Hilda? Or what if she wasn't home?" He peered toward the house. "Where is she, by the way? I thought she'd come say hello."

"I wouldn't have the milk cow 'cept for my Hilda. She wants the cream for her butter. And she went to town. Maggie called a ladies meeting to meet a new—"

"A new woman, perhaps?" He closed his eyes. Leave it to Maggie to gather the troops. No doubt the good Miss Weston was pouring out her heart, hoping to elicit enough support to justify her stay in Lyndale.

Theodore nodded. "Yah, a woman. Maybe it's this lady doctor you talk about?"

"Most likely. I don't like the idea of Hilda traveling alone though. That road is rough and she shouldn't be bouncing around on a buggy seat this late in her pregnancy."

The big man smiled. "Oh, my Hilda is strong. It will be good for her to be with other women. She gets lonely, I think, but she never complains. If this new lady she meets is that woman doctor, you want

I should not let them be friends?"

"Well, no, let's think this through. If you wouldn't tell the woman so-called veterinarian what was wrong with your cow, and Hilda wasn't here to do it for you, do you think the other farmers and ranchers would want that woman caring for their animals?"

Theodore cocked his head and studied the sky, then pulled a splinter of wood from the fence. "You want me to tell you what other men think about this lady?" He snapped a small piece from the splinter. "You already told me what John Henry wants to do." He tapped his finger against his temple. "Does he know something wrong with this woman?"

"Well...no, she's not a bad person, if that's what you mean. We just don't need a real doctor and an animal doctor both. Haven't I been doing a good job for you? Lyndale has a doctor. Why do we need a woman coming in and taking over?"

Theodore broke off another piece of the splinter. "You came back here when Leonard was the doctor. Nobody told you to go away."

"Leonard wasn't a real doctor, you know. He was a twenty-one-year-old storekeeper when the battle at Wilson's Creek was fought. I know, because my father was there and he told story after story about that engagement."

"My papa told plenty stories about that fight, too. Did your papa tell you who saved his life?"

Kyle swept his hand across his forehead. "Leonard? Was it Leonard?"

Theodore nodded. "Papa said Leonard worked day and night just like he was a real doctor. And he just kept on doctorin' when he came home to Lyndale."

"But he was never more than a surgeon's assistant. He wasn't a licensed physician."

The big man shrugged. "I don't reckon it mattered so much. People here trusted him. People, animals, I guess it doesn't make much difference. All is family. Some older folk would still call on Leonard if he'd come."

Kyle pushed away from the fence. "What do you mean, if he'd come? I didn't run him off, you know."

Theodore broke off another piece of the splinter. "John Henry wanted you to leave, too, just like he wants this woman to go away."

"He wanted to get rid of me? Why?"

The big man shrugged. "Mostly because you're a Finley."

"That's unfair. You can't judge a person by his name."

"That's the same words Leonard said. He said your name didn't matter. You were the new doctor in town, Finley or not, and we all might as well give you a chance 'cause he was through."

Kyle squeezed his temples. "I didn't know."

Theodore flipped the last bit of splinter into the dust. "I don't reckon I should've been the one to tell ya, but now it's said. I thank ya for coming to fix our animals like you do, Doc. And I'm mighty beholdin' you don't ask us to give what we ain't got. I can't say what them other folk would tell ya, but I don't hold to runnin' this woman off. Could be it might work good to have a special doctor for our animals." He grinned at Kyle. "For sure, when it comes my Hilda's turn to have that babe, I wouldn't want you off somewhere fixin' a plugged spigot."

Kyle didn't return the smile, and he couldn't answer. Theodore had just opened a wound that had never fully healed. If only he hadn't taken off that morning without telling anyone he was headed for the Crane ranch to check on a horse that had tangled with barbed wire.

No babies were due. No one near death. Nothing that needed his immediate attention, and he'd be back before dark. How could he have known Wilmer would choose that day to chop wood? And nothing could have prepared him for the slip of the axe that sliced through the man's femoral artery. Maggie heard him scream. Had screamed herself, over and over again, she told him. He should have been there. He lived at the hotel. He could have given immediate attention. But as it were, by the time anyone realized the doctor was not in Lyndale, and they'd fetched Leonard, it was too late. Wilmer bled to death while cradled in his wife's arms.

The picture would be on the wall of his mind forever. Maggie's haunted eyes as she sat beside the body of her husband in the hotel lobby, her hands reaching across the pine box to grasp those of her beloved Wilmer's. The constant flow of townspeople as they came to pay their respects. The wind rattling the fallen autumn leaves through the cemetery the day they laid him to rest.

The pounding of horse hooves blessedly interrupted his introspection.

"It's a good thing Hilda could tell us where you were, Doc Finley." Victoria Thomas started yelling before the buggy came to a complete stop. "Maggie sent me to get you both back to town as quick as possible. Hilda's having that baby."

Theodore's eyes darkened. "If something happens to my Hilda, or the babe, I'll shoot the cow, Doc. Mark my word. I'll shoot her and leave her for the coyotes." He jumped into the buggy with Mrs. Thomas. "Let me drive. Hilda's got our buggy in town. Hold on. Once we start, I won't slow down."

CHAPTER 9

Kyle wiped sweat from his bow and gritted his teeth. He hadn't expected this kind of trouble. Hilda was a strong, healthy woman. Yes, it was her first child, and they often took longer. But something more ominous loomed.

The pain on Theodore's face mirrored that of his wife, and he stood and motioned for Kyle to move away from Hilda's hearing. "Can't you do something for my Hilda? Please?"

Maggie followed them. "Are you thinking what I'm thinking, Kyle?"

"I don't know, Maggie. What're you thinking?"

"That babe has to come out."

"You think I don't know that? But how?"

"You're the doctor. And I think you know. You're going to have to do a caesarean on this woman or lose both of them."

Theodore's eyes widened. "You mean my Hilda might die? What is this thing you say Doc must do? Why is it you've wait so long?"

"It's an operation, Theodore." Maggie answered.

He shook his head. "You have to cut her? Cut my Hilda? You've done this before?"

Kyle shook his head. "I've never done it, but I've watched."

"And if you don't do this thing, my wife will die? And the babe, too?" Theodore's face crumpled. "And if you...if you cut her, she still might die? What am I to do? God help me. What am I to do?"

Maggie patted his arm. "You have to let him try, that's what. No matter what happens, Hilda deserves a chance and so does the little one."

"Will you help, Maggie? If I say Kyle can do this, will you help?"

Tears filled her eyes. "Don't ask that of me, please. I can't."

Kyle leaned closer. "You have to, Maggie. I can't do it myself."

"Then ask Doctor Weston."

"Doctor Weston?" He clenched his teeth. She couldn't be serious. He shook his head. "I'll not ask an animal doctor to assist me."

She walked to the window. "But you'd ask me?"

"I know you, Maggie. I know nothing at all about this... veterinarian."

"My dear boy, you only think you know me." Maggie swiped at tears. "Do you know how many babes I've lost? Four. Four little ones that I never got to hold in my arms. Never got to kiss the top of their fuzzy little heads. Never had the chance to nuzzle them to my breast. No, Kyle. Don't ask me to do this. If you won't let Kathleen help, then you give Theodore your reasons why. You tell Hilda you're sorry but you can't help her because you're too proud and too stubborn."

Theodore stood with his hands balled into fists. "Maggie, you tell the lady veterinarian to come in here. I say Hilda's my wife, and that wee one is mine, too. Where is the woman?"

Kyle grabbed his arm. "Have you not heard me? Her expertise is only with animals."

He turned to Kyle, a mixture of anger and anguish on his face. "It is you who has no ears. If you won't let the woman help do this terrible thing, then I'll go for Leonard. For Hilda he'll come." He nodded to Maggie. "Where is the woman?"

"She's in my parlor, Theodore, with nearly every other woman in town. They've been praying this whole time." She shook her finger at Kyle. "And if you say they should be home where the Good Lord intended, so help me, Kyle Finley, I'll—"

"Go Maggie." Theodore motioned to the door. "Get the lady doctor. And tell the women thank you."

"Do you have any idea what you're asking me to do, Maggie?" Kathleen raised her hands and stepped away from the other woman. "Why would you even suggest such a thing? You know how Kyle Finley feels about me. One mistake, and he and every other man in this town will make sure I never practice veterinary medicine anywhere."

"It's not for any of them I'm asking. It's for Theodore and Hilda and their little one."

Whatsoever you do, Kathleen. For ye serve the Lord Christ. You can do all things. Do it heartily, as unto the Lord. She pushed the admonition as far back as she could. Papa didn't know Kyle Finley. Papa had never been to Lyndale, Kansas.

Maggie put her hands on Kathleen's shoulders. "And what happens if you refuse to help? You think it would be easier to live knowing Hilda's babe didn't have a chance because no one gave him one? Surely you've done something like this in your training."

She crossed her arms to still her shaking. "Sure, on a cow in a very controlled situation. And the professors and all my colleagues were there to help if I encountered any trouble."

"Well, my dear, if you haven't figured it out by now, I'm here to tell you that there is very little in real life that's all that controlled. You're expecting the worst. But let's say you're wrong. Let's imagine, for a minute, that you go in there and the two of you work together to do what you know how to do, and Theodore and Hilda leave this hotel in a week or two with a healthy little Clements?"

"I can't imagine the good doctor wanting to work as a team with a veterinarian."

"He doesn't. But neither does he want Theodore to go for Leonard."

"Leonard?"

"It's a long story, and there's not time for that now. Neither Hilda, nor the babe, has time to give."

She took a deep breath. Maggie was right. She'd never be able to forgive herself if something happened to this young woman and her baby. "Will you promise that Kyle will be a gentleman...at least until this is over?"

"Sure, and I'll promise the sun won't rise in the east. But I'll do my best.

Kathleen closed her eyes and leaned her head against the back of the chair. Well, Papa. How'd I do?

"Mind if I join you?"

She opened her eyes. Kyle Finley...with a smile on his face. Maybe the sun wouldn't rise in the east come morning. "Mind if I don't sit up?"

He chuckled. "Would you like a cup of coffee?"

"You think Maggie will let you back in the kitchen?" She hesitantly returned his smile.

"Oh, the kitchen has been taken over by the good women of Lyndale. I think their families got tired of waiting and somehow they figured out where they were. The restaurant is up and running, without my help. But I do know there's fresh, hot coffee."

"They're all still here? That was quite a prayer meeting. And yes, I would love a cup of coffee. But would you mind bringing it in here?"

He stood and winked. "Not at all. I was hoping you would suggest that very thing."

Where was the animosity? At some point during Hilda's travail, she realized Kyle Finley was no longer throwing darts her direction. He'd actually spoken with his eyes what words he'd not allowed to leave his mouth. And she hadn't missed the raw emotion on his face when the tiny boy let out his first lusty cry. Or the obvious pride when Theodore announced they would call their son Theodore Kyle Weston Clements.

She removed her combs and ran her fingers through her hair. She was tempted to kick off her shoes, too, but Kyle returned before she could accomplish that feat.

"I hope you don't mind. I added a spoon of sugar and a bit of cream. Didn't know if you were ready to eat, but the women have fixed ham sandwiches should you be hungry."

"I'm starved, but would gladly exchange food for a good hot bath right now."

He winked. "I think this is where we met the first night you were here. Sure you don't need help drawing that bath?"

She ran her fingers along the rim of the cup. "Tell me, Doctor Finley, when did you decide to stop hating me?"

He set his cup on the floor and rested his forearms on his thighs. "You have time for a story?"

She nodded.

He related his conversation with Theodore. "Maggie has never once accused me of not being here when she needed me. The townspeople have never accused me of not being here. Not until Theodore cared enough to pull off the scab of pride I'd allowed to seal the pain, could I see what I was doing to you. Even then I wasn't ready to give up. But then you walked into the room, knowing full well, I'm quite sure, how I felt having you there. Yet you transmitted none of your own concerns to the patient, nor her husband. Did Maggie tell you I'd never performed a caesarean before today?"

"No, but I suspected it."

"You did? And what aroused that suspicion, may I ask."

She put her hand over his. "Your hands shook until the minute you made the incision. Then you looked at me, as though you wondered if you were doing it right."

"And you only nodded. It was at that moment, with that one small nod, I realized how foolish I've been to...to...actually, Miss Weston, it was at that very moment I became so enamored by you.

"Enamored?" Not since high school had anyone told her they were enamored. And then it was an underclassman.

"You find that hard to believe?"

"I do. Think about it, Doctor. You were ready to marry me off just to get me out of your way. You've observed me at my worst—hot and tired after a day of travel behind Trembley's old mare, then sitting in a heap with Prudence across my lap, no buttons on my blouse and slobber in my hair. And now here, tonight, my hair is tangled, my apron soiled, and only because you're a doctor am I willing to admit that if I took off my shoes, like I so want to do, my feet would smell."

He leaned back in his chair and laughed until tears rolled down his cheeks. "Exactly! That's why I'm so enamored. But you do know there's still a lot of hills to climb, don't you?"

"I know. I'm not expecting it to be easy. But Leonard once told me that as Kyle Finley goes, so goes Lyndale."

"Leonard said that? Then I'll make sure that Kyle Finley is going the same direction as Kathleen Weston."

"That would be Kathleen Olivia Weston, Doctor of Veterinary Medicine, Doctor Finley."

He smiled at her. Had he always had such white teeth? And to think—

"Kyle Finley, you in here?"

"In here, Leonard. Is something wrong? And by the way, we need to talk."

Leonard grinned as his head bobbed between the two of them. "Nothing's wrong, just thought you should know Prudence is about to become a mother before the night is over."

Kathleen smiled at him. "Told you."

"Yes you did." Kyle stood and pulled Kathleen to her feet. "Would you allow me to accompany you on a house call, madam veterinary?"

"Are you poking fun?"

He shook his head and put his arm around her shoulders. "Me, make fun? Never."

When they stepped onto the porch his shoulder brushed against Andy's sign and it crashed to the floor. He stooped and picked it up. "What's this?" He held it to the light that glowed from the window.

"My little brother made it for me. I promised I'd hang it by my office."

He cocked his head. Doctor Kat, huh? I like that." He brushed his hand along her cheek. "I like that a lot."

She sighed and hung the sign back on the nails.

DOKTR KAT

VETNARY

She liked it, too.

If you enjoyed this compilation of stories, please look for these other novella collections from Wings of Hope Publishing.

Threads of Time

A collection of seven Christian romantic novellas about a very special quilt—one intended to grace the marriage bed of a young couple but never fulfilling its original purpose—which travels through many hands and decades, lending comfort to its temporary owners before being passed on.

FEBRUARY 2014

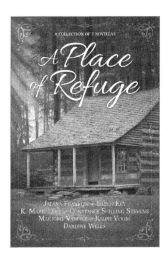

A Place of Refuge

A cabin constructed by Scottish immigrants in the mid-1870s becomes a place of rest, restoration, and refuge for weary travelers over the decades. Enjoy seven stories featuring one log cabin in the beautiful mountains of Wyoming, and find your place of refuge, as well.

MARCH 2015

www.wingsofhopepublishing.com

Made in the USA
San Bernardino, CA
16 January 2017